I0702608

WAR SONNETS

Susannah Willey

For more information, or to book an event, contact:
susannahwilley@gmail.com
https://utterloonacy.com

Book design by K. J. Harrowick
Cover design by K. J. Harrowick
Sonnets and Haikus by Allen H. Benton, writing as Albert Ezra Fitzwarren. Used with permission.

ISBN - Paperback: 979-8-9882220-0-2
ISBN - Hardcover: 979-8-9882220-2-6
Library of Congress Control Number: 2023908440

TABLE OF CONTENTS

DEDICATION

To Charlie
Aaron, Ben, Sarah, and Amelia
Without whose support and encouragement *War
Sonnets* would never have been written.

And
To Diane, who helped me find courage
To Jeff, who offered me wisdom
To Barbara, who showed me the truth

PREFACE

In the fall of 1942, twenty-one-year-old Allen Benton received his draft notice. A freshman at Cornell University, he had planned to enlist through a campus recruiter, ensuring he would remain stateside. Fate intervened and his draft notice arrived before he could enlist. He would spend his time in the United States, the Philippines, and Japan, returning home in February 1946.

Years later, Dr. Benton wrote the sonnets and haikus that inspired this novel and are included herein.

WAR SONNETS

PROLOGUE

LUZON, PHILIPPINES—JULY 1945

"Fuck this war."

Even though his BAR man was a good twenty yards behind him, Staff Sergeant Leo Baldwin could hear Filipowski muttering. He should be used to the cursing by now, but that particular word would always make Leo cringe. Truth was, he felt the same. Without the expletives but, yeah, he'd had enough of this war.

"Goddamned fucking Nips." Filipowski was louder now. Too loud for a soldier on recon patrol.

Leo turned and shot a warning look at him. "Okay, Corporal, we get it. It's no picnic." He twisted an imaginary key against his lips. "Now pipe down."

Out of the corner of his eye, Leo saw Filipowski twist his fingers against his lips and roll his eyes. He'd pretend he didn't see that for now, but they'd have words later on.

Corporal Jakob Filipowski was a city boy with light blond hair, brown eyes, and a ruddy complexion. He'd spent his youth in the Warsaw ghettos and had a scar from a street gang fight across his left cheek to prove it. His family had immigrated to the States when he was a teenager, and he'd been an auto worker in Detroit before the war.

At twenty-three years old, Leo was younger than Filipowski. He might have been a farm boy, but in the past three years, he'd seen a heck of a lot. On a good day, his brown eyes sparkled with humor, one cheek dimpled when he smiled. But today, he wasn't smiling. His thin lips made a grim line across his face, and inside, he was fuming.

Why on earth were they out here hunting stragglers when he had a bunch of raw recruits back at camp?

Besides recon, Leo trained new recruits for the upcoming assault on the Japanese island of Honshu in the fall. Unless some bureaucrat could convince the pig-headed Japanese emperor to surrender, Leo and his men would be part of the first wave. His platoon was nowhere near ready for combat—he needed every minute of the few weeks he had left to make them battle-fit. Instead, every time some local yahoo reported seeing Japanese soldiers, the army sent his squad on a wild goose chase in search of Japs half dead from starvation. Usually, it was as boring as picking rocks in a cornfield—they'd go out, patrol, find nothing, and go back to the garrison.

Mixed terrain, mostly jungle, became increasingly steep as it made its way to the east. Occasionally, they came across flatter, more open ground like they were on now, scattered with rock outcroppings and covered with thick, waist-high kunai grass. Deep scratches covered his hands where the sharp leaves raked his skin. He barely noticed as the stinging grass shushed against the stiff khaki of his pant legs.

The day was scorching; even worse was the humidity. July was the height of the rainy season, and the muddy trail was slippery and rutted with footprints. His men's boots sank in the muck, sucking and popping as if the sloppy earth had no intention of maintaining silence.

Leo reached under his helmet and wiped away the sweat dripping from his shaggy brown hair. Man, did he need a haircut. Mother would have a conniption if she knew.

Mother would have a conniption if she knew most of what had happened to her boy lately.

As squad leader, Leo was on the point. Ten yards to his left and a few paces back, his mate, Corporal Woody Grayson, matched his steps. Corporal Joe Russo took the right flank. Filipowski took the rear, sweeping his Thompson M1921 from left to right in search of the enemy. They were the last of Leo's original Luzon squad. The rest had gone home, many of them in a box. He'd lost so much in these few months.

He'd thought all it took was honesty and hard work, believed "right" was on their side.

Two years of training had made him stronger. Tougher. His time in New Guinea and en route to Luzon had accustomed him to the climate and given him a small taste of war. But nothing could have prepared him for the immoral cruelty, the back-stabbing, the betrayal of soldiers on both sides—especially the Americans.

He slapped at a mosquito that had settled on his forearm. *If the kunai grass doesn't get your blood,* the locals had warned, *the mosquitoes will.* He scanned the brush for movement, open areas with stale campsites, any lingering sign of the enemy. As usual, they'd seen nothing today. Now, late in the day, they were heading back to the outpost, and his mind wandered to the next day's training. His men would shoot for record, an official test of their marksmanship, and he worried that too many wouldn't qualify. Jones wouldn't make it—he knew that for sure. How in Hades was he going to get them ready for an invasion?

What was that noise? Leo stood still. He raised his hand to his ear and then palm out to warn the others. His armpits itched fiercely from the jungle rot all soldiers dealt with, but he pushed the discomfort from his mind as he focused his senses, eyes first, watching for the slightest movement. He strained his ears to pick out any unusual sounds, wrinkled his nose in search of odd smells, acutely aware of signs of danger.

The air was still. No rustling betrayed an enemy.

They were long gone. But he reminded himself to stay vigilant.

He took a deep breath and released the tension in his shoulders. He gestured to Grayson then to Russo and Filipowski, palm in, and pulled toward himself: *let's go.*

Then a fist: *pay attention.*

That one was more for his own benefit.

Lifting his rifle slightly to avoid more scratches, Leo took a step forward and found himself staring down the barrel of a Japanese Nambu pistol.

Susannah Willey

DRILL SERGEANT

Now this here, men, is called a hand grenade –
A deadly weapon, simple and precise;
So simple, I won't have to tell you twice.
If you can pull the pin, you've got it made.
There's just one catch—ten seconds have to pass
From when you turn it loose until it blows.
That's time for some Jap, seeing where it goes,
To grab it, throw it back, and blast your ass.
So what you have to do—it takes some guts –
Is let the handle go, then count to four.
Then let it fly, lay low, and let 'er roar.
You've got 'em then, no ifs or ands or buts,
Unless it's quick-fused; that's another story.
Before you count to four, you'll go to glory.

CHAPTER 1

CAMP HOOD, TEXAS—MAY 1944

Leo leaned against a tent post, watched the army camp come to life, and prepared for the day ahead. Camp Hood was dry, dusty, and as hot as jalapeños this time of year. The sun had barely breached the horizon, and Leo was already sweating.

He'd start training another new batch of trainees today, and every one of them would have a million questions. What a life. How many new batches of recruits had he put through Basic? Too many to count, that was for sure. He took a sip of his stone-cold coffee, grimaced, and poured the rest of it on the ground.

He tried to remember what it was like when he first got to boot camp. Was he ever as green as these guys? Maybe. But whoever that fella was, Leo had long ago left him in the dust. The move from farming to the army was jarring at first—like throwing a city boy on an unbroken stallion—but he'd adjusted, worked his way up to drill sergeant, and was now in the business of getting boys who should still be boys ready for war.

Sergeant Ronnie Lee Nelson, known to his cohorts as Dooley, threw back the flap of the tent he shared with Leo, lighting up his first cigarette of the day and inhaling deeply. "Damn," Dooley said, smoke wafting from his lips. "It's already so hot out it'd burn the black off a Darkie."

"Thought a southern boy like you would be used to it," Leo said.

Dooley rolled his eyes and took another drag on his cigarette. Two hundred pounds spread over his six feet, six inches made him sturdy but not overweight. His blond hair kinked up in the Texas heat, and the dark red tattoo on his arm stuck out like a deep bruise. Called a blood-drop cross, it was the badge of the Ku Klux Klan, tucked on the upper inside of his left bicep where it went mostly unnoticed. His blue eyes gave him a look of innocence—until they went dark with anger. Then they were frightening. His pride in hailing from "DOO-lac, Loo'siana" had earned him his nickname.

Leo had got used to Dooley's sugar-sweet southern drawl—sometimes he even understood what the man was saying. But the honeyed tone of Dooley's voice hid the venom behind it. The man was a judgmental bigot, his ignorant racism aimed mostly at Negroes and Mexicans, but as far as Dooley was concerned, anyone who wasn't from the south was a foreigner.

"Hey, Yankee boy, ain't you listenin'?" Dooley's voice pulled Leo back to the present.

"What?"

Dooley rolled his eyes. "Our new general." He glanced to his left then his right and continued. "I heard they kicked him back home from Italy."

"Is that so?" Leave it to Dooley to know the scuttlebutt.

"Yeah," Dooley said, smoke streaming from his nostrils. He pulled a folded paper out of his breast pocket, shaking it open. "And you ain't gonna believe General Italy's latest order."

"When did that come in?" Leo raised an eyebrow and leaned over to see the orders.

"Late last night." Dooley pulled the paper away. "All troops"—his tone dropped to a deep, commanding voice—"will march double-time to and from the training field."

Leo's eyes widened. "In 110-degree heat?" He shook his head. "Is he crazy?"

Dooley snorted out a laugh. "What's the trouble, Yankee boy? Afraid you gonna melt?" He feigned an aw-shucks smile and shifted to his commander voice. "Man up, soldier."

Leo crossed his arms, his body tense. "It's insane." He kicked at stray rocks, sending them flying into the brush. "You'll have men dropping like flies."

"Don't be a goddamned pussy." Dooley took another drag on his cigarette. He dropped the spent butt and ground it out in the hot Texas dirt. "We end up in some tropical jungle runnin' from a bunch of Japs, you're gonna wish you'd had some practice with heat."

Leo rolled his eyes and smirked. "I'll remind you of that when we're freezin' our tails off in Germany, southern boy."

Dooley good-naturedly slapped Leo's back. "Always a goddamned Yankee, that's whatcha are." He smiled, shook his head. "C'mon, let's get those rookies out on maneuvers."

Leo watched the other platoons disappear into the mesquite until it was his turn.

"All right, men," Leo commanded. "Head out." He launched into a double-time cadence.

The soldiers groaned in unison, but nobody protested further. As one, they scurried across the compound in perfect double-time. Twenty minutes later, they reached the training grounds, their uniforms soaked with sweat.

"Sergeant." The lieutenant nodded as Leo's men came to a halt.

Leo saluted. "With all due respect, sir." He fixed a no-nonsense look on his superior. "Marching double-time in this heat is going to kill people."

"But being a good soldier, you intend to follow orders anyway, right?" The lieutenant eyeballed him as if daring him to argue.

"Yes, sir." Leo kept his disgust from his face. Of course, the lieutenant would be long gone, relaxing under a shady tree in his civvies when the overheated men began to fall.

At the end of the day, everyone was dusty and exhausted. The weight of their gear and the heat of the day had sapped every inch of energy from them. The men were sluggish, muttering angrily as they reluctantly formed up ranks.

Dooley stared into the brush then suddenly thrust his hand into the bushes and emerged with an eight-foot-long mole snake.

Leo had seen Dooley pull this act before, and he thoroughly disapproved. Big as it was, the mole snake was entirely harmless. Brandishing the snake toward his platoon was Dooley's way of motivating his exhausted men. The resulting chaos was predictable—soldiers scattered in all directions. Dooley held out the snake, one hand on its head, the other on its tail.

"Get in line," he ordered, wrapping the snake around his shoulders. The platoon fell silent as they lined up. Dooley shouted out the double-time cadence, and the troops scuffled across the sun-parched field.

They hadn't marched fifty yards when one soldier collapsed to the ground. Dust flew in all directions as he fell, his fellow platoon mates scattered to avoid tripping on him.

"Move it, soldier." Dooley poked at the downed private with his rifle barrel.

The soldier didn't move. Dooley rolled the soldier onto his back as the mole snake slithered off to safety. The soldier's skin was red and bone dry.

"Shit," Dooley muttered. "Heat stroke." He motioned to his two closest men. "Morris, Gentry, get this man back to camp, pronto."

Already exhausted, Morris and Gentry struggled to lift the downed soldier onto Gentry's shoulder and staggered down the path to camp.

"That's one pantywaist down." Dooley held a wide stance, his chest thrust out and his arms crossed. He glared at his troops. "What? You think the Japs are gonna feel sorry for you when you pass out?" he sneered. "Move it out—double-time."

Dooley's platoon disappeared down the trail, and Leo turned to his own men. There was no way he was going to risk losing a soldier to heat stroke just to prove some idiot general's point. He shouted the order for a normal march pace.

They were the last to return to camp, and the lieutenant was waiting, his arms crossed and a scowl on his face. Leo dismissed his men then stood at attention as the lieutenant approached.

"Care to explain yourself, Sergeant?" The lieutenant glared at Leo.

"Yes, sir," Leo said. "I believed a double-time march would put my men at risk, but I followed orders until one of Sergeant Nelson's men collapsed from the heat. At that time, I decided an unnecessary double-time pace would be counterproductive."

"So, you saw fit to ignore the general's order?"

Leo felt the twinge in his stomach. He'd catch the devil from the lieutenant, but he wouldn't back down now. "I don't believe the general understood the danger he was putting my men in, sir."

"If General Saunders were here, he'd have your ass." The lieutenant crossed his arms and leaned closer to Leo. "You know you could get a court-martial for ignoring his orders."

"I do, sir." Leo kept his face expressionless. There was no way he'd let this jerk think he was afraid of him. "But I felt the personal risk was necessary for the safety of my platoon."

"Not your decision to make," the lieutenant said. "Consider yourself confined to the base until further notice."

Leo winced as the lieutenant strode across the parade grounds. He'd never get used to taking orders from the arrogant brass who were clearly out of touch.

Dooley grinned as Leo entered the mess tent.

As much as he hated Yankees—only slightly less than the Spades and the Spics—Dooley liked Leo Baldwin. Leo didn't condescend to him, didn't brag about his education; he kept quiet about his politics and his religion. He was a farm boy as much as Dooley was, loved the boondocks, and hated the city just like he did.

"Got yourself in hot water with the LT, huh?" Dooley said.

"Yeah," Leo growled, "and I'd do it again if I had to."

True, Leo was a little stiff sometimes, a little too stuck on his moral path, but Dooley admired when Leo spoke his mind and did what he thought was right. Most of the time, Leo Baldwin was just a good ol' boy.

That deal with the double-time marching: Dooley had to admit Leo knew what he was doing there. He sometimes envied Leo's calm demeanor, the way he never got mad or started a fight. Leo simply picked his battles and stood his ground. The only way Dooley knew to stand up for himself was through his fists.

But Dooley would say none of that out loud. It wasn't in him to give credit or praise, show admiration or respect. It just wasn't in him.

Instead, he poured himself a cup of coffee, and settled onto a bench.

"How's your man doing?" Leo continued.

"He'll live." Dooley shrugged. "Goddamned general. What the hell was he thinking?"

"Guess he wasn't." Leo shook his head and laughed. "They leave thinking to the noncoms."

Dooley raised his cup in salute.

"Damn right," he said, and took a long drink.

That night, Leo wrote the day's events in his diary, used his pen to keep his place, and stuck it under his pillow for the night. He stretched out on the cot, hands under his head, and thought about home. Back then, he kept his diary in a hollow tree in the woods behind his house. It was where he did his best thinking. Where he wrote the sonnets he loved.

THE FARM

I own these hills, as they in turn own me.
My kin are products of this stony earth.
We draw our strength from hill and rock and tree,
This farm's stark beauty nourished us from birth.
I learned its secrets when I was a child:
The field mouse nest, within a clump of sedge;
The dwelling place of all things strange and wild.
At dusk, in early spring, along the hedge
I heard the woodcock trill its evening song.
Along the wall, I watched the chipmunks play.
Ere winter loosed its grip, I waited long
To hear the wild geese on their northern way.
I am what I became, in large degree,
Because this farm, in early years, owned me.

CHAPTER 2

BALDWIN'S CORNERS, NEW YORK—SEPTEMBER 1940

"Leal," Leo's mother screeched from beyond the trees.

Leo rolled his eyes. Only his family still called him Leal. He hated the old-fashioned hand-me-down that belonged in the Highlands it came from. His friends called him Leo, and anyone outside the family who dared to call him Leal did it only once.

Returning his attention to the sonnet he'd just finished, he read it aloud, checking its rhythm and rhyme. Not bad. He might even show this one to his English teacher.

He looked forward to the stolen moments he spent with his notebook. He enjoyed the sense of calm that writing poetry provided. The challenge of the sonnet intrigued him, its rules of iambs, quatrains, and couplets a welcome exercise of the mind instead of the body.

A woodpecker drilled into a nearby tree then flew away, its bright red crest a beacon as it landed in a maple a few yards from him. Deer moved along the narrow trail that led to their hideout, crunching the dry leaves and twigs underfoot. Leo kept an eye on them until they disappeared into a tangle of brush. He made a mental note of the location: fresh venison was always a welcome addition to the dinner table.

Leo loved this farm. He knew each sight, each smell, by heart. He could name the trees by the shape of their leaves, the feel of their bark. He knew which birds were common to the farm, and which were visitors just passing through. He could tell the season by the scent in the air: the freshness of spring, the stale mustiness of autumn, when a winter blizzard or a summer thunderstorm was on the way.

The farm had been in his family for generations. It would be his eventually—at least that was his parents' plan. But the land he loved came with the job he loathed: farming. It was pure boredom, trudging behind a horse and plow for hours on end, planting, harvesting, baling. Day after endless day. Farming was a constant struggle against the elements— and the economy as well—since the stock market crash. Leo was tired of the battle, tired of there never being enough money for more than the necessities.

Couldn't the farm go to one of his sisters? Sure, it was always the son who inherited the land, but doggone it, Leo didn't want it. What Leo really wanted to be was a writer, but he knew better than to tell his parents that.

"There's no future in that," his mother would say. And his father would just nod in agreement like he always did when Mother passed judgment. The man needed to grow a spine.

His grandfather would roar, indignant to think his grandson wasn't interested in family tradition.

"You'll do as you're told," he'd growl.

Grandfather considered himself the ultimate authority of the family, even if it meant going against Leo's parents, which he did often enough. Leo, his sisters, and his parents had lived with his grandparents since his father had lost their house to back taxes—something both Grandfather and Mother never let him forget. His sisters had since married and moved away, but Leo was stuck.

"Leal Patrick Baldwin," his mother called again.

Swear to God, she shrieks louder than seagulls in a fresh-cut wheat field.

Leo stretched his arms, glanced at the sun that was already halfway toward the western horizon. Holy smokes! He hadn't meant to spend so much time here.

He jumped up, brushed the twigs and bits of grass from his dungarees. He was in for it now. Leo slammed his notebook shut, wrapped it in a scrap of heavy fabric, and shoved it inside the knot-hole in the ancient tree beside him.

He threw a haphazard pile of rocks on top of the covered notebook, another layer of camouflage from both human and animal invaders.

It took a good five minutes for him to get out of the woods, cross the field, and follow the path that led from the barn to the house. His mother was on the porch waiting for him.

"Where on earth have you been?" Her hands were firmly planted on her hips, her eyes narrowed in disapproval. "Your father's been looking for you."

"Uh, I must have fallen asleep." Leo winced the minute the words came from his mouth.

His mother shook her head and turned to go inside. "Lazy as the day is long," she said. "Just like your father."

Leo scuffed the dirt with the toe of his boot and stomped off toward the barn. He was *not* just like his father. He hated the comparison. Just because he had the same brown eyes and brown hair, just because he had "his father's nose" didn't mean he was one bit like the man. For one thing, he wasn't going to stick around long enough to let them bully him into staying here.

He missed the man his father had been before they'd had to move in with his grandparents. Back then, he played hide and seek in the cornfield with Leo, taught him how to play baseball and shinny up the tall oak tree in the front yard. But now that playfulness was gone, replaced by a man who was stodgy and humorless all the time.

Leo might daydream every once in a while, lose track of time, and show up late for chores. But he worked hard, and doggone it, he'd prove to both his parents that he was not lazy.

国はなれ
休み見上げる
月ひとつ

Kuni hanare
Yasumi miageru
Tsuki hitotsu

Far from my dear home
Yet the same moon above me.
Now I can find rest

CHAPTER 3

CABANATUAN PRISONER OF WAR CAMP, LUZON, PHILIPPINES—SEPTEMBER 1944

Stars dotted the nighttime sky, the bright full moon an old friend. Corporal Tadashi Abukara knelt on the hard-packed dirt inside the Cabanatuan POW Camp. To his right were the barracks where he and his fellow guards slept. To his left were the primitive bamboo huts that housed the American prisoners. The terrain surrounding the compound was flat, cleared of vegetation to make it more difficult for prisoners to escape or for the enemy to attack.

This was the night of Tsukimi, the Harvest Moon Festival. It was a traditional time of quiet reflection when one honored the beautiful moon and thanked the kami—the Shinto spirit-gods—for another successful harvest.

But tonight, his thoughts weren't about the harvest.

Tadashi gazed longingly at the worn photograph of his family, amazed at how much younger he had looked just two short years ago. Back then, he was slender, clean-shaven, his hair cropped short. Since that time, he had lost too much weight. His black hair had grown longer, stringy and dirty. A scruffy beard grew on his chin; his bayonet was the only means of keeping it trimmed. He shook his head. Sachiko and Ichiro would not recognize him.

He returned his attention to the photograph. Creased and smudged with age, it was becoming harder to see his family's faces. Soon, they would be indiscernible. This was his third Tsukimi away from home, but he took comfort knowing his wife, Sachiko, shared the Harvest Moon with him, even though they were two thousand miles apart.

His fingers gently caressed the image of his wife and child. Oh, how he missed them. His heart ached with love and longing for his beautiful Sachiko, for his cherished son.

The bright full moon drew his attention. He imagined himself under this same moon at home with his family. He and Sachiko, and perhaps little Ichiro, would kneel together in front of the outdoor shrine. Together they would read tanka poetry and eat Tsukimi Dango—moon-viewing dumplings made from rice flour—under the moonlight, accompanied by the sweet song of the nightingale.

Although the sky was bright and clear, the air was heavy with the stench of starvation and disease. The worst smell was from just beyond the wire, the deep trench where they disposed of dead prisoners. The bodies were attracting carrion-eaters. Bears, jackals, ravens, vultures, wolves—all desperate for food—became bolder as the corpses piled higher. Malnutrition and disease—scavengers of the nearly dead—invaded the prisoners' huts, taking more than twice the lives than those who died from injury.

The Cabanatuan POW Camp had once been an American military training camp and, before that, the home of the Department of Agriculture. Now it was the largest POW camp in the Philippines. When Tadashi and his childhood friend, Kaito, had first arrived, there were eight thousand American prisoners at Cabanatuan, fresh from the Bataan Death March. They had sent most of the prisoners elsewhere, often as slave labor on the Japanese mainland. Most of the soldiers who remained at the camp were too sick from disease, malnutrition, or starvation to be useful.

The camp itself covered about a hundred acres dissected by a road from north to south. Over one hundred buildings occupied the space. Twenty-six of them housed prisoners. Surrounding the perimeter of the camp were two ten-foot-high barbed-wire fences, spaced twenty feet apart, with guard towers and pillboxes in between. The front gate, made of thick wood and fitted with an enormous padlock, loomed nine feet tall.

Endless hours of guard duty had filled Tadashi's head with worries that continued long after he retired to his bed each night. Sachiko's letters were always cheerful, but he knew the hardships she must be experiencing. Were they getting enough food? Was the rent being paid?

His more important worries were less concrete.

Does Sachiko still love me? Surely, she did—but he had been away for so long. And what of his son? He was nearly three years old, but Tadashi only remembered him as an infant. He had missed so much—Icihiro's first steps, his first words. Would he even recognize his father when he returned?

Tadashi envisioned a small boy running from him, frightened by a man he didn't know. So many worries endlessly occupied his mind.

A shadowy movement from beyond the fence caught Tadashi's eye. A small group of prisoners wearing only loincloths carried a heavy bundle. Tadashi watched. He would only sound the alarm if the men appeared poised to escape. But the men stopped at the burial pit and bent to the ground.

They released their burden, a dead body, little more than a skeleton.

Tadashi stayed where he was. He looked around to see if any on-duty guards were near. Most had returned to their barracks, and the evening guard was light and had yet to arrive.

He kept watch while the prisoners gently laid the body in the ditch. They spoke as one in whispers, their voices respectful—perhaps the words of their religious burial ritual—then gestured in an up-down, left-right motion: forehead to chest, shoulder to shoulder. It was a sign he had seen often during the prisoners' worship services and prayers.

The Japanese command strictly prohibited formal burial in the camp, but how could Tadashi interfere?

How could he see these men as barbarians? Their respect and honor for their comrade did not differ from his own.

The evening breeze picked up. Tadashi wrinkled his nose, buried his face in his shirt.

The odor of death. It clung to his skin like a lingering sunburn. He longed for the unspoiled aromas of home, the freshly cut wheat, the newly turned earth, the sweet scent of his beloved Sachiko.

As the Americans quietly returned to their huts, Tadashi once again raised his eyes to the Harvest Moon as it gracefully descended toward the horizon. It reminded him of the reverence with which the prisoners had lowered their comrade into his grave. Tadashi gently kissed his magatama, sending love to his wife and son. If guarding this hell would keep him alive to return home, if it would grant his family peace and safety, he would do it for a thousand more Harvest Moons.

Please keep them safe, he prayed. He stood, bowed to the kami, and walked toward his barracks.

An autumn chill crept up Sachiko's spine as she knelt by the shrine. Her long, black hair flowed loosely down her back, wayward strands falling in her face as she worshipped. Her dark eyes beseeched the kami to protect her husband. The night was clear, and the Tsukimi moon shone brightly, obscuring even the brightest stars. Her heart ached with longing for Tadashi. Was he still alive? She heard from him rarely; the mail service was as fickle as February sunlight. Still, she faithfully wrote letters to him, full of news from home and tales of their young son's adventures.

She gazed at the brilliant Harvest Moon and imagined Tadashi kneeling in some distant place, perhaps a rice field or a jungle, watching the moon and thinking of her and their son. A long-eared owl hooted from the nearby tree, a watchful guardian believed to bring good luck, fortune and health. Was he watching over Tadashi as well?

Sachiko rose from the shrine, bowed to the kami, and remembered the day her husband had said goodbye.

Susannah Willey

大自然
離れがたきは
この景色

Daishizen
Hanare gataki wa
Kono keshiki

Glorious nature
Fills each day with such beauty—
How can I leave?

CHAPTER 4

SHINTOKU, HOKKAIDO PREFECTURE, JAPAN— MAY 1942

Tadashi woke at first light, as he did every morning. He slipped out of bed, careful not to wake his wife, dressed quickly, and hurried outside to welcome the day.

The air was still chilly this time of year. Tadashi wrapped his coat tight and settled against the large rock that was his writing place. He sat quietly for a moment, watching the sky brighten behind the distant snow-capped mountains. As the day lightened, he opened his diary and began to write. Some days, he wrote only his thoughts. Today, he added a haiku, an ode to thc bcauty of nature.

The gentle caress of brush on paper brought serenity to his worried mind. The challenge of capturing his thoughts in the simplicity of seventeen syllables often kept his mind active as he worked the fields.

On this early May morning, the deep purple lilac blooming by the shed scented the air. To the east, the hill was ablaze with bright yellow rape flowers. The plum tree, covered with deep pink blossoms, would yield a generous crop if there was no late freeze this year. A lark sang from a nearby tree, a melodious accompaniment to Tadashi's thoughts.

Tadashi closed his diary and set it aside for another day. The sky was bright now with the early morning sun. His dark hair glinted red in the sunlight, a remnant of his Ainu heritage.

It would be a good day for planting, he thought. Today, he would sow the wheat that thrived in Hokkaido's northern climate. The earth was ready to receive the seed, warm enough, moist enough for the tiny grains to germinate and grow.

He stood, stretched the stiffness from his legs, and approached the small, wooden shrine that sat near a corner of his house. Like many of his neighbors, the kami-dana was outside, set on a flat stone and swathed by a wisteria vine whose lavender flowers hung like clusters of tiny butterflies.

Tadashi knelt in front of the shrine and set down a fresh rice cake, his daily offering to the kami. He prayed to the Shinto spirits for a successful harvest and good health for his family. Today, he had an additional request.

"Dear spirits," Tadashi said in a voice that was soft and reverent, "I humbly ask for your guidance. What I must do today tears at my heart."

He pulled the bright red paper from his pocket, the kanji script stamped with the official army seal. The Imperial Army considered it a father's duty to be sure his son reported for service. As was customary for military call-up, the army had delivered the notice to his father, who had delivered it yesterday.

Tadashi remembered his compulsory military service eleven years ago. He was nineteen years old then, had never left his family home. The training was rigorous, the officers strict and swift with harsh punishment for the smallest infraction. He had returned home stronger in both body and spirit.

The army taught their men that a Japanese warrior was the reincarnation of the ancient samurai. The kami protected a samurai, a warrior who was unequaled in courage and strength and would choose death rather than suffer the disgrace of surrender. Tadashi had grown up with the legend of his young uncle, who, at twenty-two, had taken his own life rather than be captured by the enemy. From the first time Tadashi heard the story, he knew he could never be so courageous. He feared he would bring disgrace to his family, knowing that he could never choose death.

He clutched his jade magatama necklace. A good luck charm, it had belonged to his uncle and to his grandfather before that. Perhaps his uncle's spirit remained and would grant him the courage he lacked. But that choice might not be his, and there was a distinct possibility that he would never return. He imagined his wife, Sachiko, receiving the box that might—or might not—contain his remains. He could not bear the grief he saw in her face, the hopelessness of her life if she were left without a husband.

Tadashi breathed deeply, taking in the familiar scents of home. The sweetness of fresh hay, the musk of the farm animals, even the acrid tang of fresh manure, eased his anxiety. He knelt silently for a moment then rose, bowed respectfully to the kami, and moved toward the front door where Sachiko waited with his breakfast.

She nodded as Tadashi entered and hung his coat by the door. He sat at the small table where his morning tea steamed against the chilly air.

Sachiko's stockinged feet brushed against the floor as she moved across the room, bringing breakfast to her husband. Their six-month-old son, Ichiro, watched intently from his comfy perch on his mother's back, his eyes wide with curiosity. Tadashi smiled and held out a finger toward his son, who gripped it and pulled it toward his mouth.

"How is my young son today?" he asked.

Sachiko looked up from her task. "He is strong and happy, just like his father."

"He is handsome and smart, just like his mother." Tadashi's heart swelled with pride for them both. How the kami had blessed him. He had a wife he loved, a strong young son—they were all he needed to feel complete.

Their traditional marriage was not meant to be a love match, but Tadashi had loved Sachiko from the moment he saw her. She was small but self-assured, and her dark eyes shone with intelligence. She would be a worthy partner.

He saw Sachiko's beauty in his young son, and his heart ached. *Will I live to see him become a man?*

This life was everything Tadashi wanted. Money and possessions were unimportant. But today, that life had been turned upside down, perhaps forever. With tears in his eyes, he gently kissed his wife and child and headed to the shed where the ox patiently waited.

Susannah Willey

強き丑
運気を担い
共に労

Tsuyoki ushi
Unki o ninai
Tomo ni rou

My strong faithful ox
Bears my fate on his shoulders
We toil together

CHAPTER 5

Tadashi's freshly sharpened plow released the newly thawed soil from its winter bed, revealing the small creatures that sheltered below. Worms wriggled against the earth, bugs of all shapes and sizes skittered across the ground in search of safety.

The massive beast he walked behind was nearly as tall as his master and many times heavier, but he obeyed Tadashi like a devoted servant. He knew every inch of the fields he traveled. Tadashi's mind could wander, composing verse or considering the many problems his family faced—his ox would never falter.

Over ten years ago, the Japanese invaded Manchuria, and the Great Depression rocked the world. Food was scarce. The grain they grew went to delivery quotas imposed by the government; they could keep only a small personal allotment that was nowhere near enough. Without the chickens, the eggs they produced, and the small garden Sachiko tended, they would surely starve. The military-run government had put out a plea for all Japanese to tighten their belts, but Tadashi's belt was already so tight it nearly choked him. And now the war had expanded well beyond China to the United States.

Tadashi hated the Americans. A part of him yearned to fight the enemy that threatened the Japanese race with extinction. It seemed the entire Western world was against them. The westerners had invaded and colonized Asian countries yet sanctioned Japan with embargoes when Japan tried to do the same. Japan saw no choice but to withdraw from the League of Nations; the Western world branded them the "Yellow Peril."

The Americans were the worst offenders. They closed their border to the Japanese, cut them off from the world's oil supply, embargoed their exports. They'd demanded Japan reduce the size of their army. Japan had had enough of Western interference: they would claim East Asia for the emperor, fight to keep it out of the hands of the imperialists and communists.

The Japanese attack at Pearl Harbor had come days after Ichiro's birth. Most people were excited—Japan had stood up to the meddling West. But Tadashi's feelings were not as clear. Funny how having a child changed one's perspective. Before Ichiro's birth, Tadashi would not have hesitated to defend his country. But now, he had a child to protect, and suddenly defending his emperor seemed far less important. To whom did he owe his greatest loyalty? Others might say the emperor; for Tadashi, family meant more.

But that family was on the brink of disaster. There was only enough money to pay their rent, and they were always a step away from starvation. Being in the army meant Tadashi would have money to send home—far more money than he could make selling his crops. It would be a hardship, but Sachiko could manage the small garden and chickens. Perhaps he could sell the ox—without fields to plow, it would become an unnecessary expense, and its sale would provide Sachiko with much-needed funds.

The ox slowed, hesitating at the end of the field. Tadashi pulled at the reins, urging the animal to turn. Such a faithful beast. It would not be easy to lose him.

"Nii-chan!" The call came from across the field. Tadashi knew the voice; it was his best friend Kaito, who had called him "brother" since the day they'd met.

"Sachiko sent lunch with me," he said, handing Tadashi some rice balls and a small bowl of miso soup. He wore the same peaked hat as Tadashi, the same bamboo mat, worn like a shawl and tied at the neck.

Tadashi was so deep in thought he hadn't realized how high the sun had risen. But now his stomach rumbled with hunger, and he gratefully accepted the meal from his friend. "Arigato, Kai-chan."

Kaito stood a head taller than Tadashi. He was slender, not as muscular as Tadashi, although he, too, worked on his family's farm. They'd been friends since they'd first met in the schoolyard nearly twenty years ago.

They sat side by side on the ground as Tadashi silently ate his lunch.

"You are deep in thought," Kaito said at last. "What are you thinking about?"

Tadashi drained his bowl and set it on the grass beside him. "My red paper came yesterday," he said. "I leave in three weeks." Tadashi stared at the distant mountains. Tears pressed against his eyes. "I haven't yet told Sachiko."

"I, too, have received orders." Kaito pulled at the matted grass then straightened respectfully. "I am ready to give my life for the emperor." He paused a moment to make a small pile of the grass he'd pulled. "With hard work, I might become a corporal—you are smart enough to become sergeant—and when we return home, we will have greater status, more influence in the village."

"I have no desire for influence," Tadashi said. "I am no leader. I only hope to serve the emperor and return whole to my family."

Kaito brushed away the small pile of grass and stared at the empty spot. "I wonder if I will have family left when I return. My parents are old and may not live much longer."

He stood, brushing debris from his trousers. Tadashi rose from the grass and handed his empty bowl to Kaito. A small silence hung between them until at last Kaito spoke.

"We will go together, Nii-chan." He clapped a hand on Tadashi's back. "Brothers forever."

It was nearly dark when Tadashi at last released his ox from the iron plow and led him to the shed. He scooped grain into the manger, filled the water trough, and added clean straw to the ox's bedding. The doorway was just visible in the fading daylight as he left the shed and closed the door behind him. He crossed the yard to where Sachiko fed grain to a cluster of chickens gathered impatiently around her, pecking at the bits of wheat that fell on her wooden sandals. Together, they walked toward the house where Sachiko prepared dinner.

She was so beautiful. How could he leave her? He reached out, wrapping Sachiko in his arms. They silently held the embrace, neither willing to let go. At last, Tadashi pulled away, his hands gradually sliding down her arms until he held only her hands. He gently touched his son, sleeping peacefully on Sachiko's back. His eyes glistened with love and regret.

"The Imperial Army has called me to service." He choked on the words; he could say no more.

Sachiko nodded and lowered her face to hide the tears that forced themselves from her eyes. She had known this day would come; she knew her husband's duty to his emperor had weighed heavily on his conscience since the war began.

Her legs trembled, and she struggled to stay standing. The baby stirred restlessly on her back, making little smacking sounds with his lips. *Stay still a bit longer, little one.* She feared her sadness would flow with her milk; she must stay strong for her child.

"When must you go?" she asked.

"The first of June," Tadashi whispered. His voice faltered. "In three weeks, I will leave for Sapporo."

Heavy clouds hung ominously in the sky when Tadashi slipped out of bed the morning of his departure. Sachiko had been up long before daylight, preparing his breakfast of rice, miso, and pickled vegetables. Ichiro slept soundly on his mother's back, and Tadashi bent to kiss his downy, dark hair.

They spoke few words as he ate. He and Sachiko had shared their bodies last night, said their goodbyes as they held each other close. He had laid his head on her chest, memorizing the beat of her heart, melding its rhythmic pulse with his own.

At midday, in the privacy of their little home, they held a long embrace. Tadashi gently ran his hand down her face, feeling the curve of her eyelashes, the teardrops in her eyes, the full lips he would not kiss for many long months.

He lightly kissed her cheek and took a step back. "It is time."

Sachiko nodded, wiped her eyes, and solemnly followed her husband out the door.

They traveled to the village where there would be a send-off for him and Kaito. It was a small but formal ceremony, ending in a parade of sorts as the villagers followed them to the train station. Tadashi would have preferred to slip away without the fanfare. He didn't feel like a hero, felt no desire to be congratulated for being called to serve. Surely, people could see he was an imposter who was neither brave nor eager to die for his country.

But Kaito seemed to drink in the attention like a thirsty traveler. He beamed as the mayor presented him to the villagers and announced the great honor of his service. He had the warrior's spirit; he welcomed the chance to fight and kill.

The mayor presented each of them with a senninbari, a thousand-stitch belt. Made from white cloth embroidered with one thousand red stitches, soldiers traditionally wore it around the waist for protection. He handed each a hinomaru, the Japanese national flag with its crimson sun, inscribed with good luck messages from family and friends that radiated from the center.

Tadashi knew the hours Sachiko and his mother had spent collecting the many stitches for his sennibari, the custom that each person was to make one stitch only. His father would have visited many homes to gather messages on the hinomaru.

"Banzai! Banzai!" The crowd shouted their congratulations and waved send-off banners as Tadashi and Kaito boarded the train. A light rain was falling now. Thunder rumbled in the distant sky, and bits of lightning flashed behind the trees.

"We need the rain." Kaito held his hand out to feel the little drops of moisture against his skin.

Tadashi nodded. He regretted he had to leave the fieldwork undone. His father was no longer a vigorous man, and it would be difficult for him to tend and harvest every field. But Tadashi knew he would do as much as he could then sell the ox for whatever money he could get.

Their journey sent them west and south toward the city of Sapporo. An especially loud clap of thunder occasionally drowned out the clatter of wheels on steel tracks. Otherwise, there was silence. Tadashi admired the lush spring scenery as they traveled. The brown frosted grass had come alive with the warm weather and turned a deep emerald green. Once bare trees were now covered with new leaves.

The train followed a slender river on its journey west. Along its bank, a flock of red-crowned cranes fished for snails and whatever other delicacies they could snatch, undeterred by the noisy locomotive. The birds' long, black legs extended from the water, their bright white bodies accented with a black tail and neck. A patch of bare, red skin topped their heads. His body relaxed when he saw the cranes. A symbol of good luck, love, and long life—a sure sign for a safe return home.

He thought about where the war might take him. Would it be hot or cold? Rainy or dry? Flat or mountain-covered? Wherever it was, it could never be as beautiful as his Hokkaido.

The train crested a small hill, revealing the wide expanse of Sapporo in the far distance.

"It looks as if the rain is ending." Kaito broke the silence and pointed to the west where the clouds had cleared and the sky was brightening.

The sun had dipped behind the mountains when their train arrived at the army depot south of Sapporo. They would spend the next few weeks here in training, disciplined to be obedient creatures like his ox, and committed to fight a war they might not survive.

Four weeks of rigorous training had made their bodies strong. After the first week, their muscles ached—the long days of marching and practicing with both rifle and bayonet exhausted them—but at last, they completed their training. Tadashi and Kaito boarded a train and headed south.

Their train took a long, circuitous route from Sapporo, a wriggling eel as it sped down the island of Honshu. The great city of Tokyo was a revelation—so many people pushing along the streets, so many tall buildings standing like sentinels guarding the city. It was an awesome sight, but it only intensified Tadashi's ache for the peacefulness of home.

The two-thousand-kilometer trip took fifteen hours.

"It feels like we are in a different country, Kai-san," Tadashi said as they alit from the train. Although the mountains and seaside looked much the same, the climate was much warmer. The air was humid, the streets damp with recent rain. "We must hurry. Our ship will leave soon."

He and Kaito at last found their way to the port just as their ship, the *Myoko Maru,* prepared to set sail.

Susannah Willey

闇の中
運命呪う
死の世界

Yami no naka
Unmei norou
Shi no sekai

Alone in the dark
I curse the fate that brought me
To this land of death

CHAPTER 6

SOMEWHERE IN THE EAST CHINA SEA—

SEPTEMBER 1942

Tadashi's pencil skipped across the paper at the crest of every wave. His narrow hammock swayed. But he persevered, and his body at last adapted to the rhythmic rolling of the sea.

In the hammock above, Kaito tossed and turned.

Tadashi closed his notebook and playfully kicked at Kaito's wriggling backside. "We're going up on deck," he said. "The fresh air will help."

Kaito groaned. "If you say so, Nii-chan." He dragged himself off his hammock and climbed down to the deck. "But if I vomit again, it will be on you." He laughed weakly and staggered to the ladder. "Come on, brother."

Up on deck, they stood at the railing, watching the albatross and shearwaters glide across the sky in search of a snack. The occasional wind gust sprayed bits of salty water in their faces, stinging their eyes. A small school of dolphins breached the surface, happily chattering as they danced on their tails, as graceful as geishas. Their antics amused even Kaito, who forgot his queasy stomach.

"Where do you think we are going?" Kaito asked as they watched the frolicking wildlife.

Only the higher officers knew of their destination. All Tadashi could do was guess. "Somewhere south for certain." He pointed at the sun relative to the ship's heading. "But that only means we aren't going to China or Burma."

The Imperial Japanese Army had already conquered much of East Asia and had won several battles throughout the

South Pacific. In April, they had taken the island of Luzon in the Philippines and expelled or captured the Allied troops.

Tadashi gestured to the south. "I have heard rumors we will attack the northern coast of Australia or the island of New Guinea."

Kaito rubbed his palms together. "Wherever it is, I am eager to fight. I only hope there is something still left to conquer when we arrive."

Tadashi nodded, although he would never feel Kaito's excitement for war. With the current success of the Japanese armies, perhaps it would be only a few months before Japanese victory was complete.

The sun shone brightly overhead, but in the distance, heavy clouds cluttered the horizon. Their thick, dark cotton absorbed the sun, turning the sky a murky gray. Tadashi could see dense threads of rain beneath the clouds.

"Typhoon." A sailor next to them pointed at the threatening mass. "But no worries—it is going away from us. By the time we get to where it is now, the storm will have moved far inland."

"They don't seem to agree." Tadashi nodded to the pod of dolphins hurriedly swimming away.

The sailor shook his head. "They are only sea creatures," he said, "not smart enough to know they are not in danger."

Perhaps they know their home better than you, Tadashi thought.

Two nights later, Tadashi woke to the sound of the ship's alarm. The ship rocked like a runaway coal tram. He'd dreamed he was riding an angry bull intent on throwing him to the ground. Soldiers scrambled down from their hammocks, clutching whatever they could to keep from falling.

Kaito jumped from his hammock, his eyes wide with fear. "We must get out," he shouted and struggled to the ladder. "Hurry, Nii-chan."

"No." Tadashi grabbed at Kaito. "It's not safe up there."

But Kaito was already scrambling through the open hatch.

A curtain of dense fog enshrouded the ship, the skies black with the night and pelting rain.

A sailor rushed past them. "Get below," he shouted. "The typhoon has taken a sharp turn. We are directly in its path."

Tadashi spotted Kaito standing at the rail, staring into the distance. The winds grew stronger as the storm approached, and the ship rocked violently.

Wave after wave attacked the ship, each one fiercer than the last. At its peak, each wave raised the ship's bow high, leaving the stern dangerously low. When the wave moved on, the ship dropped to the trough, and its belly smacked against the water, propellers thrashing the air.

Tadashi's stomach clenched and heaved. Vomit spewed from his mouth and onto the already slippery deck. The wind gusted wildly, breaking loose a cargo winch that crashed to the deck just feet in front of them. The sailor who had warned them flew past, helplessly caught by the brutal wind and pitched into the churning water.

Tadashi grabbed at Kaito's arm. "Kai-chan," he yelled. "What are you doing? We must go below." His voice was barely audible over the roaring sea. Kaito didn't respond.

He wrapped his arm around Kaito's shoulder and pulled him away from the rail. They moved as one, dropping to their knees when they could no longer stand, and at last, descended the ladder to the hold. With no air movement, the stink was even worse than on deck. Tadashi and Kaito retched, their slimy vomit mixed with others' now coated the hold.

The ship tossed helplessly at the mercy of the powerful wind and waves. Hammocks, packs, and firearms flew about as if a vengeful poltergeist raged in the darkness. Even the heavy tables and seats came loose from their anchors, sliding across the lower deck and slamming into prostrate soldiers, crashing against the hull.

Tadashi knelt on the floor, his head against the wall. He held tight to a swaying but still tethered hammock with one hand, and his other hand clutched his magatama.

"Dear sainted uncle," he whispered. "I am no hero like you. I humbly pray for your protection from the spirits' anger.

I swear I will do my best to honor the emperor in battle if only you will help me survive this storm."

His mind raced with worry for his wife and son. How would they manage? If he died in battle, the village would take care of a hero's family. But death from drowning was not heroic; it was almost as shameful as surrender. He glanced at Kaito, who lay on the floor covered in vomit, too weak to battle the pitching ship. Together, they had come to serve the emperor. Together, they would die before they even saw combat. Tadashi clung to the hammock, praying that he would not lose his grip, and quietly wept.

The winds and the waves howled throughout the night and all the next day, finally easing toward daylight of the third morning. When the sun at last peeped through the portholes, it revealed the filthy mess the storm had left behind.

Tadashi and Kaito dragged themselves up the ladder, crawled to an unoccupied corner, and collapsed on the deck. The sun was brilliant, no clouds in sight, but the ship told the story the sky belied. The storm had ripped away the radio tower and two derrick booms, and a sizeable chunk of the bow was torn off. Seaweed churned up from the ocean littered the deck. A mass of fish, weak and dying, flopped where the storm had left them on the deck.

Tadashi gripped his magatama. His throat was raw, and his stomach was weak, its muscles exhausted from constant spasms.

Thank you, venerable uncle, for sparing my life, he prayed silently. He didn't deserve the favor, but he would do his best to honor his uncle's sacrifice in the months to come. At last, he felt strong enough to sit up. He leaned against the kingpost and took stock of his surroundings.

A few crew members were trying to clean up the wreckage, dragging it to the rail and heaving it overboard. Others did their best to stabilize the damaged bow. A handful of soldiers had regained their bearings and tentatively stood, but most of them still lay scattered across the deck, too battered and exhausted to move.

"Are you better, Kai-chan?" Tadashi gently touched Kaito's back.

Kaito moved slowly, groaning as his aching muscles reacted, and eased his body next to Tadashi. "I'll live." He grinned and touched the jade necklace. "The kami have blessed us, Nii-chan."

Tadashi struggled to his feet and made his way to the rail. The dolphins had returned, once again performing their geisha dance. Their noisy chattering filled the air.

Kaito pulled himself next to Tadashi and stood. "Even the sea creatures are grateful to be alive." He waved at the dolphins. "You may go back to your ocean homes, lovely dancers. Nii-chan and I are going to war."

A few days later, the *Myoko Maru* finally limped into port and anchored offshore. It was much too early to have arrived in Australia or even New Guinea. The soldiers boarded the landing craft, a gentle breeze carrying them to shore. They disembarked among the remnants of abandoned cargo and wrecked machinery. Beyond the beach, the ground rose to a high cliff. The mountains loomed in the distance.

"Nii-chan." Kaito caught up to Tadashi and took a minute to catch his breath. Both men were soaked to the waist from wading through the ocean surf. "Where are we?" Kaito swept his arm across the landing beach. "Wherever it is, it seems the enemy has already gone."

Tadashi nodded. "The storm has badly damaged our ship. Perhaps we are here for repairs or to board another ship."

As the soldiers formed up into platoons, word came they had landed in the Lingayen Gulf on the Philippine Island of Luzon.

"Luzon?" Kaito rubbed his chin. "The Americans have already surrendered here." He shrugged. "You must be right. We are here only until we have an able ship."

The sound of approaching trucks silenced the landing troops. Someone pointed toward the dirt road where a line of transport trucks drew near, each flying a Japanese flag.

"At least we won't have to sleep on this beach," Tadashi said, pointing to the approaching vehicles. "It seems we may have to wait awhile for another ship."

An NCO hopped down from the lead truck, approached Tadashi's lieutenant, and saluted.

"Do you have our orders?" Their lieutenant crossed his arms impatiently.

"Ah, yes." The NCO pulled an envelope from his pocket.

The lieutenant ripped open the envelope and studied it. His scowl turned into a snarl as he finished. "Guard the American prisoners." He spat on the ground, a glob of mucus that bowed the blades of grass it fell on. "We are to be watchdogs?"

"I do not make the orders, Lieutenant," the NCO said meekly and took a small step back.

A voice rose from the crowd of soldiers. "The Americans are like sheep, choosing a prisoner's shame-filled life over an honorable death."

"A Japanese soldier would take his own life rather than being caged like an animal," growled another.

Tadashi couldn't believe what he heard. Of course, he would be grateful if he could avoid combat, but he was also frustrated. His father had sold his beloved ox; and he'd left his wife and infant son, risked his life on the open sea. Had it been for nothing?

The lieutenant held up his hand for silence. "I will lodge my protest with the general," he turned to the NCO, glaring. "We are soldiers. We are meant to fight."

The NCO shrugged, regaining his confidence. "It is difficult to fight when there is no enemy," he said. "MacArthur and his underlings ran away long ago." As he returned to his transport, Tadashi heard him mutter under his breath. "Wait until you have been here a little longer. You will be grateful to have avoided your own death."

CHAPTER 7

CAMP HOOD, TEXAS—AUGUST 1944

As the summer wore on, the number of units receiving their deployment orders increased dramatically. Most went to Fort Meade and, from there, to the German front. A few went west, stopping over at Fort Ord, California before boarding a ship to the Pacific Theater. Since the Pearl Harbor invasion, both Admiral Nimitz and General MacArthur had been pushing the Japanese army back toward their homeland. MacArthur was currently in New Guinea. They'd all heard the rumors that his long-promised return to the Philippines was in the offing.

Leo, Dooley, and Jim Furness, a corporal in another training cadre, sat at a table by themselves. Most everyone else had already headed off to their daily assignments.

Dooley shoved a mound of eggs into his mouth and waved his fork at Furness. "Heard you got the high qualifying score on BAR yesterday. Congratulations."

The M1918 Browning Automatic Rifle was the army's light machine gun, whose effective firing range was as much as three times farther than the M1 carried by most infantry soldiers. It was a heavy piece of equipment and required a muscular soldier behind the trigger. A stocky farm boy from the northern Adirondacks, Furness was a perfect choice.

Furness took a swig of his coffee. "I suppose I'm good enough at it," he said. "After all, how much brains does it take to aim and shoot?" He mimed holding a rifle to his shoulder. "They even give you a little tripod to keep it steady."

"Don't short yourself," Leo said. "It takes a powerful man with a sharp eye to operate a BAR."

"I suppose." Furness shrugged. "But as far as I can see, it's just a bigger gun that fires a lot faster."

"Well, I gotta go," Dooley said, washing down the last of his breakfast with a long gulp of coffee. "Time to push around my new batch of pussy-boys." He clapped a hand on Furness's shoulder as he stood. "BAR man, huh? I'm jealous. I can just see you out there mowin' down the Krauts."

Furness lowered his voice to a whisper as Dooley left. Small beads of sweat peppered his forehead. "I gotta tell you, Leo, I can't say I look forward to mowing down soldiers, enemy or not."

"I hear you," Leo said. He and Furness had met at the induction center at Fort Niagara, just north of Buffalo, New York. Besides being a fellow New Yorker, Leo and Jim shared a common religion. They were Methodists amidst a swarm of Southern Baptists and often attended services together. Their distaste for alcohol and tobacco further separated them from the rest of the Camp Hood soldiers, and the two had become close.

Leo finished his meal and pushed his tray to one side. "Your platoon get deployment orders yet?"

"Not officially. But the rumor is we'll get sent to Fort Meade by the end of the month. From there, it's the proverbial hop-skip-and-jump to France or Germany or wherever the hell the Krauts are hiding out these days." He pushed what passed for scrambled eggs around his tray. "Your platoon get orders?"

"Not yet," Leo said. "But if my transfer back to cavalry comes through, I'll probably go to Fort Ord." He absently sipped his coffee and kept talking. "It's funny how it's still called 'cavalry.' Back home, they think we're riding horses through the jungle and all instead of jeeps and tanks." He laughed and looked at Furness for a reaction.

Furness nodded and concentrated on his plate, his eyes shiny with tears.

It seemed like Furness was even moodier than usual these days. Leo leaned closer. "Are you okay, buddy?"

Furness surreptitiously wiped his eyes and looked up with a smile. "I'm fine." He shrugged. "Just a little homesick, I guess."

"You sure?" Leo reached toward him.

"It's no big deal, buddy." Furness put his hand up, palm out. He turned toward the garbage bins, dumped his tray, and hurried out of the mess hall.

Leo watched Furness wander toward his tent, head down, feet scuffing the dirt. He was a hard one to figure out: so quiet, keeping to himself, always so humble.

No, it wasn't exactly humility—it was like Furness lacked confidence, didn't believe he was good enough. Leo couldn't quite put his finger on it, but it seemed like Furness was always glum. He mentioned it to Dooley the next time he saw him.

"Ah, he's just lookin' for attention." Dooley waved his hand. "I've seen it before, guys who go all Nellie Negative so's you'll feel sorry for them."

"Yeah, I guess." Leo wasn't so sure he agreed, and clearly, Dooley wouldn't be much help.

That evening, Leo noticed Furness walking across the compound and decided he had to say something.

"Furness," Leo called as he got closer. "Are you sure you're okay?"

"Let me be." Furness spoke without looking back at him.

Leo caught up to him and touched his shoulder.

Furness whirled around, fists raised. "I said let me be."

"I can't do that, buddy." Leo kept his voice soft and even.

"You don't understand."

"Understand what?"

"Any of this." Furness raised his voice and swept his hand in a wide arc. "The army. The war! They think I can be some kind of hero just because I can hit a target with the BAR. They don't know shit about me." He stared at the distant tree line, and his fists clenched and unclenched as he struggled to keep control. "I can't do it," he whispered. "I'll screw it up. I screw everything up."

"Aw, c'mon, buddy." Leo did his best to sound reassuring. "That's just your nerves talking—we're all nervous about it." He patted Furness on the back.

For a moment, Furness didn't move, didn't speak. He couldn't tell Leo how hopeless he felt most of the time. Leo wouldn't believe him anyway—or maybe he would and would tell Furness to get over it like everybody else did. It was just like when he was a kid and his father got so moody he'd shut himself in his bedroom. It made Jimmy feel like he'd done something wrong, and now, here he was acting the same way.

At last, he looked at Leo with a forced smile. "So, what's your plan for the day, Sergeant Baldwin? Got any new recruits to harass?"

"Takin' the boys out on a two-week bivouac in about—" Leo looked at his watch. "Holy Hannah, I gotta go." He didn't want to leave Furness, but he'd catch hell if he was late. "You sure you're okay?"

"I'm fine." Furness rolled his eyes then snapped to attention and saluted. "Good luck, Sergeant Baldwin, *sir!*"

Leo shook his head and laughed. "Yeah, you too, Corporal."

The sky was darkening as Leo headed toward the staging area where he would meet up with his squad.

Great, Leo thought. *Rain. Mud.* He pulled on his rain poncho. As if he needed anything else to make his life miserable. Hard to believe that just a couple of years ago, the most miserable thing in his life was being a farmer.

CHAPTER 8

BALDWIN'S CORNERS, NEW YORK—MAY 1942

"I saw Mr. Harrigan in town today." Leo's father looked at him from across the dinner table, waiting for a response.

Leo perked up. Mr. Harrigan had been his favorite teacher in high school. He frantically chewed the hunk of meat, swallowed hard, and willed it not to get stuck halfway. "You did?" The words came out "oo ih?" as they forced their way past the food he'd just inhaled. Leo blushed and wiped his mouth. "Excuse me."

Mother and Grandfather both scowled at him, but his father just kept talking.

"He wants you to go see him." He pointed his fork at Leo. "Says he has something you might be interested in."

"I'll do that," Leo said. His father nodded and returned his attention to his dinner.

What could Mr. Harrigan want to show him? It had been almost two years since he'd finished his schooling. The last time he'd spoken to Mr. Harrigan had been at graduation.

"Leo." His former teacher jumped up as Leo entered the classroom "Good to see you." He extended his hand. "I guess your father told you I was looking for you."

Leo shook his hand and nodded. "Yeah. It was a pleasant surprise." He sat at the nearest desk, wriggling uncomfortably in the narrow chair.

Mr. Harrigan laughed and sat at his desk. He shuffled through a tall pile of papers, pulled one out of the stack, and handed it to Leo. "I got this the other day and thought it might interest you."

Leo stood, politely accepted the paper, and squeezed back into the chair. "Sears, Roebuck and Company" blazed across the top of the page. He shot a questioning look at the teacher, who simply nodded and gestured toward the paper.

"Read it."

"Sears, Roebuck and Company and Cornell University have announced the establishment of a full-tuition scholarship for deserving young men who have graduated high school within the past two years.

"You think I can get this?" Leo wanted to jump up and shout. A full scholarship? This could be his ticket out.

"I think if anyone can, it's you," Mr. Harrigan said. "You're the smartest student I've ever had."

Leo's mind buzzed as he jogged toward home. Cornell was an agricultural school. Did that mean he'd have to study agriculture? What could he do with that besides farming? Until now, he'd seen no way of getting out unless he wanted to lead a hobo's life. The Depression had wiped out most of the jobs he could get, and he didn't know anyone outside his community who might help him. Would Cornell offer a degree in writing? Was that even a practical career?

Well, he wouldn't worry about that just yet. He had to win the scholarship first, and he'd have to convince his parents to let him go. But he knew one thing for sure: if he could get a college education, he'd take it and learn all he could.

And he'd make darn sure to turn that into a career that would get him somewhere.

Leo paced around the mailbox as the black Chevy sedan pulled up.

"Nothing for you today." The mailman handed Leo a stack of letters and the weekly newspaper. "Whatever you're expecting must be important. You've been out here every day for the last three weeks."

"Ah, it's nothin'." Leo stared at the ground, kicking at a wayward spider. He raised his hand. "See ya later, Mr. Wiggins." It had been two long months since he'd applied for the Sears scholarship. He'd told no one, didn't want to hear their arguments until he knew for sure.

He turned toward the house. The crunch of tires on gravel grew faint as the mail car disappeared down the road. Fading away, just like his chances of going to college. He felt as if he carried an extra twenty pounds in his legs as he started back toward the house.

Leo nearly jumped out of his skin when the horn beeped behind him. He swung around to see Mr. Harrigan emerge from his car.

"Got news." He waved a paper in the air. "Come see."

Leo ignored the slap of the screen door that meant someone had stepped onto the porch to investigate the noise. He raced to the car, afraid to ask if the news was good or bad, but Mr. Harrigan wouldn't have come all this way if it was bad news, would he?

"You got it." Mr. Harrigan clasped Leo's shoulder and handed him the letter. "But I knew you would."

Leo's heart pounded as he read. "We are pleased to announce..." He couldn't believe it. In less than ten weeks, he would be on a train headed to Ithaca and a future as something other than a dirt-poor farmer.

He sprinted up the steps where his mother waited.

"Aren't you going to invite your company inside?" She scowled at him and raised a hand toward the idling car, where Mr. Harrigan was just sliding behind the wheel. "Can you stay for lunch?" she shouted.

"No, thanks." He stuck his head out of the window and waved. "Got papers to grade." He honked his horn repeatedly as he headed back toward town.

Leo stood in the kitchen where his parents and grandparents were eating. He handed the letter to his father, who held the paper at a distance, squinting to read the small type. Leo's mother came up behind his father and peered over his shoulder, glaring at the paper.

"What's this about?" Dad raised an eyebrow, looked at Leo as if he were in some kind of trouble.

"It's a scholarship from Sears and Roebuck." The words poured out in a rush. He dared not stop to take a breath. "To go to Cornell. Free tuition. Mr. Harrigan helped me apply for it, and he just brought this letter that says I got the scholarship."

His mother was first to react. "You think you're too good to stay on the farm?"

Leo's stomach lurched. Leave it to his mother to find the negative side of this. "No, Mother, I don't. But—"

"Simmer down, Mary." Grandfather held his hand up. "An agriculture degree could be just what the boy needs to bring this place back up to snuff."

Leo stiffened. This was going about as badly as he'd imagined. No one had even bothered to congratulate him. "Maybe I don't want an ag degree."

His grandfather glowered, his fists clenched tightly. "Then maybe I don't want to give you permission to go."

Tears pushed behind Leo's eyes. He knew this was too good to be true. He leaned across the table toward his grandfather, put on his angriest stare.

"I don't need your permission." He turned away and stormed outside.

"Don't you run off when I'm talking to you," his grandfather roared from the kitchen.

But Leo ignored him, ignored every one of them and sprinted off toward the woods. He stumbled across the wheat field, the ground still uneven from tilling and dotted with the sprouting plants. He angrily crushed one or two of them. *I will not be a farmer.*

A pair of red squirrels scrambled out of his way as he crashed through the thick brush that bordered the woods. By the time he reached his writing spot, he was gasping for air. He dropped to the ground, shaking from both anger and adrenalin.

You can't make me stay here.

The pounding in Leo's chest slowed as he caught his breath. There was nothing he wanted so much as to be a writer. How could they take away the one thing he loved? He hated this farm, hated everything about it, including his family.

He didn't care what anyone said. He was going to college, and if he had to leave right now, that's what he'd do. He felt a sense of calm with the decision, his body relaxed.

Carefully retrieving his notebook from its hiding place, he reread his poetry, thought, *Am I good enough to be a writer?*

His stomach clenched. What if he wasn't good enough? What if the college professors told him he was a terrible writer? What else could he do?

"Leo." Dad gently touched his shoulder.

Leo jumped. "Jeepers, you scared the crawdads out of me."

His father smiled and sat next to him. "Sorry, didn't mean to."

Leo let the silence thicken between them, carefully choosing what he hoped were the right words.

His father spoke first. "I went to college."

Leo's eyes widened. "You did? You never told me that."

"No reason to," he said. "I wanted to be a musician—loved playing piano and was darned good at it." He paused, his eyes glazed as if he was watching his hands fly across the keys. "My grandfather paid my way. There was money back then." Tears glistened, and his hand trembled slightly. "When he realized my plan, he took away his money. Told me I'd take over the farm, or I'd be out the door on my keister." Dad sighed, wiped his eyes. "So, I took over the farm." He looked at Leo, touched Leo's chin and lifted it until they were eye to eye. "I've regretted that every day since."

"I didn't know." Leo wasn't sure what else to say. He'd just always assumed Mother and Grandfather's accusations that his father was lazy. Now he understood the reason behind his father's behavior. Leo pointed to the notebook in his lap. "I want to be a writer."

His father held out his hand. "May I read it?"

Leo nodded, handed him the notebook. This was the first person he'd ever shown his notebook to. Would his father hate it? Tell Leo his dream was hopeless? He studied his father, looking for a reaction—any kind of reaction. There was nothing in his father's face that gave away his thoughts.

His father finally looked up.

"This is good." He smiled, closed the notebook, and handed it back to Leo. He stood, wiped the dust off his trousers. "Take the scholarship," he said. "Go be a writer."

Mother was going to be harder to convince. "There'll be room and board to pay for. Have you thought of that?"

Leo hadn't thought about living expenses. But he had some money set by.

"I've been saving up for a while," he said. "And it's nearly haying time. There'll be plenty of farmers needing extra help before I go, and I promise not to get behind on my chores at home." He looked pleadingly at his mother and father. He'd made sure his grandparents weren't around—he wouldn't give Grandfather a chance to object again.

A smile crossed his mother's face, something Leo had rarely seen.

"Then you'd better go," she said.

"Thank you." He hugged his mother, shook his father's hand. "I promise not to disappoint you."

It was a good day for packing; the light drizzle outside made cutting hay impossible, and they'd finished the morning chores. Finally—*finally*—he was leaving home. The small suitcase bulged as Leo packed his few belongings neatly inside. He lowered the lid and leaned heavily against it as he forced the clasps to close.

Two more days and he'd be on his way to his future. He patted his pocket where he'd put the envelope containing twenty dollars from the church congregation that Reverend Hanson had given him on Sunday after services.

"Something to help you on your way," the reverend had said. "We're all praying for your success."

Out the window, he could see his mother walking toward the house with the day's mail in her hand. *It must be after eleven. I'd better get a move on.*

He jogged down the stairs, meeting his mother at the back door as she came inside.

"You got a letter," she said. "Looks important." She held the envelope out, a worried expression on her face.

Leo's heart jumped. Had something happened to his scholarship? Was Sears and Roebuck rescinding their offer? He took the envelope, turning it over to see the return address. His shoulders sagged as he opened it and removed its contents.

"Order to report for induction." The words blazed across the top of the page. "The President of the United States, to Leal Patrick Baldwin..." He was to report to the local induction board next Wednesday where he would "... be examined, and, if accepted for training and service, you will then be inducted into the land or naval forces."

Only weeks before, he had seen a rare smile from his mother. Today, he saw something he had never seen: his mother slumped in a chair, crying.

CHAPTER 9

CAMP HOOD, TEXAS—AUGUST 1944

On the practice field ahead, most of the other squads had already loaded their gear and formed up. Leo hurried his pace; he didn't want his men to be the last squad ready to go. He hoped Furness's attitude would be improved by the time he got back.

By the time he and his squad were five miles into the twenty-mile march to the bivouac site, Leo had all but forgotten Furness's mood. His knee ached—it hadn't been the same since he'd tripped into a gopher hole on a rainy day much like this one. He ignored the pain, struggled to catch up with his men.

More like boys. Not one of them had yet reached the age of twenty; the youngest was only seventeen. It was bad enough he had to take naïve boys and train them into killing machines in a matter of weeks, but most of these kids ought to still be in school, not playing soldier. And that's how they acted: like kids, full of themselves and feeling immortal.

On the trail ahead, his boys were trading playful punches, thinking he wasn't looking. Sure as heck, they were planning some sort of juvenile mischief as soon as they hit the bivouac site.

God help me, he thought.

"Line up. Today's problem is locating our new outpost." Leo distributed the maps to his squad as they shuffled into a line. "You've got our current coordinates and the coordinates for the outpost. You'll be using the skills you've learned to set your azimuth and pace." He glared at his squad. "Anyone got the nerve to admit he doesn't know how to do that?"

No one moved.

"Good. You'll have four hours to reach the new OP. And remember"—Leo raised his pointer finger—"you are under battle conditions. That means you have to be prepared for anything."

His squad studied the map and plotted their course. Within minutes, they were headed to their target, cautiously scanning for the enemy. Leo followed at a distance, keeping out of sight.

Good. At least they took that much seriously.

It didn't take long before the squad forgot his cautions. They ran across the open field like they were playing a game of tag, paying no attention to the possibility of enemy fire. Leo watched, a pinched expression on his face. Danged idiots. This was going to get ugly.

A whoop went up from the squad when they spotted the tree that marked the first checkpoint. The boy in front raced to the tree and tagged it.

"Beat-cha." He triumphantly wagged his hands in the air.

Gunfire rang from beyond the trees. The boys dropped and covered their heads. Bullets threw up bits of dirt as they hit the ground in a circle around the squad.

"Well, that was a disaster." Leo stood over his squad, hands on his hips. "You babies going to get up, or do you plan on taking a nap?"

One boy cautiously lifted his head. "What the hell—that was live ammo!"

"No kidding." Leo said sarcastically. "You think the Japs or the Krauts are shooting blanks? 'Oh, look, it's a Yank—let's not kill him just yet.'"

"Jesus Christ." One recruit cautiously stood, still visibly shaken. "I nearly shit my pants." He reached to dust off the back of his trousers and stopped. "Oh crap."

His squad mates broke into laughter until Leo's stony glare brought them back to attention. "You're alive. Which is more than you would be if it was the real enemy shooting at you."

Two weeks later, a bedraggled bunch of recruits straggled into camp. The whole thing had been a disaster for Leo's squad, ending with their failure to complete their field training successfully.

Leo dismissed his men and stormed into the barracks. He was fuming. Clearly, these guys would not graduate from Basic. He was so angry he almost walked into the soldier who paced at the door.

"Thank God you're back, Sarge." One of Furness's platoon buddies.

"Now what?" All Leo wanted was a hot shower and a long nap. "You can run right back to Furness and tell him I'm not in any mood to kid around."

"That's the problem. I can't."

"Why not?"

"He disappeared before breakfast." The soldier took off his cap and ran a hand through his hair. "We need to find him before the CO reports him as AWOL."

Leo slammed his fist against the wall. He dropped his gear in the corner. "Okay, let's go," he growled. "He'd better have a darned good reason for running off."

By late afternoon, Leo was about ready to call the MPs himself. He'd looked every place he could think of where Furness might be. He wouldn't have gone AWOL, would he? Leo shook his head. He was more worried than angry now, and he wasn't sure where else to look.

"If we don't find him by dinner—" Leo stopped abruptly and stared across the fast-flowing river. Furness stood on the opposite side and stared down at the rushing current. A pistol hung loosely from his right hand.

"Furness!" Leo shouted as loud as he could, but the noise of the current drowned him out. He waved his hands in the air, trying to get Furness's attention.

Furness didn't move.

"Stay here and keep trying to get his attention," Leo said to Furness's squad mate.

Leo raced along the edge of the river, desperately looking for a place shallow enough to cross. Finally, he plunged into the current and prayed it wouldn't get too deep.

"Furness!" he shouted as he climbed out of the river.

Furness lifted the pistol, studied it for a moment, and looked at Leo. His face was red, his eyes swollen from crying.

"What do you think you're doing?" Leo was out of breath and soaking wet. He held out his hand as he approached Furness and cautiously took the pistol from him.

Furness looked blankly at the pistol. "I'll never make it, Sarge."

"Yes, you will," Leo said. "Don't give up now. We'll find someone to help."

"I don't think so." Furness shrugged. "I'm sick of feeling like this." He gestured toward the pistol. "Just give that back to me and leave me alone."

"I can't, Jim." Leo tucked the pistol in his waistband and put a hand on Furness's shoulder. "Come on. Let's get back to camp before they send the MPs for you."

After Furness was safely tucked in a bed at sick bay, Leo played with the food on his tray. He glanced at his watch. It was getting late, and he hadn't even unpacked yet. Leo had convinced the doc to keep him overnight, but he'd avoided giving details other than to tell him that Furness was suffering from exhaustion and needed some rest.

He kicked himself for not making Furness get help. His mind had been on the bivouac and his transfer status, and he'd let Furness convince him he was okay. That was going to change.

Tomorrow they'd talk, he'd insist Furness see the doc.

Leo looked up. The mess hall was nearly empty, and his dinner was cold and congealed on the tray. *Tomorrow*, he reminded himself as he dumped his dinner in the trash, *I'm going to get Furness some help.*

"I'm fine, dammit." Furness perched on the edge of his sick bay cot. By the time Leo got there, Furness had dressed and was about to leave.

"You're not fine," Leo said. "You almost killed yourself yesterday."

"Yeah, well, I'm better now." Furness started for the door. "I just had a bad day, that's all."

Leo wasn't giving in this time. He stepped in front of Furness. "That wasn't just another bad day, and you know it."

Furness folded his arms and glared at Leo. "Listen," he said, "I told you I was fine. Let it go."

"I'm not letting it go," Leo said. "If you don't talk to someone, I will."

"No, you won't." Furness grabbed Leo's arm and leaned toward him. "I won't let down my squad just because I'm feeling sorry for myself. If I ask for help, I'll get a 4F slapped on me, sure as shit, and I won't let that happen."

Furness softened his grip, his face pale. "Please, Leo," he whispered. "I promise I'm okay."

"And if you're not?" Leo raised an eyebrow.

"Look," Furness said. "We leave for Fort Meade on Friday. If I get there and I'm still having problems, I'll see about getting some help."

"You do that." Leo stepped aside. He didn't believe for a minute that Furness would ask for help, but for now, there wasn't much he could do to stop him.

CHAPTER 10

CAMP HOOD, TEXAS—SEPTEMBER 1944

Leo relaxed under a large pecan tree in the warm September sun, pen in hand. It was a chilly morning, and he had a small fire going. No matter where he sat, the smoke blew into his face, but he didn't mind so much—it was a pleasant change from the unrelenting heat.

He paused, considering what to write next.

> Dear folks,
>
> I am going to Fort Ord, California. That, of course, means that there's no possibility of my getting home. That no doubt means action in the South Pacific, which I can't look forward to with any great pleasure. It means a return to cavalry, however, so it will be okay. I don't know exactly what my next address will be, but I'll let you know just as soon as I find out.
>
> Love to all,
>
> Leal

Another step closer, Leo thought as he tucked the letter into its envelope and set it aside. He pulled another box from the small pile beside his cot. Only things essential to battle and a few small personal items would go with him. He'd packed everything else into boxes to be sent home. He closed and taped the last box, addressed it to home, and set it aside.

He'd already said his goodbyes. Furness was leaving for Fort Meade in the morning, Dooley would be with Leo on the train to Fort Ord. Was Furness okay? He hadn't confided in Leo since Leo had threatened to notify the CO. Whenever they saw each other, Furness put his head down. If Leo asked how he was doing, Furness changed the subject. Furness *seemed* okay, but Leo couldn't forget his friend's despair, his desperation. He crawled under the covers and settled in for his last night in Texas.

The sun was barely peeking above the horizon as Leo and Dooley stood in line to board the bus to Killeen. From there, they'd board a train to Fort Ord. In less than forty-eight hours, he'd be on the west coast, farther from home than he'd ever been.

Where was Furness? He was scheduled to take the same bus to the train station, his train taking him east instead of west. Leo hadn't seen him at breakfast either. A knot formed in Leo's stomach. He didn't take off again, did he?

Ten minutes later, Furness still hadn't shown. Leo checked the time. The bus would leave soon—where the heck was he?

"Hold up."

Leo jerked his head up and looked out the window where a soldier ran across the compound shouting frantically.

"Hold up!" the soldier shouted again.

About danged time. Leo relaxed his grip on the seat in front of him.

As the soldier approached, Leo could see it wasn't Furness. The man's face was pale, his eyes wide as he boarded the bus, gasping for air.

"I need to see Sergeant Baldwin," he shouted. His body trembled as he looked for Leo.

"Hurry up," the driver growled. "I gotta get going."

Leo stood, moving to the front of the bus. He recognized the man now, one of Furness's platoon mates. "What's up, soldier?"

"Furness," the soldier's chest heaved, pulling in air. "He's dead."

CHAPTER 11

CABANATUAN POW CAMP—OCTOBER 1944

Nothing but rubble remained of Valdefuente village when Tadashi and Kaito arrived with their prisoner work details. Smoke rose from the still smoldering ruins, creating a haze that covered the barangay like a funeral shroud. Dead bodies coated with a thick layer of ash lay everywhere.

A third detail was already at work, clearing the remains from last night's bombing. The emaciated POWs crawled over the remains of burned-out buildings, picking through the debris for anything useful before hauling away the remains of both homes and bodies. Perhaps the American planes had meant to harass the prison camp; instead, their bombs fell on the innocent villagers.

Corporal Miyamoto, the guard in charge, waved at Tadashi and Kaito as they approached.

"Start on that one," Miyamoto said, pointing to an adjacent mound that might once have been somebody's home. He returned his attention to his men.

"I would like to have Miyamoto's self-confidence," Tadashi said as he and Kaito directed their men toward the work site. "Nothing frightens him."

Daiki Miyamoto was as different from Tadashi and Kaito as a peacock from a mouse. He was born to an affluent and powerful family in Katori, near Tokyo. He was well-educated and outspoken, a man whose influence could be substantial if he chose to use it. But he rarely spoke of his advantages; the only sign that he was different was the deference he received from the officers. Not one of them dared lay a hand on him.

But trouble had a habit of finding Miyamoto—or maybe Miyamoto had a habit of finding trouble. He was a risk-taker, thumbing his nose at death, daring it to find him.

"Do you think I joined the army out of duty to the emperor?" Miyamoto would ask. "Any duty I might have owed to my country has long ago been fulfilled. No, I stay for the adventure, for the thrill of risking my life every day. If I die tomorrow, at least I have lived well," he'd told his fellow soldiers. He'd slick back his jet-black hair and grin. "Besides, women love a man in uniform."

It was that devil-may-care attitude that Tadashi found enticing. Although he could never be so cavalier about life, he admired Miyamoto for his boldness. The man lived life his own way and laughed at death.

Kaito glanced at Miyamoto and spat on the ground. "I don't know why you find him so appealing. The man is nothing but a braggart. Clearly, he cares more for himself than his country."

Tadashi grinned. "You're jealous, aren't you?" He put a hand on Kaito's arm. "You will always be my closest friend."

"I am not jealous." Kaito jerked his arm away and angrily cuffed the nearest of his work crew. "Get to work," he growled, pointing at the pile of rubble.

"More bodies," Tadashi grumbled under his breath. Cleaning up after death was not a duty he imagined when he arrived in Luzon. In combat, he would have seen the remains of soldiers littering the battlefield, but these corpses were civilians: a few old men but mostly mothers and children who had inadvertently gotten in the way of war.

Clouds formed as the day progressed. The air thickened with the heat and humidity until it drenched the guards in sweat.

"I'm calling a rest break," Tadashi said as he motioned his crew to stop working. Kaito scowled but gestured to his men as well. Tadashi handed a bucket of water to the nearest prisoner, who gulped several handfuls and passed the pail down the line of men.

Shouts erupted from Miyamoto's work crew. Tadashi and Kaito jumped up, rifles ready.

"Bomb!" No one needed translation for the word. Every man in the work detail dropped to the ground and covered his head.

Everyone except Miyamoto. He approached the unexploded missile like a stray dog, curiously circling it, inspecting it from every angle. He picked up a long stick and poked at the bomb. "Huh."

Prisoners and guards alike scattered behind mounds of rubble and downed trees.

"What are you doing?" Kaito screeched at Miyamoto. "You're going to kill us all."

"What?" Miyamoto thrust his stick like a fencer, poking the bomb a little harder. "You're afraid of a little bomb?" At last, he stopped and threw the stick into the nearest pile. He pointed to an adjacent area. "Move your details over there."

Tadashi cautiously emerged from his hiding place and assembled his work crew. He looked at the unexploded shell, raised an eyebrow toward Miyamoto.

"It's not going anywhere." Miyamoto laughed. "I'll report it when we get back to camp tonight."

"The man is crazy," Kaito grumbled as he moved his men.

Tadashi wouldn't argue with that. But he would not admit it to Kaito.

By midday, the overburdened clouds could no longer hold the humidity. Heavy rains poured from the darkened sky. At first, the rain was a welcome relief, but soon the entire village was a pit of standing water and slippery mud. Already weakened POWs slid from the mountains of rubble.

Kaito stumbled back, enraged, as a tumbling prisoner bumped against his foot. He raised his foot, kicked at the man on the ground in front of him over and over.

"Get up," he shouted. Each kick increased his anger, amplified his frustration. "Get up!"

The prisoner lay helpless, covering his head from Kaito's blows.

"Kaito." Tadashi put his hand on Kaito's shoulder and spoke quietly. "You need to stop."

"This prisoner needs discipline." Kaito's voice pitched higher. "Did our sergeants take pity on us in training?" he shouted. "No, they expected us to obey."

"Kaito." Tadashi kept his voice even.

Kaito jerked away. "Why do you defend them? Because they are weak like you?"

Tadashi's jaw dropped. Kaito had always teased him for being too soft, but where had his fun-loving Kai-chan gone? When had he become so callous?

"You call yourself a peaceful man. But the truth is, you're a pushover. Your prisoners get away with disrespect. You look away when they steal food or smuggle medicine. I should tell the commander." Kaito aimed an especially brutal kick at the prisoner. "What do you think of that?"

He turned and stormed away.

Tadashi put himself and his men at the end of the line when they returned to the POW camp. He intended to keep as much distance as he could between him and Kaito. The heavy rain had stopped, but the exhausted prisoners struggled on the muddy path. It was nearly dark by the time they stumbled through the heavily guarded gate.

Most nights, the grounds would be empty except for the evening guards, but tonight, every soldier and prisoner in camp was assembled in the open area used for morning roll call. Major Takasaki, the man who had recently taken command of Cabanatuan, stood on a raised platform in front of the crowd.

Not even the crows dared make a sound. Tadashi held his breath. He knew Takasaki's reputation for cruelty to both his men and his prisoners. Who had annoyed the major this time? He shuddered and searched his memory. Had he done anything that may have angered him?

At a nod from Takasaki, two soldiers dragged a beaten and bloodied POW to the platform. A disheveled guard followed closely behind them. Tadashi recognized the prisoner. He had escaped from a work detail two days ago. It wasn't surprising that he'd been captured. Very few escapes were successful. The Americans' pale skin was a giveaway—the natives were too afraid to shelter them.

The guard approached Takasaki and bowed respectfully then turned to the half-dead prisoner. Major Takasaki removed his pistol from its harness, held it against the escapee's head, and fired. As the dead man slumped to the ground, Takasaki spoke.

"There have been too many escapes, despite the certainty of execution when they are caught." Takasaki glared at the assembled prisoners. "I will not tolerate this under my command."

He signaled to a waiting group of soldiers. Each pulled a prisoner from the crowd, dragged him to an open area, and forced him to his knees.

Tadashi watched in horror as the soldiers took a position behind their prisoners and raised their rifles. He knew a couple of the men who were dragged from the crowd. They were men he'd admired for their courage and their compassion. He thought of the quiet reverence he'd seen as they'd buried their comrades.

Takasaki spoke. "From now on, every prisoner must take responsibility for the actions of his comrades."

He raised a hand toward the soldiers.

Nine shots fired. Nine prisoners fell dead.

"Starting tomorrow, I will assign all prisoners to groups of ten," he continued. "You will be blood brothers, responsible for one another. If one of you escapes, I will execute the remaining nine." He turned toward the guard, still standing at attention next to him, lifted his pistol, and shot the guard in the head. "I will also execute the guard responsible for the offending group."

He returned his pistol to its harness, turned, and left.

Hours later, long after the bugle had called lights out, Tadashi's mind was still reeling, unable to accept what he'd seen. Executing escapees was nothing new. It was necessary. He knew that.

But this? Randomly killing good men who had done nothing wrong?

Was this what war did to people? Did it drive them to madness? He shook his head, hoping to dispel the images burned into his brain.

He'd had no appetite for dinner. His stomach growled from hunger, and his gut churned with nausea. He could not sleep, unwilling to close his eyes.

Tadashi had refused to beat his prisoners like the other guards did so easily. Even when he'd seen them as cowards for choosing capture over death, he believed they deserved to be treated better than cattle.

None of this was what he'd been taught. None of this fit his beliefs about his emperor and his country. If these were the convictions he was fighting for, perhaps he was on the wrong side.

CHAPTER 12

Boots and bare feet squelched in the mud as the work crews returned to Valdefuente the next day. The torrential rains had put out any remaining fires and washed away the remains of stick-built homes and thatched roofs. The rot of dead bodies replaced the reek of wood smoke. Work crews moved through the carnage like machines, lifting, carrying, depositing the remains: one pile for rubble, another for bodies. They would burn both at the end of the day.

Any trace of hope the prisoners might have held had vanished with the crack of Major Takasaki's pistol. Although Tadashi's English was limited, he'd understood their whispers last night.

"That crazy bastard's going to kill every last one of us."

"What's the difference? We're all dead, anyway."

They worked now in their groups of "blood brothers," each man watching the others with a pleading "don't you dare try to escape" look in his eyes.

The guards stood together as they watched their charges at work.

Tadashi took his eyes off his men and looked at Miyamoto. "Do you think the prisoners will heed Major Takasaki?"

Miyamoto shook his head. "I think he has taken what little hope they had. As much as they might have been willing to risk their own lives, I doubt they will readily risk the lives of their comrades."

Tadashi nodded and looked toward Kaito, who stayed silent, his attention focused on his crew. Their time as prison guards had created a distance between them. If any of his men acted suspiciously, Tadashi felt sure Kaito would shoot the prisoner with no questioning.

The three guards stood quietly for a few moments.

At last Tadashi spoke. "I knew two of those men."

Miyamoto raised an eyebrow. "The ones Takasaki executed?"

Tadashi nodded. "They were good men. I watched them as they ministered to their ill comrades, giving up their own rations to those who needed them more. They kept their heads down but did not hesitate to protect their friends."

Miyamoto only nodded. Kaito seemed not to hear.

"That's just not right." Tadashi shook his head. His voice rose in frustration and anger. "What did they do to offend the major? Nothing. He had no cause to execute them."

"Nii-chan," Kaito scowled but kept his eyes on his prisoners. "Are you crazy? If Major Takasaki knew your thoughts, he would kill you just as easily as he did the Americans."

Tadashi shrugged. "If it weren't for Sachiko and our son, I'm not sure I would care."

Kaito turned and glared at him. "Are the Americans any more moral when they destroy our innocents? We should kill them all right now."

Tadashi winced and shook his head. "I don't think I know you anymore, Kai-chan. I am ashamed of what you have become."

He moved away, closer to his work crew, and kept his back to Kaito and Miyamoto.

Kaito silently turned his attention back to the POWs.

"Tadashi is right, you know." Miyamoto spoke softly.

Kaito's voice rose in anger. "Who are you to know his mind better than I? Tadashi and I are like brothers. Do you think your fine reputation makes you a better friend?"

Miyamoto stepped back. "I simply meant that randomly executing good men is abhorrent."

"If you don't like the way prisoners are treated, why don't you change it?" Kaito growled. "You have the influence, the powerful family."

"I am not the enemy, Corporal Shimizu." Miyamoto shook his head and whistled at his work crew, motioning them to an area farther away.

As evening approached, the guards assembled their men and prepared to return to camp. Miyamoto was at the head of the line as they passed the area where they'd found the bomb the day before. He stopped the POWs behind him. Tadashi and Kaito came up to see why the line had been halted.

"We forgot about the bomb," Miyamoto said, pointing to the unexploded missile.

"We were occupied with other matters, as I remember." Tadashi smiled wryly. "We'll report it tonight."

Miyamoto studied the bomb from a distance. "I can take care of it now," he said. "You and Kaito go ahead with the prisoners. I'll catch up."

Tadashi nodded and returned to his men. Kaito assumed command at the head of the line. Minutes later, a thunderous blast filled the air. The ground shook. Tadashi looked back to see a thick cloud of smoke rising from the village.

As everyone realized they were not in danger, they stood, re-forming their line. Kaito gave the order to move out, with Tadashi once again in the rear. Every few feet, he turned to look behind him, expecting to see Miyamoto come running down the road.

Was he hurt? Dead? *Should I go back?*

An hour later, Miyamoto still had not returned. Tadashi decided to look for him. He was halfway back to the village when he spotted his friend weaving down the road like an intoxicated native.

Dried blood from shallow shrapnel wounds striped Miyamoto's arms and face.

Tadashi rushed to his side. "Are you okay?"

"Just a few scratches, that's all." He wiped his face and arms, reopening a few of the wounds.

"What took you so long?"

Miyamato blushed. "It was a bigger blast than I expected. It knocked me out for a while."

Tadashi shook his head. "You *are* crazy."

"I just did what had to be done." Miyamoto shrugged. "I paced off to a safe distance, aimed at the detonator, and fired. No big deal."

They continued down the road in silence for a way. Then Tadashi stopped and looked at Miyamoto.

"I don't understand your recklessness," Tadashi said. "Do you wish for death?"

Miyamoto hesitated.

"I don't invite death," he said. "But I will not hide from it either."

Tadashi thought about being killed in action. He could not knowingly risk his life when his wife and son waited at home.

"What about your family? Don't you care about going home to them?"

Miyamoto stared into the distance. When he spoke, his voice was only a whisper. "I have no family. They are all dead."

CHAPTER 13

KATORI, CHIBA PREFECTURE, JAPAN—1930

Daiki Miyamoto's head bent to his desk as he tried to concentrate on his schoolwork. Outside, the rain fell in torrents, and heavy winds shook the windows and howled like a bevy of lost souls.

When he'd left home that morning, thick clouds hung over the ocean to the east. Fog shrouded the grounds of his family's compound on a cliff high above a small fishing village.

"The storm will be quick," his father had predicted. "See how the clouds move? They will not linger."

By midmorning, the rain had started, growing in intensity along with the winds that pushed against the windowpanes, rattling the glass like a toddler's toy.

At sixteen, most boys would have finished their schooling and joined their fathers in the fields or on the sea. But Daiki's family held status, money, and power. Like most boys in his social class, he was entitled to at least another four years of education.

The school building, a large brick structure, stood firm against the pounding storm. But by midmorning, the winds had intensified, and the building trembled with the force.

"Attention everyone." Daiki looked up from his work as the headmaster spoke. "Everyone must move to the gymnasium quickly and in an orderly fashion." With no windows, the gymnasium was the safest place in the school.

Daiki looked outside. The rain fell in heavy sheets and obscured everything. He gathered his belongings and hurried with the other students to the gymnasium. Although it was the largest room in the building, there was just enough space for everyone to fit.

"Resume your work," the teacher instructed.

But before anyone could obey, the high ceiling lights flickered and went out.

Although the older boys knew better than to talk, a few of the younger students cried out, nervously chattering at one another. The teachers placed oil lanterns around the gymnasium, and the boys returned to their studies. Daiki bent to his textbook, straining in the dim lights to see the page.

Hours later, the storm still raged. Whatever food the boys had eaten at lunchtime would have to do until they could go home.

The headmaster addressed the students. "Until the storm is over, everyone will stay here. Let us pray the morning will bring relief."

Using his coat for a pillow, Daiki huddled on the floor, scrunched between two of his classmates. His stomach growled with hunger, and his mind raced with worry. It seemed he had just fallen asleep when the headmaster's voice roused him.

"The storm has passed," he said. "But there is substantial damage outside. Students in year four and younger are to wait here for family to come for them. Older students may return home with extreme care."

Trees and utility poles lay everywhere. Daiki picked his way around downed branches and wires, past houses that were now only a pile of thatch and matchsticks. He felt grateful his house was built of brick; he was sure it had survived the storm.

In the far distance, he could see the shadow of his home, the skeletal shapes of the large trees that had fallen around it. As he got closer, the near walls of the outer courtyard became clearer. Fallen trees lay everywhere, their sod-covered roots black and foreboding.

Nothing moved.

Where was everyone? Something wasn't right. His father, the gardener, *someone* should be outside. He broke into a run, vaulting over a pile of bricks where the wall had collapsed. As he came closer to the house, he realized only the nearest wall was still standing.

The house was gone, replaced by a gaping hole. The cliff's edge was twenty feet closer than before. His heart in his throat, Daiki cautiously crept to the cliff and peered over the edge.

What remained of his home lay covered in mud and debris one hundred feet below. There was no sign of the fishing village.

It seemed like hours before Daiki reached what remained of the fishing village. Heart pounding and breathless, he clawed his way to the top of the mud pile that buried his home. Daiki frantically tore at the mud, sobbing uncontrollably as he dug, until his hands were raw and bleeding. *They must be alive. Please let someone be alive.*

"You won't find anyone," a voice said from behind him.

Daiki turned around and faced the man who had spoken. "They're my family." His voice was hoarse, tears ran down his face. "They have to be alive."

The man shook his head. "If anyone survived the fall, they will have suffocated in the mud. It has been too long."

Daiki jumped up, his fists clenched by his side. "You can't know that. Maybe someone got out."

He dropped to his knees and started digging again.

A hand gently touched his shoulder. "No, son," the man said. "I saw it fall. We all saw it fall. There are no survivors." He pointed down the ridge to where a handful of people stood. "When the storm hit, most of the villagers hid in that cave. We heard the loud rumble from the cliff when it gave way. I peeked out of the cave and watched as the cliffside and everything on it tumbled onto the village, crushing what little had survived the typhoon."

Miyamoto looked at Tadashi, his eyes wet with tears. "That night I left Katori. I have not returned since."

"Where did you go? Did you have family nearby?"

Miyamoto nodded. "I could have gone to my uncles for shelter. But I decided this disaster was a sign: it was time for me to become an adult. And after losing everyone I loved, I had no desire to feel that emotion ever again."

He returned his gaze to the horizon.

"The next morning, I enlisted in the army. I arrived in Korea in time to take part in the takeover of Manchukuo. I fought at the Marco Polo Bridge and in Nanking. I took risks, put myself in danger. I didn't care if I lived or died. Because of that, they celebrated me for my courage." He frowned and shook his head. "There was no courage in my actions, only apathy."

"You have been in the army for many years," Tadashi said. "Why are you still only a corporal? Surely, by now you would have reached a high rank, especially with all of those medals."

"They were offered," Miyamoto said, "but I refused." He flicked his hand dismissively. "Why would I want responsibility for the lives of other men? Men who had wives and children, mothers and fathers. No, I am content to stay a corporal. Taking responsibility for prisoners is enough."

CHAPTER 14

SAN FRANCISCO, CALIFORNIA—NOVEMBER 1944

Leo breathed in the heavy scent of the Pacific coast. The aroma was intense, a mixture of brine and seaweed, mucky sand, stranded crustaceans, and rotting fish. A pelican gracefully glided over the sea and plummeted to the surface to scoop up a mouthful of fish. Occasionally, a seal would pop its head above water, grab a mouthful of air, and disappear beneath the waves.

The ocean reminded him of a freshly plowed field. He imagined the surf as newly turned dirt. Pelicans diving for fish became gulls in search of bugs and worms, the heady scent of salt replaced by the musk of earth.

He shot himself with his M-1, Sarge. The bullet went straight through his heart.

He'd never forget those words. They burned like a knife through his gut, and the wound refused to stop bleeding. He should have made Jimmy see the doc. Should have notified his CO.

He should have stopped him.

Could he have stopped Furness? Leo's shoulders slumped—probably not.

He wasn't sure he'd ever understand what kind of fear, what level of hopelessness, could drive a man to take his own life. Put a gun against his head and pull the trigger.

Bile rose in his throat, and his fists clenched at his side. How dare he take his own life? His anger shocked him, but yes, he was mad at Furness for giving up.

He just didn't get it. Maybe he never would.

"We're not in Texas anymore, Yankee boy." Dooley shouted over the roar of the surf.

Leo jumped. "Geez, Dooley. Sneak up on a guy, will ya?" He forced a laugh. No way was he going to let Dooley see his grief. He returned his gaze to the endless blue to the west. "I expect we'll have to get used to it. We won't see much else for a while."

Dooley nodded, sucked a lungful of smoke from his cigarette, and wrinkled his nose. "Don't think I'll ever get used to the stink."

"I kind of like it," Leo said. "Even the dead fish."

Dooley rolled his eyes. "If you say so, Yankee boy."

They stood on the dunes a hundred yards from shore, the ocean wind gusting like a poltergeist intent on pushing them back. Dooley snatched his cap off his head before it could blow away.

"I know why I switched to the cavalry, but what's your excuse?" Leo was more than a little annoyed when Dooley had announced that he, too, had transferred to cavalry and had his orders for Fort Ord. Dooley wasn't a bad guy, but Leo was tired of the way he strutted and preened like a courting rooster, the way he wore his disdain for anyone but a white southerner like a badge of honor.

"Who can resist the beautiful California coast?" Dooley swept his hand from left to right. "Besides," he said, "I figured if the cavalry was good for you, it was good for me too."

Leo raised an eyebrow. "Japs and all?"

Dooley shrugged. "I gotta fight Krauts or Japs. Don't matter to me which."

The pelican flew off, its pouch filled with dinner. Leo turned his attention to the line of troopships moored in the harbor down shore, glanced at his watch, and looked at Dooley. "Time to go. You ready?"

"Is a beaver eager?" Dooley laughed. "Let's go." He took one last drag on his cigarette and ground it into the sand.

TROOPSHIP

For thirty days our little ship has plied
The broad Pacific, and in that vast space
We've seen no ships, no island has been spied.
We float suspended, lost to time or place.
Beside the bow, a troop of dolphins break
The placid surface of the quiet sea.
Six albatrosses track along our wake,
Like us suspended, gliding endlessly.
Someone above cries "Land!" We rush to stand
Along the rail; the minutes slowly pass
Until we see the thin blue line of land
Arising from the ocean's vast morass.
Blue mountains pierce blue sky. Almost in reach
The blue Pacific laps New Guinea's beach.

CHAPTER 15

SAN FRANCISCO, CALIFORNIA—NOVEMBER 1944

The line of soldiers waiting to board the troopship out of San Francisco seemed endless. Leo and Dooley were somewhere in the middle of it, crammed in like pickles in a Mason jar. Every man struggled under the hundred pounds of weight on his back as he trudged forward, taking care not to bump into the man—or the gear—in front of him.

Their transportation was the *Poleau Laut,* a Dutch merchant ship that Uncle Sam had "borrowed" for the war effort. At 490 feet long and weighing over nine thousand tons, it could accommodate two thousand troops.

At the front of the line, soldier after soldier disappeared into the black hatch of the hulking ship. Man followed man as they climbed the gangway and wove through a maze of doors and companionways until each reached his assigned area: a vast sea of bunks supported by steel pipes. The bunks— rectangular frames of tubular steel with a canvas mattress— were tiered in stacks of six, each less than two feet above the one below it. A soldier who got the top bunk had a jungle of pipes just above his face. The soldier on the bottom had the specter of five bodies lying over him.

The soldiers' gear jammed the narrow aisles between the bunks. There were no portholes. What little air was available was thick with the odor of some previous contents Leo didn't want to contemplate. He threw his hat on the closest bunk and studied his new territory. Third tier: not too hard to climb to and only three butts to look at.

Dooley grabbed an open bunk across the aisle. He sniffed the air and pulled his shirt over his nose. "That stink's gonna make it hard to sleep."

Leo gestured toward the tower of bunks. "I can't imagine we'll get much sleep anyway."

The *Poleau Laut* was underway before dawn. There was no military escort, and that made the ship an easy target if an enemy submarine or plane attacked. All hope of survival depended on the experience, skill, and knowledge of the captain, a grizzled Dutchman who knew the Pacific well but was likely unqualified for combat.

Sailing out of San Francisco Bay, they passed Alcatraz Island. Leo studied the prison and its surrounding buildings huddled together on the pile of rocks.

"Easy to see why no one ever escapes from there," Dooley said.

"Yeah," Leo replied, "if a con could somehow get out of the jail, he's got to climb down those cliffs and then try to swim through the rip tides." He chuckled. "Not likely."

"And the sharks," Dooley said.

Leo nodded. "And the sharks."

He shook his head at the irony: he and Dooley were locked into their fates as surely as the Alcatraz inmates, sailing toward a future filled with treacherous currents and lethal predators they couldn't control.

It seemed only minutes before the California coastline disappeared. Leo and Dooley made their way to the bow, zigzagging with the rocking ship like drunken landlubbers. At last, they reached the rail and grabbed on. Leo tried to relax the muscles in his aching legs and roll with the ship rather than resisting it.

"Holy shit." Dooley stared at the distant horizon. "This damned lake goes on forever."

Leo looked up and saw nothing but blue. Blue ocean, blue-gray overcast skies. He looked behind him. That was east, right?

But their course could have already changed. They could be headed northwest or southwest or due west, and without even the sun to give him a clue, he could just as easily be on his way to the North Pole. His chest tightened as reality hit him.

This is it. I'm going to war.

An indistinct image of bodies, of blood and body parts, appeared in his mind. He was going to have to kill. Of course, he always knew that, but he hadn't really thought a lot about it. Now he was en route to almost certain combat.

Could he kill someone? Killing was against everything he believed in. His family and his church had drilled the Sixth Commandment into him, along with the other commandments. It was a mortal sin. Was there any way he could avoid it now? Any chance he could stay, say, at battalion HQ? Motor Pool, maybe? His heart pounded, and his hands trembled. The rolling ship made his stomach turn. He closed his eyes and imagined home. Opened them and saw nothing but blue.

Suddenly, he couldn't breathe. His stomach heaved and pushed up against his lungs, and vomit forced its way to his mouth. He clenched his teeth and staggered to the head.

Long after he'd emptied his stomach, the heaves continued. He sat on the floor next to the toilet. He felt weak, didn't think he could stand. His mouth tasted of rancid eggs and salt air, and sweat chilled his face.

A pounding on the door shook him to attention. "C'mon, buddy, hurry it up."

"Just a sec." Leo wobbled to his feet, willed his head to stop swimming and his eyes to focus.

The pounding on the door matched the pounding in his head. "Move it, man."

"Okay, okay." Leo inched toward the door, hanging on to whatever he could. He made his way to his quarters, willed himself to climb up to the bunk, and collapsed. Although the bunks rolled as much as the rest of the ship, as long as he stayed on his back, he could handle the nausea.

But the thoughts of killing wouldn't leave his head.

The first time he'd gone hunting with his father, they were walking across the meadow when his father abruptly stopped and laid his hand on Leo's arm, pointing at the pair of deer feeding on the cornfield remnants. He gestured, miming a raised shotgun, and pointed to Leo's firearm. Leo tensed and raised his shotgun, sighting the tip just behind the buck's foreleg.

Focus, he reminded himself. His breath came in shallow gulps, his hands trembled.

"Shoot," his father whispered.

Leo nodded. He felt like he couldn't breathe, felt too weak to pull the trigger.

The buck raised his head, scenting the air. He froze for the briefest of moments and then turned, loping into the woods with his doe right behind him. Leo had missed his chance.

"It's okay," father reassured son. "You'll get the next one."

And he had. Soon he understood that hunting meant putting food on the table. He'd learned to kill for mercy when an animal had to be put down. Any farmer did eventually.

But could he kill a person on sight? Take the life of an enemy soldier who had a family of his own praying for his return? His body stiffened as his stomach threatened to upend itself again, but he forced his muscles to relax.

Don't think that way. It's survival plain and simple. Me or them.

Leo woke at the sound of reveille. A chorus of voices growled as the men rolled out of their bunks, fumbling in the darkened hold and cursing their way to the showers. He rolled over, not willing to risk the nausea he knew would assault him if he tried to get up.

He'd lost track of time since he'd crawled to his bunk. How many days had it been? Really, he didn't care.

"You need to get your ass out of bed." Dooley handed Leo a glass of water and some saltines. "Get up on deck and get some fresh air." He leaned against the bunks across the aisle and watched Leo struggle to sit up. "The stink down here isn't doing you any favors."

"Yeah, I'll do that." Leo shook his head. The minute he climbed down, he'd puke for sure. But Dooley was right—he couldn't stay in his bunk forever.

"Come on, Yankee." Dooley grabbed Leo's shoulder and tugged. "I'll go with you, and if it doesn't get better, we'll go to sick bay."

"Not going to sick bay," Leo muttered.

Dooley tugged harder. "Move it, soldier." He stood back as Leo slowly climbed down. "You gotta puke, turn your head the other way."

"Funny." Leo inched his way to the hatch and slowly climbed to the deck.

"Now get to the front of the ship and put your face into the wind," Dooley said.

He glared at Dooley. That's what he needed all right—to puke all over himself in front of a whole danged brigade.

"Go on." Dooley steered him forward. "You'll be fine."

Leo sucked in deep breaths of the sea air, trying to ignore the nausea building in his gut. He wove toward the bow of the ship, where several men gathered. One by one, they watched him make his way forward. He'd be damned if he'd let them see him puke.

"Well, look who's rose up from the dead," one of them said. "Come up to join the real men?"

"Har, har." Leo rolled his eyes and grabbed the rail. Dang it if Dooley wasn't right. The nausea had eased; he felt almost human again.

"I can't believe I'm actually hungry," he said to Dooley. "When's dinner?"

"Like anyone wants two helpings of that slop," Dooley muttered. "Didn't I tell ya you'd feel better up here?"

Leo chuckled and turned his eyes toward the calm seas. He looked out over the seemingly never-ending expanse of water, relaxed now that the threat of sickness was gone. Albatross and petrels flew gracefully past the ship, and the sea exploded like an erupting volcano as a whale breached the surface. How many hundreds of miles had they already traveled? How many thousand more remained until they sighted land again?

It didn't matter, really. The war was still out there, and they'd find it soon enough.

Dear folks,

I have hopes that this will reach you relatively soon. I mean, a couple of weeks perhaps. I know you must wonder where I've disappeared to, but you'll have to remain unenlightened for a while. If you don't hear again for a couple of weeks, don't be alarmed. I'll just be gallivanting around the world somewhere. Don't know where I am, where I'm going, or what the future will bring forth. I'm thoroughly tired of ocean voyaging, but still it goes on.

Susannah Willey

囲まれて
死と紙一重
我ら十

Kakomarete
Shi to kamihitoe
Warera too

We are only ten,
Surrounded by enemies.
Must we die tonight?

CHAPTER 16

CABANATUAN POW CAMP—JANUARY 1945

"Is that carabao I smell?" Kaito's mouth watered as he inhaled the tantalizing aroma. A native water buffalo, the carabao would feed the entire camp. Their usual supper was steamed rice and fruit, but today, the meal included the rare treat of fresh meat.

The room was nearly empty. Ever since the Americans landed at Lingayen Gulf in early January, most of the Japanese soldiers were deployed to the front. Just over five hundred prisoners remained, all of them permanently disabled or near death.

Since the Allies' landing on Luzon, there had been rumors that there would be an attempt to rescue the remaining prisoners at Cabanatuan. The Japanese vowed that would never happen; they had already executed Allied soldiers being held at other camps. Tadashi and the remaining guards received their orders: if a rescue was attempted, they were to kill every captive before the enemy could free them.

Last night, Major Takasaki had ordered the guards to burn down the barracks that held the most critically ill POWs. They had barricaded the doors and windows and set the thatched roof aflame.

"Twenty parasites we no longer must support," Major Takasaki brusquely announced as the smoke and flames shot skyward.

Today, the stench of charred flesh still lingered.

Kaito shoveled roasted carabao into his mouth, swallowed, and smacked his lips. As he lifted another spoonful, he hesitated, sniffed the air, and wrinkled his nose.

"I wish the wind would shift," he said. "That smell from the prisoners' quarters is ruining my dinner."

Tadashi looked at Kaito. "The fire doesn't bother you?"

"What?" Kaito shrugged. "The dead Americans? What are a few less barbarians to me?"

Tadashi shook his head.

Dusk was falling as Tadashi and Kaito headed toward the guards' quarters. As they strode across the grounds, eight other off-duty guards who lived in the same barracks joined them.

"You can thank me for dinner." Miyamoto patted his full belly.

"You caught the carabao?" Kaito raised an eyebrow skeptically. He picked a stray piece of straw from the dusty ground and used it to coax a scrap of meat from between his teeth, savoring the small morsel as he swallowed.

"It was in the prisoners' pit trap. I allowed them to keep the hide when they butchered it." Miyamoto looked at Tadashi and winked. "Along with the stubborn layer of flesh that stuck to it."

A small plane droned in the distance, coming closer. Tadashi and the others raised their heads in search of the source.

"Up there." Tadashi pointed toward the eastern sky. "American." A loud backfire echoed as the plane lost altitude. "In trouble by the sound of it."

Twice more, the plane dipped and backfired as it headed toward the low hills beyond the camp and barely cleared them.

"It's going to crash," said Kaito, grinning as he pointed to the plane's staggering path. "Just watch."

The plane disappeared behind the hills. Instead of an explosion, the guards watched as the plane feebly climbed, its engine coughing and spitting smoke from the engine. It dropped again and again, each time avoiding a crash.

The off-duty guards kept their eyes on the struggling plane as they approached their barracks.

"I bet five yen he won't make it back to his base." Miyamoto pulled a few bills from his pocket and waved them in the air. Kaito added his bet, along with the other guards.

"Are you going to get in on this?" he asked Tadashi.

Tadashi held out his empty hands and shook his head. "My earnings go to my family," he said. "But I think you're right. The plane will never make it home."

All eyes in the camp were on the hapless plane as it dipped and climbed, struggling across the sky.

Suddenly, the air erupted with gunfire and mortars. The guard shack at the main gate exploded. Bits of wood and metal flew in the air. One by one, the guard towers and pillboxes surrounding the camp fell. American soldiers burst through the main gate, firing at officers and enlisted men emerging from their quarters. Japanese soldiers fell like bricks in an earthquake, some from the ruined towers, others as they ran toward the prisoners' area, determined to eliminate their captives before the Americans could rescue them.

An explosion boomed from the highway that ran in front of the compound as the Americans bombed the wooden bridge to block the Japanese soldiers in a nearby encampment from coming to their aid. A second explosion in the opposite direction destroyed the road from the city five miles distant, where a brigade of five thousand Japanese assembled.

Another explosion rocked the ground, this one much closer. The tank shed, situated in the middle of the courtyard, was ablaze. Two trucks loaded with Japanese troops had just emerged from the shed and were now engulfed in flames. The few soldiers who managed to jump free of the fire were killed as they ran for cover. A lone Japanese soldier jumped out from behind a burning building and fired two mortar rounds before he, too, was killed by enemy bullets.

Tadashi and his fellow guards watched from the rear of the compound, momentarily frozen in disbelief. One by one, they put on their helmets, drew their rifles, and ran toward the conflict. One by one, their bodies jerked back from the impact of enemy fire and dropped to the ground.

Kaito gaped at his comrades. He put on his helmet, grabbed his gun, and turned toward the invaders.

"Stop." Tadashi put his hand on Kaito's arm. "You can't save the others. Joining the fight only means certain death."

Kaito glared at Tadashi. "It is our duty to the emperor."

Tadashi held Kaito's arm tightly. "Wait, Kai-chan. Not yet."

Kaito nodded and relaxed his arm.

"Where is Miyamoto?" Tadashi looked again at the bodies of the fallen guards. "He's not with the rest of them."

A loud boom erupted from near the artillery shed as a Japanese Chi-Ro tank crawled toward the invading army, firing its fifty-seven-millimeter gun. Miyamoto briefly stood in the turret, grabbed the machine gun, and mowed down a line of advancing soldiers. He waved triumphantly at Tadashi and Kaito then disappeared into the tank's belly.

The tank lumbered forward, firing as fast as Miyamoto could reload. Tadashi wondered if the tank would make it to the front gate and what he would do then.

The air screamed as an American fighter plane raced over the compound and dropped its ordnance. Miyamoto's tank burst into flames as the bomb hit and shrapnel flew everywhere.

Black smoke rolled from the tank and rose skyward. Tadashi and Kaito huddled under the barracks as the Americans advanced down the road toward the prisoners' huts. Only a handful of enemy soldiers stayed behind, picking off the few Japanese troops that were still alive.

Tadashi looked at Kaito. "We must decide, Kai-chan. Do we run toward the fighting or away?"

Kaito stared at the bodies of the men who had just been by his side. The bright flames from Miyamoto's burning tank lit his face. Tadashi prayed his friend would see the uselessness of attack.

Kaito's cheeks flushed as his chin dropped to his chest, and he whispered. "I do not desire to die, Nii-chan."

"Nor do I." Tadashi studied the barbed-wire fencing behind their barracks. He made out the shadows of enemy movement in the distance, but he and Kaito still had time. Together, they might yet escape.

Keeping the barracks between them and the enemy, they crawled on their bellies to the fence, digging furiously with their entrenching tools until they had a hole that would just barely allow them to escape under the wire.

Free of the wire, Tadashi paused. The openness of the area around the camp that kept the prisoners from escaping made Tadashi and Kaito easy targets. They had only seconds to find a place to hide.

Tadashi tapped Kaito's shoulder and gestured toward the burial pit. Kaito grimaced, shook his head. Tadashi shrugged: where else could they go? They belly-crawled to the pit and rolled in, wriggling under the decomposing bodies as much as possible.

"We wait here," Tadashi whispered, "and pray the enemy takes us for dead."

The stench was nearly unbearable. Tadashi took small, shallow breaths to keep the odor out and to keep his chest as still as possible. They lay quietly, listening for the Americans as they passed. Tadashi stiffened his body to mimic rigor mortis as the enemy inspected the pit. He felt the poke of a bayonet against his back.

"This way," an American soldier shouted from a distance. The bayonet withdrew from Tadashi's back. The sound of footsteps moved toward the prisoners' compound.

Kaito and Tadashi huddled in the burial pit. They were soaked in body fluids, covered with maggots. But they dared not move. As the night progressed, the fires continued to burn, and the voices of American troops echoed through the empty compound.

The skies brightened with the upcoming dawn, and still Tadashi and Kaito waited, motionless, until they had heard no noises for several hours.

Tadashi extracted himself from under the pile of bodies, crept to the edge of the pit, and peeked out.

The camp was abandoned. Piles of blackened beams smoldered from what once were the officers' quarters.

Charred bodies hung from the mutilated tanks. Nothing moved. Still, Tadashi and Kaito dared go no further.

Tadashi thought he'd become numb to the odors of death, but the smoke and the odor of burned meat were nearly unbearable. He held his hat over his face, tried to keep his breaths shallow. His body ached from the rush of adrenalin, the struggle to dig under the fence. His belly growled, and he was exhausted from fear and lack of sleep.

At nightfall, they moved. They had seen no one else emerge from the camp. No Japanese or American soldiers were visible in the nearby fields.

"It seems we are the only survivors," Kaito whispered as he scanned the camp and its surroundings yet again. "Does that make us heroes for escaping or cowards for running away?"

"It makes us alive, Kai-chan."

They stayed on their bellies, crawled out of the burial pit, and crossed the open field to the distant trees. They worried that the nearly full moon might give them away, but it seemed there was no one watching. The enemy had got what they came for: five hundred emaciated and dying prisoners.

They crossed the river near the Japanese encampment. Like the POW camp, bodies littered the ground. Many wore only their undershorts and helmet, having been rousted from sleep.

"Where are you going?" Tadashi grabbed Kaito's leg as he stood.

"To the encampment, of course."

"Are you crazy? What if someone sees you?"

"There is no one here to see me." Kaito shrugged. He pointed to the jumbled remains of the encampment. "Nii-chan, there are dozens of bodies here. They have guns, ammunition, scrip, maybe even food. And those dead soldiers have no use for any of it."

Tadashi and Kaito scavenged the empty tents, filling two abandoned backpacks with as much as they could carry.

They snaked through the open fields, alert for the sound or sight of enemy troops. As dawn approached, Tadashi spotted a line of dark shadows ahead, pointed, and turned to Kaito.

"There is a forest," he said. "Maybe dense enough for us to hide in."

They hurried their pace, eager to find cover before daylight, and finally located a thick copse of brush and trees. Kaito scouted the perimeter while Tadashi set up camp. They dared not risk lighting a fire, opening up tins of the rations they'd confiscated the night before.

Tadashi hadn't realized how hungry he was. It had been two days since he'd last eaten. He thought of the roast caribao, of Miyamoto's boasts about its capture.

Miyamoto is dead.

The words startled Tadashi as they formed in his head. His friend was gone. It was an act of bravery and sacrifice.

Was it? Tadashi wondered. He must have known his actions would make little difference. Surely, he knew it would be suicide. Tadashi remembered Miyamoto's story of the landslide, of his dedication to recklessness ever since. It would be just like Miyamoto to go down in flames as he did.

Tadashi was sad to have lost his friend. But he was grateful that perhaps Miyamoto was at last at peace.

"You are thinking about Miyamoto, aren't you?" Kaito wiped his mouth as he finished his dinner. "I regret the disrespect I felt toward him. He was a good friend and a faithful soldier."

Tadashi nodded. He took out his spade, dug a shallow hole, and dropped their empty food tins into it. "I am grateful I will no longer have to witness Takasaki's cruelty," he said as he filled in the hole. "Although we will likely now face combat, it can't be any worse than what went on at Cabanatuan. Those are images I can never erase."

CHAPTER 17

REPLACEMENT DEPOT AT LAE, NEW GUINEA— DECEMBER 1944

It took a month, but at last they sighted land. By dawn the next morning, the ship had dropped anchor a few yards offshore of Lae, New Guinea. At dusk, the order came to disembark.

Hundreds of troops descended the rope ladders like columns of army ants, laden with their packs, bedrolls, and rifles. Below them the LCIs—Landing Craft, Infantry—waited to take the men ashore.

Leo and Dooley clambered onboard the LCIs with the rest of the disembarking soldiers, wedging themselves into any space they could find. In the distance, they could see the tent city that was the troop replacement depot, erected on a flat, dry plain with barely a tree in sight.

"Lousy Civilian Invention is more like it," Dooley grumbled as he squeezed between Leo and another soldier. The flat bottom that allowed the LCI to get close to shore meant that the soldiers felt every movement. "Feels like a goddamned earthquake."

The approaching beach bustled with bare-chested natives working alongside soldiers as they directed the new arrivals to a waiting transport truck.

Dooley's eyes widened. "Jesus Christ, it's an island of ni—"

"Negroes?" Leo narrowed his eyes and frowned. "They're not doing anything to you."

Dooley scowled. "*Negros*," he emphasized, "ain't supposed to mix." He crossed his arms, revealing his tattoo

90

just enough for Leo to see it. "I sure as hell wouldn't let one get within ten feet of me."

Leo sighed. "Well, you'd better get used to it. We'll be here for the next four weeks."

Four weeks of jungle training then on to the real thing in Luzon.

"It ain't right," he growled. "The whole fuckin' world is goin' to hell."

As they landed on the beach, Dooley carefully avoided the natives, making a beeline to the closest American soldier. Once onboard their transport, Dooley and Leo were carried to a remote part of the base, assigned to squad tents, and given bedding and a mosquito bar to keep the ever-present parasites from invading a soldier's sleep.

Even though he was on land, Leo's body still rocked with the rhythm of the ocean waves. He wondered how long it would take to feel steady again, but for now, he was happy to crawl into his bed and get some sleep.

"Nelson and Baldwin—why do those names sound familiar?" The sergeant scanned his clipboard list when Leo and Dooley reported the next morning. "Oh, yeah." His eyes stopped partway down the page. "We're still waiting for your orders."

"No problem." Leo reached into his pocket. "We got our orders before we shipped out."

"Nah, those ain't good anymore."

"Why not?"

The sergeant shrugged. "Shit changes."

"Well, what the goddamned hell are we supposed to do, then?" Dooley growled.

Leo suppressed a smile. Good ol' Dooley—never at a loss for words.

"Guess you'll have to hang around here until we figure out what to do with you," the sergeant said.

"You could send us home." Dooley smirked, raising his eyebrow.

"Yeah, sure." The officer smirked. "And I just got a date with Dorothy Lamour. In the meantime, the army's got lots to keep you busy."

"Dang, southern boy," Leo said as they left the officer's tent. "I'd trade this sauna for a Texas sun any day." Temperatures in New Guinea were generally in the nineties at this time of year. That was lower than in Texas, but the humidity in Lae was a good twenty percent higher.

Dooley snorted out a laugh. "You need a good dose of the bayou, Yankee boy."

"No, thanks." Leo shook his head. "I'll take a lake-effect blizzard any day."

An hour later, they were learning about their upcoming training.

"Jungle fighting is like nothing you've ever done before." The CO swept his hand across the landscape. "Some of you jocks doubt that already. You think you've done it all." He stared at one particularly fit soldier. "You'd be wrong. The jungle will fight you every step of the way. Between the slimy mud, the vines that try to eat your gear, and the dense underbrush, it'll take you twice as long to cover ground. The heat and humidity will sap every bit of your strength within the first hour, but you're just getting started." The CO pointed to a soldier who held a walkie-talkie. "You can't trust your radios to work in the dense foliage. You can't trust your eyes either 'cause there's no way to know who or what is lurking just a few yards away."

He described the plants to be avoided: ones that could cut or cause a painful rash just by brushing against them.

"And then there's the animals," he said. "The tarantulas, cockroaches, and centipedes around here are as big as your sister's pet guinea pig—and I'm not exaggerating about that. You gotta watch out for venomous snakes and biting monitor lizards. Hell, there's even a few poisonous birds in this jungle."

Leo glanced at Dooley and whispered, "Sounds like even you don't want to mess with *these* snakes."

Dooley grunted. "Ain't never met a snake I couldn't handle."

Leo shrugged and returned his attention to the CO.

"Today's bivouac is only five miles." There were scattered murmurs of approval from the soldiers. The CO held up his hand. "Don't thank me yet. Those five miles are going to feel like five hundred before you're done."

At the end of the day, Leo fell into his bed. He was drenched in sweat, covered with bites, his arms scratched and bleeding from the dense underbrush.

Two weeks into their training, Leo and Dooley sat in the mess tent, shoveling down the powdered eggs that passed for breakfast.

They'd just returned from a night hike—the training Leo hated most. It was the noise that really got to him. Back home, the woods were alive after dark, but he knew those noises and could easily identify the ones he could ignore and the ones he should heed. Here, he knew very few of the night sounds. The humid air seemed to intensify the clatter: buzzing insects, yelping frogs, shrieking birds, the rustle of something or someone scuffling through the bushes, all blending into a chorus that surged and ebbed as the night wore on.

"Heard MacArthur and his gang landed on Luzon a couple days ago," Dooley said between bites. The Allies had already retaken the island of Leyte in October and declared the end of Japanese resistance there in December. "Scuttlebutt is they're on their way to take back Manila."

Leo slurped at his hot coffee and wondered why he still drank the stuff in this heat. "Yeah, well, I'd be perfectly happy if they got that out of the way before we ship out."

He looked up as a corporal approached.

"CO wants to see you, Baldwin," the corporal said.

Ten minutes later, he stood at attention in front of the corporal's desk stood and saluted. "You wanted to see me, sir?"

"I've got your new orders here." The CO handed Leo an envelope.

Leo removed the sheet from the envelope and scanned the page, his eye pausing on "Staff Sergeant." He looked up at the CO. "Beg pardon, sir, but this is a staff sergeant position. I'm only a sergeant."

"Not anymore, you're not." The CO gestured at a folder on his desk. "Got a special request from a unit in Luzon and you got the job. You're now officially Staff Sergeant Baldwin."

"What the fuck?" Dooley shouted when Leo shared the news. He shook the envelope with his own orders at Leo. "How come you get a promotion and I don't?"

ASSAULT FORCE

The sea is calm; upon its boundless deep
Our troopship glides, lost in infinity.
Beneath her decks two thousand soldiers sleep,
Or, waking, wonder what their fate will be.
From my assigned position here on high
I peer ahead, and in the east I see
The dawn's pale fingers clawing at the sky,
And then, a speck of land. The enemy
Will not be sleeping.
Now the troops are out
And stand in little groups beside each boat.
The gunship's roar drowns out the sergeant's shout.
Rope ladders fall, the LCIs, afloat,
Receive two thousand men in war array.
Each boat, full loaded, quickly moves away.

CHAPTER 18

PHILIPPINE SEA—JANUARY 31, 1945

Dear folks,

I'm on the move again—this time en route to the Philippines. I'm not really sorry to leave New Guinea, though the next step may be worse. But in the Philippines, they at least have towns and cities and some of the important aspects of civilization. I'll be very glad when I get back to dry land again. The worst objection to my moving is that I'll have to get along without mail again for a considerable period. I haven't been seasick this trip, and unless we hit rough water, I don't imagine it will bother me. But it gets very boring for me in a mighty short time. Very few things happen on ship worth mentioning.

Very few things I can *tell* you, Leo thought. It seemed like all his letters home were full of such mundane complaints as wandering mail and seasickness. He couldn't tell them how the closer he got to the front, the greater his fear of survival. He couldn't talk about being trained to kill. Even if the army allowed it, it was not something you wanted to tell your mother when she was already afraid you'd never come home. Mail call was often the highlight of his day. It was the thinnest of threads to his home and his family, the thread that reminded him there was a normal world out there that, hopefully, he would return to. It was all he had to cling to some days.

Leo sat against a pile of life rafts, his knees bent to support the letter he was writing. Dooley perched on a pile of rafts next to him with a handful of Aussie sailors. Their ship, the Australian transport *Westralia,* was part of a large convoy escorted by agile destroyers.

They were already sweating from the sun's heat, even though it was barely an hour past sunrise. Every day was the same at sea: cloudy at dawn but clearing. Extremely hot, cooling off rapidly at night, rain before morning. The troops' schedule was just as monotonous. Other than the occasional intelligence briefing or refresher training, they spent most days relaxing, napping, and daydreaming of anything but combat. Leo wondered if the brass were trying to give their soldiers the last bit of relaxation they might have for a very long time.

"I could spend the rest of the war right here." Dooley patted the life raft. "Whatcha think, Yankee boy?" Ever since they'd left New Guinea, Dooley had acted like his outburst at Leo's promotion had never happened.

Leo set down his pen and took a moment to stretch his arms. "I think I'd rather be almost anywhere but on a ship."

Dooley took a last, deep drag on his cigarette. "With our luck," he said, exhaling smoke through his nostrils, "we'll get sunk by a submarine before we get to Luzon." He flicked his cigarette into the water.

"Not funny." Leo growled.

"More likely some crazy kamikaze," an Aussie sailor said, "locked into a bomb-loaded plane they call an *Okha*. But *Baka* is more like it: a bloody fool." His fellow seamen snickered.

"Those mates are crazy." The sailor propped himself up on one elbow. "One of 'em nearly sent us to kingdom come a couple months ago." He glanced at his fellow Aussies. "Ain't that right, mates?"

"Yeah, up in Leyte," said another. "Missed us by a wallaby's tail." He held up his thumb and forefinger, an inch apart.

"About eight of them just dropped from the clouds." The Aussie launched into his story. "Before you could blink, one of them crashed head-on into one of our carriers. Our mates couldn't do anything but watch."

Sitting on the open deck, Leo felt exposed. He subconsciously scanned the sky for enemy planes, strained to hear their engines. His brain struggled with an indistinct image of planes impacting with ships—something he'd really rather not imagine.

"Instead of cats and dogs, it was raining planes and bodies, machine-gun fire and bombs. Seemed like those bloody bastards were hell-bent on dying."

One of his mates picked up the story. "The ship next to us got clobbered. Bloody *Baka* took out half the crew. Men flyin' through the air like rag dolls, others stuck with shrapnel. They said the deck was covered with Jap guts and brains, all kinds of body parts and plane wreckage."

That was something Leo couldn't begin to imagine, and he was grateful for that. He dang sure didn't want to get obsessed about being split into pieces by a kamikaze. "Sitting ducks" was a perfect description of their situation out here in the middle of the ocean. Except a duck was a lot harder to hit than a troopship.

The Aussie storyteller looked at Dooley. "You should've seen it, Yank. Helluva mess."

Dooley bristled at that last remark. "Don't call me a Yank."

One of the Australian soldiers snickered. "Well, that accent of yours sure ain't Brit."

Dooley jumped to the deck, fists clenched at his sides. "You can call Sergeant Baldwin here a Yank cause he's a northerner. But I'm from Loo-siana, and where I come from, calling a southern boy a Yank is fightin' words."

The Aussie held up a hand. "Don't go getting your civvies wrinkled, mate. It's just what we call Americans."

"American's full of goddamned mongrels, and I ain't one of them," Dooley growled. "We got Russkies and Polacks, Wops—and *Yankees.*" He spat out the word as if it was the sourest bit of vomit. "We got so many Nips they had to build prison camps to keep 'em outta our hair. And that don't even count the spics and ni—"

Leo had about enough of Dooley's bragging and bigotry. He held his hand out for Dooley to stop. "Yeah, we get it. You southern boys are some kind of special all right."

Dooley glared at Leo and started pacing. "All's I'm sayin'"—his deep southern drawl thickened as he stopped and pointed an accusing finger at the Aussie—"is don't put me in the same kennel with the mutts."

The sailor put up his hands in a defensive gesture. "Slow down and speak English, mate. Whatever language you're talkin' sounds more like Chinese."

"Ain't no goddamned Chink, *mate.*" Dooley put up his fists, took a step toward the rafts.

The Aussie jumped off the raft, ready to fight. "You ain't winnin' this fight, *Yank.*"

Dooley snarled and lunged toward the Aussie sailor, who raised his fists and took a step toward Dooley.

"Come on, fellas." Leo didn't want any part of this fight. Dooley was being a jerk, and it embarrassed Leo. He stepped between the two men, cautiously put a hand on Dooley's chest. "You're making this a bigger deal than it oughta be. Step back and cool off a minute."

Dooley glared, but what Leo noticed was beyond Dooley: a cloud of smoke bursting from a destroyer escort in the near distance. In seconds, the air boomed with the report of multiple firing K-guns.

The harsh tones of the General Quarters alarm sent the men on the life rafts scrambling. As troops en route to the front lines, they weren't much more than cargo—there was nothing for them to do but hide.

Adrenaline surged through Leo's body as his brain went to work. K-guns fired depth charges. Depth charges meant enemy subs. Enemy subs meant torpedoes—likely the ones the Japs called kaitens, manned suicide bombs not unlike the kamikaze planes. They were notoriously inaccurate, but how accurate did a danged torpedo have to be? His mind was spinning out of control even as he fought to stay calm.

"Leo!" Dooley shouted from under the pile of life rafts and gestured for Leo to join him.

Dooley's shout got his attention.

Leo's instincts took over. He looked across the ship's deck, crowded with frantic soldiers trying to find their way, being pushed and shoved by the ship's crew trying to do their jobs.

"Come on, Yank." Dooley's voice was strained and insistent. "Get in here."

Leo scrambled under the life rafts, pushing his way well back into the pile.

All sound was muffled now, the incessant alarm, the boom of exploding missiles, the shouts of men who hadn't yet found cover. The skirmish sounded deceptively far away.

Leo's heart pounded. Every breath took effort in the suffocating enclosure created by the life rafts. Was that a plane he'd heard? He struggled to shut out the noise and concentrate. His body tensed, waiting for the explosion that would collapse the deck underneath him. He struggled to breathe.

This was too soon. They weren't supposed to fight until Luzon.

Leo thought about his future, his belief that hard work and ethics were all it took to be a success. He hadn't counted on random things like kamikaze and kaiten. He hadn't faced the fact that life and death didn't take sides. He wiped the sweat from his forehead, forced himself to slow his breathing.

I'm not ready to die. Not yet.

At last, the battleships went quiet, the General Quarters alarm stilled, and the order came to stand down.

Leo pulled himself from his hiding place, watching as soldiers slowly emerged from where they had taken cover. Many of them had merely lain prone on deck with their hands covering their head.

"Holy shit." Dooley slipped out from under the life rafts. "What in hell was that?"

Leo's hands still trembled as he brushed off his fatigues. "Too close is what that was." He scanned the ships in the convoy. "Doesn't look like anyone took any damage."

Dooley stood and turned in a slow circle as he surveyed the ships. Leo noticed that Dooley's hands trembled almost as much as his own. The sea was quiet now, the sun bright on the water as each ship sailed on its own reflection. Neither Leo nor Dooley felt compelled to disrupt the calm.

At last, Dooley completed his rounds and turned to Leo. "Yankee boy, I think we're at war."

Susannah Willey

ASSAULT

Loaded, the LCIs roar toward the beach.
The naval guns are firing in our rear.
Motors and guns and shells drown out all speech
As we move in, our bowels tense with fear.
The LCIs strike sand; the ramps go down.
We race for shore, while bullets seek us out.
Some die at once, some fall face-down and drown.
Some gain the beach, fall flat and gaze about
As though half stunned to see their buddies fall.
Then someone shouts "Move up." We reach the trees,
In squads assemble at the sergeant's call,
And inch by inch drive back our enemies.
Behind us, new waves land, and in our wake,
Secure the beach so many died to take.

CHAPTER 19

LUZON, PHILIPPINES—LATE FEBRUARY 1945

The convoy anchored off Lingayen Gulf, north of Manila. Although it was the middle of February and early morning, the temperature was already pushing eighty. Disused machinery and rotting driftwood cluttered the landing zone. Down the beach, soldiers unloaded cargo onto waiting trucks. There was no sign of the enemy.

Leo scanned the beach in the near distance. "Doesn't look much different here than it did in New Guinea."

"What'd ya expect, Yankee boy?" Dooley snorted. "A welcoming committee?"

"I don't know." Leo shrugged. "I guess I figured we'd have to fight our way to shore. Those danged Aussies told so many horror stories about Leyte."

"Yeah." Dooley snorted. "You kinda went off the deep end, Yank."

"Of course *you* weren't scared at all." Leo crossed his arms and scowled. Although he was embarrassed that Dooley had seen his fear during the submarine attack, he wasn't ashamed of it. He bet Dooley was just as panicked as he was.

By the time everyone was ashore, the day had gone from hot to scorching. Soaked in sweat and seawater, they tossed their gear in the back of the four-ton, six-by-six transports that would deliver them to the staging area at Guimba and climbed in. Although the transport's green khaki canvas protected the troops from the sun, underneath it, the air was thick and stagnant. Crowded together on wooden benches on each side, the men bounced around as the truck bumped toward the highway.

Tamarind trees towered over the ferns and lianas that hugged the edges of the dirt road leading to the highway. A familiar smell of rotting vegetation radiated from the surrounding swamps. Clouds of dust stirred up by the vehicles ahead of them enveloped the truck and made it hard to breathe. Leo glanced at his watch: 0900 hours. He wondered how long it would be before they made it to the outpost at Guimba.

The main road was a relief. Open and beautiful countryside surrounded the paved highway. The air was lighter, rid of the choking dust and reeking swamps. They arrived at the outpost before noon, were assigned to quarters, went through an equipment check, and were dismissed to lunch.

The mess tent held no tables; everything was temporary.

Dooley found a spot on the ground next to Leo and settled in. "So whaddaya think, Yankee boy?" The food he'd already stuffed in his mouth garbled his words. "They gonna give us each a squad or an entire platoon?"

Leo shrugged, raised a finger, and pointed to his full mouth. He took his time chewing, swallowed, and washed it down with a long drink of water. "Likely just a squad," he finally said. "We don't have enough rank for a platoon."

"You guys think we'll go to the front soon?" The private seated next to them couldn't have been over eighteen. He was slender, almost skinny, his figure still more that of a boy than a man. His reddish-blond hair was buzz cut close to his scalp, revealing a small crescent-shaped scar at the hairline. He looked at Leo, his green eyes wide with anxiety, and shifted uncomfortably.

"Nah," Dooley rolled his eyes. "We're just here on holiday."

The private blushed, lowered his eyes. "I was just wondering how long we've got before we have to fight."

"Ease up, Dooley," Leo said. He extended his hand toward the private. "Leo Baldwin."

"Cal Richards." He shook hands with Leo and avoided looking at Dooley.

"I heard we'll be here for at least a week," Leo said. "They'll want us to settle in and get organized before they send us out."

Richards nodded and returned to his lunch.

"What's your problem, Yankee?" Dooley growled.

"You are." Leo forced himself to keep his voice even. "Why do you have to be so negative?"

"Why do you have to be such an asshole?" Dooley glared at Leo.

"Ten-*hut*." A voice boomed across the room.

Everyone stood and snapped to attention as an officer entered the tent. Tall and slender, with dark brown hair, his steely blue eyes scanned the crowd, intimidating to even the boldest soldier.

"At ease, soldiers," he said. "Welcome to the beautiful island of Luzon."

A few of the men chuckled, like toadies bent on pleasing the boss.

"I'm Captain Mickelson," the officer continued. "Commanding officer of Troop B, 112th Regimental Combat Team."

I wouldn't want to get crosswise of that guy, Leo thought. *Sure hope he's not as bull-headed as he looks.*

"The 112th is primarily a reconnaissance unit," Mickelson said. "Our orders are to patrol into and behind the enemy outpost line and report back to headquarters on what we find. We work in four-man recon teams, and once you leave the outpost, you're on your own. You get in trouble, nobody's there to help. You'd better stay sharp if you want to survive."

Dooley was still fuming at Leo's accusations. He shot a threatening look at Leo as if he couldn't wait to get him alone on patrol.

"But for the next ten days, you'll be here," Mickelson continued. "That will give you a chance to acclimate to the surroundings and have a few days of orientation training to get you used to the team. The fellas who have been here awhile will tell you everything they've learned. After that, you'll rotate in to your position, and the rest is up to you."

Leo snuck a glance at Richards. If the boy was nervous before, he looked downright terrified now.

"Your assignments will be handed out by platoon." Captain Mickelson turned and nodded to the officer, who stood at attention behind him. "We'll start with Lieutenant Ryan."

At six feet, four inches tall, weighing a solid 225 pounds, Lieutenant Thomas Ryan's muscular body was as intimidating as Captain Mickelson's steely stare. A colorful tattoo peeked out from under his shirt sleeve just enough to reveal the words, Rarin' to Go, the motto of the 112th.

Lieutenant Ryan consulted a clipboard and barked out names. "Richards, Russo, Filipowski, Webster, Myoga—"

Dooley tensed and sent a sidelong glance to Leo. "There's a Jap in here?" he whispered. "What the hell?"

"Shut up, Dooley," Leo jabbed him with an elbow.

"—Grayson, Nelson, Baldwin," Lieutenant Ryan finished his list. "You're A squad."

"Well, hell." Dooley looked at Leo. "Somebody musta screwed up, Yank." He puffed out his chest. "Too bad you didn't get a squad of your own."

"Sergeant Baldwin." Ryan looked at Leo. "You're squad leader." He moved his attention to Dooley. "Sergeant Nelson, you're his assistant." He pointed to one corner of the room. "Squad A, assemble in the far corner."

Several men standing in the area shuffled aside to make room.

Dooley muttered as he moved toward the corner. "What the fuck, Yankee boy?" His face was red, his lips pressed together. "First you get a promotion instead of me, and now you're my boss?"

"Aw, come on Dooley," Leo said. "It's no big deal." But he knew Dooley wouldn't let go of it any more than he did when Leo was promoted, especially since Dooley would now take orders from him.

"It's a goddamned conspiracy is what it is." Dooley growled. "Course you won't see it that way—they made *you* the leader."

"I do outrank you, Dooley." Leo kept his voice low as the other squad members joined them.

"Yeah, sure. Rub that in. Gloat all you want to but—" Dooley glared at the Japanese soldier as he approached.

"Corporal Haruki Myoga," the man said, extending a hand toward Leo. "Rifleman and interpreter." At five feet, seven inches, weighing 148 pounds, Myogi's slight build belied his fighting ability.

Leo shook hands with the corporal. "Welcome to the squad." He nodded toward Dooley. "This is Sergeant Nelson. But everybody calls him Dooley."

Dooley glared at Myoga, his arms crossed defensively.

Myoga stepped toward Dooley and extended a hand. "Nice to me—"

"Nuh-uh." Dooley raised his hand, palm out. He shook his head, took a step back. "A goddamned Nip? Ain't we fighting y'all? Fuckin' army'll take anybody."

"You gotta excuse him." Leo put a hand on Myoga's shoulder and glared at Dooley. "Sergeant Dooley's a redneck and a bigot."

Dooley pulled away from Leo. "You ain't my goddamned nanny."

Myoga shrugged. "It's no big deal, really. I get that all the time."

Leo shook his head. "It *is* a big deal, Corporal, and it isn't right."

For now, he'd let it ride, but he hoped the others hadn't heard Dooley. He'd need a plan for the next time Dooley went off.

He turned his attention to his squad. "I'm Staff Sergeant Leo Baldwin," he said. He gestured toward Dooley. "Sergeant Nelson is second-in-command. How about the rest of you introduce yourselves?"

Acknowledging nods and handshakes were given as each man spoke. They came from all over the country: Los Angeles, Detroit, Chicago, the Deep South, and the Far North.

"Sergeant Baldwin," Lieutenant Ryan said as he strode toward Leo.

"Lieutenant Ryan." Leo acknowledged him and dismissed his men.

Dooley bumped into Leo as he passed. "This ain't over, Yankee boy."

"Trouble already?" Lieutenant Ryan grinned as Dooley stormed toward the door.

"Nothing I can't handle, Lieutenant," Leo said.

"Good to hear." Ryan nodded. "You and I are taking a tour of the neighborhood this afternoon. Meet me here at 1400 hours."

To heck with Dooley, Leo thought, *I'm his superior, like it or not.* The brass had given him the job, hadn't they? Now it was up to him to do it right. *It's time you act like a leader, Baldwin. Stop pussyfooting around and do your job.*

"We're headed this way." Lieutenant Ryan pointed to the left and started out. As they walked away from the cluster of tents and machinery, he started talking. "Your first name is Leal?" he asked. "Is that Irish?"

"Scots," Leo said. "But nobody calls me Leal outside my family. It's Leo now."

Ryan nodded. "You get settled in okay?"

"All stowed away."

"Great." Ryan pointed to the area in front of them as they walked. "Right here it's mostly rice paddies with a few clumps of trees scattered around. And lots of kunai grass."

He led Leo into the high grass and extended a blade of grass with the nose of his rifle. "Kunai leaves are sharp. See the teeth along the edges? There's these sharp crystals all along the blade. You gotta watch out, or it'll really cut up your hands."

"Ran into some of that in New Guinea," Leo said.

"It's all over the place here and easy to forget about when you're under fire. It's not until later that you realize how brutal the cuts can be." Ryan held out his hands, revealing deep scratches. "Out where we'll be patrolling, there's a ton of it and a fair amount of jungle. Both make good hiding places for us—and for the enemy." He pointed to the dried-out ruts across the trail. "If it's dry, it's not too bad, but in rainy season, the going is treacherous." He gestured across the rice paddy to the blue humps of mountains in the near distance. "Lots of mountains out there. Those are the Zambales." He turned around and pointed east. "Sierra Madres are east of us. Then up north you got Cordillera Central," he said, thumbing to his left. "Those are the really high buggers." Ryan thumbed with his right hand. "Down there is Bigti Ridge. Can't see it from here, but we'll be making friends with it soon enough."

Leo looked to the southern horizon. "That's over by the Manila water supply, right?"

"Yeah, Ipo Dam. Under Japanese control right now. One of our jobs will be to recon Bigti so our guys can retake the dam and restore water to the city—as soon as MacArthur's troops secure Manila."

So that was where they'd meet the enemy. He was relieved that they were just a reconnaissance troop. Or would that make them even more vulnerable?

"Bigti Ridge is riddled with caves, and the Japs have dug tunnels," Ryan said, "so the whole thing is a maze. They store munitions and machinery in the bigger caves—hell, I heard they even got a hospital in one of them. You never know when or where the big guns might suddenly appear and open fire."

"So, you wouldn't recommend the place for a honeymoon," Leo deadpanned.

That got another laugh out of Ryan. "Not exactly a romantic surrounding."

They continued their patrol of the area. Ryan occasionally pointed out an important landmark, but they were mostly quiet.

The rice paddies seemed innocent enough now, but Leo imagined what it might be like under fire from an enemy that was tucked safely in a cave and hell-bent on victory or death.

"You were a drill sergeant stateside?" Ryan asked.

"Yeah, me and Dooley—Sergeant Nelson. We were part of a cadre at Camp Hood. After that, I was an RTC instructor until we got our orders."

Ryan nodded and was quiet for a minute. "Leadership is a lot different out here," he finally said, "especially in combat. You can't be all hot shit like a drill sergeant." He puffed out his chest and strutted in pantomime. "What you say still goes. Just don't be a prick about it. It helps to let the men in on your thinking: they'll be worth a lot more to you if they realize why they're putting their lives on the line and that you're going to have your life on the line right there next to them."

Leo thought of his last group of trainees at Camp Hood. He was relieved that his squad here seemed to be a lot more mature.

"So, you and Nelson have been together awhile," Ryan said. "What's the deal with him?"

Leo shook his head. "Two words: Louisiana redneck. He's about as bigoted as they come, a wise-guy know-it-all who really doesn't know much of anything."

"And you two butt heads every now and then?"

"Ever since I got promoted and he didn't," he sighed. "It's not going to help that Mickelson put him in my squad as assistant. That's going to grate on him like crazy."

"Does he always have a bug up his ass?"

Leo laughed. "More like a hand grenade. And you don't want to be around when it goes off."

Ryan stopped, stared toward the distant mountains for a moment. "I take it he doesn't think much of Corporal Myoga."

Leo shrugged. "Like I said: bigot."

"He might be in for a rude awakening." Ryan said. "Myoga might be small, but don't let his size fool you. He's a karate black belt and a qualified sharp-shooter. Piss him off, and he'll take you down faster than you can say, 'Oh shit.'"

Leo laughed. "I'll be sure to inform Dooley of that."

"Let's head back." Ryan turned toward camp, deep in thought.

"I might be able to get him moved to a different platoon."

Leo hadn't considered that idea. It would make Dooley someone else's problem, but Leo wouldn't give Dooley the satisfaction. "Nah, I'll manage. He's a good soldier, with a big chip on his shoulder."

Ryan nodded. "There are a lot of guys out here like that. They get their nose so outta joint they forget why they're here. You just gotta make sure that chip on their shoulder doesn't hurt their aim."

CHAPTER 20

GUIMBA OUTPOST—EARLY MARCH 1945

"I can't wait to kill my first Jap." Dooley lifted his rifle, pretended to pull the trigger, and jerked backward.

The Guimba outpost, about forty miles inland from Lingayen, lay in the Central Plains, comparatively open terrain on a mostly mountainous island. Leo's newly formed squad clustered under the palm tree next to one of the few temporary shelters at the outpost. They'd settled into their tent, big enough for the entire squad, and had set to cleaning their firearms.

Myoga scowled and kept his eyes on his own rifle. His hands tightened on the oiled cloth he used to rub down the barrel.

Did Dooley really think this was a great conversation starter?

Myoga was tired of the racism, of being equated with the enemy. Dooley had made it clear how he felt about him, but Myoga wouldn't give him the satisfaction of showing how much it bothered him.

Richards watched Dooley's mime with wide eyes. He stifled the vivid image in his head of the only person he'd ever killed. It had been an accident, but death was death, and Richards had caused it. It was one thing to cause a death unintentionally, but it was another thing entirely to kill on purpose. His rifle slipped from his clammy hands and into his lap, and at that moment, Richards wished he'd never have to touch it again.

Corporal Filipowski felt differently. He had spent much of his boyhood in Poland being chased by street gangs and harassed by German soldiers. He'd enlisted just so he could kill some Krauts, but the army had sent him here instead. He sighed.

"Not as good as a dead Kraut," Filipowski said. He lifted his rifle, sighting on a distant tree. "But Japs will have to do."

A few of his squad mates muttered in agreement.

The men worked quietly, relaxed by a task they could complete in their sleep. It was comforting somehow, the slip of soft cloth down a freshly oiled barrel, the firm click of the bolt slipping back into position.

Richards's heart beat only slightly more slowly as he forced himself to ask the question that consumed him. "Myoga," he said, "you've seen combat?"

Myoga nodded.

"Doesn't it bother you?" Richards struggled to keep his body still.

"Doesn't what bother me?"

"Killing someone?" Richards swallowed hard. "Even if he is the enemy?"

Myoga shrugged. "If you can't, you're dead."

"You got that right," said Filipowski.

Richards's ears turned red. "Yeah, I know." He sat rigidly, stared for a moment. "But I worry I won't be able to pull the trigger."

"You can't think like that." Corporal Russo paused and set down his rifle. "You won't have *time* to think about that."

"Have *you* ever killed a man?" Richards stared at Russo. His voice trembled slightly. He hoped like hell no one noticed.

"Not yet." Russo didn't want to think about killing. This place was about as far away from his life in Chicago as you could get. Sure, there was violence in the Windy City, but Russo hadn't seen a lot of it in the Little Italy neighborhood where his family lived and ran an Italian restaurant. Of course, the Italian Mafia ruled Little Italy, but he was smart enough not to get involved. He wasn't afraid of killing—not exactly—but he was in no hurry to experience it.

"You don't know what you're going to do 'til it happens," Myoga said. "And when it does happen, you just do whatever it takes to stay alive." He looked at Richards, at the trembling hands Richards tried desperately to hide, at the innocence on his face, tinged with just a trace of what looked like barely controlled panic. This war was going kill him. *I just hope to God he doesn't kill the rest of us while he's at it.*

Leo leaned against the tent post, listening to the conversation. As each soldier spoke, Leo tried to gauge his personality, his intelligence, his ability. How would each one mesh with the others? Was there anyone he'd need to keep an eye on? Anyone who might become a liability? Captain Mickelson had trusted him with this squad, and he was determined to prove his CO had made a wise choice.

He'd definitely have to watch Private Richards. The kid was too naïve for his own good, and that could be a problem for the entire squad. Corporal Grayson, a Muscogee Creek Native American, would be Richards's scouting partner. Grayson was tall and slender, with a wiry frame that could slide through the underbrush unseen, find evidence of travel on the most unused trail, and sniff out the enemy from a mile away. He was quiet, soft spoken, and rarely showed anger. Leo hoped his calm demeanor and patience would be a good influence on Richards.

Filipowski, their BAR man, might be a hothead. Leo had already heard about his history of getting into fights. The last one had got him busted from sergeant back down to corporal. Could Leo direct that temper in a positive way?

For a split second, Leo thought of Corporal Furness, crouched behind his BAR. Now there was a man with skills. Jimbo could knock a fly off a pinhead at a hundred yards. Boy, he missed that kid. He shook the image from his head. *Enough dwelling on Furness. He's gone. Let it be.*

Private Johnny Webster, a skinny sharecropper from Pelahatchie, Mississippi, would be Filipowski's ammunition carrier. He was older than Richards by less than six months, stood five feet, seven inches tall, and weighed a slight 130 pounds. A quarter-sized port wine birthmark stained his neck; his father called it his "goddamned hickey."

Being a fellow southerner, Dooley would look after Webster like a big brother. It was bound to cause friction between Dooley and Filipowski. Leo would need to watch out for trouble.

Myoga was Filipowski's assistant gunner. As the only man in the squad to have combat experience and with an understanding of the Japanese language, Myoga would be a valuable resource. *If* the other guys could get beyond thinking of him as Japanese. Being Nisei—born in the United States to Japanese immigrants—Myoga was a target for those who believed no Japanese could be trusted. Like many Japanese-Americans, his family had been moved to the Manzanar Relocation Camp in the California desert. But in Leo's mind, Myoga was just as American—and just as loyal—as the rest of them.

And of course, Dooley. The man could drive a wedge between Leo and the squad, but he was a top-notch soldier. Leo had something to prove here too: that he was a qualified leader more than capable of handling guys like Dooley. The other guys might be strangers to him, but he knew Dooley well enough to anticipate what nonsense he might try.

Leo shifted his thinking. What would he need to do to get his squad working as a cohesive unit? He had only a few days to accomplish it, and if he failed, the results could be lethal.

His first task, he decided, would be a confidential chat with Private Richards. Leo understood too well the feeling of panic that came with impending battle. He was certain it was something they all felt but most kept their fears to themselves.

"Private Richards." Leo motioned to Richards. "Need a word."

"You're in the soup now." Dooley smirked, wagging his forefinger in the air.

Richards jumped up, his face flushed with embarrassment.

"Knock it off, Dooley." Leo shot Dooley a look that he hoped would shut him up. He put his hand on Richards's shoulder and steered him away from the rest of the squad.

"I shoulda kept my big mouth shut." Richards crossed his arms defensively. "It's just—"

"It's just a conversation you should save for your CO, or better yet, for the chaplain," Leo explained. "Nobody here is immune to fear."

"Dooley is."

Leo shook his head. "I doubt it. He just covers it up with bravado." He looked Richards in the eyes. "The thing is, these guys'll eat you alive if they think you're too scared to back them up in a gunfight."

"I wouldn't let that happen, Sarge." Richards's face paled.

"Are you sure?" Leo's face reflected his concern. "Because if you seriously think you can't pull the trigger, that's something Mickelson needs to know."

"Nah." Richards waved his hand dismissively. "Just a little pre-combat jitters." He managed a weak smile. "I'll be fine."

Leo and Richards were silent as they returned to the rest of the squad, who were finishing up with their weapon-cleaning.

"Security patrol at 0800 tomorrow," Leo said. "We're on the lookout for any signs of stragglers." Although sightings of the enemy in the area were rare since the Allies drove the Japanese out of Guimba, going out on patrol would be a good chance for Leo to unify his squad.

"All right!" Dooley raised an imaginary rifle and fired.

Filipowski pumped his fist. The rest of the men looked away, as if unwilling to commit to Dooley's enthusiasm. Richards was noticeably quiet, but this time, his face showed no emotion at all.

The next morning, the squad left the outpost. They traveled in groups of four, spread out across the terrain, and headed east toward the barrio. Any man who told you he wasn't scared was lying. But there was an excitement to it. This was what they'd spent months training for, and every one of them was eager to find out just what kind of soldier he was.

"Remember," Leo cautioned as they set out, "our job is to reconnoiter and report. We don't engage."

The terrain was flat, the ground covered by mostly neglected rice paddies. Leo scanned the area for clusters of shrubs or small trees, anywhere they could hide in an attack. As unlikely as it might be to encounter the enemy, he planned to be ready. A solitary mountain, several miles south of the outpost, poked through the clouds, and Leo thought of the cliffs to the southeast where the Japanese hid.

A few meters to Leo's left, Grayson stopped abruptly and held up his hand then pointed ahead. Two figures moved through the kunai grass. Two or three more followed at a distance.

Leo nodded and motioned to the rest of the squad to get low to avoid alerting the enemy of their presence.

Remember guys, he said to himself, *observation only.* He hoped they had been listening.

Using his compass to determine their coordinates, he reached into his pack for a pencil and paper. As soon as the Japs were clear, they'd head back to the OP to report.

A loud report of gunfire shattered the air.

A Japanese soldier jerked back from the impact and fell to the ground.

Leo looked around him. What idiot had fired? Now they'd have to engage. He directed the squad to a small clump of trees dense enough to provide cover.

"Banzai!" the Japanese soldiers shouted as they charged. "Banzai! Banzai!"

Leo held up a hand: *don't shoot just yet.* He watched the soldiers draw closer. What was he waiting for? They were not going to stop.

Dooley glared at Leo, his firearm aimed and ready to shoot.

When Leo gave the signal to fire, Dooley's shots were the first. Each time he killed another soldier, he pumped his fist in a silent cheer.

There was no attempt on the enemy's part to take cover. Did they want to die?

Grayson ducked as he launched a hand grenade at the advancing soldiers. It exploded, and bodies flew, many of them in pieces.

When the air cleared, the enemy was still.

Leo gathered his men and counted: all present, no injuries. At least he had that to be grateful for.

"Did you see that first bastard fall?" Dooley mimed a pistol with his hand, blowing away imaginary gun smoke. "Direct hit."

"You didn't make that shot." Filipowski huffed, hands on his hips. "I did."

Dooley put up his fists, ready to fight. "Says who, Polack?"

"Stand down, Sergeant." Leo glared at Dooley. "If I were you, I wouldn't take credit for shooting first." He pointed at Dooley and then at Filipowski. "It was a bone-headed move."

Reluctantly, both men dropped their fists and stepped back, still glaring at one another.

"We need to inspect the bodies for anything useful," Leo said. "Grayson. Webster." He pointed to the two of them. "You stand guard in case more stragglers show up. The rest of you come with me."

"Hot damn." Dooley shouted like a kid at Christmas. "Souvenirs."

Leo scowled. "We're looking for identification, documents, anything that might provide intel, Sergeant Nelson, not souvenirs."

What remained of the stragglers was a mangled mess. Helmets scattered, uniforms spattered with brain matter and soaked with blood. Some corpses were missing arms or legs, some barely recognizable.

"Russo and Filipowski, you gather up all the weapons," Leo directed. "Dooley and Webster, check the bodies for documents and IDs. The rest of you buddy up and scout the area. See what else you can find. Richards, you come with me." He wanted to keep a close eye on Richards's reactions. "And remember," he said as the men went to work, "hands off the rest of it."

More than one Japanese flag found its way from a dead man's helmet to a squad-member's pack. Russo surreptitiously slipped a confiscated pistol into his waistband.

Dooley drooled over a mouth filled with gold teeth, annoyed that there was no way to extract one or two without Leo noticing.

Richards, grateful that he didn't have to touch a dead body, couldn't tear his eyes away from the carnage. With each body he passed, he became a little paler, trembled a little harder.

"You okay, buddy?" Leo looked at Richards with concern.

"I'm fine." Richards' response was clipped, his voice shaky.

"Over here," Myoga shouted. He'd spotted another dead Japanese soldier a few meters away from the others. The rest of the squad came running.

The corpse lay in a tangled heap underneath a tree. There was no blood or tissue damage. But the odd angle of the head confirmed the cause of death.

Dooley stood over the dead soldier. The man's neck was completely broken.

"Looks like he fell out of the tree," he said, shaking his head. "Damn gook. What a fuck-up." Dooley laughed and kept walking.

Richards froze, dropped to his knees, and sobbed.

Susannah Willey

春の色
黄金の稲
冬来たる

Haru no iro
Ougon no ine
Fuyu kitaru

The green fields of spring
The golden grains of harvest;
Then comes the winter.

CHAPTER 21

BIGTI CLIFFS, LUZON—MARCH 1945

Tadashi stood for inspection with the rest of his platoon. These daily inspections were a ridiculous waste of time. Their uniforms were tattered and stained with blood. Their bodies were filthy. They stank of sweat and gunpowder. There was nothing worth inspecting.

His stomach growled. When had he last eaten? Yesterday? The day before? Whenever it was, the meal had been little more than bits of rice and whatever nourishment they could forage from the mountainside.

First Lieutenant Daisuke Inoue stood inches from Tadashi's face, his lips curled into a sneer, his eyes narrowed in suspicion. He was not a large man; his body was lean, his slender face overpowered by a large moustache. He reminded Tadashi of the Mamushi pit viper, a small but deadly venomous snake: the slit, beady eyes, the way he seemed to slither menacingly from one end of his line of men to the other. Unlike the rest of the battle-weary troops, his tattered uniform and grime-coated body evoked fear rather than sympathy.

"Corporal Abukara."

"Yes, Lieutenant," Tadashi answered.

"Are you as stupid as the ox you drive?" Inoue demanded.

Tadashi's body stiffened. "No, Lieutenant." This man was what—six years younger than Tadashi? Japanese custom would never allow an elder to be treated so harshly.

He reminded himself that his goals were simple: first, live to see another day. Second, live to see home. If all he had to put up with was an arrogant lieutenant like Inoue, he would consider himself lucky.

"And you, Corporal Shimizu," Lieutenant Inoue poked the one-star insignia on Kaito's shoulder. "Are you sure you are a corporal? Who promoted you—Abukara's ox?"

"No, Lieutenant." Kaito's face reddened. "I mean yes, Lieutenant, I am sure I am a corporal."

"Is the ox's hoof print on your papers to prove it?" Inoue snorted, moving to the next soldier.

Tadashi stole a glance at Kaito. How had they ended up in this moron's platoon?

It wasn't unusual for itinerant soldiers to wander into an outpost like the one at Angat, so when Tadashi and Kaito appeared days after the massacre at Cabanatuan, they were simply assigned to a platoon with few questions asked. The Japanese Army was losing soldiers faster than they could replace them, and no one was going to complain about two more men reporting for duty. By the end of the week, the platoon had joined the contingent of nearly ten thousand Japanese troops at the Bigti Cliff complex.

"The Americans do not know our number," Inoue had bragged to his men. "They believe we are a disorganized group of stragglers, instead of the fortified army we have become."

Tadashi winced. A fortified army? How did he explain their ragged clothing and lack of food? How did he account for their dwindling supply of ammunition?

Inoue scrutinized a young soldier's uniform. "Private— Kimura, is it?"

"Yes, Lieutenant." Kimura stood at rigid attention, his trembling hands clasped behind his back.

Tadashi risked a sideways glance at the private. He was young—couldn't have been more than eighteen. His buzz-cut dark hair gave away his recent arrival; anyone who had been in Luzon for any amount of time had not seen a razor or clippers in months. The kid was skinny, full of nervous energy, and scared to death.

Inoue tapped Kimura's name tag with the riding crop he always carried against his shoulder. "Your name tag is loose." He grasped the tag, tore it off Kimura's uniform, and threw it in the dirt. "And now your uniform is torn. This is insubordination. Repair it immediately."

Inoue struck Kimura's face with the riding crop, leaving a deep red welt on his cheek.

Do not touch your wound, boy, Tadashi thought. *It will only invite another.*

But Inoue had already moved down the line. When he reached the end, he strode to the front of the line as if deep in thought then turned to his platoon.

"Although dogs would do a better job, I am burdened with the lot of you." Lieutenant Inoue spat on the ground. "You are released to your duties." As they scattered to their assigned posts, he added, "Failure is not acceptable."

"Does he think we don't already know that?" Tadashi said.

"Lieutenant Inoue is our commander." Kaito glared, growling like a threatened dog. "He needs to know we will obey him without question." He waved his hands at Tadashi. "Hurry. We will be late for duty."

Tadashi stayed silent. Kaito's determination to defend the emperor had only strengthened since the Americans had invaded the POW camp. He seemed obsessed by the notion of death with honor and frequently volunteered for forays into American territory. Long letters from his father reminded Kaito that he must fight to the last as an honorable warrior. It seemed the same with most of the soldiers—at least publicly. Although Tadashi felt certain there were others who shared his misgivings, some days he wondered if the entire brigade thought of nothing but a martyr's death, of glory as a war god.

But he had seen the cold truth of Japan's kind of war. He'd witnessed more cruelty and death at Cabanatuan than he thought man was capable of. If this was what the emperor considered honor, Tadashi had no taste for it.

Cruelty was not leadership. Tadashi subconsciously touched his cheek as if the whip had slashed his own face. It was arrogance.

He retrieved Kimura's name tag from the dirt and tucked it in his pocket. The boy feared his own shadow. He needed guidance. He thought about his determination not to bear the responsibility of leadership and shook his head. Was taking Kimura under his wing any less burdensome? Could he do that without inviting unwanted attention from Inoue?

The path in front of him was dimly lit by torchlight. He felt the closeness of the tunnel walls on both sides, the mass of dirt and rock above him. In front of him, the three new arrivals, all young privates, were silhouetted in the slim beam of bright sunlight. Two of them, Privates Ikeda and Yamada, laughed and jostled each other like a couple of teenage boys on their way to some kind of mischief.

Tadashi recognized Private Kimura, slightly away from the other two and moving with caution rather than conceit. His cheeks were pale, his chin dotted with acne where beard stubble ought to be. His scarecrow frame seemed to jitter with a mind of its own. Tadashi caught up with him, maneuvering him away from his comrades. Kimura instinctively covered the welt on his cheek and stiffened, but Tadashi simply nodded and gestured toward their destination.

When Kimura seemed to have accepted his presence, Tadashi spoke.

"How old are you, Private Kimura?" he asked.

"Sixteen, sir," Kimura's face reddened. "Old enough to fight."

"Yes." Tadashi nodded toward Ikeda and Yamada. "Are those two as young?"

"They are older," Kimura sighed. "I wish I were as brave as them."

"That is not bravery. They are arrogant young men who believe they are invincible." Tadashi angrily scuffed the dirt with his boot. "Boys like that put all of us in danger. But you—you are smart enough to have fear."

Kimura stopped. He turned toward Tadashi, his eyes bright with anger. "I do not have fear," he growled in a low voice. "Fear is for weak boys."

"Not so." Tadashi lightly touched his shoulder. "Fear is in all of us. Feeling fear and facing danger despite the fear is what makes men."

Kimura silently clenched his fists, focused on the distant mouth of the cave, and started walking.

Tadashi stayed quiet until he felt Kimura relax. "I am sure you have seen others as strict as our lieutenant," Tadashi said. "If you are like most of us, you are no stranger to corporal punishment."

Kimura didn't answer.

"Which of us has not felt the sting of discipline?" Tadashi spoke gently. "Who was it for you? Your father? Teacher? Superior officer?"

"All of them." Kimura's voice was barely a whisper. "Our teachers had their canes for beating us, our commanding officers their fists, often the butt of their rifle." He glanced nervously at the close walls of the tunnel. "My father locked me in a dark closet for hours as punishment. I felt like I might die. It was worse than Lieutenant Inoue's whip." He stopped and stood at attention. "But it was necessary. One must learn respect, obedience, and strength of spirit, sir."

"There are many ways to gain respect and obedience," Tadashi said.

They walked silently toward the mouth of the cave. Tadashi noticed Kimura's ragged breathing. The boy gasped as if he could not get enough air. His hands trembled.

"Is it always so dark and stuffy in here?" Kimura's eyes were wide, his voice thin.

"You'll get used to it," Tadashi said. "Just don't breathe too deeply," he added, smiling. "You might faint from your own stink."

Kimura laughed nervously, forcing a weak smile. In the dim light of the tunnel, the dark gash from Inoue's whip glistened with sweat. Behind them, his young comrades laughed with bravado.

Tadashi made his decision. He would be a quiet mentor to Kimura, try to be a counterbalance to Inoue's cruelty, and keep both Kimura and him out of the lieutenant's crosshairs. He gestured Kimura to the side of the cave and waited for the other soldiers to pass them.

"Not everyone here is as harsh as Lieutenant Inoue." Tadashi kept his voice even, placing a hand on Kimura's shoulder. "If you need help, come to me."

CHAPTER 22

BIGTI CLIFFS—MARCH 1945

First, they give me leftover prison guards. Daisuke Inoue paced the wide cavern as his troops dispersed. *Now I've been handed a bunch of undisciplined children.*

How would he ever prove his worth? How would he rise in status with such imbeciles under his command?

He stopped, violently slapped the riding crop against his thigh. He winced from the pain and was reminded of himself as a youth. His father had held up the samurai and the Bushido Code as the ultimate goal. His teacher demanded intellectual prowess that Daisuke did not possess. Their beatings were frequent and severe. They called it ai no muchi, the whip of love. It was meant to make a boy stronger, in body and in spirit.

At seventeen, his father enrolled him in the military academy. Daisuke was determined to make his father proud. Academics were still difficult, but he excelled at the practice of warfare. His aim was deadly, his bayonet swift and sure. He was the fastest on the obstacle course, the winner in every contest of strength and cunning. He commanded a team of cadets and led them with confidence and authority.

When he graduated as a first lieutenant, he returned to his family, wearing his stripes and stars proudly. His father angrily spat on his brightly polished boots. *You are not fit to wipe a samurai's ass.*

Would he never be enough? Would anything ever please his father? What if he advanced to the rank of colonel? What if he became a general? Or a grand marshal, the highest rank of all? Those high aspirations could only be met by perfection. He hardened his heart and set his sights on that.

At Bigti, Inoue quickly gained a reputation for being one of the strictest and most respected lieutenants. Men who needed discipline were moved to his platoon. But it never felt like enough.

Inoue strode angrily down the tunnel toward his platoon's position. He glared at the dark, dank walls. He sniffed the stuffy air, the human scents of sweat and rampant dysentery. Living within the confines of the caves, in darkness with no hygiene and a dwindling supply of food, had perhaps made it easier to take out one's anger on subordinates.

But lately, he had realized that the soldiers who received his fury were merely substitutes for himself. It was he who was inadequate.

Who was he to beat a man for weakness when the weakness was his? Was obedience based on fear preferable to loyalty gained from respect?

But it was the behavior expected of him by his superiors. As a commander, Inoue must show no weakness, no emotion. As an officer in a *just* war, launched for a *just* reason, he must use any means necessary to achieve the army's goals. That included demanding loyalty and obedience from his men in any way necessary. To do any less would certainly cost him the promotions he so desperately wanted and maybe cost him his life.

He carried a copy of the *Bushido Code* with him always, striving to live by its eight main virtues. Every night, he wrote in his diary, describing the virtue that he had failed to exhibit that day.

Inoue lifted his hand to his cheek, feeling the sting of the welt he'd left on Kimura's face as if it were his own.

He would not write that in his diary.

CHAPTER 23

BIGTI CAVES—MARCH 1945

In the vast warren of caves, each platoon held a single entrance. Their barracks were tucked deep inside the mountain. Tunnels spread out like a spider's web connecting the many caves. A small recess away from the living quarters was piled with a variety of weapons—machine guns, rifles, mortars, grenades, and some high-velocity guns that had been captured from the American base at Clark Field years earlier. In another corner, two-hundred- and four-hundred-millimeter rockets were stored. These were used only at night so as not to reveal their location.

Their orders were simple: defend the mountain and the dam against the invading forces.

From their vantage point above the valley, they could watch the main road for approaching convoys. Even the smallest, most obscure trail the enemy might use was visible to the Japanese defenders and close enough to pick off every one of them. The cave entrance, protected by a sandbag bunker and camouflaged with fallen brush, was manned by a crew of six two-man teams, each behind a machine gun poised to fire at the lieutenant's order. The remaining twelve men supplied the teams with fresh ammunition as needed and readied the larger artillery for later use.

Tadashi positioned himself next to Kimura and handed him an ammunition belt.

"Are you prepared for the enemy?" Tadashi chose his words carefully, watched the jittery private for any sign of panic.

"Yes, sir." Kimura's hands fluttered nervously as he took the belt. "Will Lieutenant Inoue join us?"

"Soon enough," Tadashi said. "But don't worry about that right now." He motioned to the ammunition belt. "All you need to do is feed the ammunition through the machine gun. When the cartridge belt is empty, there will be a man behind you to give you another."

Beads of sweat dotted Kimura's face. He looked away from Tadashi and stared into the darkness. "It's so stuffy in here. Don't you ever think of the tons of rock and earth hanging above our heads? It feels like I can't even breathe."

"Concentrate on your job," Tadashi whispered, "and there will be no time for worry."

Private Kimura knelt beside a machine gunner and picked up the ammunition belt.

Lieutenant Inoue appeared from the tunnel as the men took up their positions. "Do not fire unless I give the order," he said. "Your shots must be deadly but brief. We do not want to give away our position."

The cave was silent, the air thick behind them. Bushes outside the cave swayed with the breeze, but none of it reached the men. Minutes felt like hours, and no one dared speak.

The men jumped to attention when Inoue thrust out his hand toward a half-obscured trail. A small recon group of enemy soldiers threaded through the brush, unaware that they had been sighted.

"Corporal Fujita." Inoue pointed at the most senior machine gunner. "You will fire at my signal."

Fujita nodded and focused his gunsight on a clearing just ahead of the enemy. When they emerged from the trees, Inoue fisted his hand, his order to open fire. Fujita fired four short bursts, each time felling an enemy soldier. He remained in ready position awaiting Inoue's orders.

"Stand down," Inoue said.

Fujita relaxed his shoulders and eased away from the machine gun. The mood in the cave lightened as the men returned to standby, anticipating the end of their shift and a chance to get some sleep.

Tadashi struggled to stay alert, but as the quiet continued, his eyelids drooped.

Suddenly the earth rumbled violently with an ear-splitting blast from just beyond the cave. Mortar fire. Tadashi covered his head as dust spit from the ground outside and the piles of spare ammunition stacked behind him shuddered. Bits of rock and dirt rained down from the earthen ceiling.

"Do not respond," Inoue shouted. "The enemy is taking random shots, looking for a reaction, but they aren't sure where we are yet. Do not give away our position."

Tadashi watched Kimura. The boy's hands trembled so violently they barely controlled the ammunition belt he still held. Tadashi moved cautiously toward him, his hand held up to calm the boy.

Don't panic before I get to you, son, he prayed.

Another mortar blast. The falling rocks rained harder, hitting Kimura's helmet.

"We're going to die in here!" Kimura jumped to his feet. He pushed Corporal Fujita away, took position behind the gun, and began firing. His body shook like a rag doll, at the mercy of the gun's power as if it were determined to escape his control.

"Stop him," Inoue demanded. He waved his pistol at Fujita.

Bullets sprayed from the machine gun, its barrel swung wildly across the entrance and angled into the cave. Fujita struggled, trying to pull Kimura away.

Another mortar exploded, this one close to the cave's mouth. More debris fell on Kimura. The machine gun cast a reddish glow from the heat of constant firing. Kimura growled like a lion guarding its prey and pushed the gunner aside.

"Enough, private." Inoue raised his pistol. "Stop firing immediately."

"We're going to die." Kimura was sobbing, his finger locked on the firing mechanism. "I don't want to die!"

Inoue took two steps toward Kimura, raised his pistol, and shot the boy in the head. The machine gun fell silent, its muzzle red and smoking. Private Kimura lay next to it, his blood and brains sizzling on the overheated metal.

Inoue glared at his men, daring them to protest. "If you cannot obey orders, you are of no use to me."

The cave fell silent as he returned his gun to its holster. "The enemy knows this entrance now." He waved his hands around the cave. "We must abandon it and seal the opening, or they will infiltrate the entire mountain."

He gestured toward the body that still lay at the mouth of the cave. "This boy's negligence has cost us a vital strategic position." His voice rose in anger. "His death was dishonorable." He motioned to two of the soldiers and pointed at Kimura's body. "Throw this body outside where it belongs. Let the vermin devour it."

As the men dragged Kimura's body toward the opening, Inoue turned back to his men.

"This is a warning to every one of you," he said, his fist raised. "I will not tolerate disobedience."

As the platoon worked feverishly to move their supplies to a new location, Tadashi was fuming. This nonsense would take them all night. How much longer could they function with no sleep?

He did his job like a robot—no thinking necessary. But his mind refused to rest. Images of Kimura sitting beside him, eyes wide with fear, would not leave his thoughts.

It feels like I can't even breathe. We're all going to die.

Pop! The single shot from Inoue's pistol, the image of Kimura, his lifeless body as it slumped to the ground.

Kimura had been a frightened child tasked with a man's job.

Had Inoue been right to shoot Kimura? The boy was clearly berserk. He was a danger to them all. Could Tadashi have done the same if he were platoon leader?

The sun had barely poked its head above the horizon when the mountain quivered with the explosion that would seal the cave. Massive stones filled the opening of the tunnel. Soldiers choked on the dust and debris that infiltrated their hiding place. Tadashi instinctively plunged his hands in his pockets, surprised to feel Kimura's name tag nestled inside.

It feels like I can't even breathe. We're all going to die.

Deep in the mountain, in the wide cavern where he inspected his troops, Inoue knelt. Vomit dripped from his chin. His stomach heaved, but there was nothing left inside him. He saw himself pointing his gun at Kimura's head and firing. It played an endless loop inside his head.

It had been necessary. He could have killed them all. He retched and spat, unable to cleanse the guilt from his tongue.

Were respect and obedience worth the price of losing one's soul?

What kind of man have you become, Daisuke Inoue?

CHAPTER 24

GUIMBA OUTPOST—MARCH 1945

"I heard there was another issue with Sergeant Nelson on the recon yesterday," Ryan said. He and Leo leaned against a transport truck with a cup of what passed for coffee. Its acrid-smelling steam rose into the chilly morning air.

"Yeah." Leo lifted his cup and sniffed it, made a face, and set it on the hood of the truck. "He fired on a bunch of enemy stragglers after I'd expressly ordered my squad not to."

Ryan raised an eyebrow. "And you didn't nail him for it?"

Leo picked up his cup. How could he explain his concerns about Dooley without sounding incompetent?

"I'm trying to find the right approach," he finally said. "Ever since I got the promotion and he didn't, he's had a big chip on his shoulder." Leo drummed his fingers against the side of his tin cup. "He's looking for any excuse to make me look bad, and I don't want to be the one to set him off."

Ryan sipped his coffee. "You're familiar with the ACP?"

"The Army Command Policy?" Leo frowned. "Isn't that for officers?"

"It is," Ryan nodded, "but it applies to NCOs too. Any relationship between a leader and his subordinate that might compromise authority is a no-go. You can get slapped with an Article 92 if you're not careful."

Leo nodded. That was one regulation he was familiar with. Article 92, Dereliction of Duty, could mean a loss of pay, a bad-conduct discharge, even confinement. There was no way Leo was going to let Dooley's antics mess up his record.

Ryan lifted his cup and paused. "You sure you don't want me to look into a transfer for him?" He sipped his coffee. "I can say something to Mickelson."

Leo considered the offer. It would definitely solve a lot of problems if Dooley was gone. But how would it look to the rest of his squad? He didn't want them to think he couldn't handle his men. Filipowski wasn't much better than Dooley at following orders, and if Leo had to get rid of him too, what would that say about his ability as a squad leader?

"Let me talk to him," Leo said. "If I remind him it's army regulations, he might not take it so personally."

"Okay." Ryan lifted his hands in surrender. "I'll let you handle it." He took a last sip of coffee, made a face, and poured the rest on the ground. "I don't know why I bother drinking this slop." He lit a cigarette, inhaled, and relaxed against the truck. "What about Private Richards?" Ryan frowned. "I heard about his reaction to the dead Japs yesterday. Is he going to be okay?"

Leo thought for a moment. Was he? "I'm not sure what happened out there." He shrugged. "But he says he's okay. Maybe the blood and bodies overwhelmed him."

"You'll want to keep an eye on him," Ryan said. "You never get used to the bodies, but some guys just can't handle it. You don't want him losing his shit in the middle of a battle."

"I'll have a talk with him," Leo said.

Being a drill sergeant was a piece of cake next to this. How was he ever going to get these knuckleheads to work together? They'd be at the front in days. There wasn't enough time to make them a smoothly working unit.

Machine-gun fire echoed from the range where the BAR men were practicing. A couple of jeeps stirred up a cloud of dust as they bumped along the rutted road. Ryan and Leo stood silently and watched them leave.

Ryan exhaled a long stream of smoke through his nostrils. "Where's home for you?"

"I'm from New York State—the rural part, not the city. Lived on the farm all my life. Got two sisters, both married with kids." Leo watched a dark cloud of smoke rising in the distance, wondered if it was anywhere near the enemy line. "How about you?"

"Boston," Ryan said. "Irish through and through. My grandparents came over during the potato famine." He pulled a photograph out of his breast pocket. "That's my wife, Anna," he said. "The older girls are twins. Nora"—he pointed to the girl on the left then moved his finger to the right—"and Cora. They're ten."

"Identical twins?" Leo shook his head. "I'd go nuts trying to tell them apart."

"Yeah, it's a challenge." Ryan laughed and pointed to the toddler on his wife's lap. "That's Kathleen. She was only a couple of months old when I left." He wiped away a tear and returned the picture to his pocket. "Loves of my life, all four of them. They keep me going."

Leo looked at his watch. "I'm supposed to meet with Captain Mickelson in ten. Any idea what that's about?"

"He likes to meet his squad leaders," Ryan said. "He's a good officer, not a prick like some of them. You'll want to listen to what he has to say."

"I can't say as I'd want his job." Leo shook his head. "I've got enough trouble with the bunch I've got. How in heck do you lead a couple hundred?"

"I've heard it called the warrior spirit," Ryan said. "It's the commitment to duty, the willingness to take risks and responsibility in impossible situations." He chuckled. "It's not for everybody."

"That's for sure." Leo finished the last of his coffee and stuffed the tin cup into his pack. "I'd better get a move on." He stood straight and slung his pack over his shoulder.

"Just remember what I said about Sergeant Nelson," Ryan said. "You want him gone, all you have to do is say so."

Leo raised his hand in acknowledgement and headed for Mickelson's temporary quarters.

Dooley emerged from behind an adjacent vehicle. He crossed his arms and glared. "I don't think so."

Mickelson returned Leo's salute as Leo entered the captain's tent. Leo's palms were sweaty despite the chill in the air, and he resisted wiping them on his trousers.

"At ease, Sergeant." The captain gestured to the folding chair in front of his desk. "Have a seat." He glanced at a paper on his desk. "I see you're a New York boy."

"Yes, sir," Leo said. "Farm boy all my life. Headed to college as soon as I get back home."

"That's Cornell, right?" Mickelson looked up.

"Yes, sir." Leo hesitated. He didn't want to sound like he was bragging too much. "They gave me a generous scholarship."

"It's an excellent school." Mickelson sounded impressed. "You have to have a few brains to get in there." He returned his attention to Leo's file. "It says here you scored high on your communications test, were all set for Officer Candidate School." He looked up. "What happened there?"

Leo blushed. The captain didn't think he got kicked out or something, did he?

"There weren't any openings." He watched Mickelson's reaction and hoped the captain didn't think he was just making excuses. "So, they put me in Motors and made me an instructor."

"You and Sergeant Nelson were drill instructors at Hood?" Mickelson asked.

"We were." Had Mickelson heard about his troubles with Dooley already? Leo clasped his hands on his lap to keep from fidgeting.

Captain Mickelson nodded. He eyeballed Leo for a moment, taking his measure. "You're in Lieutenant Ryan's platoon?"

"Yes, sir."

"He's a good man, One of our best COs." Moving the paper aside, he straightened in his seat and folded his hands on the desk. "I see this is your first combat troop command."

"Yes, sir."

"Do you have any concerns about your command here?"

Leo thought a moment. "Well, sir, this is pretty new to me. Combat, I mean. Of course, we trained in New Guinea, but..."

"This is the real thing." Captain Mickelson finished Leo's sentence.

"Yes, sir."

"Like I told the troops, Sergeant, it's on-the-job training. The first guys here blazed the trail, handed down what they learned to new soldiers as they came in. Those soldiers learned more, shared with the next group." He shrugged his shoulders. "Not the best way to wage war, but jungle warfare is unfamiliar territory for all of us."

"Yes, sir," Leo said. "I'm sure I'll pick it up as I go along. I've already learned a lot with Lieutenant Ryan's help."

"He's a valuable resource." Captain Mickelson laughed. "Heck, anyone who's been here more than a couple of weeks is a valuable resource. If you live that long, you must be doing something right."

If you live that long. Leo considered that sentence as he made his way to their tent to debrief his men. Before now, death had been an abstract concept. Now, he'd seen it firsthand. Mangled bodies, bloodied, broken, in scattered pieces. The enemy didn't look so evil when he lay dead on the ground. He was lucky to have Mickelson and Ryan as superiors. He knew they were available for guidance and support.

Leo shifted his thoughts to his squad. Private Richards's meltdown had made Leo see his command in a new light. He was not only responsible for directing his men in defeating the enemy; he was also responsible for their lives. Success was no longer about fulfilling a dream—it was about all of them staying alive.

He needed to watch out for Richards, maybe keep him away from the bodies as much as possible. Or would it be better to get him used to seeing the dead? Make him face it and teach him to control how he reacted?

Filipowski's and Dooley's spats were going to be another thing to watch. Those two apes seemed determined to bait one another, and both were easily baited. Russo seemed to be good with Filipowski. He'd keep those two together, and as far apart from Dooley as possible.

"A word, Sergeant Nelson?" Leo tapped Dooley on the shoulder as they left the debriefing.

"About what?" Dooley jerked back at Leo's touch, raised his hands defensively.

"Come on, Dooley." Leo pinched his lips together. "You don't have to make an argument out of everything."

Dooley folded his arms across his chest. "So, what's the word?"

He's not going to make it easy. Leo took a deep breath and started. "You and I have got along pretty well until lately, right?"

"Until you got a promotion I deserved," Dooley growled.

Leo started to look away but stopped short. *Don't break eye contact,* he reminded himself. *You're the man in charge, not Dooley.*

"I'm not going to argue about that," Leo said firmly. "But because I'm your superior now—"

"Nothin' superior about you." Dooley snorted.

"Because I'm your superior now," he continued, "I can't do anything that makes it look like I'm doing you favors."

"No risk of that, is there?" Dooley sneered, his fists clenched.

"Just knock it off for a minute, will you?" Leo took another breath, forcing himself to keep his voice low and even. "The Army Command Policy says a staff sergeant can't buddy around with a subordinate. I can get an Article 92 thrown at me if anybody complains."

"Wouldn't that just be a shame?" Dooley said sarcastically.

Leo lifted his hands and shrugged. "Come on, Doo— Sergeant Nelson." He had to remember that: from now on it had to be Nelson instead of Dooley. "Work with me."

Dooley worked his jaw. Leo hoped he wouldn't have to ask Ryan for that transfer.

"Listen," Dooley said. "You're not worth the court-martial I'd get for bucking your orders. I'll be your lackey, but I'm telling you now..." He lifted his fist slightly, thought better of it, and lowered it to his side. "Sooner or later, you'll take a wrong step, and I'm gonna be right there to watch you fall."

CHAPTER 25

One down, one to go, thought Leo as he tracked down Private Richards, finally spotting him about to go in the mess tent.

"Richards." Leo spoke louder than usual, but he wanted to be sure he got the boy's attention.

Private Richards jumped and turned to face him. He looked like a kid who'd been sent to the principal's office. "Right here, Sarge."

"Let's take a walk, Private." Leo gestured toward the open rice field.

Richards nodded and nervously dusted off his fatigues. Leo watched him closely, looking for any lingering signs of panic or fear. When they were a respectful distance from the tents, Leo spoke.

"You okay, private?" Leo looked Richards in the eye. "Really okay?"

Richards's face reddened. "I'm sorry about the way I reacted, Sarge. All those bodies—it really shook me."

"It's more than that," Leo said. "The way you can't let go of the idea of killing someone, the way you freaked out yesterday." He put his hand on Richards's shoulder. "It's rough. But it's war, and you're going to see a lot of death. You break down like that when we're on the line, and you could get us all killed."

Richards stared at the ground and shuffled his feet. "It's... it's just that... well, my ma died from a broken neck." He looked at Leo, his eyes shiny with tears.

Leo blushed. "I'm sorry, Richards. I didn't know. What happened?"

"What happened was I killed her."

MITCHELL, SOUTH DAKOTA, 1942

"Calvin Edward Richards." Cal's mother clung to the window frame as the truck bumped down the rutted dirt road. "Slow down."

"Aw, Ma." Cal lifted his foot off the gas pedal. "A guy's gotta have some fun, doesn't he?"

"Not when his ma's with him, he doesn't." She released her grip on the window frame, adjusted herself in the seat, and smoothed her dress. "If you can't drive like a human being, you can't drive at all."

Cal slowed the truck, pulled to the side of the road, and stopped. His mother crossed her arms and scowled at him until he made a silly face.

She dissolved into laughter. "Guess I can't stay mad at my favorite son."

Cal rolled his eyes. "I'm your only son, Ma."

She shrugged. "That's true, but you're still my favorite."

Wrinkles creased her face, even though she was barely forty. Scrabbling for a living in the middle of nowhere was a hard life, and she'd had it harder than most. Married young to a much older man who spent most of his time drinking and angry had aged her. She'd taken his abuse, even while struggling to keep their family from starving.

In his father's eyes, Cal was the black sheep. Everything Cal did was met with scorn.

"You're nothing but a fuck-up." His father said it so often, Cal had believed it.

Cal's three older sisters had married and moved on. At fifteen, he was the only one left at home, and he and his mother had become allies against the common enemy of his father.

"One last joyride?" Cal shifted the truck into gear. He winked at her and smiled.

She sighed heavily, pretending to be annoyed.

"You know you love me, Ma." he said. "Favorite son—remember?"

She shook her head and laughed. Her eyes glittered with love and mischief.

"Okay," she said, "one last joyride."

Gravel flew as Cal floored the gas pedal, and the truck's tires spun and gained traction. They fishtailed down the road, bouncing and laughing, Ma holding on for dear life.

Lush cornfields lined the roadside, separated by deep drainage ditches designed to contain the spring runoff. The land was flat almost as far as the eye could see, interrupted finally by the indistinct blue bumps of the Black Hills far to the west. Cal loved this place almost as much as he loved his ma.

Ma's hair had come loose from its pins and flew out behind her. She laughed, carefree as a schoolgirl. Cal had rarely seen her look so happy.

"O-h-h-h-h-h. We ain't got a barrel of money." She started singing and motioned to Cal for the next line.

"Maybe we're ragged and funny." Cal's out-of-tune tenor continued, and Ma joined him.

"But we'll travel along, singin' a song." They raised their heads, grinned at one another. "Side by—"

"Cal!"

Ma screeched as Cal jerked the wheel and skidded to avoid the large bison that blocked their path. He had a split-second decision to make: hit the bison or hit the ditch. The bison slowly plodded across the road—if it kept moving, there might be room to squeeze between the two.

Cal swerved to the right.

The truck's right rear tire slid off the gravel road and into the drainage ditch. Cal fought to pull the truck to the left as it teetered off balance. He floored the gas pedal, hoping to gain enough momentum to go forward. The truck jumped back onto the road and slid past the bison, who had ambled to the far side of the road.

As soon as they were clear of the bison, Cal jammed on the brakes. The truck fishtailed, and he struggled to hold the steering wheel as he bounced and slid with the truck's movement. The air clouded with swirling dust as the truck came to an abrupt stop crosswise in the road.

Cal sat straight, trembling from the adrenalin surging through his body. Blood trickled down the side of his head where it had hit the door frame, and his arms ached from trying to control the truck. He felt dizzy and disoriented. In the seconds it took for him to regain his senses, the dust was settling.

"You okay, Ma?" Cal glanced across the seat.

The passenger door gaped open; his mother was gone.

He found her a few yards away, laying in a jumbled heap. Her arms and face were scraped raw from skidding through the gravel, her head twisted at an impossibly odd angle to her body.

Was she... Cal dropped to her side.

"Ma?" He gently shook her shoulder. "Ma?"

Her body was limp, unresponsive.

He lifted her upper body, held it to his chest, and focused his senses. There was no movement, no sign of breathing. Nothing.

Cal's heart beat wildly. His body shook from the release of adrenaline as he struggled to lift her and carry her to the truck. He laid her body on the truck bed, covered her with the empty burlap bags that were scattered there. He wanted to beg her—plead with her not to die. But he knew it was pointless. He climbed into the truck and drove his mother home.

It wasn't far, but part of Cal wished it was two hundred miles away instead of only two.

This can't be happening, he thought. *Ma isn't really dead. It must have been a bad dream. I'll wake up any minute now.*

But it wasn't a dream. Tears flowed freely down his cheeks. He wiped his eyes, snuffled back the stuffiness in his nose. He was overpowered by grief, yet a small thought niggled at the back of his mind: his father was going to kill him.

He figured he deserved no less.

When Cal got home, his father was in the rocker on the front porch, his head bent awkwardly to one side as he slept. The rifle that never left his side lay across his lap. Drool dripped down his chin, his loud snoring evident even through the closed truck windows.

"Pa!" Cal jumped from the truck. "Ma's hurt!" She couldn't be dead. Maybe she'd come around on the ride home. She must have woken up by now. He'd find her in the truck bed, laughing and shaking her finger at him—*fooled you, son.*

Pa snorted a breath and sat up. "What the hell'd you say?"

"Ma's hurt!" He rushed to the back of the truck, prayed for a miracle. "We nearly hit a bison. Damn thing was dead center in the road, and I had all I could do to keep out of the ditch." His father was halfway down the steps now, but Cal couldn't stop babbling. "The door musta popped open and..."

"Why's she in the back?" His father stumbled to the truck and peered into the bed.

Pa rubbed his bloodshot eyes impatiently, tipped his head to the side to make sense of what he saw.

"She's dead, isn't she?" His jaw moved as if he were working a wad of tobacco, still uncertain he understood. Slowly, the truth got through to his addled brain. In a flash, he went from uncertainty to anger. He turned on Cal, raised his rifle, and pointed it at his son's chest. "What the fuck did you do?"

"You did this," he snarled. "You killed your own mother."

"I— It was an accident." Cal held up his hands and took a step back. "If we hit the bison, it woulda—"

"Woulda what?" Pa growled. "Woulda killed your ma?" He looked again at the body in the truck bed. "Guess you did that all by yourself." His father's drunkenness was wearing off, and his voice was even and menacing. "You get your sorry ass out of here. Don't care where you go or what you do, I want you gone." He waved his rifle toward the road. "Don't come back."

Cal figured the minute he turned his back to his father, he'd be a dead man.

It didn't matter. His life had stopped with his mother's last breath. He stumbled down the road and didn't look back.

He hid in the bushes at his mother's funeral, not wanting to disrupt the sanctity of the service by enraging his father. Later on, when his father snored drunkenly on the back porch, Cal slipped into the house, gathered what belongings he could carry, and started walking west. When he got to Montana, he stopped. Signed on with the rodeo as a hand, eventually competing in the calf-roping events. As soon as he was old enough, he enlisted in the army. Somehow, some way, he had to prove he wasn't just a fuck-up.

"She lay there with her head all bent sideways," Richards said, finishing his story. "When I saw that Jap soldier, it was like seeing Ma all over again."

Leo nodded. "I'm sorry about your ma. But you have to figure out how to set that aside if you're going to survive out here."

Richards nodded and wiped away his tears. "I can do it, Sarge." He looked at Leo, a pleading look in his eyes. "Don't send me home."

Leo laughed. "If I can't go home, *you* can't go home."

They met Ryan on the path back to the compound. He glanced at Leo, his eyebrows raised. Leo returned the look with a light nod, and Ryan continued down the path.

Leo returned his attention to Richards. "You stick with me, okay? You have any more trouble, you let me know—we'll work it out."

"Thanks, Sarge." Richards's shoulders relaxed. "I promise not to mess up again."

CHAPTER 26

OUTPOST AT BALIAUG, LUZON—MARCH 1945

"Good to have another southern boy in the outfit," Dooley said to Webster as they sat beneath a large kamagong tree, snacking on their jungle rations. Lieutenant Ryan had sent them to monitor a small enemy encampment and report back to the command post.

Dooley relaxed against the tree. It was nice to be away from the rest of the squad. They constantly complained about his deep drawl. *Can't understand a word you're saying, Dooley,* they'd whine. When it was just him and Webster, he could drop the pretense and drawl away.

"Where 'bouts ya from, boy?" Dooley popped a handful of peanuts in his mouth and kept his eye on the encampment.

"Pelahatchie, Mississippi," Webster said. "Small town a ways east of Jackson."

Johnny Webster was barely nineteen years old. He lived in the Deep South with his large family in a shack so crowded that he slept outside whenever the weather allowed. There was no plumbing, no electricity, no heat. Water came from the creek down the road.

"Me 'n my daddy do sharecroppin' out there." He lifted his binoculars to his eyes and scanned the tree line.

Dooley's eyes widened. "Ya shittin' me?" He smiled. "I did sharecroppin' in Loo-siana. M' daddy still does."

"Bein' in the army's like manna from heaven." Webster nodded. "I send most of my pay home every month—it's double what my folks earn from the crops."

"Ain't that the truth?" Dooley was lucky. He'd managed to get out of sharecropping. Got a job in a coal black plant as a warehouseman. Army pay beat his regular salary all to hell. And with only an eighth-grade education, warehouseman was about as far up the ladder as he was likely to get. "You get any schoolin'?"

"Nah. Been workin' the fields since I was a tadpole. No time for school." Webster shrugged. "Just as well—me 'n learnin' didn't get along all that good."

"I hear ya, boy." Dooley smiled. His brain worked in high gear as Webster talked about home. The boy was light between the ears, but he was a fellow southerner who probably hated Yankees as much as he did. Didn't seem like it'd be too hard to get Webster on his side against Leo. This was gonna be easier than pickin' off crows in a cornfield.

"The whole family works the field," Webster explained. "Even my four-year-old sister, Lettie." He lowered his binoculars, stared at the distance as if he could see home. "You should see her out there pickin' cotton." He chuckled at the memory. "Her hands are so little she can only hold one boll at a time. But that gal's a fireball. Works as hard as the rest of us, maybe even more so."

Dooley nodded.

Finished talking about family, Webster put the binoculars back to his eye. Dooley ate the last of his peanuts and shoved the empty wrapper in his pocket. He let the silence hang between them for a few minutes before he broached the subject.

"Whaddaya think of Sergeant Baldwin?" Dooley kept his voice even. *Just carryin' on the conversation,* he reminded himself.

"I know you and him cross horns a lot," Webster said with a smile, "but so far, I got no problem with him. He seems fair and honest enough." He chuckled. "For a Yankee."

Dooley shared the laugh for a minute. Then his voice got serious. "There's somethin' you need to know about Sergeant Baldwin." Although they were several miles from camp, Dooley looked around him and lowered his voice. "He's not a bad fella. But the reason we butt heads so much is 'cause he's a terrible squad leader." He glanced at Webster, who had set the binoculars in his lap. "The bigwigs made a' awful mistake when they made him squad leader instead of me. I've seen that boy put his men in harm's way, just to keep himself safe." Dooley sat straight, puffed out his chest. "And I call him on that every damn time. That's why he don't like me."

Webster raised an eyebrow.

Dooley looked at Webster and shook his head. "I ain't too crazy about an NCO who puts himself ahead of his men."

"I hear that."

Dooley let that sit with Webster for a minute then put on his best fatherly smile. "So, you wouldn't mind doin' me a favor?"

Webster looked at Dooley, thought for a minute. "Depends on what you're askin'."

Dooley shrugged. "All's I want you to do is keep an eye on him. Don't make up no lies or nothing, just keep an eye out. You see somethin' suspicious, you write it down—times, locations, whatever you see."

Webster looked at the ground, his cheeks a deep red. "Cain't write," he mumbled. "Cain't read neither."

Dooley put his arm on Webster's shoulder. "Don't you worry 'bout that. You got a long mem'ry?"

Webster's face brightened. He lifted his chin and gave Dooley a wide grin. "Mem'ry's sharp as a hatchet."

"Good man," Dooley said. "I'll make it worth your while too. Wouldn't you like to have some extra cash to send home?"

Webster thought for a minute. Fair and honest didn't mean shit if a NCO couldn't look out for his men. Sergeant Baldwin might be a decent guy, but if he wouldn't stick out his neck for Webster, Webster sure as hell wouldn't stick out his neck for him. All Sergeant Dooley was asking him was to pay attention and tell him what he saw. If he saw nothing, so be it. But if he did, he had no problem with reporting the truth and letting the chips—and the money—fall where they may. If Sergeant Baldwin really was a bad NCO, then he hadn't ought to be in command of anyone.

Dooley moved his face closer to Webster, scanned the area once again. "One more thing," he said. "We gotta play it cool between us. Don't want anybody thinkin' we're in cahoots." He was thinking about his conversation with Leo, about fraternizing with a subordinate. No way in hell was he going to let Leo lay that one on him. "We gotta deal, buddy?"

Webster grinned and nodded. "I can do that."

Dooley looked at his watch. "Nearly chow time," he said. "Let's head back and give our report." He clapped Webster on the back and smiled. That was easy. *Like settin' a hound on a coon tree.*

He considered his strategy as they followed the trail to the outpost. He wasn't exactly sure what he'd do with whatever dirt he could dig up on Baldwin, but goddammit, that fucking Yankee had stolen his job. Dooley had more time in than Baldwin. He deserved to be the squad leader—hell, he deserved to be a lot more than that. If he could somehow get Leo in trouble and snug himself up close enough to Ryan and Mickelson, he might even get next in line for a platoon command. Wouldn't that be sweet?

A hundred yards from camp, Dooley stopped. "Remember the plan," he said to Webster. "When we're in camp, it's all business. If you got something to tell me, tuck in the flap on your medical pouch, and I'll get back to you."

Webster nodded. "Got it, Sarge."

He fell a few steps behind Dooley and followed him into camp.

Leo leaned against a banyan tree, his eyes narrowed as he watched Dooley and Webster return from their recon. Dooley was up to something, even if Leo wasn't exactly sure what that something was. There was no way Dooley was going to let go of the fact that he was Leo's subordinate. His resentment was clear in the way his mouth pinched every time Leo gave him an order, corrected him, or called him on his bigotry.

Would Dooley try to turn the squad against Leo? Had he already started? Leo shook his head. He would not let Dooley undermine his authority. But until Leo had solid evidence, there wasn't much he could do.

Susannah Willey

RECONNAISSANCE PATROL

My jaws are clenched, my muscles taut with fear.
My heart is in my throat, my palms are wet.
We have not seen the enemy, and yet
We know without a doubt that they are near.
We labor up the steep trail, even higher.
I walk alert, expectant; on all sides
The jungle presses in, and each tree hides
A spot from which an enemy may fire.
Eight men, alone, far from our friendly lines,
We probe the outposts of the enemy,
But they watch too; they may be watching me
Behind the bushes, trees and tangled vines.
We march to ends which we cannot discern;
Perhaps to death; perhaps to safe return.

CHAPTER 27

ANGAT, LUZON—MARCH 1945

Lieutenant Ryan huddled behind the dense scrub brush well inside Shimbu territory. The Shimbu Group was one of three large contingents of Japanese soldiers that had held the island of Luzon. Since the Battle of Manila, they had dispersed into the mountains, waging a guerilla campaign. The enemy was well-organized. Besides their stronghold at Bigti Cliffs, pockets of Japanese soldiers hid in bunkers, culverts, and scattered caves. There were few places where the Allied troops could maneuver out of their sight.

Ryan's entire platoon had been out on a long-range reconnaissance for the past few days, moving from Katakti to the Angat River. Split into groups of four men each, they were scouting enemy positions, manpower, and equipment, mostly following-up reports from the Filipino guerilla patrols that supported the Allied armies. Their job was intel only—they were to avoid contact.

Although his eyes and ears strained for movement, Ryan was thinking of home. Of all his time in the United States Army, these past months had been the hardest. He'd spent the first fourteen years stateside, on various bases and always with his family beside him. The Pacific Theater was his first combat assignment—he'd been here since the beginning of 1942, shortly after President Roosevelt declared war on Japan.

Three long years away from his girls. He was afraid his daughters wouldn't know him, especially Kathleen. He wasn't the same man he'd been back then. He didn't look any different, but he'd become hardened, cynical, far less patient.

Would he be able to leave the war behind him when it was all over?

Truth was, deep down inside, he didn't really believe he'd be going home at all. He spent so much time stalking enemy territory; he knew the odds were stacked against him. Most days, he could convince himself he was going to make it okay, but sometimes—like today—he didn't buy a word of it.

He worried about Anna too. Lately, her letters had seemed strained, filled with stories of day-to-day activities but with little emotion. He'd been away so long, and if she craved affection as much as he did, maybe he couldn't blame her for accepting another man's attention. Would she do that? He didn't know, but it scared him more than enemy fire.

A rustle in the grass brought Ryan to attention.

"Grayson's got a fix on a Nip encampment." Leo crawled next to Ryan and spoke in a whisper. "He counts seven Japs."

"That's three enemy outposts so far," Ryan said. "Get the coordinates and add it to the list. We report back tonight."

Leo nodded and scrambled off. He signaled his position to Grayson and Richards, who were patrolling toward the river, and rejoined Myoga, his partner for the day.

Myoga pointed his rifle down the grassy slope to the brushy edge of the field where two small lumps lay in front of the bushes. "Looks like a couple of bodies down there."

Leo cautiously scanned their surroundings. "Cover me while I check 'em out."

He moved down the slope while Myoga watched the high grass for signs of enemy troops. When Leo reached the bodies, he carefully scanned the area then motioned for Myoga to join him.

Both bodies were bloodied, their uniforms stiff from where the blood had caked and dried. Their bellies were bloated out, their limbs no longer stiff from rigor mortis.

"Must have been here a day or two." Leo gently poked his rifle at the bodies. You never knew when an enemy body might be booby-trapped with a grenade or a bomb. Both soldiers were emaciated, their faces gaunt. "Looks like they were on their way to starvation."

"This one's a sergeant," Myoga said, pointing to the red-and-yellow-striped rectangular patch with two stars on the soldier's collar. The other soldier's collar patch showed he was a private.

They collected the soldiers' weapons and ammunition then searched the bodies for useful information, especially orders that might give away any enemy plans.

Myoga stood from the sergeant's body. He held up the bunch of papers he'd taken from the officer's breast pocket, unfolded them, and scanned the contents. "Looks like a Field Order. They expected an attack from us, and these guys"—he gestured to the two soldiers—"were on a patrol to determine our strength and location."

Leo took the orders and tucked them in his breast pocket then knelt to search the private. In his pack, Leo found a diary and a half-finished letter.

Myoga scanned both briefly. "This is all personal stuff. Nothing for HQ here."

Leo stuffed the items into his back pocket. Maybe later he could get Myoga to translate them for him.

As darkness fell, the reconnaissance patrol gathered in a dense pocket of trees, well out of sight of the enemy.

Ryan held a map and a compass. "We've got a good ten miles to cover before we get to the command post," he said, tucking the map and compass into his pack. "In the meantime, we're behind enemy lines with precious little cover. You know there's Japs everywhere. Japs with machine guns and an itch to kill, so let's be sure to keep things quick and quiet."

He motioned his hand forward and started walking.

Each man memorized their current position and destination in case they were separated. Ryan led the way, and Grayson brought up the rear. The skies were mostly clear; there would be enough moonlight to help guide them, but it would also make them more visible.

An hour into the hike, Leo was beginning to relax. The trail was narrow, bordered by steeply eroded gulches too deep to be useful. But the terrain flattened out ahead, and they'd soon be clear of the enemy line. The last few miles would be in their own territory.

There was a flash of light from across the ridge, followed by the sound of gunfire. The men scattered, dropped to defensive positions, staying low in the grass and returning fire.

"I'm hit!" Richards yelled from behind.

"How bad?" Leo crawled back to Richards, scanned his body for blood, and saw a large stain forming on his sleeve.

"Bleeding like a son of a gun and hurts like all good get-out." Richards managed a weak smile. "But I think it looks worse than it is."

"Stay low." Leo pulled out his first aid kit and wrapped gauze tightly around Richards's arm. "That'll have to do for now."

Grayson crept closer, pointing at Ryan and then to a dark patch to his left. It was only a couple of bushes, about ten yards away, but it would be better cover than they had now.

Ryan nodded. He pointed at Myoga and Grayson then to his eyes: *Watch the Japs. Keep them occupied.* He pointed at Leo and Richards, then at himself, and finally at the bushes: *you two and I will find cover.*

Enemy fire whizzed over their heads and ricocheted off the dirt as the three of them crossed the paddy. Leo kept his eye on their objective, praying that Myoga and Grayson would make it too.

From the relative safety of the bushes, Leo threw a grenade toward the Japanese gunfire and away from Myoga and Grayson. Clumps of dirt and grass flew into the air as it exploded, followed by enemy fire as the Japanese responded.

Myoga and Grayson ran to the bushes, crouched low and rifles ready.

"Most of the fire is coming from over there," Ryan whispered as they crawled into the bushes.

Leo pointed to what looked like a stand of trees across the rice paddy. "Too far for grenades. But if we can't hit them, they can't hit us."

"There's a rock formation over there that'll give us better cover." Ryan pointed to a spot away from the Japanese position. "Stay low and run like hell. I'll be right behind you."

Clouds shrouded the moon as they ran to the shelter of the rocks.

Ryan appeared a minute later. "Hold fire for now."

Leo tended to Richards's arm, treating it with sulfanilamide and wrapping it with a bandage. The wound was shallow, not much more than a graze.

"Thanks, Sarge." Richards leaned back against a rock as Leo finished the dressing. "Guess it's not too bad, eh?"

"You'll live." Leo rolled his eyes and smiled. "That little scratch won't even get you an R&R."

The enemy fire was only sporadic now. Intelligence found that these pockets of resistance rarely attacked unless they felt threatened. Japanese prisoners had reported that morale was low, and many of their soldiers were weak, dying from starvation.

After twenty minutes of silence, Lieutenant Ryan gave the order to move. Confirming their position, the platoon headed west toward safety.

Leo and Myoga sat against the rocks drinking what passed for coffee and chewed on hard biscuits from their mess kits. They'd reached the command post shortly after midnight and hunkered in their foxholes for a few hours of rest. Orders for their next patrols would come soon, and they'd be off again, scouting for the enemy and dodging hostile fire.

"How's Richards doing?" Myoga lit a cigarette and sipped his coffee.

"All patched up," Leo said. "The bullet just ripped a hole in his uniform and grazed his arm. He won't even have much of a scar to brag about." He pulled the diary and letter he'd found from his pocket. "Remember the stuff I got off that Jap private yesterday?" He held the letter out to Myoga. "Think you could translate some of it for me?"

"Lemme have a look." Myoga reached for the envelope. "Looks like a letter home," he said, "to his family in Sapporo."

"Dear Father and Mother," Myoga began reading. The characters on the page were uneven and ragged, as if the writer had little strength.

> *I am writing this letter to bid you farewell. I do not expect to live much longer. Every day there is bombing by enemy airplanes and artillery fire. Three soldiers in my squad are dead and four wounded. There are only four of us left who can still fight. We have been cut off from our supplies and are weakened considerably. I have not eaten properly in two weeks. Most days I have had nothing to eat.*
>
> *Father, I beg you to comfort Mother in her grief. Hug my sisters for me and know that I died an honorable death.*
>
> *Farewell from your devoted son,*
> *Eiichiro*

Myoga handed the letter back to Leo and picked up the diary. Its pages were dank and grimy, the writing smudged. He skimmed through the entries, stopping at the last two.

"There's nothing useful here, intelligence-wise," he said. "Just the words of a homesick soldier who knows he will not be returning home." He read a few paragraphs aloud. "We are unable to find food except a few roots and tree bark. Two more are dead from starvation. Only Sergeant Kurosawa and I remain, but we are determined to complete our mission."

Leo thought of the two emaciated bodies lying in the tall kunai grass. It had been a miracle that their bodies had been intact, unbothered by scavengers. He was already getting hardened to seeing bodies, but the private's letter and diary were troubling. Before now, the enemy had been a faceless evil bent on destroying his men and his country. But this—this was just a lonely young man fighting for his country, the same as Leo was doing.

... know that I died an honorable death.

Farewell from your devoted son.

Leo thought of his own mother and sisters. His "final letter" was already written and in the hands of his CO. Before the war was over, would his father be reading his last words?

CHAPTER 28

ANGAT/NORZAGARAY REAR AREA—MARCH 1945

Dear folks,

We've been having a little rain for a couple of days—not much but a few light showers. In between times, it's been pretty hot, and I've been walking a good deal, not enough, however, to do any permanent damage to my physique. I'm feeling very well, though a little tired. The only thing I'd really appreciate at the moment is a good hot bath and a day or two of undisturbed rest. We've got the next week off, so maybe I can catch up on my sleep. But the bathing facilities are sorely lacking, and for now I'll have to settle for a cool dip in the Angat River instead of the hot bath.

Love to all,
Leal

They were desperately in need of rest. Aside from a brief twenty-four-hour break, the 112th had been in combat since they'd landed on Luzon in late January. Their temporary location might only be a rear area outpost, but it was safe—and quiet.

With little threat of enemy attack, Leo and his squad could relax for a few days. That meant good food, good drink, and an honest-to-god bed. Not a sleeping bag inside a rain-drenched foxhole—not crammed into a pup tent with another soldier who stunk as badly as you—but a proper bed that was soft, comfortable, and dry.

The break had come just in time for Richards. Although he hadn't had a blackout since their first mission on Luzon, every dead body haunted him. He fought off the images of the accident that killed his mother, fought to banish the words "fuck up" from his head. With each battle, it became increasingly difficult to disassociate the bodies from his mother's.

He'd had little sleep. His dreams were of mangled soldiers, severed limbs, eviscerated bodies. The first night of R&R, he dreamed the squad was hit by mortar fire. He dropped for cover, shielded his head. With a thud, a body landed crosswise on top of him. He twisted around until he could see that it was Russo, bloodied, his hands blown off. Another body fell on him. Then a third and a fourth until every one of his squad mates lay dead on top of him, trapping him underneath, unable to escape. The next thing he knew, the bodies were all his mother, their necks impossibly bent and broken. He woke to his own screams, Grayson desperately trying to shake him out of it.

"Richards, wake up." Grayson sat back when he realized Richards was fully conscious.

Richards looked around the tent, trying to get his bearings. His heart pounded, and he was drenched in sweat.

"That must have been one hell of a nightmare, huh?" Grayson said.

"Yeah." Richards struggled to calm himself. "I guess it was." It scared the bejesus out of him—these nightmares were getting out of hand. He had to talk to somebody.

The next morning, he approached Leo in the mess hall.

"Sarge, can I talk to you for a minute?" His face was pale, his eyes puffed by dark circles underneath. Breakfast was just finishing up, and the few remaining soldiers were leaving.

Leo swallowed the last of his coffee and eyeballed him. "Sure, Richards. What's up?"

"Hey, Leo." Dooley swaggered over to the table. "Hi-yo, Cowboy." He good-naturedly slapped Richards on the back and returned his attention to Leo. "Webster's gettin' up a poker game later on. You in?"

Leo shot a look at Richards, who had turned his head away, staring at the table as if he were trying to disappear. Though the day was not yet hot, beads of sweat dotted his forehead.

"I'll get back to you on that." Leo tipped his head toward Richards, a signal to Dooley to give them room.

Dooley raised his eyebrows and nodded. "Game's at two if you're interested." He turned to leave. "Later, Cowboy."

He patted Richards's shoulder and strutted out of the mess hall.

While they waited for the room to empty, Leo got coffee for both of them. Finally, the last soldier left.

"Okay, Richards," Leo said. "Spill it."

Richards fidgeted with his coffee cup, watching it intently, as if debating whether to speak.

"Do you get nightmares, Sarge?" His voice was shaky as he looked up at Leo and quickly looked away again.

"Sometimes," Leo said. He took a sip of his coffee and looked at Richards. "What are the nightmares about?"

Richards's cheeks reddened. He sipped his coffee and kept his eyes down. *Tell him.*

He raised his eyes toward Leo.

"Bodies." Richards whispered. He felt as if saying the word would make them appear. "Dead soldiers. Sometimes it's Japs, sometimes our own. Last night it was all of you guys. I was the only one left alive."

A group of soldiers entered the room, laughing as they got coffee and settled at the table next to Leo and Richards. Richards stiffened.

"Let's take a walk," Leo said.

Richards nodded and stood. Without a word, he hurried out the door. Leo met him outside.

"How about the chaplain's office?" He spoke softly to avoid calling attention to them.

"I don't need to talk to the chaplain." His voice was quiet but urgent.

"Not suggesting that." Leo put a hand on Richards' shoulder. "But he might let us have some privacy to talk."

Richards nodded and followed Leo to the chaplain's office.

"Could we borrow your office for a while?" Leo asked the chaplain. He nodded toward Richards.

The chaplain looked at Leo for a moment and consulted his calendar. "I've got nothing planned until this afternoon," he said, getting up from his chair. "I'll just go get some coffee."

"Thanks, Father," Leo said. When the door closed firmly behind the chaplain, Leo sat on the small sofa next to the chaplain's desk and motioned for Richards to sit next to him. "Tell me about these dreams, Richards."

"I told you all I can." Richards fidgeted, picked at his fingernails. "Sometimes I can't remember the faces and other details, but there's always bodies."

He watched Leo's face. *Please don't send me home.*

"Is it always soldiers?" Leo asked.

Richards lowered his head, unsure of how much he should tell. Leo was like a big brother—a man Richards admired. What if he thought he was a fuck-up too?

"Mostly," Richards whispered.

"Cal, look at me."

Richards lifted his head.

"We all have nightmares," Leo said. "Anybody who says they don't is either lying or not human. Every one of us carries pictures in our head that will never go away. Trick is, you have to learn how to shut that out, especially when you're facing the enemy. You gotta learn how to shut off your mind and just let your instincts take over. If you stop to think of the bodies and the ugliness of it, you're going to drive yourself crazy."

Richards nodded. His hands still trembled, and the fear hadn't left his eyes.

"I know you said you didn't want to talk to the chaplain," Leo said, "but that's what he's here for."

"Nah, I'll be okay." Richards stared at the opposite wall where a large crucifix hung. More death.

"We got seven days of R&R," Leo said as he stood. "You get some good rest and food in your belly, and maybe you'll feel better."

"Okay." Richards had desperately hoped Leo would have an answer. But what could Leo do anyway? What could anyone do?

"I might get you assigned to a rear area," Leo said. "You might still see bodies but not so many."

Richards's eyes brightened. He could be away from the death, away from the noise of grenades and mortars. But what did that say about him? He shook his head. No, he wouldn't be one of those guys who wimped out. "I can't let down my buddies, Sarge."

"Okay," Leo said. "But it's always an option if you change your mind." He stood, preparing to leave.

"Sarge?" Richards got up, nervously rubbed the back of his neck. "Please don't tell anybody. I'll get a handle on it, I promise."

Leo raised an eyebrow. "You sure?" he asked. "There's no shame in asking for help."

"Nah," Richards forced a smile. "I got it."

"I'll keep it to myself for now," Leo said, "but if you keep having trouble, you gotta let me know."

"Thanks, Sarge," he said as they left the chaplain's office. "I'll see you later."

As he headed off to the barracks, Leo was already deep in thought. Should he have promised not to say anything? It didn't seem right not to tell Ryan or Captain Mickelson, but he felt sorry for Richards. He was just a kid. Besides, it wasn't like they all didn't have nightmares about death. Richards was just the only one to admit it.

He thought about Jim Furness back at Fort Riley. He'd let that slide too. Oh sure, eventually he tried to do something, but even then, he hadn't tried hard enough. Would Furness still be alive if Leo had reported his concerns?

Jim's dead. Leo envisioned the day he'd found Furness by the river, gun at his head. He should have stopped it then, but he'd convinced himself it was just a fleeting moment of despair on Furness's part. When Furness said he was okay, he let himself believe it. He wouldn't do the same with Richards. He'd talk to Captain Mickelson in the morning.

When Leo got to the barracks, Dooley was waiting.

"What's up with the kid?" He tilted his head to one side. "He looks like hell."

Like I'm going to tell you, Leo thought.

"Ah, nothing," he said. But he knew if he didn't get out of there, Dooley wouldn't let up. Leo picked up his binoculars and headed out. "Off to do some bird watching."

Later that afternoon, Dooley pulled Webster aside.

"I got a new job for you," he whispered. He looked around for eavesdroppers. "Keep an eye on Richards too. I think he's losin' it, and I think Baldwin knows, but he ain't tellin'."

Webster nodded.

"If we play this right," Dooley said with smirk, "we might get rid of both of them."

Susannah Willey

五の兵が
死する田の上
雲雀鳴く

Go no hei ga
Shi suru ta no ue
Hibari naku

Five brave young soldiers
Lie dead in the rice paddy
Above, a lark sings.

CHAPTER 29

CAVES AT BIGTI—EARLY APRIL 1945

"We have a new mission." Lieutenant Inoue strode from one end of the line to the other, twenty-five gaunt, exhausted soldiers at rigid attention. They were all that remained of Inoue's platoon.

No one would say it aloud, but everyone knew the truth: they were losing this war, not from enemy fire but from starvation and disease. More than one soldier in the line welcomed combat, praying that this would be the mission to relieve him of his suffering and earn him his place among the kami.

The lieutenant scrutinized each soldier, ignoring their tattered uniforms, their reeking bodies—they were no worse than his own.

"We have been chosen to be part of an attack force tasked with taking control of the enemy ridge eight miles to our south." As the lieutenant passed down the line of soldiers, he tapped many on the shoulder, including Kaito.

"You, over there." He pointed his riding crop across the room. The men moved to where Inoue had pointed, forming a rigid line. When Inoue finished, he turned to them. "You soldiers will be under my leadership."

He pivoted to face the remaining men. "Corporal Abukara."

"Yes, Lieutenant." Tadashi's muscles tensed. What kind of trouble was he in now?

"I have promoted you to sergeant." Inoue handed him a blood-spattered sergeant's patch. The patch was rectangular. Its yellow horizontal stripe bisected a red background that featured two yellow stars instead of the single star of a corporal. Inoue nodded at the soldiers behind him. "These men are your responsibility now."

Tadashi tipped his head in a modified bow as he took the patch from Inoue. He scanned the row of men who were now under his command. Corporal Fujita, the machine gunner: arrogant but deadly behind a gun. He might make a reliable second-in-command. Corporal Sato was a good mentor for the newer men—just enough older for their respect but young enough for them to listen to him. Privates Ikeda and Yamada had come in with Kimura. Reining in their youth and bravado would be a challenge. He knew little about the rest of his men. Like him, they had kept their heads down and their mouths shut. They might not have any special training, but they would follow orders without question.

He had promised himself he would not refuse a promotion. He thought of his worries that he would not have the courage to lead. He remembered the attack at Cabanatuan, how he and Kaito hid rather than defend the camp.

"Sergeant Abukara." Inoue glared at Tadashi, as if defying him to decline the promotion. "You and your men will booby trap the enemy supply road and destroy the river bridge. No supplies must get through. As many times as the Americans repair the road, you will damage it once again."

"Yes, Lieutenant."

At dusk, Inoue and his men prepared to join the attack force. The plan was to leave the mountain in small groups to hide their numbers.

"Stay safe, Kai-chan." Tadashi clapped Kaito's back as the order came to form up.

Kaito hoisted his rifle on his shoulder. "You too, brother."

They would be apart for the first time since they'd left home, and there was always the chance one of them would not return. Tadashi touched the magatama on his chest, asking the kami to protect his friend.

When Inoue's squad had left the cavern, Tadashi spoke to his men. "Corporals Fujita and Sato will be team leaders." The two corporals stood on opposite sides of Tadashi as he assigned four men to each of them. "Fujita and Sato, you will remain here for further instructions. The rest of you get some rest while you can."

The young soldiers hurried into the tunnel that led toward their sleeping quarters. Tadashi turned to Fujita and Sato.

Sato was the older of the two and had several years of experience handling explosives. His close-cropped hair showed specks of gray. Age lines had sprouted around his dark eyes, making him look much older than his twenty-five years. Not surprising for someone constantly playing with explosives. He was an unpretentious man, following orders with a nod or a brisk salute.

Corporal Fujita, the eldest of five children from a wealthy Tokyo family, was a natural leader. His dark, deep-set eyes peeked out from under the net-covered helmet he always wore over his wool cap, earning him the nickname Turtle. But unlike that slow, plodding creature, he was an outspoken and charismatic man who easily gained the loyalty of his men. He was only a corporal now, but he was still young. He would go far in the military if he so wished.

"Since both of you have been with Lieutenant Inoue and in combat since arriving in Luzon," Tadashi said. "I have assigned each of you one of the new recruits. They will need special attention. I expect you to mentor them, to make these boys into warriors."

Both men nodded respectfully. The three of them spent the next several hours planning their mission. Corporal Sato's team was tasked with placing the explosives and detonators. Fujita and his team would act as scouts and provide cover when necessary. It was nearing dawn when Tadashi dismissed them with a reminder to be mission-ready by nightfall.

Tadashi followed them to their sleeping quarters but sat just outside in the dim light of a sputtering torch. He removed his shirt and retrieved the sergeant's patch from his pocket and his sewing kit from his pack. He removed the corporal's insignia from his shirt, carefully keeping the thread intact—the one spool of thread they had provided him was long gone.

He squinted in the dim light, trying to thread the tiny sewing needle he kept in his kit. The silence of the cave, the repetition of the needle sliding in and out of fabric relaxed him, and he thought of Sachiko. He pictured her in front of a sunlit window, perhaps with her own mending while little Ichiro teased Chiyo, their Hokkaido hunting dog. The winter would still have its grip on their little farm, but soon it would once again be planting time. Ichiro would be big enough to help his mother plant the fragile seeds in the earth and harvest the ripened vegetables in the fall.

Tadashi tried to reconcile the image of the infant son he knew with the toddler Ichiro would have become. Did he still look like his mother, or had he taken on a resemblance to Tadashi? As hard as he tried, he couldn't form an image of him. Without the tattered photograph he now carried in his helmet, he feared he would not even remember Sachiko's face.

The following night, Tadashi gathered his squad of ten and waited for full darkness before setting out. The sky was heavily overcast as they left the mountain. A good sign. They would be well hidden.

Armed with land mines, explosives, and trip wires, they were a crew of ghostly skeletons as they crept across an abandoned rice paddy toward the supply road. Their first target was the bridge that crossed the river to the south. Sato and his men cautiously set the land mines on both sides of the bridge to be certain it would be completely destroyed.

They stayed close to the road on their return to the caves, stopping occasionally to place hidden switches just under the surface. The switches were wired to explosives in the nearby trees. When the passing vehicles rolled over the switches, the detonated charges would fell the trees and further block the road.

Dawn was still hours away when Tadashi and his men returned to their mountain bunker. Their callused hands were covered with dirt, their legs and arms scratched from crawling through brush, their bellies empty. One by one, they found a place to lie down. Most were asleep in seconds. Only Tadashi was awake to hear the explosion as the enemy supply trucks attempted to cross the bridge.

At dawn, he roused his men. Hard rain, the first in many days, pounded the earth. It was unlikely the enemy would inspect their damaged vehicles before dark. It provided a perfect opportunity for Tadashi and his men to scavenge the wreckage for any surviving supplies.

The damage was evident as soon as they stepped out of the tunnel. The heavy odors of diesel fuel and burnt rubber hung in the air. Wisps of black smoke slithered sideways, pushed by the gusting wind. By the time Tadashi and his men reached the river, they were soaked. The bridge was destroyed, the road littered with fallen trees and smoldering vehicles. Tadashi sniffed the smoky air. His stomach growled, and his mouth watered as he recognized the odor of roasted meat.

What he wouldn't give for a bellyful of proper food. How long had it been since he'd tasted anything but roots and bark? His thoughts went to the carabao they'd feasted on at the POW camp—he could almost taste it.

Tadashi recoiled as he realized he was drooling over human flesh.

"Search the trucks," he ordered. He desperately needed to take his mind off his hunger. "Look for food, ammunition, anything we can use. Do not," he warned, "touch the bodies."

Twenty minutes later, his men, exhausted and discouraged, returned emptyhanded. They had done their job too efficiently: nothing had survived the explosions.

Tadashi called them together. "There is a small chance that the blast blew some supplies into the forest."

The soldiers whispered excitedly at the thought of finding anything edible. They had nearly given up when Corporal Sato shouted excitedly. Tadashi followed Sato's voice to a small clearing where the shattered remains of a wooden crate littered the muddy ground.

"Food." Sato pointed proudly at several canisters of rations, still intact. "A feast to celebrate our success."

A short distance away, they found a box packed with cigarettes and another with ammunition. Tadashi touched his magatama and whispered a small prayer of thanks. They had successfully completed their mission and would bring home much-needed supplies.

"Fill your packs with as much as you can carry," Tadashi ordered. "We must leave immediately. We have been here much too long."

They stayed just inside the tree line until they reached the abandoned rice paddy. Its open field left them vulnerable to enemy attack, but it was the fastest route. Tadashi gestured to his men—*spread out*—and nodded to Fujita. *You take point. I will take the rear.* At Tadashi's signal, they moved cautiously across the barren field, rifles ready, ears and eyes alert.

As Fujita reached the far side of the rice paddy, he signaled the *all-clear* to Tadashi and descended into the irrigation ditch well ahead of the rest of the squad.

Tadashi signaled his men: Move. Cautiously.

Sato's team went first. Loaded down with the extra supplies, they hurriedly crossed the field in a low crouch. Corporal Sato, carrying the heaviest load, was in the rear.

Tadashi looked around him, saw no evidence of enemy soldiers, and motioned Fujita's men ahead. Instead of containers, they carried their rifles, alert for trouble. As Tadashi came nearer to Sato, the corporal made eye contact with him, grinned, and rubbed his stomach in anticipation of their upcoming feast.

Sato's team had just reached the irrigation ditch when machine-gun fire rang across the rice paddy. Soldiers fell to the ground, some hit, others taking cover.

Tadashi dropped and shouted, "Get to the ditch."

As his men scurried forward, Tadashi sensed the enemy moving through the field. He knew he must get to the ditch, but there was something he had to do first. Creeping as quickly and as carefully as he could, he inspected the injured soldiers. The first body was Corporal Sato. Blood seeped from a bullet hole in his temple. Three bullets had pierced his back and exited his chest, ripping open the container of supplies he'd carried. Ration packets and cigarettes lay scattered in the mud. Four more of his squad lay nearby. Tadashi checked each for a pulse. Finding none, he removed their name tags and sprinted toward safety.

When he reached the irrigation ditch, Tadashi took stock of his squad. "Is anyone injured?"

One soldier nodded, pointing to a bloodstain on his shoulder. The rest were not hurt.

"We will follow the irrigation ditch around the paddy," Tadashi said as he examined the wound. "There is a hidden cave near to here. Stay low. The enemy will not be far behind."

They waded through knee-deep water, grateful that the pounding rain muffled their movement. By the time they reached the cave, they could hear enemy voices behind them.

Tadashi stayed back, motioning to Fujita to take the men inside. He dropped to his knees, struggling to keep his rifle above water, and stood guard. When the last soldier had disappeared down the tunnel, Tadashi checked once again for enemy soldiers, crawled to the entrance, and slipped inside, where he located the explosives that were stored near every cave's entrance in case of enemy attack. He set the charges, lit the fuse, and hurried down the tunnel as the dynamite exploded. Bits of dirt and rock pelted his helmet, and he turned back to see the opening fill with rubble.

The mood was somber as the remains of Tadashi's squad gathered in their sleeping quarters, the excitement of success replaced by shock and disbelief. Ikeda sat against the wall, his hands covering his face, his chin wet with tears. They stacked the recovered supplies in one corner. As famished as they were, no one was much interested in food.

Tadashi sat against the bunker wall, smoking a cigarette. He had not been a smoker before the war, but today the bitter taste of tobacco seemed fitting.

How could he lose half of his men on his first mission as a leader? What was Inoue thinking when he gave Tadashi such responsibility? He glanced at Fujita, who sagged against a box of rations, staring at his hands as if they had held the gun that had killed Sato. Fujita had more expertise. They should have given the command to him.

Tadashi felt impure, inside and out. He was soaked, his body caked with mud. The memory of drooling over burnt flesh seared his brain. He was grateful that he had not seen the soldiers in the supply convoy die, had not seen faces that resembled the American POWs he'd admired for their courage.

He may have proven to himself that he was not a coward, but he had failed miserably at protecting his men. Sato was gone, his explosives expertise gone with him. It was a critical loss.

The men had begun drifting off when Fujita stood. He wiped his hands against his pant leg and bent over the ration boxes.

"Let's not waste the supplies our comrades died for," Fujita said. "Let us instead feast in their honor and nourish our wasted bodies." He glanced at Tadashi, who nodded in approval and distributed the rations among the remaining men. "It's too bad the explosions burned the Yanks to a crisp," Fujita said, licking his fingers. "We could have had meat for our feast."

Tadashi glared and set down his tin of biscuits. "You will not speak of eating human flesh again," he growled. "We are neither animals nor cannibals."

Long after his men had satisfied their hunger and fallen asleep, Tadashi left the safety of the caves and returned to the rice paddy. The rain had stopped, and stars began to appear in the twilight sky. As he crawled across the rice paddy, he envisioned Sato, his playful grin, rubbing his belly in anticipation of the feast he would never enjoy. When he reached his fallen men, he removed a knife from his pack, unsheathed it, and cut a piece of fabric from each man's uniform. He carefully took hair and nail clippings from the soldier, lay it on the fabric along with the man's name tag, and wrapped them securely. They would send these small remains to his family for cremation and burial.

As the days passed with no sign of Inoue, Tadashi's squad continued to booby trap the road, spreading out in groups of two to avoid discovery. Without Sato, the traps were less effective, but Tadashi was determined to carry out Inoue's orders.

Aside from the incident in the rice paddy, what his squad had accomplished encouraged him. As much as his men hated Lieutenant Inoue, they trusted Tadashi, looking to him for direction, obeying his orders out of respect instead of fear. For that, he was grateful.

Susannah Willey

SURROUNDED

Beyond the outposts of the enemy,
Surrounded and besieged, we stood at bay,
And as the furtive twilight slipped away
We waited. Darkness fell, and suddenly
The quiet night erupted with the sound
Of bursting mortar shells. Then all was still,
But we could hear a rustling down the hill
As they advanced. We hugged the stony ground
And peered into the darkness. To my right
Some soldier threw a phosphorus grenade,
And in the sudden brightness that it made
We saw our foes, in unexpected flight.
The grass caught fire, the bamboo thicket flared.
For one more night, at least, our lives were spared.

CHAPTER 30

"HOT CORNER," LUZON—APRIL 1945

On the top of the ridge, there was nothing but rocks. Rocks piled everywhere. Leo and his men had spent their first night trying to dig in, only to hit bedrock six inches down. The rock piles would have to be their chief protection.

The Bigti Cliffs towered in front of Leo and his troops, less than a mile across the valley from where they watched for enemy movement. A menagerie of caves nestled along the rock face, and tunnels from a main shaft provided clandestine exits along the slopes.

Two roads surrounded by thick jungle snaked across the valley between the Allies' position and the Bigti Ridge. Route 52, also known as the Metropolitan Road, came alive with Allied military traffic at nightfall. The Japanese moved supplies and artillery along another heavily guarded road between Bigti and Ipo Dam. But in daylight, nothing moved.

Captain Mickelson's B-Troop was part of the 112th RCT reconnaissance-in-force (RIF) responsible for tracking enemy movement to and from the Bigti compound, estimating their size, strength, and weaknesses. There must have been a couple hundred soldiers on their mountain ridge, positioned behind the enemy lines. Leo's troops grouped up in pairs and scattered behind the massive rock formations.

For days, there had been no visible changes at the enemy encampment. What were they doing over there? Word was the Japs were preparing to attack. But when?

Leo watched along with the others, occasionally checking his troops and assigning relief. With Myoga's help, he had read most of the diary he'd recovered from the

Japanese private. What struck Leo the most was that he might have written the entries himself. His thoughts and feelings—about the war, about home—were essentially the same. Somehow, it had not occurred to him that the Japanese enemy wasn't much different from the American soldier.

It was a disturbing discovery. It made the enemy more human, gave him a face and a personality. Killing was easier when you saw the objective as a dangerous target instead of a person.

A few yards away, Dooley and Webster also watched for enemy action.

"Goddamn, I'm bored." Dooley lowered his field glasses and rolled behind the rocks. He dug a cigarette out of his pocket, lit it, and inhaled. "Stay here." He tapped Webster's shoulder. "I'm takin' a break."

Webster adjusted his binoculars, scanning the cliffs across the valley. He watched for movement: artillery, a soldier, a rifle. He listened for the sound of tanks or bombers—any clue to the intentions of the enemy.

Without Dooley breathing down his neck, he could relax and concentrate. Dooley was a good guy, but he was way too intense for Webster's liking. He jumped at the smallest sound, his finger always on the trigger of his rifle. Webster's attitude was more pragmatic. There was no point getting all het up about dying—it would happen or not, and there wasn't much he could do about it either way.

Webster watched the shadows grow longer as the sun lowered toward the western horizon, casting a bright light across the enemy-filled cliffs. He'd be off duty soon, relieved by Russo and Filipowski. He shook his head and smiled—who would have thought he'd look forward to crawling into his rocky foxhole? But he'd been sitting in one place for hours, and his limbs were stiff from inactivity. He was tired and hungry, and even a shallow, rock-filled bed sounded pretty good right now.

For the umpteenth time that day, he slowly scanned across the enemy-occupied mountain. The movement was so routine he almost missed the glint of bright light that flashed from the trees.

He focused on the spot, watching for another flash. What he saw instead was a Japanese soldier, followed by another. And another. He counted at least a dozen before he sounded the alarm.

"Sarge." Webster's voice was quiet but urgent as he gestured to Leo. "Enemy movement."

Leo crawled to Webster's position and raised his binoculars.

"Over by that clump of trees." Webster pointed as Leo focused the lenses.

"Good work, Webster." Leo stayed focused on the enemy troops. "Russo's on the other side of that rock formation." He pointed to his left. "Tell him to radio the info to HQ."

By late evening, a line of Japanese troops zigzagged down the mountain, occasionally revealing their position as they emerged briefly from under the trees. They were too far away for mortar fire, too protected for an aerial attack.

There was nothing the Allies could do but watch and wait.

As darkness fell, the men from Troop B changed shifts and dug in for the night. Some settled in their foxholes, grateful for whatever rest they could get. The others took over surveillance. Both were restless and bracing for what seemed like an inevitable attack.

Leo and Richards took the overnight watch.

"Keep your ears peeled," Leo reminded Richards as they settled in. "We're more likely to hear them before we see them."

Three hours later, Leo was struggling to stay awake. He jumped when Richards poked his arm and put a finger over his lips, put a hand to his ear, and pointed down the slope. Leo listened carefully.

A nearby grove of bamboo rustled softly.

Something was moving up the ridge.

He held up his hand and signaled Richards to alert the rest of the squad. As Richards crawled to spread the alert, Leo saw them: a Japanese squad armed with machine guns.

Something thumped as it hit the ground behind Leo. He jumped and turned as the Japanese smoke grenade hissed, exposing the Allies' position. The Japanese squad moved up the hill, firing across the ridge. Artillery fire rang out from across the valley.

The Allies returned fire. Leo's men were at the edge of the ridge where the enemy approached, close enough to take gunfire but too close for the arc of the Japanese mortars. The brightness supplied by the smoke bomb made it difficult to see.

Leo lobbed a phosphorous grenade off the ridge toward the approaching enemy squad. The thick smoke it produced would provide cover for his men and severely burn any Japs close to the explosion. A fire erupted in the kunai grass as the grenade exploded.

Japanese soldiers scattered across the ridge, easy targets for Leo's men.

"How do you like that, you dirty Japs?" Dooley shouted from a nearby position. As the enemy retreated, he smiled triumphantly at Leo. "Hoo-ee! I got three of 'em."

Leo nodded, held up his hand for silence, and signaled his men to stay in position. After a few minutes, the fire in the kunai grass died out. But before anyone could relax, machine-gun fire erupted from beyond their position.

The radio crackled. "Troop A is taking heavy fire."

Leo scrambled his men and prepared to provide support. The air boomed, and the ground shook as the Allied camp fired mortars at the advancing enemy, drowning out all sounds of gunfire.

"Jesus!" Grayson ducked behind the rocks as a stray mortar exploded not ten feet away. A fireball leapt into the air, followed by billowing smoke. Rocks and shrapnel flew everywhere. "We're fuckin' goners."

Leo's ears rang from the blast. Instinctively, he checked each man's position, taking a mental roll call of his squad. Everyone was accounted for and uninjured, but Webster had been the closest to the detonation point. Now he lay curled in a fetal position, hands over his bare head, his eyes squeezed shut as if he was waiting for another hit. His helmet lay behind him, knocked off by the mortar's impact. For once, even Dooley was speechless.

"All good?" Ryan had crawled to Leo's position.

"Still got everybody," Leo said. "Just a little shook is all."

Along the mountainside, the brush was ablaze, this time from mortar fire. From the rocky summit, Leo and his men would be safe. They watched as the enemy retreated. They didn't come back.

Leo gathered his men. "Filipowski, Russo, you take first guard duty with me. The rest of you get some sleep if you can."

He watched as the rest of the squad stretched out in their shallow foxholes, knowing that nobody would get much sleep. Their ears were still ringing from the mortar blast. The stink of burning grass permeated the air and made it hard to relax. But at least they'd get some rest. Leo joined Filipowski and Russo, already settled in for guard duty. Filipowski sat propped up against a rock, holding what looked like a scrap of fabric in one hand and stroking it with the other hand.

"Something from home?" Leo nodded toward the fabric.

"My wife made it," Filipowski said. "It's a hair weaving—she stitched it to this cloth and made a little bag for it so it wouldn't get wrecked."

Leo extended his hand. "Can I see?" He carefully took the scrap from Filipowski and examined it. The hair was intricately braided and made into the shape of a heart. Three distinct hair colors were visible: brown and two shades of blond.

"The brown is hair from my wife, the blond is from my children," Filipowski explained. "I have a piece of each to keep near me."

"It's beautiful," Leo said as he handed it back to Filipowski.

"It's tradition." Filipowski tucked the fabric into its bag, pulled the drawstring closed, and tucked it in his breast pocket. "My wife says it's for luck. To bring me safely back home."

Russo reached into his pocket and pulled out an intricate rosary. "My mother's," he said, holding it out for Leo and Filipowski to see. "She asks about it every time she writes."

Leo pulled a necklace from under his shirt. A lump of agate the size of a half-dollar, etched with the image of an eagle. It had been polished to a high sheen, fitted with a delicate piece of copper wire, and slipped onto a strip of rawhide.

"Indian relic," he said. "My father gave it to me when I left for boot camp."

It seemed like a lifetime ago—that day his parents took him to the train station and said their goodbyes.

They'd started out just after morning chores. The sky was hazy, the midsummer humidity already bordering on intolerable. His mother chattered nervously all the way to the station, random motherly reminders like, "Don't forget to brush your teeth," and "I packed lots of clean underwear for you"—her way of saying, "I am scared to death for you, son. Please come home alive."

His father insisted on carrying Leo's single suitcase when they arrived, each stride shorter than the last, as if he could delay his son's departure. His mother, still nattering, kept pace. Her voice was hoarse from the talking, quivering ever-so-slightly with the promise of tears if she dared go quiet.

At the platform, Father insisted she sit while they waited, reminding her that trains were rarely on time. He put his hand on Leo's shoulder and steered him around the knots of waiting families, keeping his back to Mother to make his words private.

Father reached into his pocket, removed his clenched fist, and held it out to Leo. When Leo opened his hand, his father placed an object in it that Leo recognized immediately: his grandfather's agate. Grandfather had discovered it one day when he was plowing; it had been his good luck charm ever since.

"I was going to give this to you anyway," he said in a ragged voice. "Now seems as good a time as any." He wrapped Leo's hand tightly around the amulet. "Tuck it in your pocket, son, as a reminder of home."

Leo's father held his arms awkwardly, as if he wanted to hug his son but was reluctant to show the emotion.

"Thanks, Dad." Leo rarely called him Dad, but the word slipped out on its own, as if it was the only one appropriate for the occasion.

The train's mournful whistle signaled its approach. The little family bundles became bigger as they merged at the edge of the platform and waited. An uneasy quiet fell over the crowd as the train drew near. Anxious looks flitted from family members to the train.

Leo's father gathered his mother from the bench, her eyes red but her face dry. They made their way to the waiting train, embraced their son with every last ounce of affection and courage they could muster and then let him go.

Russo laughed nervously. "I guess we all have good luck charms."

They sat silently, each fingering his talisman.

"Any movement?" Leo broke the silence. He peeked over the rocks and focused his binoculars down the ridge, unable to see much in the pre-dawn darkness.

"They're out there somewhere." Russo swept his hand in a broad gesture. "They won't stay still forever."

Leo nodded. How long had it been since he'd slept? His bones ached, his mind sluggish and unfocused. In the distance, he could hear the grinding motors of the supply trucks, once again plodding down the road. It was a familiar sound, and Leo relaxed. The situation must be under control for the trucks to be moving again. He felt the shape of the agate under his shirt and leaned back, half listening to Filipowski and Russo as they whispered to one another and willing his eyes to stay open.

Suddenly, the air boomed, and the ridge shook. Leo jerked up—had he been dreaming? He looked for Filipowski and Russo. Both stood beside him, Russo pointing to the northeast and the supply road, shrouded in smoke and lit up with flames. Through the haze, Leo could see the supply trucks, all of them ablaze.

A second explosion rocked the air, this time closer to the ridge. Leo could tell from the location that it was the bridge that the trucks had to cross to reach their location. Shouts and screams echoed in the clear night air, the sound of men caught in the flames, unable to escape.

When daylight came, it revealed what the darkness had only implied: the smoking wreckage of the supply convoy and the destruction of the Metropolitan Road and the river bridge.

Leo's squad, and most of the Allied troops on the ridge, squatted behind the rocks and stared across the valley.

"All troops are to meet at the assembly area," Ryan said as he approached his platoon.

"What's up, LT?" Russo asked.

Ryan just shook his head. "There's news," he said, "and you aren't going to like it."

At the assembly area, the men crowded around the officer in charge. "I don't need to tell you what happened on the supply road last night," he said. "But we've just received word from our scouts down the ridge. We are surrounded by Japanese forces."

"We're fucked," Grayson whispered.

Nobody argued with him.

CHAPTER 31

"We're nearly out of rations." Leo made his report to Ryan. It had been two weeks since the enemy attack. Although there had been no more direct confrontations, the supply road was still cut off, and enemy artillery kept the supply planes from making emergency air drops.

Ammunition was running low. Morale was even lower. Water was scarce. If the 112th didn't stop the Japanese soon, the hill would be lost, and they'd all be prisoners—or dead.

"Command has sent volunteers down to fill water from the spring three times," Ryan said. "Every time the men have to turn back."

Leo gazed at the cloudless sky. "Where the heck is the rain when you really need it? Last month was a monsoon. Now it's dryer than a cornfield in a heat wave."

"Lieutenant Ryan." Russo peeked his head around the giant boulder that shielded them. "Captain Mickelson on the radio for you." He handed the walkie-talkie to Ryan.

Ryan put the radio to his ear and moved away from Leo and Russo.

"The boys are getting restless." Russo nodded toward the foxholes. "Any news on supplies?"

Leo shook his head. "Nothing yet. Maybe Mickelson's got some answers for us."

"Captain Fyke is leading a rescue operation to get us out," Ryan said as he rejoined them and handed the radio back to Russo.

"What's he going to do?" Russo smirked. "Tell the Japs to lay off 'til we get free?"

Ryan rolled his eyes then said to Leo, "Get your men ready."

The men were packed and ready to go within the hour. While they waited, they took their regular turns at guard duty and getting some rest.

Six hours later, they were still waiting.

"Where the hell are they?" Dooley kicked at small rocks, launching them off the edge of the ridge. The sun was high in the sky—they wouldn't leave before nightfall, but the men were eager to get started.

"What's your hurry?" Filipowski spat into the dirt. "The Japs'll wait for us."

"Here we go." Webster raised his chin toward the staging area where Ryan was talking to Leo. The men grabbed their gear, ready to go.

Leo shook his head and walked toward his squad. "Rescue squad only got about a quarter of the way up before the Japs opened up on them," he said. "We're on our own."

Dooley dropped his gear. "Figures," he growled. "Another damned Yankee that don't know how to do his job."

Leo ignored the comment. "Bugout starts at dark."

It would be a very long night: several hours just to get down the mountain and then whatever time it took to get to their new location, what was known as an OLR, or Outpost Line of Resistance.

The order to move out came at 2100. The night was overcast. That gave them more cover from the enemy, but it also made finding their way almost impossible.

An artillery battalion kept the enemy at bay as Leo and his men moved down the mountain, followed by Troops A and C. The path—basically the parts where the trees weren't—was steep and rocky, treacherous in the pitch black of night. They made their way by feel and sometimes simply by placing a hand on the soldier in front of them and following, trusting that the man ahead of him wouldn't falter and take them both down.

Twenty minutes into their march, all hell broke loose.

Fifty yards to their left, a mortar exploded, filling the air with a white-hot light that temporarily blinded them.

"Ambush!" The alert came from behind them, perhaps the leader of Troop A.

Every man, maybe a hundred troops, fell to the ground, rifles ready to fire. As their eyes adjusted to the light, shadows appeared beyond the flames.

Machine-gun fire rattled the air. More mortars exploded. Trees crashed to the ground, and shrapnel pierced the air. There was nowhere for them to go.

"Find cover," Leo shouted, knowing there was precious little cover available.

Now gunfire came from every direction. But the Japanese attackers had made a fatal mistake: the bright flames had illuminated them like searchlights on an escaped convict. There were far fewer of them than there were Allied soldiers. In minutes, most of them were dead, and the rest were in retreat.

One by one, the troops stood. Just enough light remained from the fire for them to find the trail and re-form. Leo looked up the trail, counting his squad.

"Sound off." He listened as each of his men answered, relieved that everyone was okay.

Seven hours later, Leo and his men emerged from the jungle into the flat plain of the rice paddies. Gathering at the edge of the tree line, the clouds had thinned just enough for starlight to illuminate the various squads as they assembled. Leo's squad gathered near a clump of trees, Grayson bringing up the rear.

"Grayson," Leo whispered. "You the last one?"

"Yes, sir," Grayson said. "But Troop A isn't behind me."

CHAPTER 32

"Where the hell is Troop A?" Captain Mickelson paced in front of his men and glared at the mountain path where it emerged from the trees. Troop C had arrived minutes earlier. They'd been behind Troop A on the mountain.

Troop C's lieutenant looked around him and shrugged. "I dunno, sir. We couldn't see shit up there. One minute they were in front of us, and then they weren't."

"Are all your men accounted for?"

"Yes, sir."

"Form up with the rest of the men." He pointed to a well-worn trail where officers were lining up their squads. "Sergeant Baldwin." Mickelson eyeballed Leo. "Take two of your men and patrol into the jungle. See if you can spot any of A Troop."

"Yes, sir." Leo saluted, tapped Grayson and Myoga, and headed down the path.

"Don't go too far," Mickelson said. "I don't want to lose you too."

Five minutes passed. Then five more. Mickelson paced restlessly, glancing at his watch, at the sky, toward the jungle path.

At last, Leo and his men returned.

"No sign of 'em, sir," Leo said.

Mickelson looked at his watch again. "We can't wait around any longer," he said. "But somebody has to stay here for A Troop and lead them in to the new OLR." He gestured to Leo. "That somebody is you, Sergeant."

"Yes, sir." Leo suppressed a groan. Why did he have to be the one to stay behind? It wasn't like he'd let Troop A wander off like a herd of wayward sheep or something.

"Keep four of your men with you." Mickelson said. "I'm taking the rest to the OLR." He pulled a map from his breast pocket, unfolded it, and smoothed it out against a rock. "We're here," he said, pointing to the map. "The new OLR is over here, about five miles to the southwest." He refolded the map and stuffed it in his pocket. "When you make contact with A Troop, bring them in."

Leo watched as the rest of the RIF moved out toward the rear and safety. They were still several miles inside enemy territory, and now there were only five of them, each armed with only an M-1 rifle. He'd kept Russo, Filipowski, Grayson, and Myoga with him. They were the most experienced—and the most reliable—of his men.

"We'll wait over there." Leo pointed toward the deep shadows that indicated a line of trees, just west of the trail. Daybreak wasn't far off now. Although that meant their movement would have to be limited for several hours, it also meant that they would have a clear line of sight in both directions down the trail when Troop A showed up.

There they were, behind enemy lines waiting for a bunch of soldiers that were who-knew-where and about to be listed as "missing in action" if Leo didn't find them.

He thought about what Captain Mickelson had said when they'd first met. *On-the-job training.* That was certainly putting it mildly. Had it really been only two months since they'd landed on Luzon? In Guimba, they had assigned him as combat squad leader. Now it was his job to collect Lord-knew-how many soldiers and get them safely home. He wasn't even twenty-five years old, for God's sake.

But they had trained him to be a leader. He'd been responsible for his squad since he was in the cadre back at Fort Riley. It was his job to train them. To protect them. To lead them.

Whether he liked it or not.

Leo sighed and watched the trail. He glanced at his watch. He'd give them thirty more minutes. If they hadn't shown up by then, chances were they weren't going to.

Each man found a spot where he could rest and watch the trail. Myoga settled on a rock that was just big enough for sitting and pulled out what was left of his K-rations. As much as he craved a hot cup of coffee, there was no time to make a fire. He grabbed a dried fruit bar and a couple of biscuits, washing them down with warm water from his canteen.

Grayson leaned against a nearby tree. He pulled out his pack of cigarettes, offered one to Myoga, and took one for himself.

"Wonder how long we'll be stuck here," Myoga said.

"As long as it takes to find the wanderers, I suppose." Grayson carefully crushed his spent cigarette against the tree and tucked the butt in his pocket. "Let's hope that's before the Japs get here."

Forty minutes later, there was still no sign of them.

"I've got a feeling they bypassed us already," Leo said. Heavy clouds shrouded the sky, and he was anxious to make the OLR before it rained. "Russo. Filipowski." He gestured to his men. "Scout down the trail a mile or so. I don't want to run into any more surprises today."

The men nodded and headed off.

"As soon as they get back, we're heading out," he said. "If anyone else is left out here, God help them."

Ten minutes later, Russo came jogging down the trail with Filipowski tight behind him.

"Bunch of Japs up ahead." Russo caught his breath as he whispered to Leo.

"How many?" Leo asked.

"Ten. Maybe twelve. They seem to be searching for stragglers—"

"Like us?" Leo smiled as he finished Russo's sentence.

"Yeah, exactly like us. And coming this way."

Leo turned to Grayson and Myoga, encircled his right wrist with the thumb and forefinger of his left hand—*enemy*—and pointed down the trail. Then he pointed toward his men and then to the trees. They'd no sooner settled into their hiding place than the enemy appeared.

Everyone held his breath as the Japanese soldiers stopped, halfheartedly poking the high grass in search of concealed Americans. An officer barked out an order. The group seemed to relax, not in any hurry to move on.

For a long time, they stood on the trail smoking cigarettes, talking and laughing as if it were break time at the office. Leo watched the soldiers. Some of them looked like they were only teenagers, like Richards and Webster. He thought about the letter he'd taken from the Japanese private. Any of these boy-soldiers could be just like that private: acting like brave warriors and knowing they would likely die. Honorable or not, it was a terrible waste.

The Japanese finally moved on just before dawn. The sky was heavily overcast with the rain they'd so desperately needed on the ridge. Leo held his men; he wanted to be absolutely sure the enemy soldiers were gone.

They'd just started out again when the clouds let loose.

In minutes, the trail had turned into a muddy bog. The men slogged on, their waterproof gear providing little protection from the driving rain that poured off the soldiers' hoods and under their slickers. In the heavy rain, nothing looked familiar. Leo stopped to consult his compass. They'd been moving at least an hour; they should've found the OLR by now. Did he somehow miss it?

Russo caught up with him. "Are we lost, Sarge?"

Leo scratched his head. "Not really lost," he said. "Seems like that new OLR is well hidden."

"So we're lost."

"Temporarily, soldier." Leo shrugged and looked at the skies to the west. The clouds hung ominously close over the mountains. It would probably rain like this all day. He scanned the area and pointed a few yards down a steep hill to a small cluster of trees. "We'll hole up here for a while. It's far enough down that no one is likely to see us from up here. I'll take first watch. The rest of you try to get some sleep."

By nightfall, the rain had stopped. A multitude of stars twinkled in the clear skies. Leo studied his compass, located the Southern Cross constellation, and plotted a path that he hoped would lead them into the OLR. It shouldn't be more than a couple of miles away.

Another hour elapsed before they finally struggled into camp. Troop A had arrived there hours before.

Figures, Leo thought. *We risked our lives and got soaked to the skin to boot, all for no good reason.*

"Hey, Sarge." Richards had spotted Leo and ran to meet him. "We thought you guys were dead."

Leo nodded. "I see Troop A made it without me."

"Well, sort of." Richards scuffed at the dirt. "They took some serious losses. Six dead, a bunch of wounded, and eight still MIA."

"I'll catch you later," Leo said. "Right now, I need to report to Ryan."

It was only a few hours until dawn by the time he made his report. He was beyond exhausted, but he still had one more job to do before he could sleep. He scanned the area, found a suitable spot, and dug a new foxhole.

CHAPTER 33

BIGTI OUTPOST—APRIL 1945

Leo stuffed the last of his gear into his pack and hoisted it over his shoulder. After a ten-day break, Troop B would return to the Bigti area for another recon assignment.

Across the compound, Dooley crawled out of his tent and stretched. Webster was just returning from the latrine and lifted an eyebrow at Dooley.

He had information.

Dooley gestured to a rock pile a few feet away. Webster nodded and followed. When they got there, Dooley extracted his cigarette package from his breast pocket, took out a cigarette, offered one to Webster, and lit both of them. He casually took a drag and slowly exhaled.

"What's goin' on?" Dooley asked.

Webster shuffled from one foot to the other like he might explode from excitement. "Saw Richards over by the latrine. I been keeping an eye on him like you said."

"Good man." Dooley relaxed against the rocks, gesturing for Webster to sit. "What happened?"

Webster sat down and inhaled deeply from his cigarette. "So, I'm headed out to take a dump, but on the way there I spot Richards, talkin' to himself." He rolled his eyes. "Like a crazy man. So's I stepped behind a tree to watch him."

"Yeah?" Dooley's eyes brightened. This was gonna be great. "What was he sayin'?"

"Talkin' to his ma. Sayin' how he's sorry, how he won't fuck up no more." Webster spat in distaste. "That boy was cryin' his eyes out. It was like he thought nobody was there 'cept him and his mama. Well, I stepped out from behind the tree," Webster continued, "made a little grunt so he'd know he wasn't alone. He just took off like I wasn't even there."

"Sounds like he's gone around the bend." Dooley lowered his voice and glanced around. "Here's what I need you to do."

The next morning, Webster was pacing by Leo's foxhole when Leo returned from guard duty. "Can we talk a minute, Sarge?"

Leo sighed. He'd hoped he could get to his foxhole and snugged in before someone noticed him. "Sure, Webster." He gestured to sit. "What's up?"

Webster sat, nervously tracing patterns in the loose dirt with his finger. "It's Richards."

"You got a problem with him?" Leo crossed his arms. It was bad enough Dooley kept ragging on Richards. Knowing how buddy-buddy Webster and Dooley were, he figured Dooley'd put him up to this.

"I'm worried about him is all." Webster picked up a small rock and rolled it around in his hand. "I caught him talkin' to himself yesterday just before we left Guimba—no, that ain't quite right. He was talkin' to his ma like she was right there in front of him." He rubbed his face. "Sarge, I think he's losin' it."

Leo stared across the compound and found Dooley watching from a distance. Dooley abruptly turned his head and walked off. Leo glared at Webster. "I don't suppose Sergeant Dooley had anything to do with your concern?"

Webster's ears reddened. "I mentioned it to him. But only 'cause I didn't want to bother you with it if I didn't have to."

And Dooley told you to run right over here and rat on Richards, didn't he? Leo was getting tired of the infighting within his squad. They were like a bunch of brothers duking it out for the last scraps at the dinner table. But he was their leader, and it was his job to see to their complaints, no matter how flimsy they seemed.

"I'll look into it," Leo said. "Now let me get some rest." He flicked his hand in dismissal, not willing to take Dooley's bait.

"Yes, Sergeant." Webster saluted stiffly and walked away.

As much as Dooley's nonsense rankled him, Leo knew he'd have to have a talk with Richards. But first he'd get some rest and talk to him when he was more clearheaded and patient. He curled up inside his foxhole, tucked his pack under his head for a pillow, put a spare sock over his eyes to shut out the sunlight, and set his raincoat within reach for the rain that would surely appear before he was ready to get up.

Just as he was nodding off, the voice of some soldier preparing for his day's mission jarred him awake. He recognized Richards's high tenor. It sounded like he was talking to Filipowski—the deep, gravelly voice was a giveaway.

Might as well get this over with. Leo set the extra sock aside and scrambled out of his foxhole.

"Private Richards." Leo motioned to Richards.

Russo and Filipowski, his teammates for the day, looked up as he spoke.

Leo walked Richards a few paces away from the other men. "I'll have him back to you in just a minute."

Richards's cheeks reddened, arms crossed against his chest. "Webster talked to you, didn't he?"

"He did," Leo said. "Do I need to be worried?"

"That damned son of a bitch." Richards clenched his fists. "He's been sticking to me like a gnat on flypaper." He looked down then off into the distance. He stayed quiet, as if deciding what to say next, and kept his focus on the distant terrain. "Are the guys over there listening?"

Leo glanced at Russo and Filipowski. They had their heads together, talking about one thing or another. "Nope." Leo turned his back on them to be sure they couldn't try to read his lips. "Go ahead, Richards."

"Sometimes it gets to me, Sarge." Richards's eyes were teary. He struggled not to cry. "I think of Ma, laying there in the road, and how it was all my fault 'cause I just had to show off. When I feel it coming on, I try to go off by myself, get it outta my system. I didn't see Webster there at first, and when I did, I was so embarrassed I just took off."

Leo raised an eyebrow. "Are you sure that's all there is to it?"

Richards nodded. "I'll be more careful." He traced an X across his chest. "Cross my heart."

"What you need to do is let go of it," Leo snapped. "Obsessing about your ma is going to get you killed. If you can't get it under control, I'll have to see about taking you out of combat."

Richards' eyes widened. "Don't do that, Sarge." He straightened his body. "I'm as good a soldier as anyone. I promise I'll handle it better."

"You be sure you do, Private," Leo said. He knew he shouldn't have been so brusque with Richards, but the boy reminded him more and more of Furness. He put a hand on Richards's shoulder. "You *are* a good soldier, Richards. Don't forget that." He turned toward his foxhole. "Russo and Filipowski are waiting for you, and I need to get some shuteye."

NIGHT PATROL
LUZON, 1945

Outside the closed perimeter, we wait
Until full dark; then, at a word, we go
Like green-clad ghosts to stalk the distant foe.
Still harbingers of death, grim tools of fate,
Beside a road, we crouch in silent dread
As files of soldiers pass, and never know
That Nemesis is watching. If they show
Some signs of knowing, many will be dead.
Most of us, too, will die, for we are few,
And far from any help; but we sit tight.
We come to watch their movements, not to fight,
Though, if they see us, we will do that too.
But they pass on into the midnight murk,
Past this dark place where death and horror lurk.

CHAPTER 34

BIGTI OUTPOST—MAY 1945

Dear folks,

I have all the necessities for writing airmail letters now—if my ink holds out. This may reach you ahead of a V-mail I wrote a few days ago. I hope you haven't worried much about not hearing from me for a few days. I just couldn't get the necessary materials. I haven't received the stationery yet. You don't realize how slowly packages come. The stamps came O.K. and will surely be useful.

Your spring weather sounds marvelous. Here it's pretty warm most of the time, occasionally a thunder shower, and really not too bad altogether. Today there's a cool breeze, and it's quite comfortable in the shade. In the sun, it's plenty hot. I wish I could tell you a little more about what's happening and how I'm getting along. I'm feeling quite well, and while accommodations could be better, I suppose they could be much worse. I'm just hoping and praying that I can sweat out this campaign and maybe get a good vacation. I'm afraid the war is far from over yet, regardless of what the papers say. It isn't all as easy as they make out. I don't want to seem pessimistic, but there's too much complacency in the States. I hope I'm wrong.

Hope this finds everyone well. Keep an eye on the birds for me.

Love to all,

Leal

Leo sealed the letter and fidgeted. He looked at his watch and sighed—only ten minutes since the last time he'd checked. He was caught up on writing letters, had read every magazine within reach, even dashed off a poem or two, and there was still an hour to go before nightfall and patrol.

Night patrol was the worst. The enemy would be on the move, probably patrolling just as Leo's squad was. The last thing either side wanted was to stumble into one another.

At last, the patrol left the outpost. Dooley and Myoga were Leo's only companions. They fanned out as they moved down the trail, alert for any sound or sight of the enemy. The night was clear, the sky peppered with stars, a waxing moon hanging high. They cautiously crossed a rice field, crouching low and ready to respond to any threat.

Leo spotted a large hayrick on the far side of the field. He held his hand out, signaled for Dooley and Myoga to stop, and knelt on the ground.

"That hayrick's a good Jap hiding place," he said. "We need to be extra cautious. Keep an eye out for movement."

Dooley and Myoga nodded, and the squad continued, rifles loaded and ready.

Myoga stopped abruptly, touched his nose, and pointed across the field. A glint of reflected moonlight flashed from the hayrick, perhaps a Japanese bayonet. The men dropped to their bellies.

"Let's see if we can get close enough to get a count." Leo scanned the area for cover, anyplace they could retreat to if the Japs opened fire. "There."

He pointed to a rock pile, probably cleared from the rice field. It was close enough to get a good look at the hayrick and tall enough to provide cover for all three of them.

As the three crawled closer, several Japanese soldiers burst out from behind the hayrick, led by a man frantically shouting orders. As if in response, the soldiers threw their packs to the side, using all their energy to escape.

Dooley lifted his rifle to his shoulder, aiming toward the fleeing enemy.

"Not yet," Leo cautioned. "We only engage if we have to, remember?"

Dooley grunted but kept his rifle aimed and ready. When the last of the Nips disappeared into the darkness, Leo signaled his men to advance, cautiously moving toward the abandoned hayrick and at last getting to his feet when it became clear that no soldier remained.

"Gather up their gear." Leo showed the direction in which the soldiers had fled. "That ought to give us a pretty close count."

Leo moved closer to the hayrick to search for anything useful the Japanese soldiers might have left behind. As he drew closer, he heard a low moan coming from the nearby tall grass. Leo dropped to the ground, signaling Myoga and Dooley to do the same. He crawled the remaining distance, following the sounds. Occasionally, he heard weak, frantic words as if someone were trying to yell for help.

"Kōsan!" Leo shouted. *Surrender!* The voice went silent, Leo shouted again. "Kōsan!"

"No shoot." The frail voice filtered through the tall grass. "I surrender." The wounded soldier had propped himself against a rock. His rifle lay across his lap.

"Rifle." Leo held out his rifle, pointed to the soldier's rifle, and then to a point a good three yards away. He doubted the soldier had enough strength to use his weapon, but he wasn't taking any chances.

"Got it," Dooley said as the wounded soldier weakly tossed his rifle aside. Dooley retrieved the rifle from the tall grass and headed toward the hayrick.

Leo kept a close eye on the soldier as he approached, alert for any movement that might reveal a hidden grenade or knife. The soldier lay still, his breathing labored and shallow. Leo pulled his medical pouch from his belt and dropped to his knees next to the Jap, performing first a visual and then a hands-on survey of his injuries.

The wound was in the soldier's thigh, a gaping hole that was poorly bandaged. Leo drew in his breath, recoiling from the stench as he removed the dressing. The wound was deep, the skin around it red and hot with infection. Leo filled the wound with sulfanilamide and gauze, gently wrapping it with a fresh bandage.

"Is he going to live?" Myoga asked.

"Holy smoke!" Leo jumped. He hadn't heard Myoga approaching. "You trying to get yourself shot?"

"Sorry, Sarge," Myoga mumbled, pointing to the wounded leg. "You get him patched up okay?"

"Wound's pretty bad," Leo said. "But I think if we get him back soon enough, he'll be okay."

"I wouldn't count on that." Dooley held the Japanese rifle pointed down as he stepped over the wounded soldier. "We oughta put him outta his misery."

Dooley raised the bayoneted rifle and plunged the spear into the soldier's chest.

"There," he said, jerking the bayonet free. "Dead is the only way I want to see a Nip." He removed the dead man's helmet, retrieved the Japanese flag tucked inside, and slipped it into his breast pocket. "And a souvenir to boot," he said as he turned and headed back to the path. "Don't that beat all."

"Sergeant Nelson." Leo spoke as loudly as he dared. "Stop right there." As he ran toward Dooley, he looked back where Myoga stood over the lifeless body. "Check him for important documents and catch up to us."

Dooley stood on the path, hands on his hips and legs spread defiantly.

"What the heck do you think you're doing, Sergeant?" Leo said. "There was no need to kill the man—he'd already surrendered."

"Oh, c'mon, Baldwin. He was a dead man anyway. I just saved us a lot of trouble tryin' to haul him back."

Leo's face reddened. He'd had enough of Dooley's nonsense. "Listen, soldier." He stood nose to nose with Dooley. "You don't call the orders around here. I do. I don't care how good you are with a gun. I won't have a subordinate who disobeys orders."

Dooley grabbed Leo's shoulder and shoved. "You think you're all hot shit, but I'm telling you now, *Sergeant*, you're just another pansy-ass playin' at war."

Leo knew Dooley was baiting him, but he couldn't let this one go. He was Dooley's superior, whether he liked it or not. Myoga came down the path, his face pale, his eyes wide as he watched Leo and Dooley. Leo got back in Dooley's face.

"You listen to me, soldier." He poked Dooley's chest. "I'm putting you on report." He clenched his fists and paced then turned back to Dooley. "You're here to follow my orders, Sergeant, and if you can't do that, I'll have you up on charges of insubordination."

"I was doin' the guy a favor," Dooley grumbled as they headed back to base.

All the way back to the command post and half of the next day, Leo thought long and hard about Dooley. He'd report the altercation to Ryan and Mickelson as required, but should he request that Dooley be transferred?

No, he finally decided. Getting rid of Dooley felt like admitting defeat. *I may be digging my own grave, but I'm not letting him think he's won.*

Susannah Willey

そよそよと
揺れる木の葉は
敵か風

Soyosoyo to
Yureru ko no ha wa
Teki ka kaze

Leaves rustle softly
Is it enemies passing
Or just the night breeze?

CHAPTER 35

BIGTI CLIFFS—MAY 1945

"I was beginning to think I would not see you again, Kai-chan." Tadashi embraced his friend as he entered their sleeping quarters.

Kaito laughed. "It will take more than a little gunfire to stop me, Nii-chan." He dropped his pack to the floor, rested his rifle against the wall, and squatted on the cold dirt. "We kept them surrounded for nearly two weeks. No supplies could get to them, even by plane, and finally they were desperate enough to give up. The ridge is ours, but most of the enemy escaped." He frowned and lowered his head. "Corporal Araki was killed."

Kaito and Tadashi paused in silent respect for their platoon mate.

"But I killed two Americans." Kaito lifted his head and thrust out his chest. "Two for one is not a bad trade, don't you agree?"

"Not bad, Kai-chan. Now hurry, or we will be late for assembly."

Tadashi and Kaito crowded into the mountain's largest cavern with the rest of their battalion. The air echoed with the joyful sounds of over one thousand men who embraced one another, shared stories of their missions, and bragged about their conquests.

The room fell silent as soldiers snapped to attention when the battalion commanding officer, Lieutenant Colonel Wada, entered the cavern.

"We welcome back our comrades from their successful mission to take the southwest ridge." Wada raised his fist triumphantly. "The destruction of the enemy supply road is complete. The remaining soldiers huddle in their foxholes with no food or ammunition. Any day now, they will surrender like the cowards they are."

The assembled soldiers cheered in response. "Banzai! Banzai! Banzai!"

Wada held out both hands to silence the men. "But I have even more glorious news to report. President Roosevelt, the leader of the United States, is dead. It won't be long until America surrenders completely."

The crowd went wild. For a moment, the stench of unwashed bodies went unnoticed. The anticipation of victory overrode the ache of starvation. The men cheered, cried silent tears, allowed their minds to fill with thoughts of home and family reunions.

Tadashi silently watched the men around him, amazed at how many of his comrades actually believed Wada's propaganda. Kaito stood beside him, his fist raised in victory, his chest puffed out in pride.

Even Kaito had swallowed the lies. Tadashi shook his head. *When did I grow so cynical?*

President Roosevelt was indeed a formidable enemy, and now he was dead. Tadashi was grateful for all of this, but he doubted the death of one man would deter an entire army. At least it might put Lieutenant Inoue in a forgiving mood when Tadashi shared the details of his first mission as Sergeant.

Tadashi stood at attention as he made his report.

"My men destroyed the bridge, along with four supply vehicles and all of their cargo," he said. "In two weeks, we planted twenty-three bombs. All were detonated by enemy traffic."

Inoue nodded. "Good work, Sergeant."

Tadashi frowned. "I have lost five men, Lieutenant. Enemy soldiers attacked as we crossed the rice paddy."

He stared at the wall, prepared for Inoue's anger.

Instead, Inoue waved his hand dismissively. "It was unavoidable," he said. "But we have no one to take their place."

"Understood, Lieutenant." The tension left Tadashi's shoulders.

Inoue studied his fingernails for what seemed like several minutes as Tadashi stood rigid and stone-faced. "On second thought," Inoue said at last, "you can have Corporal Shimizu. He is useless to me."

"Thank you, sir." Tadashi was careful to let no emotion betray his relief at having his friend beside him again. Kaito was a valuable soldier, and as a part of Tadashi's squad, he would avoid much of Inoue's hostility.

Inoue returned his attention to his hands, idly picked loose threads from his uniform, and looked around the cave as if he was bored.

Did he take pleasure in making Tadashi stand here?

Finally, the lieutenant spoke. "I have a new mission for you."

"Our new mission is reconnaissance." Tadashi scrutinized his men, much like Lieutenant Inoue did. He spoke with the same authority, but there was no swagger, no sneer. "There will be no aggression on our part. We will divide into two groups for scouting and attack only in defense. Our commanders need to know how many enemy soldiers remain. Are they well supplied? Do they have the means to take the dam, or have they moved on to bother someone else?"

"Yes, Sergeant," the men answered in unison.

He was overjoyed at having the chance to leave the cave for several days instead of the few hours at a time he could get laying booby traps. Scouting the area for enemy movement meant having fresh air to breathe instead of the odors of death and decay that filled the tunnels. If all went as planned, there would be no enemy contact, no fighting, and he would return with valuable information.

The oppression of the mountain hideout lifted from Tadashi as he stepped into the night air. The breeze was gentle and warm, the night sky bright with a nearly full moon. He gazed at the twinkling stars, identified Ryuu, the dragon constellation. It had been his favorite since he was a child. His father had pointed it out, told him the ancient legend of the dragon.

Tadashi imagined his farm in Hokkaido and his beloved Sachiko. It brought a pang of longing to his chest. Longing for Sachiko and Ichiro. Longing for his faithful ox and his fields of wheat. It brought a closeness to his home and family that he couldn't find inside a darkened cave. He whispered a brief prayer to the kami to return him safely home when this war ended.

"Are we going to gawk at the moon all night?" Kaito's voice startled Tadashi from his thoughts. "Is star-gazing our mission?"

"I am thanking the kami for their protection." Tadashi smiled and gestured toward Japan. "And wishing I were home." He stiffened and made his face expressionless as the rest of his squad joined them and formed up for marching.

The air sang with the hum of insects, of hooting boobooks and calling nightjars, as Tadashi and his squad of six approached the rice field. His senses were sharpened; he felt certain the Americans were not far away, perhaps hiding in the jungle thickness beyond the field. The last time he's crossed this paddy, he had lost half of his squad—he could afford to lose no more today.

"Corporal Fujita," he said and motioned to a small copse of trees, "your team will search the trees and surrounding area to our north and west. Corporal Shimizu, you and your men search to the south and east. We meet back here in three hours."

As the teams headed off, Tadashi scanned the immediate area. On the other side of the rice field, kunai grass covered the flat ground. The jungle shadows loomed only a few meters beyond. A good place to find adequate shelter for the day.

"Nigeru!" *Run!* Tadashi jumped and raised his rifle as voices shouted from the kunai grass. He fought the instinct to follow the command, crouched, and prepared to defend himself.

The kunai grass swished loudly with movement. Tadashi strained to listen, recognizing frantic whispers in Japanese. Their accent was too perfect to be Americans. He stood cautiously, keeping his rifle pointed toward the ground.

"Nihongo. Tomodachi." *Japanese. Friends.* Tadashi raised his hand in the air and spoke in a loud whisper. He prayed the men would recognize that his accent was genuine.

The fleeing soldiers froze. They held their rifles close but did not raise them to fire.

"I am Sergeant Abukara," Tadashi said as they approached.

The soldiers lowered their weapons, and Tadashi motioned for them to crouch in the high grass.

"We must hide." The lead soldier gasped for air as he pointed toward a pile of rocks near the tree line. "The enemy is just over there."

Tadashi nodded an acknowledgement. He wasn't ready to run just yet. "Are there more of you?"

"There are others who ran." The soldier's breathing slowed. "I don't know where they went." He nervously looked around him, as if the enemy might crash through the kunai grass at any moment. "But there is a wounded soldier," he said. "We had to abandon him when the Americans discovered us."

"How far?" asked Tadashi.

The soldier pointed to the left of the trees. "Half a kilometer, maybe. We were resting near an old hayrick when they attacked."

"Take me there," Tadashi said. The rest of his squad had come running when they heard the shouts and now crowded around him. "You will come with me." said Tadashi, pointing to Private Ikeda. "Corporal." He nodded toward Kaito. "You and the rest stay here."

The three men stayed crouched behind the kunai grass as they hurried toward the hayrick.

When they came within sight of it, Tadashi motioned toward a massive dipterocarp tree. "We will hide there."

Three Americans stood over a wounded Japanese soldier. Tadashi could not understand their words but recognized the insignia that identified the leader. He spoke to another soldier—a sergeant, Tadashi thought. The third American stood nearby.

Do not engage. Tadashi recalled Inoue's orders. It would be an even battle, but it relieved Tadashi that he did not have to fight. What he saw next made him reconsider.

The sergeant abruptly straddled the wounded soldier and raised his bayonet. Their leader raised his hand, perhaps in a motion for him to stop, but it was too late. The sergeant violently stabbed the wounded man, kept stabbing until he seemed satisfied. When he finished, he lifted the dead man's helmet and extracted the rising sun flag many Japanese soldiers carried for luck. As he disrespectfully crumpled the flag and shoved it in his pocket, he laughed derisively, said something Tadashi couldn't understand, and walked away with an arrogant swagger.

The soldier who had led Tadashi to the hayrick snarled and raised his rifle.

"Stop." Tadashi put his hand firmly on the rifle and pushed its muzzle toward the ground.

"He killed my comrade." The soldier's eyes blazed with anger.

"Our orders are to observe only." Tadashi forced out the words. He wanted revenge as badly as anyone, but he would not defy orders.

He thought of the POWs at Cabanatuan, their gentle treatment of their dead and wounded comrades, their reverent worship. Why did he believe the Americans were not capable of cruelty? They watched as the American leader searched the dead soldier, rummaged through his pack, picked through his belongings. Tadashi grew angrier and angrier as he watched the Americans scavenge the dead soldier's effects.

The Americans were long since gone when Tadashi and his men went to retrieve the dead soldier's body. Tadashi noticed the fresh dressing on the soldier's thigh. Had the Americans done that? Why would they tend to his wounds if they intended to butcher him?

Tadashi shrugged. None of that really mattered, did it?

He searched through the soldier's pockets, emptied his pack in search of anything he might send to the man's family. He found nothing.

Tadashi's squad kept watch as he dug a shallow grave. He would not dishonor this man by allowing his body to be eaten by scavengers. Before he and his men rolled the body into the ground, he cut off some of the soldier's hair and took clippings of his fingernails, cut a piece from his uniform, and reverently placed the hair and fingernails inside, just as he had done for Corporal Sato. He could at least return that much to the man's family.

At dawn, he took first watch, allowed his men some sleep. He couldn't erase the memory of the American, brutally stabbing an already wounded man.

I was wrong. He clenched his fists. The Americans were no better than Takasaki.

Before today, Tadashi simply wanted to go home. Now he wanted revenge.

CHAPTER 36

NEW BOSOBOSO AND HILL 1200—MAY 17, 1945

Dear folks,

Its a damp evening and a little nasty. However, if our tent doesn't leak, it will be O.K. Glad the war in Europe was over before Hayden was there too long. I hope he didn't see too much action. No doubt he'll be over in this part of the world before long. However, he may have a good long vacation before he sees any more action anyway.

Things are going pretty well with me, though I have a sore heel just now. I'd like to tell you more about what's going on, but I can't tell you much, and there's no use worrying you with what little I can say. When I get home, I'll tell you all you want to know about it.

Leo set down his pen and took a drink of his coffee. It seemed like it was all he drank anymore, and he was beginning to hate its acrid taste. Even the smell was becoming offensive. But it was hot, and it kept him going, especially on days like today when he was stuck in his tent.

He'd seen so much, but he couldn't speak a word of it. Would he tell his family even if he could? No, but it would be nice to have someone hear it. Rudd, his close friend at home, would listen. Then again, he wasn't sure he could even tell Rudd.

There was one image that would never leave him.

Two weeks previously, they'd been on a regular recon mission, tasked with weeding out enemy stragglers. Leo's men had located a small cave—just the sort of place where Japs might be hiding. Creeping to the entrance, they could hear voices inside, although they were not much more than muffled noises.

"Kōsan," Myoga shouted into the cave's opening.

The voices fell silent.

"Kōsan," he said again, this time more forcefully. Still no reply.

At Leo's signal, Myoga and the rest of the men pulled back.

"Let's give them some time," Leo said. Their orders were to call in the flamethrowers to destroy any caves or tunnels suspected of hiding the enemy. But Leo had smelled enough burning flesh in the past weeks to know that he never wanted to smell it again. He would wait and hope they'd surrender.

Thirty minutes passed before Leo had Myoga issue the command again. "Kōsan."

The only sound from inside was the drip, drip, drip of water seeping through the cave's ceiling.

"Russo." Leo turned to his radioman. "Call HQ for orders." *And pray they don't send the flamethrowers.*

Russo pressed the transmit button and relayed Leo's request.

After three tries with no response, Russo lowered the handset and shrugged. "No answer, Sarge," he said. "I can keep trying, but we're probably out of range."

Reluctantly, Leo sent Grayson and Richards to the command post to report their findings and receive orders. It was an hour before they returned.

"No flame squad," Grayson said as he reached Leo. "Cap says grenade it."

Leo felt his shoulders relax. He was relieved that they wouldn't be using napalm that day. Even if the Japs hid far back in the cave, the concussion of several exploding grenades should be enough to kill most of them.

Leo silently signaled his men. Each one pulled the pin from his grenade, counted four seconds, and lobbed the charge into the cave.

The ground shook as the grenades exploded one after another. Smoke poured from the entrance. They waited a few minutes, listening for movement inside before tossing in another round.

"Huwag mo aking shoot!" The voice from inside the cave spoke in Tagalog. Leo recognized the plea—*don't shoot me*!

"Russo." Leo gestured to the corporal. "How many grenades did you hear go off?"

Russo thought for a moment. "Five, I think. Four I'm sure of."

"Myoga?"

"I got five."

"Grayson, Richards, what's your count?"

"Definitely five," Grayson said.

"Agreed," said Richards.

Leo had counted five as well, but he wanted to be sure there weren't any unexploded grenades in there before they went in.

Leo gestured to the Filipino guerilla that often traveled with the squad.

"Tell them to come out," he said.

"Lumabas," the Filipino shouted into the cave.

Long moments passed, and finally a figure appeared at the cave entrance.

"Huwag mo aking shoot!" Dust and soot streaked the old woman's face. Her clothes hung in tatters on her bony frame. She held her hands high in surrender.

"Mas?" *More?* Leo gestured into the cave.

The woman nodded. "Si. Mas."

"Tell her to show us," Leo said to the Filipino. "Russo, I want you and Richards to stand guard. The rest of you come with me." The last thing Leo wanted was for Richards to flip out over a dead body inside a cave.

The old woman rushed ahead, jabbering in Tagalog and waving her arms toward the back of the cave. Bodies lay everywhere, some in pieces. Grenade fragments protruded from arms, legs, torsos. Some had no obvious injury, likely dying from the force of the explosion.

Leo and his men paused only long enough to check each body for a pulse, less if death was obvious. There was no need to search for important papers or weapons, and Leo was grateful for that.

The old woman, still talking incessantly, still waving her arms, seemed not to be affected, almost as if she didn't even see the bodies around her. As they approached the back of the cave, her voice became more urgent. There were survivors here, some badly injured—others, like the old woman, merely stunned by the explosions. She scanned the bodies as if she looked for someone in particular.

"Alon?" she called. "Alon? Alon?" She was near hysteria as she moved through the bodies of living and dead. "Nasaan si Alon?"

A small voice came from the rubble. "Lola?"

The old woman rushed toward the voice, gesturing for the men to follow. Myoga and Grayson carefully dug through the fallen stones and bodies, at last uncovering a boy, maybe six or seven years old. Cuts and bruises covered his body, most of them superficial. Ending up at the bottom of the pile had probably saved his life.

The old woman clutched the boy to her chest. Tears streamed down her face as she whispered in his ear. The boy sobbed, holding tight to the old woman. After a few moments, the old woman gestured to Leo and said something to the boy.

The boy looked at Leo. "We saw bad soldiers. We hide."

Leo nodded. "Check for more wounded. I'll send for help."

He hurried outside as the rest turned their attention to the bodies.

"Radio for medics," Leo said to Russo as he emerged from the cave. "Try going up the ridge a ways. Maybe you can get a signal." Russo shouldered the heavy radio unit. "Tell them we've got civilian causalities, three critical."

With medics finally en route, Leo and his men did their best to triage the wounded and prepare them for transport. The Filipino guerilla gently coaxed the old woman as she told what had happened. A group of Japanese soldiers had invaded their nearby village, burning their houses and killing everyone in their path. A few of the natives had escaped and hid in the cave. When Myoga ordered them to surrender, they thought it was the Japanese soldiers come to slaughter them. They silently huddled as far back in the cave as they could and prayed the soldiers would leave.

Twenty civilians had hidden inside the cave. Only five survived the initial blast. Three died later from their injuries. Only the old woman and her grandson survived.

The army higher-ups deemed it "collateral damage."

They didn't see what we did, Leo thought. He had nightmares for a week. It wasn't like he hadn't seen bodies, but those were enemy soldiers—men who deserved to die. These were civilians just trying to survive.

No matter how he looked at it, he couldn't reconcile his actions. He had always understood that death was a part of war. He knew in his mind that innocent people would die. But he always imagined those deaths at the hands of the enemy. It was logical to believe that the Allies had caused civilian deaths too. But those deaths were accidental. He and his men had thrown their grenades into the cave, intending to kill. That they thought they were killing enemy soldiers seemed moot.

People were dead—the people they were supposed to protect.

Leo struggled to still his shaking hands as he took another sip of coffee. When he'd finally controlled the trembling, he picked up his pen and continued.

We filled out our cards for rotation recently. Of course, I stand pretty low on the list, and I'm afraid it will be a long time before I get enough points to do me any good. However, its encouraging to know that they're doing something along that line anyway. Hope it works out fast.

Joe E. Brown was here recently with a USO show. It was pretty nice to get a show like that. He was good and so was the rest of his show. They had a juggler, violinist, and accordionist. Guess thats all for now.

Love to all,

Leal

Leo placed his letter in its envelope and sealed it shut. He capped his pen, tucking it into his knapsack.
There were some things he would never tell.

Susannah Willey

囚われて
息をしつつも
余は死人

Torawarete
Iki o shitsutsumo
Yo wa shibito

Wounded and dying,
I am taken by my foes.
I live, but am dead.

CHAPTER 37

AMERICAN FIELD HOPITAL, LUZON—MAY 1945

Lieutenant Inoue struggled to open his eyes. It felt like they were held together with glue. He cautiously touched his face; it was covered in bandages. Two tiny holes for his nostrils, one, slightly larger, for his mouth. His lips were a mass of blisters, his mouth gummy with saliva. His hands stunk of burnt flesh and gunpowder.

The fire. Was it still burning? He needed to get out. He thrashed on the narrow cot, nearly fell off. His legs refused to move. A hand touched his shoulder, speaking gently in a language he didn't know.

Inoue's heart fell as he understood his situation: he was a prisoner, probably in an enemy field hospital. Whatever had happened, there hadn't been time to kill himself rather than be captured. How could he have allowed that? He forced his body to be still, focused on his thoughts, trying to remember what had happened. How long ago had it been? Days? Weeks?

Two weeks after the Japanese attack at Hot Corner, the Americans had repaired the Metropolitan Road. Now, a large contingent of U.S. Army soldiers was seen moving in from the northwest. Inoue and the other officers were summoned to the command bunker deep inside the mountain to plan their next move.

They had one card left to play: Ipo Dam.

"We must hold the dam at all costs." The general in command had not spoken of retreat—it was not an option. "The Americans and Filipinos are desperate to restore water to Manila. As long as we control Ipo, we control the city."

The rumor was that a new American Army division, with the help of Philippine guerilla forces, was planning a massive assault on the caves. Before either side could mount an attack, the rain had come. It was relentless, confining the Japanese to their mountain tunnels. The downpour slowed the American forces; their ordnance was mired in the muck. But today, the rain had receded, the skies were cloudless, and the Americans would soon resume their advance.

"Colonel Nakamura." The general nodded to the man on his left. "Where are the bodies of our deceased brothers stored?"

"For that, we have built a special tunnel," Nakamura said, "away from the others." He showed the tunnel's location on the tattered map he held.

"And how many bodies do you estimate are there?"

Nakamura thought for a moment. "Several hundred, I'm sure."

"There will be a special mission tonight." The general pointed to an entrance on the north side of the mountain. "This entrance is as yet unknown to the enemy. All soldiers who are not assigned to guard duty will remove the bodies and transport them to the dam, where they will be disposed of. The contaminated water will be useless to drink, even if the Americans open the access pipe. Our lost brothers will be heroes even in death."

As they discussed their plan, the mountain suddenly shivered.

"An earthquake," the general said calmly. "We are safe here. We have specially reinforced our bunker against earthquakes."

"General." The voice from outside the bunker was frantic. "We are under attack!"

The officers rushed to the observation entrance. The sky was dark with enemy planes, hundreds of them, releasing bomb after bomb that exploded into a storm of flames when they hit.

Napalm.

With each strike, a cave or tunnel was silenced, the earth beyond it scorched and obliterated. Screams echoed from the caves below. Burning soldiers ran outside to escape the flames, only to be killed by machine-gun fire. Columns of heavy smoke from each entrance rose high into the sky.

Lieutenant Inoue hastily gathered his soldiers, moving them toward the cave they defended. They ran past the adjacent cave just as it burst into flames, the stored ordnance hit by enemy fire. Ammunition bounced off the walls and into the corridor, ignited by the explosion.

"Our orders are to seal our entrance," Inoue said as they entered their cave. "We will keep open only the entrances on the north and east sides that are more difficult for the enemy bombs to reach."

They held fast for nearly a week. Whether the enemy had run out of napalm or believed they were dead was unclear, but at last, the bombing stopped. By then, only a few hundred soldiers remained of the original nine thousand Japanese forces.

By daybreak, it was apparent the massive enemy army was preparing to assault the Japanese fortress.

Colonel Nakamura, the highest-ranking surviving officer, assembled his remaining soldiers. "Tonight, we will leave." He paced across the room and back. A dirty and bloodied bandage covered a deep wound on his face. "Our mission now will be to hide in the mountains, in the valleys, in the forest, and kill enemy troops as they pass by. We may die in the end, but we will die with honor."

In a small corner of the cavern, Inoue gave his orders. Their backs laden with all the supplies and munitions they could carry, his men formed up at the northern entrance. Inoue stepped outside the cave, scanning the darkness for enemy movement. The air was still heavy with smoke and the stench of death. He turned, beckoned to his troops.

The night sky erupted in bright light—a white phosphorus grenade exploded feet in front of him. The impact knocked Inoue to the ground, his body on fire. He vaguely remembered being pulled across the rocky ground, hands covering his body with mud to stop the burning.

"Rikugun-Chūi." The man speaking used Ikeda's proper title. Was he Japanese? Was this some kind of enemy trick? "I am Lieutenant Sasaki of the American Army," the man said. "You are in an American field hospital."

"And you are a traitor." Inoue's throat was raw, his voice raspy. "Let me die with honor."

"You may get your wish. You are badly burned. We amputated your legs. There was nothing left of them."

Inoue pretended he hadn't heard the lieutenant. He was grateful his bandaged face would not reveal his shock.

"My eyes won't open," he said.

"Your facial burns were severe, especially your eyes. They must stay bandaged until you heal more."

A voice spoke in English.

Sasaki answered then spoke to Inoue. "Captain Morris has some questions for you."

"Captain Morris can go to hell. I will speak to no one."

"As you wish."

Inoue listened as Sasaki translated Inoue's response to the captain. He felt more contempt than ever for the Americans. What kind of weak officers were they? If Inoue were questioning the enemy, there would be violence, whatever sort of torture it took to get the soldier to speak. But each time someone approached—each time Lieutenant Sasaki translated their questions—Inoue refused to speak, and the officer left without so much as an angry reproach. Inoue shook his head. These Americans were not worthy to polish his shoes.

He lay rigid in his bed until he was sure both men were gone then tentatively examined his body. He felt the catheter inserted in his left arm, gently touched the thin tubing that probably attached to a bottle of intravenous fluid. It intrigued him he was not restrained.

Not that I'm going anywhere, he mused.

Moving his hand down his side, he felt more bandages, smaller cuts, and bruises. Slowly, slowly, he slid his hand below his waist and to his legs. When he reached his knees, there was nothing.

This couldn't be right. He could sense them—he could almost *move* them. He reached lower and felt only air. Despair flooded his thoughts.

He was no good to anyone now. Not his men, nor his father, nor even his mother.

Hara-kiri, he thought. Suicide. It was the only option left. He would have to wait, at least until he could see, and then figure out how. *Perhaps I will be fortunate and die from my wounds.*

In the darkness behind his bandages, Inoue strained for details of his new surroundings. The room stank of blood, urine, feces, vomit, and disinfectant that would never dissipate the foul odors. He thought, perhaps, he even smelled the sour stench of fear. Uniforms swished as their wearers moved between the cots, instruments clanked. A soldier moaned. Another wept. Rain thundered against the canvas roof, and Inoue prepared his plan.

Slowly, his cuts and bruises healed. The blisters on his lips disappeared. Every day, the doctors removed another dressing. The last were the ones that covered his eyes. He cursed the kami for not allowing him to die.

They uncovered his eyes gradually so as not to overtax them. They burned from the bright light of day when the last layer came off. It took hours before they stopped tearing and he could focus.

"We'll send you to rehab soon," Lieutenant Sasaki told him. "Probably to a detention center in the United States."

That will never happen.

Alone again, he surveyed the cavernous room. All around him were cots. Most held men with injuries, some severe, others less so. There were both American and Japanese soldiers, many attached to intravenous lines, some attached to handcuffs.

A table sat by each cot. Some contained medicine vials, bandages, scissors, and other equipment. His was empty. He scanned the room for guards but saw only doctors and nurses. Good. They wouldn't be armed. It would be easier to implement his plan. He visually checked each bedside table in the room until he found what he would need.

Inoue waited until late at night. Only a handful of nurses remained to monitor the most critical patients. Little by little, he maneuvered his body to the side of the cot. He twisted his torso until what remained of his legs hung over the edge. Lifting his body with his arms, he slid over the side. The pain was excruciating as what remained of his legs touched the floor, but he stayed silent.

He dropped to his belly and pulled himself under the cot next to him and under the one next to that, until he reached his destination.

A glance around the room told him no one had noticed.

Slowly, he turned his body to a sitting position. He reached up to the table beside him, felt around until he found what he needed, and pulled it down.

Grasping the scissors in his fist, Inoue shouted, "Banzai!" and plunged them into his heart.

CHAPTER 38

SANTA INEZ—JUNE 1945

Not much remained of the adobe structure. Three battered walls stood. The other had crumbled. The remains of the straw-thatched roof hung precariously overhead. The enemy had spared no building in the barrio. The entire village stank of death: the putrescence of decaying flesh, the combined stench of feces, mothballs, rotten eggs, and a foul, garlicky odor, all the result of various chemicals escaping the decomposing bodies. It was a smell that had become all too familiar to Leo and his squad.

They called it a "mop-up" mission. A civilian might envision a crew equipped with mops and pails, shovels to move the rubble, brooms to sweep up dust. There were no mops. No brooms. Their tools were the same ones they always carried: grenades, rifles, bayonets. They were there to clean up the aftermath of Japanese destruction.

One never knew where the enemy might hide or what had been booby-trapped. Although the silence was deafening, it was still a combat zone.

Most of the Japanese were scattered now, on their own and desperate for food. Captured prisoners reported that morale was low among what remained of the Japanese Army. They took no aggressive action against the Allies. In fact, they did their best to avoid confrontation. Their major concern now was survival, and they spent their sapping energy on foraging raids against the outlying barrios, eliminating as many natives as possible.

The Japanese were brutal in their quest. They burned villages, raped and killed the women, executed the men, tossed small children into the air and impaled them on their bayonets. Bodies lay strewn in the streets, amidst the rubble, in burned-out buildings.

After the cave incident, Leo thought he'd never see anything worse. What he saw now was nothing less than wholesale slaughter.

The natives had done nothing to invite disaster. Their country was under siege by two foreign armies, and the locals were merely in the way. How many Filipinos had been killed by the Allies' stray bullets and misdirected bombs? Where was the morality in any of this?

It all made Leo feel dirty somehow. He hadn't been responsible for the killing this time. But that he was any part of the deaths of innocents was becoming more and more intolerable.

Searching through the rubble for survivors, Private Richards struggled to remain calm. After weeks of combat, everyone's nerves were on edge. He couldn't get the annoying ringing out of his ears, and his eyes ached, his vision slightly blurred. His whole body felt deadened, floating as if he were a wandering spirit in search of his soul. He'd lost all track of time, moved in a slow-motion world. Nothing felt real.

Leo watched Richards carefully as the squad approached a demolished home, worried Richards might panic again.

Moving ahead of the squad, Richards was the first to see the two bodies in the stone rubble. A woman, positioned on her side, clutched a young child. Both had been bayoneted and shot. Fallen straw partly covered their bodies. Bloated from the heat, flies clustered in the surrounding air.

Richards's eyes went wide, and his body visibly trembled.

"Holy shit." Dooley stood beside Richards and muttered something unintelligible in his ear.

Richards's face went white. His eyes lost focus, and when he blinked to clear them, he was standing over his mother's body, bent and broken in the South Dakota road.

"Ma!" Richards started toward the bodies.

"That's not your mother," Leo said, grabbing at Richards's arm.

Richards pulled away from Leo's grasp, ran to the two bodies, and dropped to his knees.

"Richards, get back," Leo shouted. He took a step toward Richards, reaching for him.

Richards twisted toward Leo, using his rifle to deflect Leo's arm.

"You stay away from my mother," he growled and pointed the rifle at Leo. His jaw clenched with determination, his eyes wide, darting from one person to another.

Leo stepped back, holding his hands at shoulder height, palms out. "Get the men out of here," he said to Dooley. "Take cover." As the rest of the squad scrambled toward a burned-out truck that lay on its side across the street, Leo tried again. "Cal." He kept his voice low and calm. "You need to step back until we clear the area. There could be booby traps."

Richards didn't answer. He'd lowered his rifle and turned back to the bodies.

Leo cautiously backed toward the truck. "Cal, you need to listen to me. That's not your mother."

Richards gently touched the woman's face, stroked her hair, felt her chest as if she might be still breathing. "Ma." He lowered his head and started weeping. "Ma, I'm sorry." He tenderly lifted the body into his arms.

"Richards, d—"

Leo ducked behind the truck just in time. Dust flew, chunks of concrete and metal scattered as a hidden grenade exploded.

When the smoke cleared, Richards lay a few yards away, his body riddled with shrapnel. His neck was bent at an awkward angle, broken by the impact of the explosion. His face and chest had taken most of the flying metal from the exploding grenade.

Leo raced toward Richards, kneeling by the ravaged body. He knew it was pointless to check for a pulse, but he did it anyway. Leo felt numb, unable to feel grief or anger or guilt or whatever he ought to be feeling. He knew the reality would hit soon enough, but for now, he felt nothing.

He stayed with Richards's body until the medical transport arrived. Why hadn't he sent him home sooner? How could he have let Richards talk him into letting him stay? *Didn't I learn anything from Furness?*

Leo thought of Dooley, whispering in Richards's ear, and the more he considered it, the angrier he became. He caught up with Dooley, who had already started back to the command post.

"What the heck did you say to Richards that got him so riled up?" Leo demanded.

Dooley shrugged. "It was no big deal. I just said to watch out for grenades."

"Why'd you have to whisper it?"

Another shrug. "Dunno. Didn't want to embarrass him, I guess."

"I'm not letting this go, Sergeant Nelson." Leo glared at him, but Dooley turned as if he hadn't heard him and walked away.

A wave of exhaustion swept over Leo as Richards' body was loaded into the back of the transport. Who was he kidding? It wasn't Dooley's fault.

It's nobody's fault but my own.

He'd felt guilty for not doing more to help his buddy when Furness died, but this...this was all his fault. He knew how unstable Richards was, knew about the visions and the nightmares that plagued him. He'd ignored his instincts—and why? Because he didn't want to send home the man who was like a little brother to him? He'd wanted to keep Richards, plain and simple. He'd kept him here out of selfishness, and it had gotten Richards killed. He should have gotten Richards away from that body somehow, should have tried harder. But no, he'd only thought of his own safety. What the hell kind of leader was he?

As the truck disappeared in a cloud of dust, Leo shook himself from the trance that had overtaken him. He looked back toward the ruined home. The explosion, the image of Richard's broken body replayed in his mind like a dispassionate newsreel.

The only thing he felt was a desperate need for sleep, but when the chance finally came, his mind was uneasy, cluttered with indistinct images, with a terror he couldn't see but most definitely felt. He couldn't see Richards's face—only knew that it was Richards who lay in pieces in front of him.

The next morning, Leo remembered the dream, but the reality was slowly fading along with the numbness that had overtaken his body. It was as if the entire scene had happened in slow motion and yet so fast that he had no time to react. Did it really happen?

Of course, it did.

Richards was gone.

But the memory was slipping away fast, and Leo wasn't ready to lose it—not yet.

Susannah Willey

枝広げ
追手惑わす
マンゴの木

Eda hiroge
Oite madowasu
Mango no ki

The great mango tree
Hides me from my searching foes
Under wide branches.

CHAPTER 39

SOMEWHERE IN THE SIERRA MADRES— JUNE 1945

Tadashi's bayonet scraped against the remaining nub of his pencil. It was so worn, so small that he could barely grasp it. Soon he would have to rely on a blackened stick to write with. The pages of his diary were damp and crinkled, soiled with bits of dirt and mold. His words were faded, but he knew them all by heart.

He was the platoon commander now, although the "platoon" numbered less than a squad. Most of the rest were dead, a few captured, one or two last seen fleeing into the jungle.

Tadashi was unsure of the lieutenant's fate, but his last vision of Inoue was burned in his mind: The enemy attack. A desperate attempt to escape. The explosion of napalm. Inoue in flames.

"Kill me." It had been more of a plea than an order. Bits of Inoue's singed uniform clung to his body. Blackened blisters covered his face and torso, and the smell of burnt flesh was overwhelming. But the worst of the damage was to Inoue's legs, dotted with gaping holes where the phosphorus had burned through his uniform and melted his skin down to bone. He lifted his blistered hand and grabbed Tadashi's wrist. "Please. Kill me."

Tadashi had hesitated. As much as he hated the lieutenant, could he bring himself to kill him? He would likely die whether or not Tadashi helped him, but Tadashi could not bear to see this once powerful soldier lie helplessly on the ground. He reached for his bayonet and raised it over the lieutenant, only then seeing the bits of oily burnt flesh on his wrist where Inoue had grabbed him.

You can do this. You must help Lieutenant Inoue to die with honor.

The ground shook as a mortar exploded nearby. Mud and debris flew in the air. Too close.

"Take cover!" Tadashi motioned to his men to take refuge between two rock formations. He looked back to where Inoue lay, splattered with mud.

I haven't forgotten, Rikugun-Chūi. I won't let the enemy take you.

It was an hour before the enemy withdrew. Another before the smoke cleared and the napalm burned itself out.

Tadashi gathered what was left of the platoon and motioned to Corporal Fujita. "You are in temporary command. Take these men to safety. I will be right behind you."

He hurried to where he had left Lieutenant Inoue. He was likely dead already. If not, Tadashi would finish the task. Would there be something left to return to his family as a memento? Something that wasn't burned away or blackened by fire?

Rocks and mud were the only thing that remained where Inoue had lain. Had the bombing destroyed his body? Tadashi turned in a circle, searching for clues, and found nothing. By the time Tadashi rejoined Fujita and the rest, they'd found refuge under an enormous mango tree. Two more soldiers had gone missing along the way. Tadashi and four others were all that remained.

Tadashi sat under the mango tree, reliving the images of Inoue's charred body. The lieutenant's plea for death echoed in Tadashi's mind. The images competed with visions of the hayrick, where he'd watched the Americans brutally murder a wounded soldier. All he could think about was revenge.

The thought startled him. When had he descended to such a mindset? He'd seen the humanity in Americans at Cabanatuan, realized they were no less human than him. But now he'd witnessed their depravity. He clenched and unclenched his fists. The more the vivid scenes looped in his mind, the angrier he became. He would no longer dismiss these vicious acts; he would avenge them.

He studied the branches above him. The vast mango tree provided the perfect opportunity. Sixty feet tall and fifty feet wide, its thick, ground-hugging branches gave them a place to hide. The broad leaves kept them dry from the unrelenting rain, and it offered sustenance, its branches covered with dangling mangoes. The top branches would provide a wide viewpoint for enemy reconnaissance teams as they traveled the nearby trail.

Tadashi nodded. Yes, it was the perfect setting for his plan. The only thing that could make it sweeter was if his rifle could fire napalm instead of simple bullets.

Tadashi divided his four men into teams: Kaito and Private Ikeda, and Fujita and Private Yamada. Together they would become sugekihei, sharpshooters and experts at killing the enemy.

The persistent rain delayed his plan. No enemy soldiers passed. In the meantime, he kept his men busy with target practice, being careful not to waste too much of their valuable supply of ammunition. At last, the rain eased. Tadashi looked at the clearing skies and smiled: His revenge would start today.

High in the mango tree, Tadashi and his men settled in the crooks of the sturdiest branches. Private Ikeda, now the youngest in Tadashi's platoon, was the lookout. Small and wiry, he easily scrambled to the top and claimed a spot on the highest branch.

Ikeda was a year older than Kimura. Still just a kid and eager to please, he reminded Tadashi of Kaito at that age—his devil-may-care outlook, his innocent grin. He had the characteristic Japanese kurokami, the jet-black hair common to East Asian natives. But his eyes were lighter than most, a hazel-brown-green that was not unusual in his native Kyushu. They gave him a mischievous look when he smiled.

Ikeda scaled the slenderer branches and settled into a tiny nook. The boy took out his binoculars and scanned for enemy movement. With his rifle slung across one shoulder, his pack balanced on his back, he looked as comfortable as an eagle chick perched on a rocky crag.

"Can you imagine what Sachiko would say if she saw me up in a mango tree?" Tadashi laughed softly, adjusting the rifle that lay on his lap.

"You might wish you didn't have to climb down and find out." Kaito grinned from his branch a few feet away. "I would not want to anger her."

"Nor would I," Tadashi said. "But right now, it would be worth the scolding just to hear her voice."

Leaves shivered as Ikeda banged on the branch above. Four knocks—that meant an enemy sighting. The men came to attention and peered at the boy, who pointed to the west, then held up three fingers on his right hand and motioned twice with a fisted left hand. *Three hundred meters away.* Ikeda stared at the distance once more and signaled with five fingers—the number of soldiers who approached.

Tadashi made eye contact with each of his men, holding up his fingers to assign a target. He had the sharpest aim and would take the first soldier then be ready in case anyone else missed their man. He watched as the recon squad came closer, waited until they were well within range, and fired.

Four shots rang out immediately after Tadashi's. All five enemy soldiers fell. Tadashi's men stayed in position, ready to fire if more soldiers should appear. At last, Ikeda signaled—three knocks—all clear.

"Corporal Fujita," Tadashi said when they assembled under the tree. "you and Private Yamada retrieve the bodies. Corporal Shimizu, you and Private Ikeda build a fire."

As Yamada dragged the last of the bodies to the hideout, Fujita angrily scuffed the dirt to remove as much evidence as possible. *Abukara gives me the dirty work to do,* he mused, glaring at his blood-stained boots, *while his buddy Shimizu keeps his hands clean.* That wouldn't happen if he was in charge.

At the mango tree, Fujita directed the men as they stripped the bodies: one pile for uniforms, another for boots, a third for packs. Kaito collected firearms and ammunition. They would bury both for later use. Insignia and identification tags were removed. Anything Tadashi and his men couldn't use would burn with the bodies.

When they finished, Tadashi ordered his men to take off their tattered clothing. It would make excellent kindling for the fire. He distributed the enemy uniforms, with no identifying insignia. They looked no different from their own. Each man received a pair of boots. No one seemed to care if they fit poorly.

Each man lit a match and touched them to the discarded clothing. The burning fabric ignited the small twigs and branches. Once the flames took over, they dragged the bodies to the pit and tossed them on the fire.

Tadashi noticed Fujita surreptitiously pull something from his pocket. It was a name tag, scavenged from one of the bodies.

"That belongs on the fire," Tadashi said. "We will keep no evidence that American soldiers have been here."

Corporal Fujita glared at Tadashi, emptied his pocket, and threw the tags into the flames.

Smoke stung Tadashi's eyes as the fire consumed the enemy. The crackle of roasting fat, the odor of charred flesh, filled his nostrils. Sharp hunger pangs pierced his belly, evoking an even sharper image of the burnt human remains at the supply road bridge.

"I would give these new boots for one bite of meat." Corporal Fujita stuck out the American boots on his feet, licked his lips, and stared into the fire. Yamada glanced at Fujita and discreetly nodded.

"Not another word." Tadashi glared at Fujita. "There will be no talk of eating human flesh." Tadashi's cheeks flushed as he recalled his first reaction to burning flesh, and he looked away.

One at a time, the men returned to the tree and assumed their watch position. Tadashi stood by the fire a while longer and considered their actions.

Overall, the mission was a success. Five enemy soldiers were dead. Tadashi's men had clothing, footwear that wasn't cracked and leaky for the first time in months, extra weapons and ammunition. He had killed an enemy soldier, watched him die. Of course, it wasn't the first enemy to die at his hands, but this was the first time he'd actually *seen* the man he'd killed. A small pang poked his stomach. Perhaps he should feel remorse, but he felt nothing.

He glanced up at the tree toward where Fujita sat. He worried about the corporal's increasing hostility, worried about his influence on Private Yamada. With only five of them left, Tadashi couldn't afford dissension. He frowned, wondering if Lieutenant Inoue was still alive. He shook his head. Impossible. If they had captured him, he would have found a way to commit hara-kiri. If he hadn't been captured, he would have surely died from his wounds. He never thought he'd miss Inoue, but right now he wished the lieutenant was here to witness this minor victory.

On his perch in the mango tree, Fujita fumed. *Who is this country bumpkin who thinks he can boss me around? Why did Lieutenant Inoue make him a sergeant instead of me? I am smarter. I have more combat experience. I was meant to be the leader.*

For now, there wasn't much he could do, but he would keep his eyes open and wait. Eventually, he would take his rightful place. In the meantime, he patted the pocket he hadn't emptied and the American pistol hidden inside.

CHAPTER 40

NEAR ANTIPOLO, LUZON—JUNE 1945

Outside Captain Mickelson's tent, Dooley prepared for his role. He set his face with the proper amount of concern mixed with nervousness. This would be his most important scene, and he couldn't fuck it up. He lightly knocked on the tent pole to announce his presence.

"Come." The captain's voice was stern and commanding.

Dooley approached Mickelson's desk and stood at attention.

"What is it, Sergeant Nelson?" Mickelson didn't bother to look up from the report Leo had written providing details of Richards' death.

"Well... sir." Dooley fidgeted with his cap. He wanted the captain to think he was hesitant to rat on his squad leader. "There's something I think you need to know about Private Richards's death."

"You need to bring that to Lieutenant Ryan," Mickelson said.

"I did, sir," Dooley held his body rigid, focused his eyes on the wall behind the captain. "All due respect, sir, I don't think Lieutenant Ryan is taking the problem seriously enough."

"Ryan and Baldwin have already filed their reports." Mickelson gestured impatiently toward the folder in front of him. "What do you think I need to know that isn't in here?"

"Well, sir, Private Richards was having mental problems."

"This war has been tough on everybody. What was so different about Private Richards?"

"May I speak freely, sir?" Dooley asked.

"Go ahead, Sergeant."

"The thing is, Private Richards was a lot worse off than Sergeant Baldwin wanted to admit. Richards went a little crazy every time he saw a dead body, like he went off in a fog for a while." Dooley frowned and briefly pursed his lips before he continued. "He shoulda gone home a long time ago. But Sarge let him stay, and it got Richards killed."

Mickelson folded his hands on the desk, leaning forward. "What's your point, soldier?"

"Well..." Dooley took his eyes off of the captain, staring into the distance as if in thought. He looked at Mickelson, a mask of concern on his face. He lowered his voice to a whisper. "Sir, I have to wonder if Sergeant Baldwin is fit to be a squad leader. Seems to me he's putting his men in danger unnecessarily. I mean, that grenade coulda killed us all, not just Private Richards."

"Nobody ever said combat isn't dangerous."

"No, sir, they haven't." Dooley paused as if he didn't really want to say what he was about to say. He carefully worded his tale. "But this ain't the first time Baldwin's been involved with a suicide. One of his guys back at Fort Riley killed himself. Baldwin knew he was struggling and didn't tell nobody."

"And you want me to relieve Sergeant Baldwin of his command, right?" Mickelson raised an eyebrow, crossed his arms, and leaned closer to Dooley. "Look, Sergeant Nelson, I know all about the animosity between you and Sergeant Baldwin. Are you sure that has nothing to do with your 'concern'?"

Dooley cleared his throat and held his hands up in defense. "All's I'm sayin' is I think it ought to be looked into, sir."

"You'll need to file a formal complaint, Sergeant. Then I'll take it under consideration." Mickelson returned his attention to his work. "You're dismissed, soldier."

Dooley saluted, made a sharp about face, and left Mickelson's tent. *My finest performance.* He'd make the formal complaint today, get that knucklehead Webster to add his two cents.

Dooley smiled as he entered his tent. Leo was already torn up by Richards's death; an inquiry would destroy him. The rank of staff sergeant and the job of squad leader would be Dooley's.

"Sarge." Webster was out of breath as he burst into the tent. "You talk to the captain?"

"Is a Jap mortar fodder?" Dooley smirked and stood straighter, his chest puffed out like a triumphant rooster. "You're lookin' at your new squad leader."

Webster's jaw dropped. "Already?"

"Nah, it ain't quite that easy." Dooley shook his head. "But I got him wondering." He smirked. "All's I gotta do now is put it in writing. You're gonna back me up, right?"

"Course I will." Webster shook his head, scuffed the toe of his boot against the floor. "It's too bad. I mean, the Sarge is a nice guy and all. But you were right all along. He's got no business callin' the shots. He just ain't got the chops to be a leader."

"Yeah. Too bad." *Too bad everyone ain't a dumb shit like you.* It'd take some work, but he'd get the rest of them in line soon enough. Hell, look at the bunch: a Wop, a Polack, an Injun, even a goddamned Nip. They got too soft with Baldwin in charge, but he'd have them whipped into shape in no time.

"You suppose I could get a promotion too?" Webster looked at Dooley, his eyes bright. "I mean, you might need an assistant or something, right?"

"Sure, why not?" Dooley smiled and clapped Webster's shoulder. Who knew what else he could get Webster to do for him? "C'mon. We got a complaint to write."

In Mickelson's tent, Ryan frowned as the captain relayed Dooley's concerns.

"Sergeant Baldwin informed me of the issue the first time it happened," Ryan said impatiently. "He was keeping an eye on Richards and noted it in his report."

Mickelson stared at Leo's report. He'd read through it several times; the incident in Santa Inez seemed straightforward enough. Too many soldiers suffered from battle fatigue. In fact, it surprised Mickelson that more men didn't have mental breakdowns. They withstood daily bombing, constant gunfire, a lack of sleep. They watched as their buddies died, the man beside them suddenly dropping from a bullet or a grenade, body parts flying and scattered across the battlefield. It was a wonder anyone survived it.

"At ease, Lieutenant." Mickelson closed the folder and motioned for Ryan to sit.

"Sir," Ryan said, "I don't trust Sergeant Nelson as far as I can throw him." Ryan had thought the problem was resolved. He'd seen no need to bring Private Richards's issues to the captain and was annoyed that Dooley had gone over his head.

Mickelson took a moment to reflect on what he'd read as he finished the coffee that was already stone cold. Finally, he sat back, lit a cigarette, and offered one to Lieutenant Ryan.

"What's your take on Sergeant Baldwin?" he said as Ryan lit his cigarette.

Ryan inhaled and set his cigarette in the ashtray in front of him. "I've never known him to be anything but a highly responsible and capable leader. He knew Private Richards's struggles were ongoing, encouraged him to talk to Father Sabbatino, and kept a close eye on him. He could have recommended the private for a medical discharge. But Richards was adamant that he could control his reactions, and Baldwin wanted to give him every chance he could to prove himself."

Mickelson thought for a moment. "It has to be looked into," he said, tapping Dooley's complaint. "You know it'll get around anyway, and we can't let the men think we're pushing something under the carpet."

"Agreed, sir," Ryan said.

"But for now, let's not advertise it." Mickelson scribbled a few sentences on the paper in front of him. "I want you to stick with Sergeant Baldwin, watch how he interacts with his men, especially under stress or combat situations. Let's give it a couple of weeks. Then report back to me, and we'll go from there."

"Yes, sir." Ryan saluted and left the captain's tent. He'd keep an eye on Dooley too, although he was sure Dooley would be on his best behavior as long as Ryan or Leo were around.

Leo stood in front of Ryan's desk and handed him the daily patrol report from his squad. Ryan had carefully monitored Leo's interactions with his squad for over two weeks now. He'd seen nothing to make him think the sergeant was not doing his job effectively. Sergeant Nelson, on the other hand, was clearly up to something. Every time Ryan was around the squad, it seemed Dooley was lurking—behind a tree, just inside a tent—and "just happened" to nonchalantly appear. He'd noticed Private Webster sneaking around too. Leo hadn't mentioned it, but Ryan couldn't believe he didn't see it.

Ryan scanned the report.

"You doing okay?" he asked, keeping his eyes on the paper.

"You mean, am I getting over what happened to Richards?" Leo was getting tired of people asking. Of course, he wasn't okay, but he wasn't going to broadcast that. "I guess so." He shrugged. "Trying to convince myself I did right by the boy."

"There isn't one of us who doesn't worry about our men," Ryan said. "It's part of being a leader."

Leo looked off into the distance and chewed on his lip. "Do you think I did the right thing?"

Ryan kept his eyes on the report for a moment then folded his hands on his desk and looked at Leo. "You made what you thought was the right decision. The best thing you can do is learn from it so it doesn't happen again."

Leo nodded. He shifted his feet nervously and wished Ryan would change the subject.

Ryan returned his attention to the report. "Looks good," he said, setting the papers to the side. He lit a cigarette and leaned back, motioned for Leo to take a seat. Ryan tried to sound casual. "How are things with Dooley?"

"What do you mean?" Leo asked. It was another subject he was getting tired of.

"Just wondering how he's doing with the other men. Seems as if they're all getting along okay."

"He and Webster are pretty tight. Both being southern boys, they have a lot in common, I guess." He shrugged. "It's like they're planning something, but I can't figure out what."

Ryan took a deep drag on his cigarette, exhaling the smoke through his nose, and picked up another report. "If I were you, I'd keep an eye on the two of them."

Leo stepped out of Ryan's tent, squinting in the bright sunshine. He headed for his tent, going over their conversation as he walked across the small compound. It seemed like Ryan was trying to warn him. Did he know something about Dooley and Webster he wasn't telling?

He looked at his watch. He was on recon again tonight and had just enough time to catch a quick nap before they had to move out. Leo stretched out on his cot, but every time he closed his eyes, he felt certain someone was watching.

敵の血を
流し生き延び
でも涙

Teki no chi o
Nagashi ikinobi
Demo namida

My enemy slain,
I shall survive for today
Why, then, do I weep?

CHAPTER 41

JUNE 1945

Tadashi straddled the broad branch on the mango tree, his rifle slung over his shoulder. For the first time in months, he wore a uniform that wasn't torn and grimy, although it hung on his gaunt frame like a gunny sack.

The last of the mangoes were overripe and on the ground, the flesh soft and inedible. However, both the leaves and the rain were still plentiful, and they subsisted on mango tea and grubs. What once had been unimaginable had become routine. Tadashi shrugged. His body was so shrunken a cup of tea and a handful of grubs was plenty to fill it.

What was more important was that he was exacting his revenge on the enemy. There might be only a patrol or two every week, but he estimated they'd killed over twenty Americans so far.

The revenge had felt sweet until the last kill. As the bodies burned, Tadashi's spirit had fallen, and a sense of hopelessness had overtaken him.

He adjusted his position to get a better look down the trail. His eyes fixed on the blackened spot where the ashes still smoldered. What had happened to his sense of morality, his belief in the righteousness of their cause? Had any of this killing eased the pain of seeing Japanese soldiers mutilated by the enemy? Had it exorcised the image of Lieutenant Inoue's burned and battered body?

He didn't like the man he'd become, the cold and ruthless killer who was no better than the enemy he sought revenge against. He thought of home, of his sweet Sachiko and dear Ichiro. He would be shamed if they knew what he'd done.

The sun set, the western horizon ablaze in deep reds and violets. The light slowly faded. The men shimmied down the tree and prepared for tea and sleep.

"I have something to show you," Kaito whispered, swallowing the last of his tea.

Tadashi followed him to a pile of brush big enough to shield them from the other soldiers. Kaito crouched, shifted a large rock, extracted two large hip flasks, and handed one to Tadashi.

"Where did you get this, Kai-chan?" Tadashi felt the weight of the flask. "It must be almost full."

Kaito smiled. "I found it on the last batch of enemy soldiers we ambushed." He opened his flask, took a deep drink, and wiped his mouth. He tipped his flask toward the one Tadashi held. "Try it."

Tadashi opened his flask, peered inside, sniffed the contents. He hesitated; he rarely drank alcohol. What did it matter? He'd already done so many things he would never have believed. He took a small sip then a larger one and wondered how much he would have to consume to forget his misery.

But the more Tadashi drank, the more miserable he felt. Tears fell from his eyes as he tried to recall the Tadashi who was gentle, who cared about all living things. In this land torn by war, virtually nothing remained: trees, animals, humans—all destroyed. Even the earth was scarred and broken. And he had willingly become a part of the destruction.

"What troubles you, Nii-chan?" Kaito was as gaunt and grimy as Tadashi, but to Tadashi, he would always be the chubby-cheeked boy he'd first befriended. Only the hardened look in Kaito's eyes said otherwise.

He still worries over his big brother. Only Kaito knew everything Tadashi had gone through. Only Kaito had been with him since the beginning.

Tadashi checked to see if Fujita or Yamada were nearby. He dropped his voice to a whisper. "This war has cost too much destruction. It's not just the dead. We are still alive, yet I feel dead." He looked at Kaito. "Don't you feel it too?"

Kaito hesitated, gazed toward the sky. "Sometimes I do. Of course, we must defend our country, but I wish I could go home to my old life." He took another long drink. "I know it's impossible."

They sat silently against the rocks, drowning their despair. Tadashi stared into the distance, his eyes filling with tears.

"Why did Lieutenant Inoue ever promote me?" his voice quivered. "I have lost nearly all of my men. Now it seems Fujita and Yamada are against me. Perhaps they should be—I am an unworthy leader." He emptied his flask and hurled it into the brush. "My wife and son will hate me for what I have done." His shoulders shook as he struggled to continue. "Kai-chan, I will lose the only two things that matter to me."

Kaito moved closer to Tadashi. "Sachiko loves you, Nii-chan. That will never change. She knows we do what we must. We're fighting for our empire. It is a worthy cause."

"Is it?" Tadashi wiped his face and stared into the distance. "Perhaps now I understand why the great samurai took their lives. For honor, yes, but also perhaps in despair." He stiffened and wiped his eyes. "Forgive me, Kai-chan. I'm exhausted. I can barely sleep. Dead men and burning bodies haunt my dreams."

CHAPTER 42

U.S. ARMY BATTALION HEADQUARTERS, ANTIPOLO, LUZON—JUNE 1945

Lieutenant Colonel Harrington scanned the troop reports. Five recon squads—twenty-five men—had gone missing. And it had been going on for weeks?

"What the hell," Harrington growled at the lieutenant who had delivered the report. "Why am I just now hearing this?"

The lieutenant nervously shuffled his feet. "It just got lost in the chaos, sir. Anyone who might have noticed their absence just assumed the squads were on a longer mission. No one thought much about it until we realized how many men were gone."

"Tilson," Harrington shouted impatiently to his aide in the adjacent room. "How soon can we get a recon plane?"

Corporal Tilson appeared in the office doorway and saluted. "Usually takes about twenty-four hours, sir. Shall I order one?"

"Do that. I want pictures of the eastern trail all the way to Infanta. And send out a memo that there are to be no more recon squads to the east until we figure out where the hell they're disappearing to."

"Yes, sir." Corporal Tilson saluted and left the room.

Harrington scrutinized the map behind him. Since the napalm attack at Bigti, the enemy had all but vanished. Reports were that most were in small, disorganized groups, uncontrolled and wandering. Could there be a larger, more organized group they didn't know about?

Two days later, he held the photographs from the plane's reconnaissance mission. He read the intelligence report that accompanied them. There had been no sign of American troops there, no sign of prisoners. The only suspicious thing they'd seen was a large, charred circle near a massive mango tree. The pilot was certain he'd seen movement in the tree. Was it wildlife? Could it be enemy snipers? The photos revealed nothing conclusive.

"There has to be something going on there." Harrington spoke to his intel officers. "Even if it has nothing to do with our missing squads, I'll bet my shirt there are Japs nearby."

"What do you want to do about it, Lieutenant Colonel?" one of the intel officers asked.

All eyes were on Harrington.

"It's not safe to send more men out there," he said. "But if there are Japs in that tree, I want them flushed out. If we destroy the tree, they'll have nowhere to hide."

Harrington's second-in-command raised an eyebrow. "How? A bomber run?"

Harrington nodded.

"What if we destroy the tree and nobody's there? We'll look like paranoid idiots."

"What if there is and we do nothing?" Harrington retorted. "All we have to lose is a mango tree. For that, I'll risk looking like an idiot." He leaned away from his desk and shouted to the outer office. "Tilson, get General McKinnon on the horn."

CHAPTER 43

JUNE 1945

Tadashi glared at the enemy plane as it buzzed overhead and disappeared to the east. A reconnaissance plane—had they been found out? He'd ordered his men out of the tree, ordered silence and absolutely no movement. Had they abandoned their branches in time to avoid the camera?

Perhaps he worried too much. The plane hadn't circled as it would have if they were suspicious. Twenty minutes later, he sent Ikeda up the tree. When he signaled the all-clear, Tadashi released his men. Everyone jumped and cheered.

"We have fooled the enemy," Ikeda shouted.

Tadashi shook his head. "Don't be so sure, Private. The Americans are not the fools you think they are."

There had been no enemy recon squads for at least a week. It seemed certain the Americans were on to them.

"Kuso," Tadashi swore under his breath.

But it also relieved him—he'd had enough of killing. This way, he could suspend their operation and still keep his honor.

He called his men together. "If they have discovered us, we must abandon our tree." The men groaned. Tadashi scowled. "We have gained our revenge. Twenty-five enemies are dead thanks to us. That is enough. We will watch and wait. In the meantime, we will plan our escape. If there is no enemy response in seventy-two hours, I will reconsider."

The next day, they returned to their high branches. No enemy appeared either by land or air. On the third day, Tadashi considered his plans. He wanted to be done with the killing, and it appeared the Americans had abandoned this route. But the tree gave perfect shelter—could they still use it as a base?

A distant droning sound caught his attention. Was that a plane?

"What do you see, Private?" he called to Ikeda.

"A plane." Ikeda shouted from his perch. "But too far away to tell who it belongs to."

The men sat stiffly, their ears focused on the approaching aircraft.

"Reconnaissance again?" Tadashi asked Ikeda.

"Not reconnaissance," the private answered.

For a moment, there was silence as Ikeda waited for the plane to get close enough to identify. At last, he spoke.

"American," he said. "Bomber."

The branches shook as Tadashi's soldiers hustled to get to the ground.

Tadashi held up his hand. "Go cautiously. The plane may not be for us, but if we make too much movement, it will attack anyway."

One at a time, the men moved down the tree. Kaito went first to organize them once they were on the ground. Ikeda was last except for Tadashi.

"It's definitely coming toward us," Kaito reported when Tadashi jumped from the lowest branch. The men wore their packs, ready to leave.

"Everyone to the shelter," Tadashi ordered. "On your bellies." He was grateful he'd thought to dig a hiding place.

One at a time, the men crawled through the small opening to the shallow bunker a few yards away. When everyone was safely inside, Kaito covered the small opening with brush. The five soldiers sat shoulder to shoulder and covered their heads with their hands.

The ground shook as the first bomb exploded. There were loud *thunks* as something large hit the ground—large branches? Unexploded bombs? Tadashi's heart pounded as he realized their shelter could be closed off by falling debris. The few inches of soil above their heads wouldn't withstand a direct hit. And if the entire tree fell in their direction, it would likely crush them.

A second bomb exploded, and a third. How many bombs were they going to use? The tree must have been destroyed by now. Flames roared from beyond the bunker, and tree limbs cracked and popped as they burned.

The fourth bomb hit dangerously close to their shelter. Clumps of dirt rained down on the soldiers. The acrid smoke told them the source: napalm.

"Move!" Tadashi shouted.

He had to get them out before the napalm ignited. The last man scrambled from the shelter just as it detonated.

The burning branches shrouded the entire area in smoke. *This is good luck,* thought Tadashi. *The smoke will hide us.*

The bombing had stopped. He couldn't hear the plane.

"Dear spirits," he prayed as he searched for an escape route, "protect us from our enemies."

"Over there," shouted Kaito. He pointed to a densely treed area, not too far away but far enough to escape the flames that were already dying out in the rain-soaked ground. The men dropped to their bellies and crawled across the open field, staying as close as they could to the shroud of smoke.

They hadn't gone ten yards when they heard the plane's engine. The air reverberated with the sound of machine-gun fire.

"Run!" Tadashi yelled and got to his feet.

Bullets strafed their path, but safe cover was seconds away and he kept his focus on it. There was no time to look around and see who was still with him.

He reached the trees, gasping for air. As he caught his breath, he looked for his squad and spotted Kaito, Fujita, and Yamada.

"Where's Ikeda?" Tadashi turned to scan the open field.

The enemy plane swooped past them, preparing to turn for another pass. It rose and banked, out of range for a moment. Tadashi carefully stepped out of the trees and spotted Private Ikeda not twenty yards away. He dropped to the ground and belly-crawled toward Ikeda. The plane was completing its turn now, and its engine roared louder.

"Hurry, Nii-chan," Kaito whispered loudly from the trees.

As Tadashi moved closer to Ikeda, he could see his mission was futile. Ikeda's helmet tipped to one side, a stream of blood pooling beneath it. Tadashi quickly ripped off Ikeda's name tag and turned toward the trees just as the enemy plane began its pass.

There was no time to belly-crawl back. Tadashi stood and ran like hell.

"Follow me," he shouted as he passed his comrades. The clatter of bullets rang through the air as the plane made its run and lifted away.

Tadashi and his men crashed through the underbrush until they were all gasping for air. He put up his hand. "Stop here. Stay quiet."

He listened for any sound of the plane but heard nothing. Perhaps the enemy had moved on, but he and his men would stay put until nightfall.

Now they were only four.

CHAPTER 44

NEAR ANTIPOLO, LUZON—JUNE 1945

"You wanted to see me, sir?" Leo stood at attention as he addressed Captain Mickelson. The summons had come after a long night of recon patrol. He was hot and dirty, and all he wanted was a little sleep.

"I did, Sergeant." The captain set aside the papers he'd been reading. "At ease." He gestured toward the empty chair and waited for Leo to sit. "We've got a problem."

"Sir?" Leo searched his brain. Had he made a misstep somewhere? Did this have something to do with Ryan's sudden interest in Dooley?

"There's been a complaint." Mickelson lifted the paper in front of him. "Someone thinks you're putting your soldiers in harm's way unnecessarily."

Leo's eyes widened. He opened his mouth to speak.

But Mickelson raised a hand to stop him. "The formal charge would be reckless endangerment."

A wave of cold electricity spread through Leo's body. According to the *Uniform Code of Military Justice*, that could mean a dishonorable discharge, maybe even confinement. Could he be subject to criminal charges? He trembled slightly as the adrenaline diffused. He clasped his hands together to steady them and took a slow, deep breath.

"May I ask who filed the complaint?" It had to be Dooley—didn't it? Leo ran through the names of his men, trying to remember any beefs they might have. He came up blank. He couldn't imagine any of them not coming to him first.

Could it have been someone outside of his squad? Possibly, Leo thought, but who? And why?

"All I can say at this time is it's one of your men." Mickelson closed the folder and set it aside. "This will be an Article 15 investigation for now. I'll be the one to decide if the charges are legitimate. If our findings support the claim, a court-martial under Article 114 may be in order."

Leo's mind was reeling. An Article 15 was meant for a minor offense and usually resulted in not much more than a slap on the wrist. At worst, he might be demoted or lose pay. What bothered him most was the stain it would bring to his service record, but it was better than going to jail. Still, if he should have done something more to prevent Richards's death, he deserved to be punished.

"This meeting is simply to inform you of the complaint," Mickelson said. "For the time being, you'll remain in command. This is still a war zone, and we can't afford to take anyone off duty. Lieutenant Ryan and I will look into this matter further and advise you when we've reached a decision."

Leo felt as if he should say something, but what? That Dooley was out to get him? Should he tell the captain he thought Richards's death might be his fault? Would that be considered an admission of guilt that would bring criminal charges? Maybe the best thing was to say nothing.

"Do you have any questions, Sergeant?" Mickelson asked.

"No, sir." Leo shifted nervously in his chair. He so wanted to tell the captain how he really felt, but he knew that now was not the right time.

"You're dismissed."

Leo stood and saluted, waited for Mickelson to return the salute, then turned and left the tent. He might not be able to say much to the captain, but he sure as heck had words for Dooley.

"What the heck are you up to, Dooley?" Leo stormed into Dooley's tent, his fists clenched, his eyes ablaze.

Dooley looked up from his cot. "Whaddaya mean, buddy?"

"That's Sergeant Baldwin to you," Leo growled. He struggled to control the shaking in his body, to contain the anger and feeling of betrayal.

"Okay, *Sergeant* Baldwin." He waved his hand dismissively. "What's the problem?"

What's the problem? Could Dooley seriously think Leo didn't know? He desperately wanted to grab him by the shirt, throw him up against the tent, and beat the tar out of him. Instead, he took a deep breath and forced the tension from his voice.

"You filed a complaint, didn't you?"

"What complaint?" he said, feigning innocence. Dooley suppressed a smirk.

Unbelievable. Leo pushed down his anger. "You know damn well," he said. "Nobody else would have done it."

"Maybe nobody else had the balls to do it." Dooley didn't try to hide the triumphant grin. "Course Richards ain't got balls at all anymore, does he?"

Leo lunged at Dooley. "So, you *are* the one who complained."

"Cool it, man," Dooley leaned back and held his hands up. "I never said I filed any complaint. But I *am* sayin' I ain't surprised." He crossed his arms. "That was a pretty bone-headed thing you did with Richards. You coulda got us all killed just 'cause you didn't want to get rid of your little buddy."

"He wasn't my little buddy." Oh, how he wanted to punch that smirk off Dooley's face. "He was a kid in trouble, and I did what I thought was right."

Dooley raised an eyebrow. "Like you did with your pal Furness?"

Leo took a step back. "You'd better stay out of my way, Nelson."

He stormed out of the tent, picked up a rock, and threw it as far as he could, wishing it was Dooley.

Dooley waited until Leo was out of earshot. "It's a little too late for that, buddy."

Leo passed by the mess tent and recognized Russo's voice. "I hear Sarge is in big trouble with Mickelson."

Leo stopped short and scowled. Oh great. It was out already. Of course, his troubles were the major topic of conversation. What else did the men have to do besides gossip? He scanned the compound—no one else was around—but he ducked behind a tree, just in case. He had to know how the rest of his men felt about the accusation.

"What kinda trouble?" Myoga asked.

"Somebody filed a complaint against him. Claims he should have got rid of Richards a long time ago. That keeping him put us all in harm's way."

"I'll bet a dollar Dooley's behind it." Filipowski grunted.

"Fuckin' asshole," Myoga snorted.

"It's not completely untrue." Grayson's voice held no emotion.

"What's not untrue? You saying Sarge is at fault?" Myoga glared at Grayson. "Was it you that filed the complaint?"

"I would not file a complaint against the Sergeant." Grayson's voice remained calm as he spoke. "He's a good man."

Several of the men voiced their agreement.

"What I am saying is that maybe Sarge should have done something about Richards sooner," Grayson continued. "We all know Richards was on the edge and that it wouldn't take much to set him off. None of us wanted to be around when it happened either."

"I sure didn't," said one of them.

"Sergeant Baldwin is our leader," Grayson said. "He had a soft spot for Richards, and he let that override his responsibility to protect the rest of us."

"It's easy to say what he should have done now that it's all over," Myoga said. "Maybe he made a mistake, but I don't think he ought to get court-martialed for it."

"Who said anything about a court-martial?" Russo said. "It'll be an Article 15, a slap on the wrist like nothing really happened."

"Grayson's right." Filipowski spoke up. "Sergeant Baldwin's our leader. That means he's responsible for the decisions he makes. If he makes a bad one, he has to take the heat that goes with it, even if it means a court-martial."

"It'll never happen," Webster piped up. "Ryan will stand up for him, and so will Mickelson. They both think he's hot shit."

A couple of men grumbled their assent.

"Maybe Ryan and Mickelson shouldn't be the ones who decide," Grayson said. "Sure, they know everything there is to know, but they're also too close to it."

"That means there'd have to be a formal hearing, and that means a court-martial for sure." Myoga hesitated. "You think that's right?"

"I think it should be an impartial judgment," Grayson answered.

Leo had heard enough. He stepped out from behind the tree and headed toward his tent, mulling over what he'd heard. Grayson was right: it was his responsibility to protect his men—all of his men. He'd focused on Richards instead and put the rest of them in jeopardy. There was a kernel of doubt among his men, enough of a kernel that might cause them to question his orders in the future. That was no way to lead a combat squad.

That night, Leo lay awake on his cot. The shock of the accusation still shook him. He was sure Dooley was behind it, but the claim that he was unfit to lead rattled him. It felt like a betrayal of the worst kind.

Sure, he blamed himself for Richards's death. He *should* have known, should have had him taken out of combat, gently but firmly.

But this? This was more than he could take. He'd believed in the rightness of what he'd done, carefully considered every option before making any decision. He'd led with integrity and fairness—and it had gotten Richards killed.

Leo fell into a restless sleep. A picture of Richards's wrecked body burned into his mind.

"Richards, don't!" He tried to yell, but his voice wouldn't come. He tried to run to help, but his feet wouldn't move. Richards looked up at him, reached under the woman's body, pulled out the grenade, and hurled it at Leo.

Leo jerked up in his bed. His heart pounded, and his hands shook violently. He looked around, trying to ground himself, trying to convince himself it was just a nightmare.

It was his fault.

Tomorrow, he would make it right.

"I'd like to request a summary court-martial, sir." Leo stood at attention in front of Captain Mickelson and Lieutenant Ryan. He'd asked both of them to be present to hear what he had to say.

Captain Mickelson's eyes widened. "Are you sure, Sergeant?"

Leo swallowed hard. He had to make this right. "Yes, sir."

Mickelson spread out his hands. "There's a good chance you'd be cleared of all charges as it stands now. If it goes to trial, it's out of my hands. Why take the risk?"

"It's a matter of integrity, sir." Leo stood stiffly, clenching his fists behind him. "I'm being accused of not doing my job. Worse than that, I'm accused of causing the death of one of my soldiers and recklessly putting the others in harm's way." He paused and thought about the conversation he'd overheard. "I can already see a difference in my men's respect toward me. As long as there's any question in their minds, that won't change, and it's going to hamper my authority as their leader."

The captain's voice softened. "Son, you understand that if you're found guilty, it could mean prison time?"

"Yes, sir." Leo paused, envisioning what remained of Richards's body after the explosion. "I take my responsibility as a combat squad leader seriously. I did what I thought was right where Private Richards was concerned, just as I would do with any of my men. If there is a chance my decisions caused the private's death and put my men in undue danger, then I deserve to be punished for it." His heart beat faster at the thought of jail. He took another deep breath. "But if I'm found not guilty, my men will know for sure I did right by them."

Ryan tilted his head toward Leo, his eyes filled with concern. "Leo, you don't have to do this."

"Yes, sir, I do. If what I've done is morally wrong, I'm no better than the Japs."

Susannah Willey

愛し国
親、妻、子供
いざ帰国

Itoshi kuni
Oya tsuma kodomo
Isa kikoku

Beloved homeland
Parents, dear wife, and children,
I return to you!

CHAPTER 45

SOMEWHERE IN LUZON—JULY 1945

No matter where they wandered, the situation was always the same: There was no food. The water was contaminated, and they drank it anyway. They'd had nothing to eat but insects and grass since abandoning the mango tree. All over southern Luzon, the trees were stripped of fruit and bark. There was not a pig, carabao, or dog left alive. Even rats were scarce, and those that remained seemed to know to stay well away from starving humans.

Shimbu Group—the fifty thousand-member Japanese division tasked with defending southern Luzon—now numbered less than eight thousand. Broken up into small groups like Tadashi's, they foraged for food and struggled to make their way north, where the rest of the army still fought.

Tadashi had long since given up any hope of winning the war. He was far more occupied with simply staying alive. Two days ago, they had encountered a Japanese platoon and learned that Germany had surrendered. The platoon leader encouraged Tadashi and his men to join them, but Tadashi had an uneasy feeling that they might end up as food instead of recruits.

The effects of starvation ruled them now. Their bodies were emaciated. They stumbled along the trails, their progress slow and aimless. Their metabolisms weren't working properly—they were constantly too cold or too hot, their bodily functions erratic. Their muscles were so shrunken that movement was painful, and their skin cracked from dehydration. Even their minds were affected. They felt sluggish and apathetic—sometimes they had hallucinations.

There were days Tadashi wanted nothing more than to sleep. He wasn't even sure if he cared whether or not he woke up.

"Do you ever wonder why we still fight?" Kaito's voice was weak and raspy as they settled on a downed tree for their third rest of the morning.

"You—the man who pledged undying loyalty to the emperor—ask this?" Tadashi smiled weakly. "You must be hallucinating."

"The army may have surrendered for all we know," Kaito said. "And if they go, why should we stay?"

Would the great Japanese Imperial Army surrender? Hundreds of officers would be required to honorably fall on their swords. Tadashi couldn't imagine that. And how would they know if there *was* a surrender unless they ran across someone else who knew?

"Nii-chan," Kaito said but kept his eyes focused on the now-distant mountains. "Have you ever thought about quitting this war?"

"Desertion?" Tadashi started to protest, but he stopped himself and thought about it. Was it desertion if the army didn't even know whether they were alive or dead? Was it desertion if they were simply trying to survive? He saw no honor in dying of starvation. "Where would we go? Would you surrender to the enemy?"

Kaito's eyes went wide. "Never. I would take my own life before I would allow myself to be captured." His face reddened. "How could you think I would dishonor the emperor like that?"

"No need to get agitated," Tadashi said. "I simply wondered, what are your plans?"

"I don't have any plans." Kaito looked at the ground for a moment then looked up, his eyes filled with tears. "I just want to live. May the kami forgive me; I just want to go home."

Tadashi touched Kaito's shoulders. "You do what you must, Kai-chan. I cannot abandon what remains of my squad."

"Then I will stay too, Nii-chan. We are brothers, and we stay together as brothers should."

Tadashi stood, brushing the dirt and grass from his trousers. "Rest time is over," he said. "Everyone, get ready to move out."

He reached for Kaito's hand and helped him up.

The day was unbearably hot as they wandered along the trail. There was little shade, and their gaunt bodies dripped sweat and soaked their clothes. By midafternoon Tadashi stopped, pointing to a small forest in the distance.

"We march to those trees," he said. "Then we will look for food and take our rest."

An hour later, they reached the trees. Exhausted, they dropped their packs and collapsed on the cool forest floor. They were silent, each man grasping for enough strength to move.

It was Tadashi who spoke first.

"We must look for food." He struggled to his feet, urging the others to get up as well. "You two search to the east," he said, motioning to Fujita and Yamada. "Kaito and I will go west."

"What do you expect to find?" Kaito asked as they scoured the brushy ground. He shrugged. "You know there will be nothing, just like everywhere else."

"You don't know that," Tadashi answered. "Would you simply lie on the ground until death comes to take you? There may be a nearby stream with fish to catch. We may find a nest of rodents in the bushes."

"Now you're the one who is hallucinating, Nii-chan." Kaito grinned and playfully slapped his friend's shoulder.

"Sergeant." Private Yamada's voice pitched high with excitement.

Tadashi and Kaito hurried across the field where Fujita and Yamada crouched over their find.

"What is it?" asked Tadashi. "Did you find a rat's nest?"

"Human rats," replied Fujita. Tadashi could see now that they were tearing the uniforms off two dead enemy soldiers. "They have not been dead for long. Their meat will still be fresh."

Tadashi took a step toward Corporal Fujita. "You will not eat human flesh. I forbid it."

He reached for his rifle, but Fujita already had his aimed at Tadashi's head.

"We will not die because of your morals," Fujita said. "Food is food, and this food, we're going to eat." Tadashi started to speak, but Fujita shoved his rifle closer. "Do you want to be a part of our dinner too?"

Tadashi put down his rifle, held his hands up, and stepped away, motioning to Kaito to do the same.

Yamato guarded Tadashi and Kaito while Fujita pulled out his bayonet and began hacking at one of the bodies. Like a feasting animal, he tore away a hunk of bloody flesh, devoured it raw, then cut off another chunk, and tossed it to Yamato. Keeping his rifle and his eyes on Tadashi and Kaito, Yamada stooped to retrieve the meat and hungrily took a bite.

Tadashi and Kaito sat at a distance as the two soldiers built a small fire, cut the bodies into pieces and threw them on the burning branches. The fire crackled and spit dripping fat. As soon as one of them finished a chunk of meat, he grabbed another from the fire.

Tadashi looked away. He would not be a part of this.

The men ate nonstop, gorging themselves, licking every last bit from their greasy fingers. Their bellies visibly expanded, and they kept eating.

As night approached, Tadashi spoke. "You should slow down. Your shrunken bellies will rebel if you continue. Rest a while. The food will still be there in the morning."

"You think we don't know you'll steal it as soon as we fall asleep?" Fujita waved his rifle at Tadashi and Kaito. "It is ours, and we will eat as we please."

Tadashi raised his hands in surrender and backed away, careful not to rile Fujita any further. He swallowed his revulsion and fear, forcing himself to speak calmly. "As you wish, Corporal."

Keeping an eye on Fujita, Tadashi gestured to Kaito to follow him, and moved to the far side of the encampment.

"Let's get some sleep," he said as they settled against the trees. "I will stand the first guard—it wouldn't surprise me if they tried to eat us too."

Kaito glanced toward the feasting soldiers. "Without our guns, we can't stop them even if they do."

Tadashi nodded. "But we will try."

Kaito snored softly as darkness overtook them. The temperatures dropped with the sunset, and Tadashi shivered in his sweat-soaked uniform. What kind of madness had brought them to this point? He made a vow to himself: if he and Kaito survived the night, they would find a way to get home.

The bright morning sun woke Tadashi with a start. He eyed the campfire, still smoldering, and piled with bones picked clean. He roused Kaito, who still slept beside him.

"They're asleep," Tadashi said. "Let's get our rifles and get out of here."

They rose quietly from the ground and crept toward the campfire. Kaito retrieved their weapons while Tadashi watched the sleeping men for movement.

Something wasn't right. The soldier's chests weren't moving, their bodies seemed strangely discolored. He moved closer.

"They're dead," he said to Kaito. "I think they ate until their bellies burst."

"Is that possible?" Kaito asked.

Tadashi thought quietly before he spoke. "I don't know. Perhaps the spirits were angry with them for their actions."

Kaito nodded. He gestured to the still smoldering fire. "Should we cremate them?"

"I don't think I can bear any more burning flesh." Tadashi scowled and crossed his arms. "Nor do they deserve it. They gave no sacrifice. They honored no one."

"You will let the wild animals eat them?"

"What wild animals?" Tadashi snorted. "They're all dead too."

"Then I will bury their bodies myself." Kaito pulled his spade from his pack and began to dig.

Tadashi watched as Kaito wiped sweat from his brow and struggled with the root-filled soil. Here was his friend, respectfully burying the dead. Kaito did what was right without judgement. Tadashi's stomach twinged with shame. *Who am I to say who is worthy of burial?*

He retrieved his spade, knelt next to Kaito, and began to dig. By the time they finished, they were both panting.

"I don't think I can travel today, Nii-chan," Kaito said, "but I cannot stay among so much death."

Tadashi nodded, pointing northward. "Let's go as far as the end of this forest. Then perhaps we can rest."

It was still early when they stopped for the day. They found a dead tree and tore at the spongy wood, finally uncovering a nest of insects. Tadashi thought of Fujita and Yamada, their dead, swollen bodies. It was what they deserved.

A part of him feared that he too might die; the handful of bugs he ate was meager. Would he ever resort to eating human flesh? What would it take for him to fall so low?

He hoped he would never find out.

CHAPTER 46

NEAR ANTIPOLO, LUZON—JULY 1945

"Sergeant Baldwin and me, we've been together since Camp Hood, nearly three years now." As the primary plaintiff, Dooley was the first witness called. "We were both drill sergeants until we got our orders to ship out, and then, after he got promoted, I was part of the combat squad he was in charge of."

The case had been assigned to Major Reginald Grissom from the 8th Cavalry. Grissom had a reputation as a by-the-book commander, but he was also known to be fair and impartial. Leo knew that, although the major might take a hard line in his case, his ruling would be respected.

"I have thoroughly reviewed this case," Grissom had said as the trial began. "Both sides will have the opportunity to speak and present witnesses. At the end, I will consider all the evidence and make my decision accordingly."

Now, he scanned Sergeant Nelson's dossier before he asked his next question.

"Did you and Sergeant Baldwin get along?" Grissom knew there had been friction between Baldwin and Nelson. He watched Nelson closely, looking for any signs that the sergeant was not being truthful.

"We got along good enough." Dooley shrugged. "Course, once he was my squad leader, we weren't so close."

Grissom pursed his lips. "I heard you gave him a hard time for it."

Dooley nodded slightly. "I was mad he got a promotion and I didn't." He shrugged. "But I got over it."

"What made you bring this complaint to Captain Mickelson?" Grissom asked.

Dooley looked at Leo, dramatically took a sip of water, and played to the crowd. "Sergeant Baldwin's not a terrible leader, but he had a big blind spot when it came to Private Richards. When the private started havin' his little fits, Sergeant Baldwin should have sent him home, but he didn't." He put down his glass and continued in a louder voice. "That got Richards killed and darn near killed the rest of us. In my mind, Sergeant Baldwin should have been relieved of his command then and there."

Leo scanned the crowd as Dooley finished his testimony. Lieutenant Ryan nodded his support as Leo caught his eye. Captain Mickelson listened intently, his face impassive. What bothered Leo most were the members of his squad. Not one of them would look at him. Some already stared at the floor, and the rest turned their heads as soon as he looked at them.

Leo's stomach clenched. Did every one of them blame him too?

Private Webster took the stand. "Sergeant Nelson asked me to keep an eye on Private Richards," he explained when the major asked for his story. "He was worried that Richards was going to have a breakdown and that Sergeant Baldwin wasn't taking that seriously enough."

"Did you see evidence Private Richards was unstable?" Grissom asked.

"Yes, sir, I did." Webster straightened in his chair. "I saw him talk to his dead mother more than once."

"What did he say?"

"He told her he was sorry. He said—pardon the language, sir—'I'm sorry I fucked up.'" Webster blushed and shuffled uncomfortably. "He bawled like a baby."

Grissom nodded. After a few more questions, he dismissed Webster and called Russo to the stand. "Were you concerned about Private Richards's state of mind?"

"I was, sir." Like the rest of Leo's squad, Russo respected his leader. But he believed the sergeant had made a mistake with Private Richards.

"And why was that?" Grissom asked.

"Well, sir, Private Richards had this thing about bodies." Russo shifted in his chair. "Rumor was it had something to do with his mother and how she died from a broken neck. Whenever he'd see a body where the neck was broken, he'd go a little crazy."

"In what way, Corporal?"

"He'd go blank, like he was somewhere else. Then he'd start crying and telling his mother he was sorry."

"Did that behavior worry you?"

"Sure, it did. We were all worried Private Richards was going crazy."

"And were you concerned for your own safety if that happened?"

Russo hesitated, looked at Leo apologetically, then looked away. "To be honest, sir, I was."

Leo's heart was racing. He'd known from the day he'd overheard his men in the tent that they were worried about Richards, but it still stung that no one thought to bring their concerns to him. Why had no one mentioned it to him? Because he was their CO? Now, here he was, facing a possible prison sentence.

"Did you tell Sergeant Baldwin your concerns?" Grissom asked.

Russo's head dropped. "No, sir, I did not."

"Why not?"

"He and Private Richards were close." Russo shook his head. "I think Private Richards was like a little brother to Sergeant Baldwin. Sarge felt like he had to protect him." He looked at Leo apologetically. "Sergeant Baldwin is a good leader," he said. "Nobody wanted to tell him he was making a mistake with Private Richards."

Grissom dismissed Russo and called the next witness. Russo averted his eyes as he walked past Leo.

As each of Leo's men testified, their stories were much the same: they knew Richards was on the edge mentally, they were afraid he might have a breakdown and that other people would get hurt, and nobody wanted to be the one to tell Leo.

By midafternoon, testimony was nearly finished, and Leo was called to the stand.

"Sergeant Baldwin." To Leo, Major Grissom's voice seemed louder, more stringent. "Did you know Private Richards was having mental issues?"

"I did." Leo knew better than to volunteer his thoughts.

"Did you consider that his behavior could be detrimental to your men?"

"Yes."

"And what did you do about it?"

"I talked to him, urged him to talk to the chaplain. I suggested that combat might not be the best place for him." Leo shared the events that followed, Richards's nightmares, his reaction to dead bodies, and his adamance that he could handle his emotions and didn't want to let down his squad mates.

"And you never thought to force the issue?" Grissom asked. "Never reported it to your CO?"

"Lieutenant Ryan knew," Leo said. "But I assured him I could handle Private Richards, and I thought I had."

Grissom nodded. He looked at his notes and added a few lines.

"You're dismissed, Sergeant Baldwin. I'll announce my decision by the end of the week." Major Grissom addressed the crowd. "The principal parties will meet here at 0900 hours on Friday."

Russo approached Leo as he returned to his tent. "Sarge, I—"

Leo waved him away. "Not now, Russo."

Once inside his tent, Leo collapsed on his cot. The next four days were going to be unbearable. He hadn't been able to read Major Grissom's face, couldn't tell which way he was leaning.

He'd done what he'd felt was the ethical thing to do. *Integrity takes courage*, he reminded himself. But had he made the right decision when he'd insisted on a court-martial?

追われる身
枝葉の陰で
休息を

Owareru mi
Edaha no kage de
Kyuusoku o

I will rest awhile
Among the cool leafy trees
Enemies seek me.

CHAPTER 47

SOMEWHERE IN LUZON—JULY 1945

Tadashi's and Kaito's goals now were nothing more than finding food and evading their enemies. But there were two enemies now: the American Army they battled for land and the remaining Japanese soldiers they battled for sustenance.

It had been two months since Tadashi and his men were forced from their mountain hideout. A few weeks later, their mango tree fortress was destroyed. From a contingent of thousands at Bigti, the Japanese Army in southern Luzon was now reduced to a few scattered pockets of resistance.

Tadashi leaned against the rubber tree and stared at his swollen and wrinkled feet, the skin white and peeling from being constantly wet. The sturdy American boots had long since rotted from slogging through mud and water. Their shoes now were nothing more than whatever grass and moss they could gather.

They were all that were left of Inoue's platoon. All the rest were dead. Why did they keep going? What were they searching for? He frowned and shook his head. They wandered aimlessly, like sheep in search of a shepherd.

We will not surrender. Beyond that, he could not see.

He tried to envision Sachiko and Ichiro, imagine his homecoming, the joy of reuniting with his land and his family. No picture came to mind. Even his brain was starving.

Kaito sat beside him. His face was gaunt, his eyes sunken. His shaggy, matted hair clung to his collar. What remained of his tattered uniform reeked. Everything—*everything*—was covered in mud.

"You look like hell, soldier." Tadashi tried to laugh but managed only a raspy grunt.

Kaito struggled to lift his head but did not try to smile. "We are no longer soldiers," he said. "We are walking skeletons."

Tadashi scrutinized his childhood friend. He had never seen Kaito so discouraged—Kaito was the joker, the one who kept Tadashi's spirits high.

"Shall we travel today?" Tadashi hoped that would keep Kaito's mind off his misery.

"Who cares?" Kaito answered. "We are already dead."

"Kai-chan." Tadashi gripped Kaito's arm. He would not let his friend know he felt the same. "You can't think like that. We have to stay alive."

"Why?" Tears shone in Kaito's eyes. "Do you honestly believe we will ever go home?"

"I have to believe that," Tadashi said. "My wife and child need me."

"And who do I have? My parents are likely dead." Kaito wept openly now. He leaned toward Tadashi and clung to him. "You are all I have left."

"Oh, Kai-chan." Tadashi embraced his friend tightly. "You are weak from hunger. Your spirits are low. You aren't thinking rationally, brother. We will survive."

Kaito sat up, wiping his eyes. "Promise me something, Nii-chan." Kaito looked at him pleadingly. "If I die before you, you must eat my flesh and keep fighting."

"Kaito." Tadashi's body stiffened and jerked back. "No—" His gut clenched, and bile rose in his throat. "How can you say this?"

"I have this feeling." Kaito looked at Tadashi intently. "I will not survive. You must—for your wife and child. "Nii-chan." Kaito reached out, touched Tadashi's shoulder, and drew him closer. "We are brothers, aren't we?"

"Yes, of course we are brothers." Tadashi's voice pitched higher. "But what you are asking is repulsive."

Kaito looked into Tadashi's eyes. "We are kindred spirits. Brothers bound by loyalty instead of blood." He looked away, staring into the distance. "Eating my flesh will nourish your body and join our souls. Please promise me."

"And could you eat my flesh if I were to die first?" Tadashi asked.

Kaito kept his eyes on the horizon, staying quiet for a moment. "I don't know," he whispered. He looked at Tadashi, a pleading look in his eye. "Please, Nii-chan, promise me. You must live."

"You will not die." Tadashi knew he shouldn't be angry with his friend, but that was how he felt. "We will both live to see home."

"You can't know that." Kaito smiled weakly. "Just promise. If I live, it won't matter."

Tears fell as they embraced each other fiercely. Tadashi felt certain this request came from Kaito's despair. Surely, he would not ask this if he were himself.

"I promise," Tadashi said. He could never eat human flesh, but he hoped the promise would ease his friend's mind. "But you will not die."

Neither moved. It was as if, by staying in their embrace, nothing could happen to either of them. At last, Tadashi pulled away.

"So, shall we travel today, Kai-chan?" He grinned mischievously.

Kaito stood and pulled Tadashi to his feet. "We travel, Nii-chan."

A hollow tree beckoned them—there might be insects inside. If not, they would eat the moss-covered bark. Either way, it was a meal. As they got closer, Kaito put his arm in front of Tadashi.

"Something is moving in there, Nii-chan." He crouched low, quietly creeping to the tree. Slowly, he rose, peeked into the rotted hole, then dropped to the ground.

"What is it?" Tadashi whispered.

Kaito moved toward a nearby clearing and motioned Tadashi to follow.

"You won't believe what I found." His eyes were wide with excitement.

"Enough insects for a feast?"

"Better," Kaito said. "A family of giant cloud rats sleeping soundly." He spread his hands wide apart, an estimate of the rat's size. "Even one will feed us for a week."

"They are sly creatures," Tadashi said, "and difficult to trap."

"Bayonet?" Kaito asked, removing the blade from its sheath.

Tadashi nodded.

Kaito crept back to the tree. He knelt quietly for a moment, listening for movement. When he heard nothing, he stood cautiously, keeping to one side of the hole where the cloud rats slept. With one swift movement, he thrust his bayonet into the tree. A piercing squeal erupted from the hole as an adult rat leapt out, carrying a baby in its mouth.

Kaito smiled, raising his bayonet triumphantly. He reached into the tree and pulled out the giant rat. "It must weigh nearly five pounds," he shouted. "We live a little longer."

"Not so loud," Tadashi warned. His stomach growled as he studied Kaito's catch.

A good thirty inches from nose to tail, the rat had long, dense fur as soft as a duckling. Kaito and Tadashi knelt, saying a prayer for the animal's spirit and thanking the kami for their bounty. They carefully removed the pale gray fur then slit the rat open from throat to belly, carefully extracting the guts and scent gland.

"We will have to eat this raw," Tadashi cautioned, "and bury everything we don't eat. We can't risk attracting attention."

Kaito nodded and cut off the rat's forelegs, giving one to Tadashi and keeping the other for himself.

"Eat slowly," Tadashi said. "Remember what happened to Fujita and Yamada."

That night, with sticky hands and satisfied bellies, they slept soundly. The meal had nourished their spirits as well as their bodies. Tadashi dreamed of home.

He crossed the overgrown pasture toward his house. Sachiko wept for joy, as beautiful as ever. A young man stood beside her—could it be his son? No, Ichiro was barely four. Tadashi's mind was playing tricks on him.

As he came closer, the young man approached him. Tadashi held out his arms to embrace his son just as the boy plunged a bayonet into his leg.

Tadashi woke, screaming. His leg felt like it was on fire. A gaunt Japanese soldier stood over him, bayonet in hand and ready to strike again.

A shot rang through the air, and the soldier fell.

Kaito rushed to his side. "Are you okay?"

Tadashi touched his leg and felt the blood. The wound was not deep—perhaps the soldier was too weak to do better. "It will heal."

Kaito reached into his pack. "It's a good thing I still have my medical kit." He poured antiseptic on the wound and wrapped a bandage around Tadashi's leg. "Let's pray it won't get infected." He reached for Tadashi's rifle and laid it on his lap. "I'm going to be sure there are no others. Can you defend yourself while I'm gone?"

Tadashi nodded weakly.

A few minutes later, Kaito returned. "If he had friends, they have run away."

"We have learned a costly lesson," Tadashi said, rubbing his bandaged leg. "From now on, one of us will stand guard while the other sleeps."

Kaito sat down at Tadashi's back so they could watch from both directions. "I think neither of us will sleep tonight."

CHAPTER 48

NEAR ANTIPOLO, LUZON—JULY 1945

Lieutenant Ryan stood at attention and saluted as he entered Captain Mickelson's tent. The command post "office" was sparsely furnished: a metal desk and chair stood opposite the tent flaps, and the captain's cot and a small stand were tucked away to Ryan's left.

"Reporting as ordered, sir." Ryan focused on the wall behind the captain's desk as he waited to be acknowledged. It wasn't unusual for him to meet with his captain, but normally Ryan had notice and a pretty good idea of the purpose. This time, he didn't.

Mickelson straightened the papers in front of him, placed them in their folder, and set it aside. The captain's face held no hint of emotion. His body was relaxed, a sign that this meeting wasn't related to combat or discipline. "At ease, Lieutenant."

Ryan relaxed, spread his legs comfortably apart, and clasped his hands behind him. His eyes remained fixed on his superior.

Mickelson leaned back in his chair and took a drink of his coffee. "How's Sergeant Baldwin holding up?"

"Holding it together." Ryan shrugged. "I just hope his determination to do right by his men doesn't cost him his freedom."

"I've seen men far guiltier than him get off." Mickelson shook his head. "But Baldwin seems determined to go through with this, come hell or high water. "But that's not why you're here." He smiled. "I got word from division HQ this morning."

"Sir?" Did they have new orders? How would that apply to him but not to the other platoon leaders? His stomach clenched—was he being transferred?

"You've been promoted to first lieutenant." Mickelson stood and extended his hand. "Congratulations."

Ryan accepted the handshake. He struggled to remain stone-faced, but a small grin forced its way out. "Thank you, sir."

"You'll report to division HQ for further instruction. Your transport leaves at 1600 hours." Mickelson tipped his head to dismiss Ryan, but as the lieutenant saluted and turned to leave, the captain spoke. "And while you're there, Lieutenant, take a couple days of R&R."

Ryan's grin bloomed into a full-blown smile. "Yes, sir. Thank you, sir."

As he crossed the compound toward his tent, his mind was racing. Would he be assigned to a specialized platoon now? Made executive officer of a company? Whatever it was meant more pay, more perks, and more stability, if there were such a thing in a war zone.

He could get used to that idea.

Ryan packed his gear and checked his watch. He worried about leaving Baldwin in the middle of his trial and had sent word for Baldwin to see him. It was getting late—he should be here by now.

Leo stuck his head into Ryan's tent. "Grayson said you're looking for me."

"I am," Ryan said. "Let's take a walk." As soon as they were clear of the tents, Ryan started talking. "I got orders to report to HQ. I leave tomorrow."

Leo stopped. "Now?" He lowered his head, closed his eyes, and took a deep breath. "It's just that you've had my back since this whole complaint thing started. The judge is going to decide any day now, and you won't be there when it happens."

Ryan put a hand on Leo's shoulder. "Don't worry, Baldwin. You'll be fine. There's no way Grissom is stupid enough to take Dooley's word over yours."

Leo nodded. It wouldn't be the same without his mentor there.

The two men crossed an open rice paddy. When they reached a small clump of trees, Ryan casually leaned against the largest one, took out a cigarette, lit it, and inhaled deeply. He raised an eyebrow and grinned. "Aren't you going to ask *why* I'm going to HQ?"

Leo leaned against a tree, his arms crossed. "Sure, Lieutenant, why are you going to HQ?"

"Got myself a promotion, that's why." Ryan tipped up his chin, thrust out his chest. "And a little R&R."

"Congratulations, Lieutenant." Leo shook Ryan's hand. "I guess this means we won't be seeing you around anymore."

Ryan shook his head. "Depends on where they send me, but no, I don't imagine I'll be coming back. That reminds me"—he pointed toward camp—"I got a bunch of stuff all ready to send home. Could you make sure it goes out?"

"Will do, Lieutenant."

Ryan put a hand on Leo's shoulder and took a step toward him. "Listen, Baldwin." He kept his voice low. "This court-martial stuff is a bunch of shit. I may be going somewhere else, but if you need anything, Mickelson will know how to get a hold of me."

"Appreciate it, Lieutenant." He hugged Ryan briefly and slapped him on his back. "We'll miss you, Ryan."

"Yeah, like the plague." Ryan laughed.

The next morning, Leo watched as Ryan hoisted his duffel into the jeep that would take him to division HQ. Now that was what success looked like. Ryan had done his job and then some, and it had gotten him a promotion. Ever since they'd met, Leo had admired Ryan's leadership, intelligence, and dedication to his family and his country. He was everything Leo aspired to be.

Division HQ was stuck out in the middle of nowhere in what had been a rubber tree plantation. A few trees still dotted the landscape like scattered sentries. The remains of a small barrio were nearby, reduced to rubble from a recent skirmish.

The camp was a mass of Quonset huts, wooden buildings fitted with sheet-metal roofs and set on a concrete slab. There were openings near the top of the building for ventilation, covered with screens to keep out the mosquitoes. A concertina-wire barrier surrounded the perimeter. Sand-bagged bunkers were scattered around the grounds and inside the barracks, many of them inhabited by officers. Although the war was winding down, they still had their share of rocket and mortar attacks, and personnel were not allowed outside the perimeter at night.

Ryan settled into the barracks, unpacked his duffel, and relaxed on his bunk. First thing he was going to do was get a long, hot shower—it seemed like forever since he'd bathed, and now that he was away from the stink of battle, he could barely stand himself. He'd get his clothes washed, wear clean underwear for once. Maybe there'd be a good movie tonight.

He'd barely soaped up when, outside, the air whistled as enemy artillery flew over the base. Ryan instinctively crouched in a corner of the shower stall, hands over his head for protection. It took him a second to realize that he wasn't on the battle lines. It took another second to realize he was okay.

His legs still trembled as he got to his feet.

Jesus Christ, he thought, *the last thing I want is to be found dead and naked in the shower.*

This long, hot shower was going to be cut short. He stayed long enough to wash the grime out of his hair and scrub off most of the stink then stepped out of the stall, wrapped himself in a towel, and went back to his bunk.

The air felt cool against his damp skin—maybe he'd stay in the towel awhile longer. He grabbed his duffel, dug out paper and his fountain pen, settled on his bunk, and started writing a letter home.

Dearest Anna,

I got a surprise couple days off and here I am at division HQ, freshly showered, wrapped in a towel, and wishing you were here.

At the end of the first page, Ryan paused and chewed on his pen. How soon would he see his girls again? Operations might have been winding down here in Luzon, but the next battlefield would be Tokyo itself. How long would it take for them to bring the Japs to surrender?

He glanced at his watch—almost chow time, and he wanted to get his letter in the mail. He hurriedly finished the letter, placed it in its envelope, and sealed it then set it on the bunk while he got dressed. He was just putting on his boots when mess call blared across the compound.

Lieutenant Ryan picked up the letter and kissed it gently, tucked it in his breast pocket, and headed for the mess hall. Artillery fire continued in the distance as he crossed the compound.

Just keep away from here, he thought. *I could use a couple nights of uninterrupted sleep.*

At the 112th outpost, the shelling had been intermittent since nightfall. Artillery fire would pummel their position for maybe twenty minutes then stop. Just when Leo's squad relaxed, it would start up again.

He had to be quiet—listen carefully—to hear the faint popping sound when the enemy fired their artillery. A few seconds after that, maybe ten if he was lucky, the shell would explode. If he heard a long whistling sound, it was a good thing. The shell was going over his head and would land several hundred feet away. A short whistle, lasting less than a second, was the one that got his attention. He had just enough time to determine the length of the sound, decide how close the shell would land, and wonder whether he'd live to hear the next one.

There'd be a muffled thump as the shell hit the ground, the whoosh of air as it moved out from the impact, the sound wave of the explosion that followed it, the strange noises as pieces of shrapnel tumbled through the air. In the quiet that followed, he'd realize he was still alive.

He'd never forget the sound.

In Ryan's dream, the fighting was intense and constant. The distant pop, the whistling shell as it passed, the explosion that rocked the ground. His platoon was being decimated, one soldier after another flying in front of him, sometimes a piece at a time, and he could do nothing but watch it happen.

He tossed and turned in his bed, struggling to run to their aid but unable to make progress. They just kept flying by: Russo grasping his mother's rosary, Filipowski holding his hair weaving, Leo's eagle stone without its owner. All gone.

Ryan jerked upright. Drenched in sweat, he threw off his blanket and was running toward his men when he realized where he was and that his men were dozens of miles away. He breathed deeply, exhaled slowly, and forced his heartbeat to slow. He scanned the bunks. Everyone else was asleep. It was just a bad dream.

You're fine, and God willing, so are they, he reassured himself.

As the pounding in his heart receded, he turned his attention outward to a noise that lay just outside of his perception. He listened closely, heard it again: a very faint pop.

Ryan shook his head in case it was a remnant of his nightmare. Instinctively, he counted the seconds. Five, six, seven... the wisp of a whistle that he wasn't sure he even heard, a muffled thunk.

"Oh, shit." Ryan heard his voice as if the words were coming from someone else. He grabbed the picture of his girls from under his pillow and held them tight.

CHAPTER 49

NEAR ANTIPOLO, LUZON—JULY 1945

Leo murmured a prayer of thanks when the enemy shelling stopped at dawn. No one was seriously injured, and they had turned away the Japs. He desperately needed something to eat and some decent sleep. But his stomach was too nervous for food, his brain too active to rest. The verdict was still a couple of days away, and that might as well be forever.

He thought of Ryan and smiled. That lucky son-of-a-gun was probably stretched out in the sun right now. But he'd earned every minute of it. Leo tried to imagine himself at Ryan's age. Would he have a wife? Children? Would he be a successful writer? If anyone was proof that it was possible, it was Ryan.

"Sarge." A hand gently shook Leo's shoulder. Leo woke to see Grayson standing over him.

"What?" Leo jerked upright and shook himself awake. "Geez, Grayson, you scared the bejabbers out of me."

"Captain wants to see you." Grayson jerked his head toward the tent flap. "Says it's urgent."

Leo rubbed the sleep from his eyes, ran his fingers through his hair. Had Major Grissom made his decision already? It seemed odd the order to report wasn't from Major Grissom, but maybe Mickelson wanted to prepare him for the worst. As Leo hurried to the captain's tent, his mind raced with the possibilities. The verdict had to be not guilty. Didn't it? He did what he thought was right. Wasn't that enough? What if they found him guilty? Would he receive a dishonorable discharge or a prison sentence? That couldn't happen—could it?

Leo entered Mickelson's tent, came to attention, and saluted. The captain returned the salute and motioned for Leo to sit. His face was drawn and tired, his eyes filled with sympathy.

"I have news, Baldwin," he said, his voice barely above a whisper.

Leo's chest tightened. Dear God, had Grissom found decided he was guilty? He straightened in his chair, took a deep breath. "Is there a verdict?"

"Not that I know of." Mickelson shifted uncomfortably. "I have news from HQ."

Leo wracked his brain. What could news from HQ have to do with him? Was it something from home? His heart pounded. Was someone hurt? Or dead?

"Lieutenant Ryan died in a mortar attack last night." He scrubbed his hand over his face and looked at Leo, a pained expression on his face. "It dropped on the barracks he was sleeping in, killed almost everybody inside."

Leo blinked. His brain felt full of lead, his body frozen. The room moved in slow motion. He heard Mickelson speak, his voice distant, deep and sluggish. What had Mickelson said? Ryan? Ryan's dead?

"... know you looked up to him."

Leo looked at Mickelson, his eyes dull and uncomprehending.

"Sergeant Baldwin." Mickelson's voice was normal now. "Are you okay?"

Leo stared at the captain. He shook his head, trying to stop the ringing in his ears.

"Yes, sir," he said at last. "I'm good." An image of Richards's mangled body appeared in his head, morphing into what Leo imagined was left of Ryan's torn and bloodied corpse. Leo swallowed and whispered, "Were there any remains?"

Mickelson sat silently, as if contemplating what to say. He finally chose the simple truth. "I don't know."

Leo pushed up from his chair, forced his trembling legs to hold the weight of his body. He came to attention and saluted. "Permission to return to my tent, sir?"

"Granted." Mickelson returned the salute and nodded. His face wrinkled with concern as he watched his sergeant for signs of a breakdown. "Baldwin?"

"Yes, sir."

"Try to get some rest."

Leo stumbled across the compound on auto-pilot. How much more was he supposed to take? He struggled to process what Mickelson had told him. Was Ryan really dead? It had to be a mistake; the captain would call him back any minute now and tell him it wasn't Ryan after all.

The next morning, Leo sat on the floor in Ryan's tent. Ryan had carefully packed his few extra belongings to send home. There wasn't much: a few souvenirs, some well-read books, an old watch.

Leo still couldn't believe Ryan was gone. Maybe it would have felt more real if he'd been killed in battle—Leo had seen plenty of that. The only thing that kept him from breaking was his responsibility to his men. He struggled to stay focused, to keep his mind on his job. But in the rare moments when he dared let down his guard, it felt like he might go crazy.

Could it have been only a few months since he and Ryan had met? The city boy and the country boy had bonded from the start—so little in common yet so much the same. Leo thought back to the day his draft notice came, the day that would forever change him.

He'd found an escape from the life of a farmer. God laid a college scholarship in front of him and said, "Go find your future." Leo's spirits soared. He could've been anything he wanted to be.

And then God, in the form of Uncle Sam, pulled the rug out from under him, threw him completely off balance. He was so naïve, so sure of everything, and yet so wrong about it all.

Being deployed to the war front was terrifying at first, but it gave him a chance to prove himself. He saw his future once again, held to his mantra that hard work and integrity were the pathway to success.

Then Richards went down. A man who had once been his friend betrayed him. He'd seen the war from the other side, the destruction of innocents, the Japanese soldiers' belief in the rightness of their cause.

Who was right? Were there any winners in war?

Leo closed the box with Ryan's belongings and taped it shut. He stood, surprised to feel his legs wobble beneath him, sighed, and suppressed another tear.

The truck idled across the compound, waiting for this one last parcel before it headed out. Leo's legs felt leaden as he trudged the hundred yards to where it waited.

Tommy Ryan—the man Leo looked up to, the man who was a living example of hard work and integrity—was gone. Killed by a random missile that didn't care how right or virtuous he was. Leo was not the kind to give up, but right now, he struggled to see the point of living. Any other time, he might have prayed to God for guidance, but he wasn't sure anymore whose side God was on.

Leo hoisted the box into the back of the supply truck and watched it disappear, along with the last remnants of Lieutenant Ryan, into the dust.

伝えよう
永遠に続くは
愛だけよ

Tsutaeyou
Towa ni tsuduku wa
Ai dake yo

Of this I am sure—
Love lasts when all else is gone
Give love while you may.

CHAPTER 50

NEAR ANTIPOLO, LUZON—JULY 1945

The full moon shone through the gray evening mist, surrounded by a faintly colored ring. Tadashi and Kaito sat at the mouth of the cave Kaito had found. Dry and sheltered, they could stay there until Tadashi's leg had healed.

"Do you see the halo?" Tadashi pointed toward the moon. "My grandmother called it an omen of misfortune."

Kaito laughed, gently patting Tadashi's injured leg.

"What misfortunes haven't found us already, brother?" Kaito was startled by his own laughter. It reminded him of the day he was so low he wanted to die. But food in his belly and Tadashi's faith in him had changed that. They would make it home—together.

Tadashi shook his head. "Do not laugh at omens, Kaito. You are tempting the spirits."

"And you are far too serious, Nii-chan."

By moonset, the sky was clear and dotted with starlight. Kaito stood and stretched his legs. "It's safe for me to go look for food," he said. "Will you go inside?"

Tadashi peered into the darkened cave. "I think I will stay here. The night sounds inspire me, and there is just enough light to write."

Kaito placed Tadashi's rifle on his lap. "Stay alert, Nii-chan."

"Stay safe, Kai-chan" Tadashi pulled his diary from his pack and opened it.

"I won't be long," said Kaito.

He emerged from the rocks and looked back. He could no longer see Tadashi in the dimness—he would be safe.

In the days since Kaito moved them to the cave, they'd seen several small squads of American soldiers scouring the area. When it was daylight, Kaito disguised the cave entrance with brush. He and Tadashi took turns sleeping until dusk, when the Americans would have returned to their outposts. As soon as darkness came, they moved the brush away.

Their first few meals at the cave were giant fruit bats. Weighing as much as two pounds each, they were a hearty meal. But the meals ended abruptly when the bats got wise and abandoned the cave.

Now Kaito went out nightly in search of food. He often came back emptyhanded.

Tadashi listened to the sounds of the night and began a letter to Sachiko. Although he couldn't mail it to her, they would share his words when he returned. He kept his ears tuned for any unusual noises and thought of the sounds of home. Sachiko would be sleeping soundly now, but perhaps earlier, she too had sat and listened to the buzzing cicadas and howling wolves, each singing their own unique song.

Dearest Sachiko,

The night is cloudy and cool, but I am warmed by thoughts of holding you in my arms. I will come home soon, dear wife, and I promise I will never again leave your side. So much has been lost here, and I am afraid I have become a hardened and cynical man, but I dream of the day I can cover your face with a thousand kisses, the day I can hold my son in my arms.

Stay strong, my love. Do not give up hope. I will come home.

The sound of something crashing through the brush made Tadashi drop his pencil and grab up his rifle. He crept to safety and peered out into the darkness. He recognized the silhouette loping across the field—in a few seconds, Kaito scurried into the cave.

"Enemy." Kaito gasped for air as he pulled the brush across the opening. "Night patrol."

They sat silently, not daring to move. They listened for voices, watched for movement. The eastern horizon was gray with the approaching dawn when they at last relaxed.

"I think it is safe," said Tadashi. "You sleep, and I will watch awhile longer."

The sun was high and scorching when Kaito woke and Tadashi lay down, but inside the cave it was cool, and Tadashi was soon asleep. He dreamed of the thousand kisses he would give his wife, and when he smiled in his sleep, Kaito smiled too.

In his dream, Sachiko gently skimmed her fingers on his thigh. He woke with a start to find Kaito's hand on his leg.

"I am sorry to wake you," Kaito said. "I was trying to check your dressing."

Tadashi sat up and extended his leg. Kaito had moved most of the brush from the cave's entrance. It was nearly sunset. There was still plenty of light for Kaito to assess his wounded thigh.

"You were having a delightful dream." Kaito grinned as he removed the soiled dressing that covered Tadashi's wound.

"I was dreaming of home," Tadashi said.

"You were dreaming of your lovely wife."

Tadashi blushed. "I was dreaming of my lovely wife," he admitted, "and of how we will greet one another."

"So first you will plant your seed." Kaito winked. "And then what?"

"Are you jealous?" Tadashi raised an eyebrow. "Perhaps you wish for a beautiful geisha to greet you?"

Kaito gazed into the distance. "I would like a wife someday. But the first thing I will do is find my parents. I pray they are still alive." He moved his attention back to Tadashi's wound. "Your leg is healing nicely," he said. "I think we can leave this cave soon."

"Happy news indeed." Tadashi looked at the darkly scabbed wound. He would have a story to tell his son of how he fought off an enemy, but he would not tell him they were Japanese cannibals.

The sky was starless two nights later when Tadashi and Kaito made their plans. They would travel at night, only a few hours at first, until Tadashi's leg was stronger.

"Tonight, I will scout the trail," Kaito said, shouldering his rifle. "If it is clear, we can leave tomorrow at dark.

"Stay alert, Nii-chan," he said as he headed out. It had become their ritual.

"Stay safe, Kai-chan."

Kaito moved silently on the northward trail. He shut out the noise of the wildlife, listening for human sounds. It wouldn't be long before he would walk trails back home. He would find a good wife and start a family, just like Tadashi. He said a silent prayer to the spirits that he might find the same love Tadashi had.

"Don't move."

To Kaito's ears, the words were senseless, but the rifle pointed at him told him all he needed to know. Kaito's stomach sickened. For one minute, he had dared to dream of home—his foolishness had walked him into the enemy's arms.

He froze, extended his arms out slightly. The Americans were still a short distance away, close enough to kill him but too far away to lay hands on him. Three against one. Kaito's mind reeled with possibilities. He could try to defend himself and die right here, or he could surrender and possibly live.

He couldn't surrender.

"Banzai!"

Tadashi jumped at the sound of Kaito's voice. Two shots rang out, followed by shouting—Americans.

Tadashi sprang to his feet, wincing at the sudden pressure on his wound. Grabbing his rifle, he rushed toward the voices. His heart pounded, and his weakened legs ached. As he ran, he made out the silhouettes of the soldiers, one bent to his knees.

Tadashi ducked behind a tree and took aim. Three quick shots, three dead Americans. He dropped to his belly and crawled to where Kaito lay, blood pumping from his midsection.

"Kai-chan." Tadashi cradled Kaito's head in his lap, his eyes filled with tears. "You cannot die."

Kaito smiled weakly. "But I am dying all the same." He grimaced in pain and looked at Tadashi. "You remember your promise?"

Tadashi nodded then shook his head. "I can't."

"Yes, you can, Nii-chan. We are brothers." Kaito looked up at Tadashi. He spoke in a whisper, his voice trembled. "Tell my father I died with honor."

He clutched Kaito. There was no pulse in Kaito's neck, no beating in his heart. His chest was still, his lips a darkening blue.

Tadashi lay across Kaito's lifeless body and sobbed.

CHAPTER 51

NEAR ANTIPOLO—JULY 1945

"Here's to your new squad leader." Dooley lifted his cup to Webster. "I earned it." He brought the cup to his lips, tipped his head back, and drained it in one long drink. He'd invited Webster to his tent to celebrate, and, although Webster didn't feel much like a celebration, he felt like he couldn't say no.

"Now that's some good hooch." Dooley slammed his cup on the table, refilled it, and offered the bottle to Webster.

Webster waved it away, shook his head. His mind was muddled enough without liquor making it worse. When Dooley had first talked to him about Sergeant Baldwin, Webster was only supposed to watch the Sarge and report back to Dooley—nothing more. How could he have known it would turn into a court-martial? Of course, he wanted to move up, be Dooley's assistant, but not at the cost of another man's freedom. It seemed to him Dooley was getting just a little too giddy at Sergeant Baldwin's misfortune.

Webster shifted uncomfortably. "You really think the Sarge deserves a court-martial?"

"Hey, that's not my decision" Dooley shrugged. "I'm just glad he'll be outta my way." He emptied his cup, lifted the bottle to his mouth, and downed the last few drops.

Webster stared at the ground. The more Dooley bragged, the more Webster questioned his motives. The tent suddenly felt hot, the air heavy. All he wanted was to get out of there, go back to his own tent, and try to forget about it.

"'Nother dead soldier," Dooley said, tossing the empty bottle aside. He stood and staggered across the tent to what remained of his stash, opened the last bottle of hooch, and chugged. He wiped his hand across his mouth, lurched toward his chair, and fell into it. "I am a master of deception, even if I do say so myself."

Webster lifted his head, his eyes widened. What had Dooley said?

"Deception?" He scowled at Dooley. "Who you lyin' to?"

"You know." Dooley surreptitiously shifted his eyes right then left, as if someone else might be within earshot. He leaned toward Webster and whispered, "You and me, we pulled a fast one on the brass."

"We did?" Webster didn't like the way this conversation was going. He hadn't pulled a fast one on anybody.

"Yup. You and me." Dooley waved his bottle in the air. "And that day Richards blew himself to kingdom come was our finest moment."

Webster felt his belly tighten. Was Dooley taking credit for Richards's death? And if it was true, what did that make him? He thought about the day Richards died, remembered Dooley whispering something in his ear just before he went bonkers.

"Sarge?" Webster's voice was low, almost a whisper. He wasn't sure he wanted to know, but he had to ask. "What did you say to Richards that day?"

"That was my coop dee grace," Dooley took another hit on the bottle of hooch and chuckled. "I told 'im that dead bitch looked like his mama."

Webster's jaw dropped, and his stomach clenched. "Why'd you do that for?"

"Aww, he was goin' over the edge anyways. I was just givin' him a little nudge." Dooley snorted. "I'm a goddamned genius." He took one last pull of liquor, capped the bottle, and stuck it under his cot. "Gotta take a piss." Dooley pushed up from his chair. "Then I'm hittin' the hay." As he staggered out the door, he muttered, "Goddamn genius."

As soon as Nelson was gone, Webster hurried toward his own tent. He felt like he was going to puke. How could he have been so stupid? Dooley was a southern boy just like him, and southern boys had to stick together, didn't they? He'd made Webster feel important, and Webster believed everything Dooley told him.

Webster peeled off his fatigues and crawled into his cot. How had everything got so screwed up? And what could he do about it now? It wasn't right, what Dooley did. Sergeant Baldwin was going to go down for something that was never his fault. Should he tell Major Grissom about Dooley? But then he'd have to admit that he was spying on Baldwin and Richards, and that would make him guilty too, wouldn't it? Would he get busted for it? But the major hadn't delivered his verdict yet. Maybe he'd find Leo innocent of the charges. And if that happened, everything would go back to normal, and nobody would ever know what Dooley had done.

Webster relaxed, reassured that he was just overreacting. He looked at his watch—0200 hours—he still had time to get some decent rest. He closed his eyes, tried to will himself to sleep.

What if the verdict was guilty?

As the thought hit him, he jerked up. He couldn't just let an innocent man go to prison. He had to tell Grissom the truth, no matter what happened to him.

"I have something to say about Sergeant Baldwin's trial." Private Webster nervously stood in front of Major Grissom two hours before time to deliver the verdict.

"The trial's over, soldier. It's a little late to add anything." Grissom scowled at the report he'd been working on, impatient at the interruption.

"Understood, sir, uh, your honor, uh Major, sir." Webster wiped his palms on his pants. "But this is really important."

"What is it then?" the major put down his pen, rubbed the tension from his neck, and glared at Webster.

"Well, sir." Webster swallowed hard. "I got some new information."

"Spit it out, soldier," Grissom snapped. "I've got better things to do than watch you fidget."

"The thing is..." Webster hesitated. "The thing is, Sergeant Baldwin ain't responsible for Private Richards's death."

There—he'd said it.

Grissom crossed his arms and raised an eyebrow. "And how do you know this, Private Webster?"

"Doo—Sergeant Nelson—told me." Webster's heart pounded. He'd catch hell from Dooley.

"Go on." Grissom gestured impatiently.

Webster took a deep breath and told his story.

When he'd finished, the major looked at him, his lips pressed tight. "That's a serious charge you're making. Can you prove it?"

Webster looked at his boots. He wiped his palms again and looked at Major Grissom. "No, sir, I can't. There wasn't nobody there last night but me and Sergeant Nelson."

"And, of course, he'll call you a liar?"

"Yeah." Webster dropped his head then stiffened to attention. "But, Major Grissom, sir, I'll swear to it on my mama's grave."

Grissom sat quietly for a moment then straightened in his chair. "Thank you, soldier," he said. "I'll take this into consideration."

"Sir?" Webster had one more thing to get off his chest. "Sergeant Nelson promised I could be his assistant when he got made squad leader."

"You know he couldn't do that, don't you?" Grissom scowled. "You don't have the rank."

Webster pursed his lips, his face reddened with anger. "No, sir, I didn't know."

He was still trembling as he left the judge's office, in a hurry to get back to his tent before anyone saw him. How could he have been so stupid? He'd let Dooley hoodwink him just because he was a fellow southerner, just because he couldn't believe anyone would be that mean. It could cost

Sergeant Baldwin his freedom—and it would be all Webster's fault. He rounded the corner of the mess tent and ran smack into Dooley.

"Where the fuck you been?" Dooley crossed his arms tightly against his chest.

Webster's cheeks blushed a deep red. "Uh, I was... I mean, I had a meeting."

Dooley grabbed Webster's shoulder and pulled him close. "With who?"

"Uh, with..." Webster stared at the ground. "With Major Grissom. He wanted to ask me some questions. You know."

"About what?" Dooley snarled and tightened his grip.

Stay calm, Webster thought. He fought to keep his face from giving away the guilt he felt. "About the trial, what else?"

"Then why're you so fuckin' jumpy?" Dooley leaned in, grabbed Webster's chin hard, and pulled until he and Webster were nose to nose. "You didn't rat me out, did you?"

"Don't wanna talk no more about it." Webster tried to pull away. "Now lemme go."

Dooley let go of Webster's chin and grabbed him by the shoulders. "You slimy little bastard." His grip tightened. "You told him."

"Leave me go, Dooley." Webster twisted in Dooley's grip. "You lied to me. You told me it was Sergeant Baldwin's fault Richards got killed."

"So what?" Dooley sneered. "I wasn't wrong. Richards needed to go home, and I needed to be squad leader."

"I can't believe you did that to Sarge." Webster was nearly in tears. He'd looked up to Dooley, thought Dooley cared about him.

Dooley's face reddened, and his body shook as if he were a volcano about to erupt. He squeezed Webster's shoulders harder.

"Stop it, Dooley. You're hurtin' me." Webster twisted and pulled frantically.

"I'll do more than that, you fuckin' hillbilly." Dooley pushed Webster to the ground.

Susannah Willey

"If I go down, I'm takin' you with me."
He aimed an imaginary rifle at Webster and stalked off.

CHAPTER 52

ANTIPOLO, LUZON—JULY 1945

At 0900 hours, the entire camp congregated to hear Major Grissom's verdict. Leo sat alone. He hadn't felt this vulnerable since the submarine attack.

If only Ryan were here, I'd be okay.

Major Grissom entered the room, his face not giving a clue to what he'd decided. "This morning, crucial evidence was brought to my attention," he said. "I want this evidence to be an official part of the record, and therefore am re-calling a witness."

Leo's heart pounded. Hadn't everything already been said? What didn't he already know about? There was a whisper throughout the crowd as everyone looked around, wondering who would be called.

"Private Webster," Grissom announced.

Webster approached the witness table, his head bowed as if he wished he could hide.

When he was seated, Grissom began. "Private Webster, I'd like you to share what you told me earlier this morning."

"Yes, sir." Webster squirmed in his seat. "Sergeant Baldwin wasn't responsible for Private Richards's death." He looked at where Dooley sat glaring at him, looked away, and continued. "Sergeant Nelson was."

Dooley jumped from his seat. "That's a goddamned lie!" He pointed a finger at Webster. "That fuckin' little cocksucker's got it in for me, and he's lyin' like a fuckin' bearskin rug."

A sentry appeared next to Dooley, ready to restrain him.

"Sit down, Sergeant," Grissom growled. "You'll have your turn." He turned to Webster. "Private, please continue."

Webster's face was pale, his eyes wide. He took a deep breath and recounted what had happened between him and Dooley. Once Webster got started, the words came in a rush.

Dooley jumped out of his seat and into the aisle. "He's lyin', Major." Dooley took a step forward. The sentry roughly grabbed Dooley's arms, restraining him. "He's nothing but a lyin' son of a bitch."

"Remove Sergeant Nelson from the room," Grissom ordered. He pointed at Dooley. "You need to shut up and go with the corporal."

"Hell, no." Dooley struggled against the sentry's grip. "I gotta right to hear what this lyin' sack of shit is sayin' about me."

"You're not on trial—yet," Grissom said. "You've got no rights until then."

Everyone's attention was on Dooley as he fought and cursed at the two burly sentries who hauled him out of the room. The audience's low murmur became a buzz of voices, growing louder as one voice out-shouted another to be heard.

When Major Grissom ordered quiet, the voices went silent. All eyes returned to the major, all ears listened for what he would say.

"Sergeant Baldwin," he said, giving Leo a slight nod.

"Yes, sir," Leo stood at attention.

"Given this recent evidence, I am ordering all charges against you be dismissed."

"Thank you, sir." Leo didn't move a muscle, but inside, he felt lighter than he had in months.

Leo sat next to Captain Mickelson at breakfast the next morning. He pushed scrambled eggs around his plate, stirred them as if that might improve the taste. "What's going to happen to Sergeant Nelson, sir?"

"They sent him down to HQ last night," Mickelson said. "Right now, he's in the brig for disorderly conduct and insubordination, but there will be formal charges."

"Do you know what the charges will be?"

"Besides the misconduct charges, he'll probably be charged with involuntary manslaughter." He took a drink of his coffee and winced at its bitterness.

"Will he get time for that?"

Mickelson stared at his coffee cup for a moment then set it on the table. "Hard to say, Sergeant. Most likely, he'll get a dishonorable discharge. The maximum sentence is confinement for ten years."

Leo nodded. He really didn't care about what happened to Dooley. Whatever justice the army imposed was good enough for Leo. He was just grateful he'd never have to see the man again.

When he returned to his tent, his knees went weak. He dropped onto his cot and released the emotions he'd withheld for so long: His grief at losing Richards, at losing Ryan, his anger and disbelief at Dooley's betrayal—most of all, his relief that he hadn't caused Richard's death after all.

"Sarge?" Russo spoke from outside Leo's tent.

Leo took a deep breath, stood, straightened his uniform, and went outside. "What is it Corporal?"

Russo looked at his feet, kicking bits of stone and dust. "What I said at the trial..." He looked up at Leo. "I just want you to understand—"

Leo held up his hand. "You told what you saw, Corporal. You were being honest. I understand that."

"I didn't want to believe it, Sarge." Russo's voice wavered. "I know you would never purposely put us in harm's way."

Leo nodded, his face emotionless. "Better get a move on, soldier. Recon patrol in ten minutes."

As Russo walked away, Leo returned to his tent. What was he supposed to say? That's okay? No big deal?

Neither was the truth.

Webster took one last look around his tent as he grabbed his gear and prepared to leave. He was grateful that most of the platoon was out on a training maneuver. They had avoided him ever since he'd testified, gave him an angry glare, and made a wide circle around him if they saw him coming.

He didn't blame them. He might have been the one who'd saved Leo in the end, but he was also responsible for the charges in the first place. He'd gotten off lucky with just a transfer.

The rumble of the jeep coming into the compound shook Webster from his thoughts. There was one more thing he needed to do before he left.

Leo stared at the tiny silver cross, remembering the day Private Richards had given it to him.

"I wore this on my cowboy hat. It's supposed to be good luck," Richards had said as he'd handed it to Leo. The mop-up mission in Santa Inez was scheduled for the next day.

Leo held back. "I've got a good luck charm. Don't you want to keep it for yourself?"

Richards shrugged. "I dunno. I just got a feeling I oughta give it to you." He nervously rolled the cross in his hand. "I want you to remember me."

"Why? You going somewhere?" Leo didn't like where this conversation was heading. If he accepted the gift, was he putting fate into motion?

Richards stared into the distance, his eyes bright with tears. "Only the good Lord knows that, Sarge." He took Leo's hand and placed the cross inside. "Keep it safe, will you?"

The next day, Richards was dead. Did he intend to die at Santa Inez, or was it just a premonition? Leo closed his eyes, seeing what remained of Richards after the explosion. It was one image he was sure would never leave him.

"Sergeant?" Webster entered Leo's tent. "Jeep's here," he said. "I'll be leaving now." Wearing his dress uniform, he had removed his hat and nervously fiddled with it. "Uh, Sarge?"

Leo's stomach clenched. He'd hoped he wouldn't have to deal with Webster again.

"What is it, Private?" It wasn't that he really blamed the boy. Nelson's forceful personality could sway just about anybody.

"I wanted to tell you..." Webster's voice was a whisper. He kept his head down, scuffed his just-shined shoes on the dirt floor. "I wanted to say I'm sorry."

Leo stared at Richards's cross. He should tell Webster he was forgiven. He wanted to tell him. The words stuck in his throat like a lump of oatmeal that refused to go down.

The jeep's horn sounded from across the compound.

"I gotta go, Sarge." Webster raised his head and turned to leave.

Say something. Richards's cross dug into Leo's clenched fist. His innocent face flashed in Leo's mind, quickly replaced by the image of his broken body. Leo fought back tears. *Say something!*

The canvas tent flap rustled against Webster's uniform, thumping softly as it closed behind him. A few seconds later, the jeep whined as its driver put it in gear and drove away.

Susannah Willey

悪溢れ
毒す思いは
詩を汚す

Aku afure
Dokusu omoi wa
Shi o kegasu

A world filled with evil
Poisons my thoughts, fills my dreams.
How can I write verse?

CHAPTER 53

SOMEWHERE IN LUZON—LATE JULY 1945

The ghostly half-light of daybreak filtered through the rubber trees. Thick morning mist clouded the landscape. Tadashi sat in front of their cave, his friend's lifeless body stretched out beside him. He gently removed the one boot Kaito wore and put it on his own bare foot. He removed what remained in Kaito's pack and tucked it in his, emptied all the bullets from Kaito's rifle except for one, and placed the rifle in Kaito's hands.

There were no tears left to shed. Tadashi felt no emotion, had no goal beyond honoring his brother. He didn't care what happened after that.

If I die, eat my flesh and keep fighting. Kaito's words would not leave his head; his friend had made him promise.

Tadashi took out his bayonet. He laid the sharp edge against Kaito's thigh, drew the blade deep into Kaito's flesh. There was no reaction from the body, although Tadashi half expected Kaito to jerk and yell. Without thinking, he looked at Kaito's face. He saw not the blue emaciated face of a dead man, but the round, laughing cheeks of his Kai-chan on the day they first met.

"Move over, farm boy." The shout had caught Tadashi's attention as he approached the schoolyard. At eleven years old, this would be his last year of schooling; children of farmers were rarely allowed to move to the next level.

In the queue ahead, Tadashi recognized Haru, one of his classmates, towering over a much younger child sprawled on the ground. A group of the older boys formed around them as the young boy struggled to his feet.

"Show the baby who's the boss," one boy shouted.

Haru stepped toward the youngster, his fists ready to fight. "You want your spot back, baby?"

The circle of boys tightened around him as he grabbed the boy's shirt.

"Who said you could touch my little brother?" Tadashi pushed through the crowd and confronted Haru.

Haru glared at Tadashi. "You don't have any brothers."

"I do now," Tadashi said, putting his arm around the young boy. "My name is Tadashi," he whispered. "We are brothers now."

The young boy beamed, and his cheeks puffed up like a chipmunk. "Thank you, brother. My name is Kaito."

They had been together ever since. Kaito had been there when Tadashi and Sachiko married. He'd been the first to congratulate Tadashi on the birth of his son. Together, they'd reported for military duty, clung to one another in the hold of their transport, praying for the typhoon to pass. They'd survived the enemy attack at the POW camp and the napalm bombs at Bigti. It was Kaito who'd saved him from being someone's dinner, who'd protected him until Tadashi was healed enough to travel.

And now he was gone.

Tears streamed uncontrollably down Tadashi's face. He looked at Kaito's lifeless body, at the exposed meat where he'd cut Kaito's leg.

He couldn't do it. He didn't care what he'd promised.

But he hadn't eaten in nearly two weeks. He was once again weak from hunger, spent from emotion and exhaustion.

You promised, Kaito's voice admonished him.

Tadashi removed his shirt and covered Kaito's face. He closed his eyes, imagined it was a carabao he carved instead of his friend, and cut a small bit of stringy muscle from the leg. Trembling violently, he put the meat in his mouth. His stomach growled with hunger and clenched with revulsion. He steeled himself and swallowed. His stomach heaved and purged itself. The bit of meat fell to the ground.

You promised.

Tadashi picked up the bit, swallowed it once again. This time, it stayed down. He cut off another small piece, swallowed it whole. Raw meat for the raw ache in his heart.

When the leg was bare to the bone, he stopped.

Enough. He carried Kaito's soul with his own now. He held his brother's flesh within his own. It was enough.

His soul ached as he built a small fire and waited for the heat to build. He didn't care if the fire attracted unwanted attention—he would give his brother a proper cremation, a hero's send-off.

When the fire pit glowed with blue-hot coals, he added more wood and gently placed Tadashi's body on the fire. He clutched his magatama, prayed to his uncle's spirit to protect Kaito in the afterlife.

He fiercely guarded the roasting body from scavengers until it was nothing but ashes. Then he collected a handful of the still warm remains and lovingly placed them in Kaito's kit, along with the hair and nail clippings he'd cut earlier. He would return them to Kaito's family so they could be interred at Yasukuni—the soldiers' shrine—in honor of Kaito's dedication to the emperor. Finally, he wrote a letter to Kaito's parents, telling them about their son's heroism and honorable death.

That night, nightmares controlled Tadashi's sleep. Kaito lay in the dirt, his blood pouring from his body. Tadashi begged him not to die, but Kaito was already gone. In his dream, Tadashi's body changed to that of a wild animal. He held down Kaito's body with his hairy paws, opened his massive jaws, sank razor-sharp teeth into Kaito's body, tore a chunk of flesh from his friend's leg, and chewed it hungrily. He took another chunk. And another. A growl caught his attention. He looked up as a snarling mob of emaciated soldiers charged to take Kaito's body from him.

Tadashi jerked awake to the sound of a buzzing plane. It was low, its engines loud. He crept to the edge of the cave and peered at the sky: American. He scrambled back into the cave, covered it with brush, and crawled as far back as he could go. He removed Kaito's remains from his pack and clutched the tin kit to his chest. He might yet die with his friend.

Although the plane's sound was muffled inside the cave, at last, he heard it fade in the distance. He waited until he was certain it wouldn't return. When he left the cave and carefully slipped to the edge of the trees, he saw that the open field was littered with bits of paper. He crawled to the nearest one, grabbed it, and hurried back to his hiding place.

The white sheet of paper was striped with red and blue in one corner. The left side contained a message in English, the right side was written in Japanese.

"Kōsan," the text read. *Surrender.*

Never, thought Tadashi. But he read the message.

Your situation is definitely hopeless. This is not your fault, just your fate. It is Heaven's gift that your life has been spared. You will still be able to serve your country for a long time if you accept the inevitable today. In order to avoid misunderstanding, come over to us unarmed with your hands up today. You may come over individually, in small groups, or in large numbers. You will not be humiliated, and it will not be long before you are taken to an interpreter who can speak your language.

Once again, the tears flowed as he tucked the leaflet inside his pack. Why shouldn't he surrender? He had given his country everything he could. They had given him nothing. To hell with honor—it was an empty word. The only thing that mattered anymore was his family, and he would return to them any way he could.

He sat on the ground and retrieved the leaflet, holding it against his chest as if he were meeting an American soldier.

"Kōsan." It startled him to hear his own voice, but he said it again, practicing his surrender. He stood, raised his hands in the air. "Kōsan."

He would stay still and wait for them to take him. It was the only chance he had to see his wife and child again.

But what if Sachiko rejected him? What if his village branded him a coward? He could never live with the shame. It would be better to choose death rather than humiliate his family with the unforgiveable disgrace of surrender.

Tadashi thought of Kaito, his plea that Tadashi live to return home to his wife and child. Had he eaten Kaito's flesh for nothing?

Late that night, Tadashi took out his diary. He lifted his pencil to the page and wrote his last letter to his love.

Dearest Sachiko,

The happy dream is over. When I think of your future, it tears at my heart. Be strong. Honor the kami. Teach our son dignity and grace.

I will love you forever.

Tadashi

There would be no surrender. With tears in his eyes and prayers to the kami and his loved ones, Tadashi stood to confront his fate.

Susannah Willey

CLOSE COMBAT

We met upon a narrow jungle trace.
He aimed his gun at me, I aimed at him.
There in the silence of the jungle dim
One shot rang out;

CHAPTER 54

ANTIPOLO, LUZON—AUGUST 1945

It was almost like being back at Camp Hood. Leo was once again training recruits: eighteen- and nineteen-year-old kids fresh out of high school and Basic Training. Back in Texas, he was sure he knew what those kids were in for. Now he understood no one could know, and there was no way you could prepare raw recruits for what awaited them on the front lines. Although he was only a few years older than them, the only thing they had in common were pimples.

Much of Antipolo was in ruins after the battle in June that finally liberated the Filipinos from Japanese occupation. It had been a bloody and devastating conflict, and many innocent villagers were tortured and killed. But the barrio was slowly recovering. Those families who remained were rebuilding, erecting simple thatch-roofed huts on plots surrounded by the debris of ruined homes. Even a few concrete buildings were going up. The army garrison was a typical village of its own, with prefabricated Quonset huts and flat, open training grounds.

After mornings with the recruits, most of his afternoons involved mop-up and reconnaissance. He was tired of beating the bushes for half-starved Japs. The surrender of the Philippines had been official for weeks, but many of the enemy either hadn't gotten the message or weren't listening. It was boring work, and although Leo wasn't exactly complaining, he was eager to finish his time in the army and go home.

Leo mentally ticked through the list of his Luzon squad: Richards and Ryan dead, Dooley dishonorably discharged,

Webster moved to a different unit. Myoga was one of the lucky ones—he'd earned enough points and received his honorable discharge last month. They had recently released his family from the internment camp at Manzanar, and together, they would return to discover what remained of their home and their grocery store. Grayson, Russo, and Filipowski were still with Leo.

He'd made the mistake of letting himself get close to his men once, and he was determined never to do it again. As far as the recruits went, Leo was their drill sergeant, the man who would train them ruthlessly and send them into battle. Their happiness was not his concern.

Leo watched the recruits practicing hand-to-hand combat. He noticed one young man halfheartedly sparring with his opponent. This guy needed a wake-up call. Leo maneuvered behind him, watched him for a few moments, pulled out his pistol, and held it against the soldier's back.

"You're dead, private," Leo said.

The young soldier froze then turned to face Leo. "What'd you do that for, Sarge?" He shrugged, as if the interruption annoyed him. "I was fighting Jonesy like you said."

"If that's the best you can do, soldier, then you deserve to die. You think the Japs are going to look at you fighting some other guy and say, 'Oh, never mind, he's busy'? No matter what happens in front of you, you have to be aware of your surroundings every second. You have to fight like your life depends on it—because it does. And you *never* forget about the guy behind you just waiting to shoot you in the back."

Leo snorted his disgust, holstered his pistol, and stalked away.

"Filipowski, Grayson, Russo, you're with me." Leo nodded to all three of them as he outlined the duties for the day. There had been a report of a Japanese encampment in a gully several miles from the garrison. The entire platoon was going out. They'd establish a base camp and spread out in small groups to recon the area.

As the men readied themselves for patrol, Leo prepared himself for another unsuccessful day. Of course, they had to investigate, but he was certain that once again they'd be chasing the wind.

The encampment was where intel had reported. It was no surprise that it was now abandoned. Leo hoped that meant the Japs had moved on and out of his territory.

"Back to camp." Leo waved his hand in a forward motion. "Let's find out what other dead ends they've got for us to follow."

As they headed back to the outpost, Leo took the point. He knew this trail by heart, knew they'd just come down it and found it empty. He relaxed his arms, dropped his rifle to his side, and let his thoughts wander.

It had been nearly three years since he'd boarded the bus to Fort Niagara. Until then, his life on the farm had been the only world he knew. He understood the rules, the routines, the way life was supposed to be. He saw clearly now that hard work and success didn't always get you what you want. As much as he had once believed that a college degree and maybe even a career in writing was his future, he was now convinced that there was no point in chasing that dream.

Leo sighed and pushed away the pressure of regret. When this war was over—if he survived it—he would go home where he belonged, take up the plow, and accept his fate.

CHAPTER 55

ANTIPOLO, LUZON—AUGUST 1945

Tadashi stumbled along the northern trail, dragging his wounded leg. He was drenched in sweat and weak from his long day of traveling. He hadn't waited for nightfall, instead starting out as soon as he made his decision. He had many miles to cross before he would find his comrades in the north—there was no time to stop for sleep.

When he came to a small stream, he paused, knelt beside it, and filled his canteen. He lifted it to his lips and guzzled. The cool, sweet water soothed his parched throat and satisfied his empty stomach. He filled the canteen again and sipped its contents this time, feeling the liquid run down his throat and into his belly.

The third time he filled the canteen, he capped it tightly and slung it across his shoulder. With effort, he stood and scanned the trail in both directions. He wanted so badly to stop, to rest his aching leg.

But he couldn't. He had to get north. Had to get home. Had to hold his wife and son in his arms.

He pictured his family. His faded memory produced only shadows, but he filled in the rest with his imagination. Sachiko in the fine silk kimono he would buy for her, her long dark hair arranged on top of her head and held with ornate combs. Next to her stood Ichiro, nearly four years old now. In his imagination, Ichiro resembled his mother—the porcelain skin, the deep, dark eyes. He wore the jade magatama that had belonged to Tadashi's venerated uncle.

Tadashi clutched the magatama and nodded. Yes. His son would have the keepsake when Tadashi came home. He vowed to keep these images in his mind as he traveled north. They would be his beacon.

He started out again. This time, his steps were firm and determined.

It was late in the day when he finally gave in to exhaustion. His wound was bleeding, his leg so weak it collapsed every few steps. Ahead of him, the trail became steep and rocky as it wound up and into the mountains. He could not go on until he regained the strength to climb.

Tadashi unwrapped his senninbari, the thousand-stitch good luck belt, from his waist. Before now, he'd stubbornly refused to remove it, unwilling to risk negating its luck. But blood flowed freely from his leg now, and he needed something to bind it with.

The minute he stopped walking, he heard them: American soldiers, too far away to see, but their voices carried on the breeze. He stepped off the trail and crouched in the tall kunai grass.

His mind raced. *I want to live to see my family,* he reminded himself. *I will not surrender, will not confront them unless I have to.* He knew his chances of survival were slim, but surrender was worse than death.

The Americans came closer, their voices louder now, as if they were unconcerned about attack. Tadashi kept his body still, held his breath, and hoped they would pass by without noticing him. The soldiers tramped through the kunai grass, its rough leaves swishing against their uniforms.

They were close. Too close and there was nowhere to hide.

Tadashi had to decide—life or death. Honor or disgrace.

CHAPTER 56

ANTIPOLO, LUZON—AUGUST 1945

"I wonder what sort of gourmet feast they'll have waiting for us back at the outpost," Russo said. It was getting late. It had been a long day, and everyone was ready for chow and sleep.

"Maybe your mom sent lasagna," Filipowski deadpanned.

Russo chuckled.

"Okay, guys, can the chatter," Leo said. "We're not home free yet." But almost. He'd never had lasagna, but any hot meal would be a welcome change. Like Mother's pot roast. His mouth watered as he followed the trail around a bend and came face to face with a Japanese soldier.

獣道
染めゆく我が血
是迄か

Kemonomichi
Someyuku waga chi
Kore made ka

Blood! It is my blood
Staining the jungle pathway.
Is this, then, the end?

CHAPTER 57

ANTIPOLO, LUZON—AUGUST 1945

"Kōsan," Leo shouted as he lifted his rifle.

Tadashi raised his pistol, shoved it at Leo, and fired.

Leo shot once, twice, then leapt behind a rock on the side of the trail.

A torrent of gunshots rang through the air. When the firing stopped, Leo peeked cautiously around the rock to see Filipowski standing over the body of the Japanese soldier.

"You hit, Sarge?" Grayson stood over him.

Was he? Leo felt his uniform. No blood. No pain. How had he escaped what should have been a fatal bullet?

"Nah, I'm good." Leo stood up, brushed the dirt from his trousers, and re-holstered his pistol.

"Was that you, Filipowski?" Leo gestured toward the tommy gun.

Filipowski nodded. "I heard two shots and saw you fall. Figured you were a goner." He gestured down the trail. "You hit the damn Jap, but he was still alive and trying to get away. I took care of that." He held out his gun. "Emptied the whole damn cartridge into that mother-fucking Nip."

Filipowski retrieved the soldier's pistol. "Bad round." He tipped it so Leo could see the bullet was still in the chamber but hadn't gone off then offered the pistol to Leo. "Your lucky day."

Leo shook his head. "That's yours," he said to Filipowski. "You earned it."

Filipowski nodded. "But this is yours."

He removed the defective bullet and handed it to Leo, set the gun's safety, and tucked it in his pocket.

Russo searched the dead soldier's body, retrieved Tadashi's diary and papers, and handed them to Leo. He removed the jade necklace from Tadashi's neck and was slipping it in his pocket when Leo stopped him.

"No." Leo held out his hand. He thought about the papers he'd had Corporal Myoga translate. He'd eventually sent all of that to HQ, but he'd always felt guilty that he didn't return them to the soldier's family. He wrapped the cord around the diary and carefully stowed them in his pack. "This belongs to his family. I'm going to make sure they get them."

That night back in the camp, they went out to the range and fired the rest of the bullets in Tadashi's pistol. Every round went off.

After the rest of his men had bunked down for the night, Leo stayed up to watch the stars. He located the Southern Cross and, moving his eyes across the sky, mentally named the constellations. His confrontation with the Japanese soldier played in his head like a newsreel, looping endlessly across the milliseconds elapsing between life and death.

As his eyes scanned north, he recognized Ursa Major, Ursa Minor, and Draco, the dragon, the familiar constellations he could see from home.

Home. How long now before I can go home?

Although he prayed each night, it had been a long time since he'd had a conversation with God. If ever there was a time for giving thanks, it was now.

Susannah Willey

...he died before my face.
For forty years since then I've wondered why
My rifle fired, his pistol somehow failed,
And still the endless guilt his death entailed
Possesses me, and will until I die.
The world at large might very well have won
Had his gun fired and my gun failed instead.
If he had lived, and I had long been dead,
Who knows what worthy things he might have done?
I bear a guilt that cannot be denied.
I've lived for him; it was for me he died

HIROSHIMA
AUGUST 6, 1945

The awesome power of death, this day uncaged,
Will, like the weak Pandora's box of woes,
Be with the world wherever war is waged,
And dog man's footsteps everywhere he goes.
That it, this day, has claimed ten thousand lives,
And saved, perhaps, a hundred thousand more
Who poise in waiting till the day arrives
When they must strike Japan's unfriendly shore,
Gives little comfort. This atomic blast
Is but the first. There will be more to come
Before the end. The fateful die is cast
And no man yet can calculate the sum
Of death and hate and misery and pain
That was released on Hiroshima's plain.

CHAPTER 58

SHINTOKU, HOKKAIDO PREFECTURE, JAPAN— AUGUST 15, 1945

Sachiko reported for training every Wednesday and Friday morning to prepare for a last defense of the homeland, just like every other able-bodied woman in Japan. While she marched and practiced, little Ichiro played in the dirt. He imagined himself a Japanese soldier shooting down enemy planes, bayoneting enemy soldiers. It pained Sachiko to see him mimic the violence of war. She prayed her son would never have to face the reality of it.

The war had come too close a few weeks ago when American planes bombed the nearby city of Obihiro. The distant sound was like a massive drum, a devil's call to death. Sachiko had clutched Ichiro as they watched the heavy cloud of smoke choke the sky.

After that day, Hokkaido had been left alone, but the bombings on the southern islands were devastating. There was talk of surrender, although no one believed that was possible. People prepared for death. Perhaps they would be crushed by enemy tanks, bitten to death by military dogs. They would take their own lives if necessary, rather than surrender.

"I heard they dropped firebombs in Tokyo," reported one woman at training. "Everything burned. Even the local citizens were on fire as they staggered down the road trying to escape."

"My sister was a nurse in Iwo Jima," another woman said. "She told me of the many injured soldiers there who lost their limbs, some who even lost their faces."

Sachiko listened to the women. She prayed there were no firebombs where Tadashi was, that he still had all of his limbs and all of his face. The last letter she'd received from him had come months ago. He had become a sergeant, holed up with his men deep inside a mountain. Although she knew he tried to hide it, she could tell even then he was losing hope.

Nine days ago, the unimaginable had happened: the city of Hiroshima had been destroyed—reduced to ashes and rubble by a single explosive device. Three days later, Nagasaki was decimated, again by a solitary bomb.

Today was the first day since then that the women had trained. They whispered among themselves. How could one bomb be so powerful that it could destroy an entire city? There were rumors that Japan would surrender, but no one believed it. Surrender was worse than death—they all knew that. When the radio announced that Emperor Hirohito would address the nation at noon that day, the women nodded knowingly.

"He will protect us," they said, "as he always has."

As the hour approached, Sachiko and her companions huddled around the radio. Her heart beat wildly. She prayed the rumors were wrong. Surely, the emperor would never surrender.

At precisely twelve p.m., Hirohito spoke. It was a voice most Japanese had never before heard, a monotone that was emotionless and measured.

"To our good and loyal subjects: After pondering deeply the general trends of the world and the actual conditions obtaining (sic) in our empire today, we have decided to effect a settlement of the present situation..."

The speech was a short four minutes. The word "surrender" was never spoken, nor the word "defeated," but the emperor's intention was clear. When it ended, many of the women wept quietly. There were murmurs of despair, frightened talk of what the enemy would do to them once they took power. Would it be better to take one's own life now rather than to submit to what they could only imagine would be cruel, inhuman revenge?

As the women quieted, gathering their emotions, one of Sachiko's companions shook her head. "I can't believe the emperor has abandoned us."

"I believe he has saved us," another woman said. "Should he have waited for more cities to be burned? More women and children to die? Even the emperor knows when it is hopeless."

A third woman nodded. "We can only pray the Americans will not mistreat us. What else can we do?"

Sachiko didn't know whether to weep in despair or for joy. She thought of Tadashi coming home at last. She would embrace him tightly when he walked in their door, cover his face with a thousand kisses.

There had been too much despair, she decided. She would choose joy.

That evening, she told her son a bedtime story of his father, a brave war hero who loved his family. She described his face, every detail that was etched in her mind.

Ichiro's eyes widened.

"But how will I know him?" he whispered timidly.

She showed him the photograph of their wedding day as she had a hundred times before.

"He will seem a stranger," she said, "but you mustn't fear him." She smiled and took his tiny hand. "When you see him, perhaps you will show him what a strong young man you are becoming. He will be proud of you."

Sachiko kissed her son gently and tucked the covers around him. When he was asleep, she prepared herself for worship and knelt at their small kamidana.

"Dear spirits," she prayed. "Bring my husband home to me."

TOKYO BAY
SEPTEMBER 2, 1945

From shore to shore in this once peaceful bay
Is gathered all the might of the Allies.
A thousand ships, uncounted men this day
Have gathered to receive the victor's prize.
On the Missouri, just beyond our bow,
The great and mighty gather for the rite
Of the surrender. Grim MacArthur's brow
Is furrowed with the strain; his mouth is tight.
This is the goal of all his cares and fears.
For this, some fifty thousand men have died.
The men he led for these five awful years
Surround him now on ships on every side.
God grant that we may never fight again
A war like that which has destroyed Japan.

Susannah Willey

CHAPTER 59

TOKYO, JAPAN—SEPTEMBER 2, 1945

Leo paced the perimeter of the *Lavaca*, enroute to Tokyo Bay. He stepped around the mass of soldiers sleeping shoulder to shoulder on deck. His armpits itched and burned like crazy from the chronic jungle rot. His mind would not let go of the images of his brush with death.

For days after Filipowski killed Leo's Japanese attacker, Leo had paged through the diary. Although he couldn't read the words, he recognized the poetic form of haiku, the triplet of lines, written vertically as was the Japanese custom. He stared at the creased and faded photograph of a young woman and child, perhaps the soldier's wife and son.

A fellow poet. A husband and father. Dead.

Why wasn't it him instead?

Nobody had much cared about Leo's determination to return the soldier's belongings to his family. He didn't trust the motives of the few who volunteered to take the diary and the necklace. They seemed far too interested in souvenirs, and Leo needed to be certain he'd done everything he could to get the items to the soldier's family. At last, Captain Mickelson gained access to the U.S. Army record that identified the soldier as Tadashi Abukara, from the Tokachi district in Hokkaido. Leo carefully packaged the belongings and sent them off in care of the local Hokkaido post, hoping they'd find their way home. He'd included a brief note expressing his sympathy, written with Myoga's help, but no amount of goodwill on his part would make up for what Abukara's wife and child had lost.

It was a clear night onboard ship. Leo gazed at the night sky, naming the constellations as they appeared. When he got to the Southern Cross, directly in front of him, he realized with alarm that the ship had turned south.

He approached the nearest sentry. "What in the heck are we going south for?"

"Typhoons," the soldier replied. "There's a couple of them between here and Tokyo. Orders are to return to Subic Bay until the coast is clear."

Two days later, the *Lavaca* set out for Tokyo once again, this time at flank speed. When they reached Tokyo Bay on the morning of September 2, it was blanketed with ships. One of the few remaining buildings that survived the Allied bombing bore a large cloth banner: "Welcome American Troops." Leo wondered how welcome they really were.

The *Lavaca* had been anchored only a short time when everyone was called on deck and ordered to stand at attention. There was no explanation. The soldiers stood in silence for what seemed like forever.

"At ease, men." The release came from the ship's loudspeaker. "You may stand down."

Leo relaxed and looked at Grayson. "What the heck was that all about?"

Before Grayson could reply, the speaker barked again. "The surrender agreement has just been signed on the *USS Missouri*. This war is officially over."

Cheers erupted from the troops. Hats flew in the air as a formation of Allied planes roared overhead. The soldiers waved and cheered when the pilots dipped their wings in recognition.

Grayson grabbed Leo in an enormous bear hug, lifting him off his feet. "We made it! We're still alive. Can you believe it?"

Each of Leo's remaining men embraced him then embraced each other. Leo could almost see the ghosts of Richards, Lieutenant Ryan, and the comrades he'd lost. They were here in spirit; he was sure of that.

朝日告ぐ
戦の終わり
嬉し泣く

Asahi tsugu
Ikusa no owari
Ureshi naku

Today they told me
The war has come to an end.
My heart weeps for joy

CHAPTER 60

SHINTOKU, HOKKAIDO PREFECTURE, JAPAN— SEPTEMBER 2, 1945

It was a day of mourning. Sachiko watched the newsreel with her friends, watched as Emperor Hirohito signed the formal document of surrender. The great Japanese Empire had fallen.

Thousands of people flocked to the Shinto shrines, offered gifts to the kami, prayed for their protection. Bombing was one thing, but Japan had never before been conquered by the enemy. Many chose death instead.

Would the Americans come to Hokkaido? Sachiko prayed Tadashi would return to her before then. He would know what to do.

Every day, she tended her garden, harvesting the late season vegetables with Ichiro. Today, she moved along the rows of corn, picking the last golden ears. Behind her, Ichiro pulled a basket, now nearly full of ripened corn that would be hung to dry. They would shell some and set it aside for the chickens, and the rest would be ground into meal. As for tonight, their corn would be fresh and roasted.

Sachiko stopped at the end of the corn row.

"Let's rest," she said. She gathered her kimono around her legs and sat on the ground.

"May I go explore?" asked Ichiro, dancing impatiently.

Sachiko smiled. "You may, but stay near the garden."

He scampered away. Her baby was no longer a toddler. Already, he was growing too fast, and soon he would be a young man, ready to make a life of his own. She vowed to cherish the years until then.

She looked up at the sun, its path drifting southward. In a few days, it would be autumn and, soon enough, winter. Ichiro would be four years old. Would his father be there to celebrate with them? She wanted to believe he was still alive, even now finding his way home, but her hope was fading.

Her thoughts shifted to the task at hand. After they finished with the corn, they would harvest the last of the broccoli. The only thing that remained would be the potatoes, and those wouldn't be ready to dig up for another few weeks. Then their root cellar would be filled for the coming winter. There were enough chickens and a few young pigs that would provide enough meat for the two of them.

No, she reminded herself—the *three* of them. Tadashi would be home soon.

"Okaa-san." Ichiro breathed heavily as he raced down the row of corn. "Someone is coming."

Tadashi! Sachiko's heart leapt as she jumped to her feet. She smoothed her windblown hair, straightened her kimono, and brushed the grass away. Ichiro raced down the path toward the village, toward the uniformed soldier who approached. Sachiko followed him, her heart beating wildly, her hands trembling with excitement.

"Hurry." Ichiro beckoned to her. As he got closer to the soldier, he slowed, moving cautiously, until he stopped a few feet away as if he were waiting for the man's permission to approach.

The soldier addressed her son. "Hello, boy."

The voice wasn't familiar, but she wasn't close enough to know for certain.

Ichiro took a few steps closer to the soldier.

"Otou-san?" He spoke so quietly Sachiko could barely hear him.

The man knelt in front of Ichiro, spoke to him, and held out his arms. Ichiro stepped back, shaking his head.

Oh, no. He was afraid. She imagined how hurt Tadashi must feel. She quickened her steps and ran. When the soldier saw her, he stood, and Sachiko knew the truth: it was not Tadashi.

Her legs convulsed, the adrenalin rush of excitement turning to despair. She dropped to her knees, bent her head until it touched the ground, and sobbed.

"It is not my father, Okaa-san." Ichiro crawled into his mother's lap. "But he asks for you. He says he has news."

The soldier reached into his pack and removed a large, square box made of wisteria wood. Sachiko didn't need to read the inscription written in calligraphy on top to know what was inside. It was the traditional means of returning a soldier's remains.

Sachiko shook her head violently at the soldier. She did not want this box. Accepting it would mean accepting her husband was dead.

The soldier waited silently, the box still extended toward Sachiko. At last, she took it, bowing her head in thanks. He bowed respectfully, turned, and walked back the way he came.

After she had tucked Ichiro into his bed that evening, Sachiko carried the box outside and knelt at their small shrine. Her hands trembled as she opened the box. On top was a letter explaining that Tadashi's belongings were being returned to her by the Japanese Army.

There were no ashes, no remains to bury at the soldiers' shrine in Tokyo. Instead, she found what remained of his belongings: the tattered Japanese flag, his sergeant's insignia, his uncle's magatama, and his diary. At the bottom of the box was a small package with Western writing on it, and Kaito's name scrawled next to it in kanji characters.

What would she do with Kaito's belongings? Both his parents were dead now, victims of starvation and old age. She closed her eyes for a moment to gather her emotions then set the package aside. She would deal with that later.

Sachiko unfolded the Japanese flag. It was creased and dirty, the good luck messages faded and unreadable. His senninbari was covered with dried blood, its stitches worn and broken. She rubbed her fingers across the stars stitched on his sergeant's insignia, feeling the weight of responsibility that Tadashi never wanted.

The jade magatama glinted in the sunlight as she raised it to her lips and kissed it gently. She held next to her heart, willing his spirit to meld with hers, then carefully placed it on the shrine where it would sit, an homage to the spirits, until Ichiro was old enough to have it.

That night, she opened his diary. The pages were wrinkled and faded, flecked with mold. She read of his hopes and despairs, the loss of comrades. She read about Inoue's mistreatment and his fiery end, about the cannibal who nearly killed her husband and the American soldiers who killed his best friend. The next night, she read more, the third night the same. Every night, she relived the war he had endured for over three years.

When she reached Tadashi's last letter, she wept uncontrollably. She would do as he asked. She would honor the kami. She would teach their son dignity and grace, tell him that his father was an honorable man. She would cherish this diary and one day pass it on to Ichiro.

Sachiko took a deep breath, wiped her eyes, and turned the page to the last entry, a final poem.

最後の句
賢者は語る
命は詩

Saigo no ku
Kenja wa kataru
Inochi wa shi

A wise man once said
Every life is a haiku
This is my last line.

Susannah Willey

TOKYO

Once lovely jewel of the Orient,
This battered city is a pile of ash,
Of twisted metal, burnt-out buildings, trash.
I pause to wonder where its people went.
Among the ashes, here and there, a shack
Of metal sheets and broken parts of boards
Shows where one person of the displaced hordes
Is starting Tokyo on the long road back.
In some undamaged streets the people roam,
Or wait beside a little sidewalk stand
To offer anything they have at hand
As souvenirs to soldiers far from home.
The Japanese were beaten in the field,
But here their dauntless spirit will not yield.

CHAPTER 61

TATEYAMA, JAPAN—OCTOBER 9, 1945

Dear folks,

I'm enclosing a couple of pictures we took in Antipolo–Luzon–in August. The boys with the flag, sabers, etc. are my squad. We had just been on a four-day patrol on which we got a whole mess of souvenirs–and on which I darn near got myself shot by that Jap pistol the soldier on my left is holding. Fortunately for me, the pistol misfired, and we got the Jap before he had a chance to reload. Be very careful not to lose these pictures. They're the only ones I have of my squad, and I want to keep them. If they reach you, let me know it in your next letter.

Susannah Willey

When the *Lavaca* at last docked at Tateyama, at the southern end of Tokyo Bay, Leo was nervous. Would the Japanese disregard the surrender and start shooting? It was an eerie feeling as they disembarked: no kamikaze planes, no artillery, no banzai attacks. Their regiment was quickly divided into small units and scattered along the eastern shore of Tokyo Bay, from its southernmost end to the Tokyo suburbs. They had no opposition—in fact, the Japanese seemed happy to see them. Their bodies were gaunt, their faces worn and tired. They were sick of war.

> *Still no news on discharges. Today's*
> *paper said that two-year men will be*
> *eligible by March, but I'm hoping that my*
> *fifty points will get me out a little sooner*
> *than that. Naturally, no one knows, and no*
> *one is telling anything except rumors. I'm*
> *just hoping and praying for the best.*
> > *Love to all,*
> > *Leal*

Across Tokyo Bay, Leo could see the skeletal remains of the tall buildings that once dominated the landscape. The Allied bombing raid earlier that year had destroyed much of Tokyo. As many as one hundred thousand people were killed and nearly a million left homeless. Leo had seen postcards of the once beautiful city. What remained was a neighborhood of charred wood and flattened concrete, trees whose trunks were blackened and scarred, whose once green leaves were seared from heat and flames, and a few lone buildings that appeared mostly untouched. Leo couldn't imagine the city in flames, engulfed by a firestorm.

Leo's unit ended up near the naval air base at Kisarazu, assigned to find and destroy Japanese stores of ammunition and war materiel. Leo was promoted to technical sergeant and made sergeant of his platoon.

After six months of constant danger, flying grenades, exploding bombs, and incendiary napalm, he should have been able to finally relax. But the war came with him, entrenched in his brain like a relentless enemy. They'd been in Tokyo for two months now, but the bang of a backfiring engine or the roar of a plane overhead still sent Leo frantically searching for cover.

He hadn't let himself think too much about how he'd escaped certain death. There were nightmares—scenes he'd never forget—but he'd pushed those to the back of his mind and sealed them away in a vault he hoped never to have to open.

The guilt of losing Richards, the feeling of hopelessness at Ryan's death, the bitterness that surrounded his trial made him want to run away, run back to the drudgery of farming, and pretend none of the past few years had happened. He hadn't written in months—wasn't sure he ever wanted to write again.

It was early December before he began to find any peace at all. The end was in sight, and for the first time in forever, he felt an optimism he'd thought was gone forever. One thing was clear to him: he was getting a second chance, and he needed to make something of it.

Dec. 12, 1945

Dear folks,

I have some reasonably straight information today. The colonel (our regimental commander) was up yesterday.

and he told us quite a lot. First of all, the outfit is to leave Japan from Jan. 1 to Jan. 5. I feel sure that I'll be with it unless some unforeseen difficulties arise. Within a week or so, I should know for certain.

It seems too good to be true, and I won't believe it till I land in Frisco. I've been wondering if my old clothes will fit me, and if not, whether I'll be able to get new ones. I don't want to wear this uniform any longer than necessary.

He couldn't wait to get out of the army, couldn't wait to see his mother and father, his grandparents, his sisters. But there were days when Leo almost dreaded going home. He'd changed so much in these three years. He might look the same, although he doubted even that, but the Leal his mother had known was a boy—naïve, sure of life and the goodness of the fight he was about to enter. The Leo who was going home was a man. He knew far too much, and he was sure of nothing.

It was early January when Leo's Liberty Ship finally arrived. Waiting for orders to board, he worked on one more sonnet. He was sick of writing about fear and death, about wars and fighting, yet documenting combat in poetry had been cathartic. When he composed sonnets, the words flowed in ways that seemed otherwise impossible.

But the war was over now. Combat and death were behind him—he hoped forever—and he looked forward to the day he could write about the beauty of life instead.

This war sonnet would be his last. It was for the young boy-soldiers, returning home to an uncertain future. He thought about all the nineteen-year-olds who would not be going home. An image of Richards's ruined body burned his brain. Could Cal have survived the transition back to home? Maybe it was better that he wouldn't have to.

Leo finished the poem, tucked his pen and notebook in his pack, and boarded the ship that would take him home.

HOME
DECEMBER 1945

Home! Going home! I'm going home today.
War's brutal horrors past, I've lived to see
The happy faces of my family;
But I am not the boy you sent away.
I am a well-trained killer; I have seen
Men die in fearful agony, while I
Have killed in turn, so that I might not die.
I am a killer. I am just nineteen.
I have no other marketable skill.
I went from high school straight into the war.
Now I am going home, to fight no more.
Now I must learn the work of shop and mill.
And leave behind the bayonet and gun.
A killer, yes; but I am still your son.

ABOUT THE AUTHOR

Susannah Willey is a baby boomer, mother of four, grandmother of three, and a recovering nerd. To facilitate her healing, she writes novels. In past lives, she has been an office assistant, stay-at-home-mom, Special Education Teaching Assistant, School Technology Coordinator, and Emergency Medical Technician. She holds a Bachelor's Degree in Computing from S.U.N.Y. Empire State College, and a Master's Degree in Instructional Design from Boise State University. She grew up in the New York boondocks and currently lives in Central New York with her companion, Charlie, their dogs, Magenta and Georgie, and Jelly Bean the cat.

ABOUT THE POET

Sergeant Allen H. Benton served in the United States Army from October 1942-February 1946. He was a member of the 112th Cavalry Regimental Combat Team and saw action in Luzon and Japan.

Twenty-one years old when he joined Uncle Sam's Army, he spent two years at Fort Riley, Kansas and Camp Hood, Texas. In late September of 1944, he received his deployment orders and traveled to Fort Ord, California and in November of the same year he shipped out, landing in New Guinea around Christmas time.

In February 1945, he arrived in the Philippines and stayed there until the Japanese surrendered. He was onboard the *Lavaca* at Tokyo Bay for the formal surrender ceremony and served occupation duty near Tokyo. He left Tokyo in January 1946, arriving home about a month later.

After his return from service, he completed his college education at Cornell University in Ithaca, New York where he earned BS, MS and PhD degrees. He taught biology at SUNY Albany for 13 years and at SUNY Fredonia for 22 years, where he was the first professor to receive the New York State Distinguished Teacher award. He was the co-author of a highly successful field biology text-book published by McGraw-Hill. While in Albany, he appeared on television in a weekly show on bird-watching on WRGB TV and published a weekly newspaper column, "On the Wing," in the Knickerbocker News. In Fredonia, his weekly nature column, "World of the Wild," appeared for two decades in the Dunkirk OBSERVER. He also self-published several books including "Slivers of Jade" and "Sonnets from Nebraska and Beyond" under the pen name of Albert Ezra Fitzwarren, and "The Wheel of Life: Haiku by Followers of Basho" which he published under his own name.

Allen Benton died September 29, 2014 at the age of 93. His poetry is included in this novel with permission from his family.

AUTHOR NOTES

When I decided to write a novel based on my uncle's poetry, I wanted it to show both sides of the war: Sonnets from an American point-of-view, haiku from a Japanese. I do not assume that I know what Japanese life is like but this story is incomplete without the character of Tadashi Abukara, a Japanese soldier. I have researched diligently and tasked sensitivity readers with checking Tadashi's story for accuracy and authenticity. I also recruited readers to confirm the accuracy of the male perspective, of military life, and of combat. Huge thanks go to Dr. James Huffman, Samantha Hakoyama, Dr. Jonathan Damiani, and Charles Crary for their expert guidance.

I have tried to maintain historical accuracy as far as dates and important battles by consulting a number of print, video, and online resources (see below). For the sake of clarity, I have chosen to write the Japanese characters' names using the American tradition of first name, surname, rather than the Japanese convention.

Thanks to my wonderful editor, Jeni Chappelle and to my beta readers: Brenda Marie Smith, Sandy Roffey, Janis Robinson Daly, Tinthia Clemant, Erin Litteken, Malve Von Hassel, Emily M., Leslie C., and Jennifer Lane. Thanks also to K. J. Harrowick for her cover and interior design talents and advice.

Most importantly, my eternal thanks to Marjorie, Tom, and Holly Benton without whose support and permission this story would not have been possible.

PACIFIC WAR RESOURCES

WEBSITES

The Pacific War Online Encyclopedia
http://pwencycl.kgbudge.com

United States Army in World War II The War in the
Pacific "Triumph in the Philippines" *by* Robert Ross
Smith http://www.ibiblio.org/hyperwar/USA/USA-P-
Triumph/

HyperWar: A Hypertext History of the Second World
War, "Handbook on Japanese Military Forces (1944)"
(U.S. War Department Technical Manual TM-E 30-480)
http://www.ibiblio.org/hyperwar/Japan/IJA/HB/
index.html

BOOKS

Unbroken, Laura Hillebrand

*Grassroots Fascism: The War Experience of the
Japanese People*, Yoshimi Yoshiaki

Japan at War: An Oral History, Haruko Taya Cook and
Theodore F. Cook

The Great Raid on Cabanatuan, William Breuer

MOVIES

Fires on the Plain (*Nobi*), directed by Ken Ichikawa, based on the novel by Shohei Ooka
> An account of the desperate measures Japanese soldiers in the Philippines were forced to take to survive in the closing days of World War II.

The Great Raid, directed by John Dahl
> The story of the American/Filipino effort to rescue five hundred prisoners from the notorious Cabanatuan Prison Camp.

PRAISE FOR WAR SONNETS

"[Ms. Willey] does an amazing job capturing the emotions and interactions of the people involved as well as the historical facts about the war... "War Sonnets" receives five stars from The Historical Fiction Company and the "Highly Recommended" award of excellence."

The Historical Fiction
Company

"Compelling depiction of the Pacific theater of WWII through the perspective of an American soldier and a Japanese soldier.

Inspired by the poems written by Allen H. Benton, this is a moving tale of Tadashi and Leo, two young men who share similar backgrounds and a passion for writing, but are separated by war, fighting on opposing sides. The story builds gradually toward a horrifying climax and is hard to forget. It brings home the horrors of this war and indeed that of all wars."

Malve von Hassell, author
of *The Amber Crane*

*"Susannah Wiley has written a lovely book of grand
scope and has done a standout job of bringing the
Pacific Theater of World War II to life and showing us
its sheer heartbreak. The poignantly drawn American
and Japanese characters continue to stick with me. I'm
particularly fond of the poetry pieces that open each
chapter, which were written by the author's own uncle
during his stint in the very same war. War Sonnets will
deepen your understanding of this very important
chapter of our collective history. I highly recommend
it."*

Brenda Marie Smith, author of *If Darkness
Takes Us* & *If the Light Escapes*

*"A powerful, dual-narrative novel, War Sonnets probes
an underlying truth of war: those on either side of the
line are more alike than not; their fears and hopes, the
same. Extensive historical detail places readers on
those lines, building a sense of sympathy for both
sides."*

Janis Robinson Daly, author of *The Unlocked Path*,
#1 New Release for U.S. Historical Fiction, Kindle
version, 08.30.22.